KILLER

J.A. K... ...
ar... p...u..... before his w... demanded he quit work and write a novel, which he thought a fine idea. The result was *The Hundredth Man*, the first in the Carson Ryder series. An avid angler, canoeist and hiker, Kerley has traveled extensively throughout the South, especially coastal regions such as Mobile, Alabama, the setting for many of his novels, and the Florida Keys. He has a cabin in the Kentucky mountains, which appeared as a setting in *Buried Alive*. He lives in Newport, Kentucky, where he enjoys sitting on the levee and watching the barges rumble up and down the Ohio River.

Also by J.A. Kerley

J.A. KERLEY

THE MEMORY KILLER

HARPER

Harper
An imprint of HarperCollins*Publishers*
77–85 Fulham Palace Road, London W6 8JB

www.harpercollins.co.uk

A paperback original

1

First published in Great Britain by
Harper, an imprint of HarperCollins*Publishers* 2014

A catalogue record for this book
is available from the British Library

ISBN 9780007493678

Set in Sabon Lt Std by Palimpsest Book Production Ltd, Falkirk, Stirlingshire

Printed in Great Britain by
Clays Limited, St Ives plc

MIX
Paper from
responsible sources
FSC
www.fsc.org FSC™ C007454

FSC™ is a non-profit international organisation established to promote the responsible management of the world's forests. Products carrying the FSC label are independently certified to assure consumers that they come from forests that are managed to meet the social, economic and ecological needs of present and future generations, and other controlled sources.

Find out more about HarperCollins and the environment at
www.harpercollins.co.uk/green

To Mary Jane,
Who made me laugh

Thanks to the fine and hard-working folks at the Aaron M. Priest Literary Agency and HarperCollins UK – special high-fives to Sarah Hodgson and Anne O'Brien – for again helping to bring another of my stories to fruition. I'm backed by the best.

1

"You're beautiful, sweethearts! Brianna thanks you for coming tonight. And if you haven't come yet, there's always later!"

The performer blowing extravagant, double-handed kisses from the red-curtained stage would have been a stunning woman if she were a woman: large dark eyes with heavy lashes, delicate features, plump and roseate lips. Her hair was a wild, piled-high stack of scarlet, her gown built from chips of orange flame, sequins flashing as she kicked a long leg from the thigh-high slit, the slender ankle ending in a glittery, sling-back stiletto heel.

"You go, girl!" someone called, and the crowd roared approval as the sound system played the signature sign-off, Elton John's "The Bitch is Back". Brianna Cass – né Brian Caswell – winked to the crowd and ran caressing hands down the deep-cut décolletage of the

1

gown to cup breasts built of neoprene foam. Her eyes widened in mock surprise.

"*I think they love you! They've grown a full size tonight!*"

Raw, raucous laughter and good-natured catcalls accompanied Brianna's stage-step descent into an adoring crowd of gay men, the air a mix of alcohol, cologne and pot. Brianna flamboyantly sashayed to a large table beneath the stage. Someone handed her a Japanese fan, and she sat, fanning herself as laughing men clamored to buy her drinks.

"Hey, waiter. Hey!"

Alone at a tiny table in the corner of the shadowed club, Debro waved his hand to catch a server's eye, but the waiter ignored him to take orders from a quartet of fortyish queens partying in a nearby booth. Debro's table initially had three chairs, but he'd pushed two to another table. He had things to do and tablemates couldn't be allowed.

The waiter took the queens' orders and angled toward the bar.

"Hey, you," Debro called. "Waiter!" Debro hated to yell – it garnered attention, which caused his invisibility to falter – but now that Brianna had finished her ridiculous, mocking act, he had to move fast.

"Waiter!"

The waiter looked toward Debro, sighed, walked over. "Yaas, do you need zomething?" he said in a faux accent, nose in the air. For a split second Debro imagined punching the man's face and raping him on the floor of the nightclub. Instead, Debro nodded to Brianna, surrounded by well-wishers.

"What's Brianna's favorite drink?"

The twink gave Debro an appraiser's stare, but Debro knew the waiter could only see himself in the wide mirroring lenses of his outsize sunglasses, the black knit hat pulled almost to the tops of the shades, a turtle-neck tee snugged beneath his chin. It helped make him invisible.

"Chom-pine," the waiter said. "Brianna like z'chom-pine."

"Champagne? What's her favorite?"

"Z'most expensive, of courz. Creeesh-*tal* . . . Two-hondred-eighty dollars." The waiter barely avoided sneering at Debro's drink choice: Miller Lite beer.

"Bring me a bottle of the stuff," Debro said, reaching for his wallet. "And one of those long champagne glasses."

The server regarded Debro with new eyes. "A bottle of Creees-tal and a flute, zen?"

"Yeah, a flute. Whatever."

The man bustled away and Debro shot a glance at Brianna, standing and waving at well-wishers before turning for the hall leading to the restroom. "Do you see the bitch, Brother?" Debro whispered into the darkness. "Will Brianna come home with us tonight?"

The waiter returned with the champagne and glass. "Do you vish me to pop z'cork?"

Debro nodded and the man unwrapped the wire and

3

tugged the cork without success. "Goddamn things are impossible," the man muttered in his real voice, Midwestern nasal, probably Ohio. Debro took the Cristal and his strong hands easily twisted the cork loose, wisps of vapor floating from the bottle. The waiter bowed and backed away, money in hand.

Sitting and sliding the table a foot deeper into the shadows, Debro reached into his jacket for his cell phone. Taped behind it was a tiny vial of amber liquid. His fingernails pried the cap from the vial and he tapped the phone above the flute as the vial emptied. Anyone looking his way saw only a man appearing to send a text.

Brianna re-entered the room, a half-dozen full glasses on her table, gifts from admirers. Her long red nails began doing an eenie-meenie-miney selection of what to drink first.

Time.

Debro took a deep breath and stood, snugging his collar higher and hat lower as he crossed the crowded room. Four young males were at Brianna's table, but they took a single glance at Debro and turned away. Debro was not trendy. It was part of his invisibility.

The only eyes on Debro belonged to Brianna, her head cocked as if finding Debro a curious intrusion on her space. He pushed a false and adoring smile to his face, feigning embarrassment as he held the bottle and flute to his side.

"Great show," Debro said. "You're so nasty and fun. May I offer you a drink?"

"Is that champagne?" Brianna said. "Brianna *loooves* the bubbly."

Debro displayed the label and Brianna trilled her delight. Debro poured, his hand hiding the amber viscosity at the bottom of the glass. The champagne mixed with the fluid and bubbled to the mouth of the flute.

"From a grateful admirer," Debro said, handing Brianna the glass. She batted big eyes, emptied it in three seconds, then held the flute toward Debro to return it.

"Thank you, sweetcakes," she said. "That was dee-double-licious."

"I bought it for you," Debro said, setting the champagne on the table. It had done its work.

"Aren't you the darling boy," Brianna chirped, crossing the long legs and pouring another glass. "Have we met before, sweet prince?"

But Debro was already moving away. He returned to the table in the shadows and stared at the drag queen drinking his champagne, a mean and insulting bitch who – like the two other nasty boys hallucinating on the floor of his home – was long overdue for punishment.

He checked his watch. All that remained was the waiting.

2

Ten days later

Call me, Jeremy, I thought, sitting on my deck on Florida's Upper Matecumbe Key and pressing my fingers to my temples as my eyes squeezed shut with effort. *Skype me. Text me. Write me.* I opened my eyes and stared at the smartphone on the table beside my deck chair.

Nada.

My friend and former colleague, Clair Peltier, a pathologist in Mobile, Alabama, is as pure a scientist as ever conceived. Yet Clair believes in synchronicity, a metaphysical linkage of time and space and energy, where wishes, dreams, actions and events form alliances unfathomable to the human mind, but totally logical within the universal matrix. I'd spoken to her last night, explaining that a person close to me seemed to have vanished from the planet and I was worried.

"*Think about the person, Carson. If they're part of you they'll feel it.*"

"*I have been, Clair.*"

"*Think harder.*"

I looked up to see a fat white moon in a cobalt sky, low enough to be enhanced by the atmospheric lens, its light broken into diamonds atop waves shivering across the three-acre cove behind my home. It would be a beautiful night if I knew my brother was safe.

I'd not heard from Jeremy in seven weeks. Though I'd once gone a year without word from my brother, he was then twenty-five and in an institute for the criminally insane, imprisoned for the murders of five women and I, ashamed, didn't visit the institution for twelve months. He'd also been belatedly indicted for killing our father, who he tied to a tree and disassembled with a kitchen knife; I had just turned ten at the time, Jeremy was sixteen.

Jeremy spent almost a decade in incarceration until the director of the institute, Dr Evangeline Prowse, broke every rule in her life and profession by sneaking Jeremy to New York. In a bizarre twist of fate – since those knowing Jeremy Ridgecliff was my brother were countable on one hand – I, Detective Carson Ryder, having a record of apprehending psychotics, was summoned to either catch him or kill him.

During the journey I discovered my brother's role in

the women's murders was ambiguous, and not deserving of death or life-long incarceration, and I helped Jeremy elude the police, a breach of my professional oath that troubled my conscience to this day. Jeremy's killing of our father likely saved my life, and troubled my conscience not the slightest.

After his disappearance in New York, I again had no contact with Jeremy for over a year, until he called from an isolated rural community in Eastern Kentucky, where he'd assumed the identity of a retired Canadian psychologist named Auguste Charpentier, living in a well-appointed cabin and growing wealthy using an un-orthodox analysis of the stock market. Since he'd surfaced, we'd communicated enough that I knew something was amiss if he'd gone this long without acknowledging my calls, texts, and e-mails.

I also knew that nothing good had ever come of my brother spending too much time alone with his thoughts.

Call me, Jeremy, I thought, one final time, adding *You thoughtless bastard.*

The phone lay dead and I glanced at my watch; four minutes past midnight. I checked the beer bottle on the table beside my deck chair; empty. Both indicated it was time to totter to bed. I took another look at the moon and whistled. Mr Mix-up, my huge pooch, ran up from hunting crabs in the sandy backyard. I yawned and scratched his head and we headed inside.

As I latched the door my cell phone trilled the opening riff of Elmore James' "Dust My Broom". My heart paused mid-beat: Had I conjured up my wayward brother? I checked the screen and frowned – Roy McDermott, my boss at the Florida Center for Law Enforcement.

"Carson, it's Roy," he said. "I hope I didn't wake you."

Roy always identified himself, as though I could forget any voice attached to a ceaselessly grinning jack-o'-lantern face topped by a hay-bright shock of unruly hair, an untamable cowlick floating above like antennae.

"I'm sitting on the deck and enjoying the moon, Roy," I semi-lied. "What's going on?"

"Viv Morningstar just called. She was looking for you, but couldn't find your number."

Dr Vivian Morningstar was the Chief Forensic Pathologist for Florida's southern region. We'd worked together several times and I'd found her as attractive as she was professional. I'd made a few attempts at flirtation, but her eyes had told me I was dancing in the wrong ballroom.

"What does the Doc want, Roy?"

"She'd like you to meet her at MD-Gen first thing in the a.m. It involves a poisoning."

MD-Gen was Miami-Dade General Hospital, Dade being the county. A hospital – with its emphasis on the living – seemed a bit far afield for the forensic pathologist.

"She doesn't want me at the morgue?"

A chuckle. "It's Viv, Carson. She basically ordered me to send you to MD-Gen."

Vivian Morningstar on a case was like Patton on the

march . . . all ahead full, damn the bombs and bureaucrats. Her staff revered her, but tempered their love with terror.

"And you told her . . .?" I said.

"Only that I'd pass the message on. Say hello to the moon for me."

3

I awoke an hour before my 6.00 a.m. alarm and jumped through the shower, pulling on jeans and a blue Oxford shirt, grabbing a coral linen jacket to keep the shoulder-holstered Glock from startling citizens at stop lights.

I went beneath my home, stilted to ride above storm surges, and climbed into a fully outfitted Land Rover Defender originally confiscated in a drug bust. Colleagues called me *Sahib* and *Bwana,* but having the only veldt-ready copmobile in the country, I laughed it off.

I turned on to Highway 1. An hour and two coffee stops later I entered Miami-Dade General and elevatored to a room in the Intensive Care section. Doc Morningstar was leaning against the wall and studying reports, her dark and shoulder-length hair fallen forward. She was slender and athletic and appeared taller than her five ten, the effect of improbably long legs currently hidden under khaki slacks. Her blouse was a silky purple, the sleeves rolled to her elbows, her only ornamentation a pair of small enameled earrings, purple coneflowers to match the blouse.

Morningstar glanced up, brushed back the errant hair, and nodded, any potential smile damped by the patient centering the room, a young man, late teens to early twenties, blond, with sunken and lifeless eyes and flesh so pale as to seem blue. A mask covered his nose and mouth, so many tubes and hoses running to the mask it appeared a mechanical octopus was clinging to his face.

I gave the doc a *What's-up?* look.

"Name's Dale Kemp," she said quietly. "Hikers found him three days ago near the Pahayokee overlook in the Glades. He's been raped, semen found, but nothing in the database."

DNA sampling used to take weeks, but recent technology made it a matter of hours with one of the new machines, and we'd recently added one to our arsenal. But if there was no match for the perp in the database, it was still a dead end.

"What's wrong with him?" I asked.

Morningstar set aside the reports. Her eyes were huge and the kind of hazel that seems pale one moment, dark the next.

"An overdose seemed indicated, but nothing showed. The attending physician, Dr Philip Costa, knew I had a sub-specialty in toxicology and called yesterday. I suggested a more complex series of tests, initially thinking scopolamine or atropine, and my preliminary tests found a massive quantity of *datura stramonium* in his blood, among other things."

"Datur-strama . . . what?"

"You might know its plant source: Jimson weed."

My mental Rolodex whirred. "Also called Loco weed?"

She nodded. "I also found robitin, a phytotoxin from *Robinia pseudocacia,* or black locust tree. When it's ingested by animals, they become stupefied, unable to recognize their surroundings. They often die."

"Jeee-sus," I said.

"There's probably more in this crazy cocktail, Ryder. But the datura and robinia seem the main components."

"What's the effect of the Loco weed?"

"In controlled quantities, datura has medicinal uses. Larger doses create delirium and fearful hallucinations. It can result in odd behavior, such as stripping off clothes, picking at oneself, staring into space. A person dosed with datura can look in a mirror and see a complete stranger. Or a cow. Or nothing at all."

Hallucinations atop stupefaction. "Where was he last seen, anyone know?"

"He was ID'd via Missing Persons at Miami-Dade PD. Last sighting was at a Miami Beach bar. He didn't come to work the next day."

"When'd he disappear?"

"Ten days ago. There's something else I wanted to show you. Take a look at his back."

We gently rolled Dale Kemp over. I saw bruises and

scratches and an odd pattern between his shoulder blades: a pair of coupled circles etched into the skin, as if a tenpenny nail had been drawn across his flesh hard enough to welt, but not break, the skin. Two vertical lines fell below, the tops of the lines touching the ovoids. A horizontal line fell between the verticals.

"A figure eight," I said. "On top of some lines."

"Or, looking from below . . ."

"Yeah," I nodded. "A freaking infinity symbol."

We rolled him back. I looked between the kid and the readings on the monitor. "He'll always be like this?" I asked. "It's permanent?"

"There aren't a lot of field trials to draw from, as you'd expect." She nodded at an array of prepared syringes on the bedside table. "The robinia inhibits protein synthesis, so we've concocted a treatment to enhance reactions. It also contains physostigmine, an acetylcholinesterase inhibitor."

"Uh . . ."

"Sorry. The first to reduce toxic effects of the black locust, the second helps reduce the hallucinations."

I found it odd Morningstar used the word *we're* and *us*, as if Kemp were her patient. The only course recommended for Morningstar's standard "patients" was burial or cremation.

"Where could you get these plants, Doc?" I asked.

"Jimson weed grows wild across the country. Black locust grows in most states east of the Mississippi."

I made a pouring motion. "What . . . someone just

14

dumped twigs and leaves into a blender and made this stuff?"

"The active chemicals were likely extracted from the plant sources and concentrated. That would take a knowledge of chemistry. But probably basic."

"As basic as jurisdictions?" I said, growing puzzled by Morningstar's request that I be here. A rape, though horrific, was not reason to call me, the FCLE's specialist in psychotics, sociopaths and other mental melt-downs.

"Jurisdictions?" she said.

"You said Kemp was found by Miami-Dade cops, was in their Missings file. Why did you call me, Doctor?"

Morningstar walked to the window and gazed down on the parking lot, forlorn in its dawn emptiness. Not only was I uncertain why I was here, I was also puzzled at her involvement. When she had solved the toxicology problem, her work was over, time to return to the dead. She seemed more like an attending physician than a pathologist.

Morningstar turned back to me. "I, uh . . . it's not a typical case, is it, Detective? The combination of substances seems so calculated and cold that it feels . . . evil."

Another anomaly. *Evil* was not a word normally used in the clinical halls of Morningstar's pathology department. Had the bizarre methodology of the case unsettled the usually imperturbable pathologist?

"So you'd prefer the FCLE to investigate? Me in particular?"

"It's your world, right, Detective? Who else but a psychopath might, uh . . ."

Words failed and she stared at the body motionless amidst the tubes and wires, his thoughts turned to nightmares and even the nightmares burned away, perhaps forever, by a combination of toxins you might find in your own backyard.

"Who else but a psychopath might turn common plants into Satan's private date-rape drug?" I said.

Morningstar nodded. "I figured you'd have the right words."

4

"You want to grab a case from Miami-Dade?" Roy McDermott said from behind his broad desk, patting down the straw-hued cowlick that immediately bounded back in defiance. "What? We don't have enough cases of our own?" Outside his twenty-third-story window the Miami skyline was a study in muscular architecture. The FCLE was in the downtown Clark Center, and was the state's top investigative agency, usually summoned when special expertise was needed. We stayed busy.

"Doc Morningstar thinks it's the way to go."

"Correct me if I'm wrong, partner, but she's a pathologist, not an investigative professional."

"We can do it, right? Assert jurisdiction?"

Roy nodded reluctantly. "We're state, they're local. But it's basically a missing-persons case that'll probably get

17

filed as a sex crime. I don't see the reason, Carson. It's not like we're begging for work."

My phone rang and I checked the caller: Morningstar. I made notes as she detailed her latest findings.

"That was the good Doc herself," I said when we'd finished.

Roy clapped his hands in mock delight. "Goodie. Does she have any more cases to add to our list?"

"She has a newly isolated agent in the tox combo. Something called raphides. Given the plant-based nature of the other toxins, Morningstar thinks it came from dieffenbachia."

"The houseplant? I used to have one in my office until it died. Probably had something to do with stubbing out cigars in the pot."

"Dieffenbachia is also called dumb cane. Seems the raphides cause paralysis of the vocal cords."

Roy spun to study the skyline. "So the perp drops this nastiness in a drink. The black locust makes the target head home with cramps and muscle weakness, the datura makes him hallucinate like Timothy Leary squared, and this last stuff . . ."

"Makes it impossible to call for help," I said.

Roy turned back to his desk and picked up the phone.

"You're tight with Vince Delmara, right?"

I nodded. Vince was a senior investigator with the Miami-Dade County Police Department. We'd worked together on my first case in Florida last year, and I'd found Delmara a first-rate detective, old school, the kind to visit a crime scene just to sniff the air. We'd hit it off from the git-go.

"Good," Roy said. "Let Vince schmooze you through the transfer and it'll go easy."

"You think?"

He grinned. "Unless some honcho has a burr under his saddle, they'll be delighted to pass the potato to us."

My partner in most operations was Ziggy Gershwin. I gave him a call and was outside his Little Havana apartment minutes later, waiting until a slender man with coal-black hair pushed from the door, jamming a scarlet shirt into tan chinos, his cream jacket hanging across his shoulder, a rolled tortilla in his mouth like a cigar. An ancient woman was walking a tan puff of dog down the sidewalk and Gershwin's cordovan boat shoes leapt over the bewildered canine, earning an icy glare from the woman. I filled him in as I drove, as much as I knew.

"*Oy caramba*, Big Ryde," Gershwin said as he buttoned his cuffs. "That's some crazy cocktail."

A few months back Ziggy Gershwin would have been wearing threadbare jeans, a T-shirt advertising a beer brand, and orange skate shoes, but becoming an active agent in the FCLE had upped his fashion game. The product of a Jewish father and Cuban mother, his full name was Ignacio Ruben Manolo Gershwin, and he'd been Iggy as a child. But a teacher had started calling the hyperactive, darting kid Ziggy, and it stuck.

"Morningstar thinks Kemp received repeated and heavy doses of the tox mix, Zigs, maybe starting at a bar."

"What, we're doing legwork for Miami-Dade?"

"We're appropriating the case. The Doc figures it'd take a psycho to sicken and weaken people, turn off their screams, then fill their head with hallucinations while he rapes them."

"No matter how lovely Señorita Morningstar may be, isn't she a pathologist and not a—"

"Heard it from Roy," I said, cutting him off.

I called and found Vince at his desk in MD's headquarters and said we'd be by in minutes. He had two words: *Bring coffee.* He meant real brew, not the stuff cooked up at cop houses across the land, desiccated brown crumbles boiled into a bitterness no sugar could blunt. We stopped at a bodega and filled my large Zogirushi with righteous espresso thunder and were at MD in minutes.

Vince Delmara was in a cluttered cubicle in the Homicide unit, his wingtips on his desk as he reviewed jai-alai scores in the *Miami Herald*. He looked up, saw us approaching, and folded the paper. Vince was medium height and slender and his dark complexion was marred with acne pocks, his black hair brushed straight back. His dark eyes were large and piercing and with his prize-sized proboscis Vince called to mind a thoughtful buzzard. He always dressed in dark suits, white shirts and neon-bright ties, capping the ensemble with a Dick Tracy-style fedora to enter the bright Miami sun, which he regarded with vampiric suspicion.

I poured his ceramic mug full of caffeine and Vince's toucan-sized beak sniffed. He drank, leaned back his head, moaned, then, as if his day had been re-booted, set his eyes on Gershwin and me. "Jesus . . . too much Scotch last night. I'm surprised I didn't wake up wearing a fucking kilt."

"Your wife still make you stop and get a few pops before you come home?" Gershwin asked.

He nodded. "Says it makes me easier to live with."

"She must have found you real easy to live with last night," Gershwin said.

"Beatrice is in Tampa visiting her sister. *I* had to live with me last night." He took another blast of java. "What can I do you gents for?"

"We've got a guy who was a Missing, Vince. He'd been drugged, kept for a week, then dumped. We're planning to pull the case into our purview. Doc Morningstar thinks it's a psycho at work."

Vince gave me a raised eyebrow. "Last I noted, Carson, the gorgeous doc was a pathologist and—"

I sighed and raised my hand. Had everyone been handed the same libretto? "I know, Vince. But I figured you might smooth the way, politics-wise."

He sucked coffee and thought. "Well . . . given that

details are just getting clear, the case will transfer from Missing Persons to Sex Crimes, but I'll bet it's still officially in MP. Lemme see what Missing Persons has listed." He sat at a blank screen, pecked the keys. Nothing happened.

"Works best when you turn it on, Vince," Gershwin said. "Let me do the honors."

Gershwin flipped the switch and seconds later we saw a photo of Dale Kemp in the corner of a screen of missing persons. His well-attended blond hair sparkled with highlights above sculpted cheekbones and penetrating gray eyes. His occupation was listed as medical-products salesman, and I figured his good looks created a buzz among the female staff when he entered a physician's office.

Vince read the investigative report: "Moved here last April from Minneapolis. Liked to hit the beach and bars, but who doesn't when they're twenty-seven and in Miami."

"Gay?" I asked.

"Yep, but you got to read between the lines. Lemme see who owns the case."

Vince expanded the screen to the full report, tapped a bottom line. "The case is still in Missings, headed by Katey Beltrane, twenty years in the biz, eight in MP, and a pro. She'll thank you for lightening her case load. Step in and snatch a case from an insecure pissant and you'll—"

"Wind up in shit-fight corral," Gershwin finished.

22

Vince tipped back the fedora and nodded at Gershwin. "For a young buck, you know a couple things. Let's get it done so I can see how much I lost on jai-alai last night. Here's a tip, never call your bookie when you're smashed."

5

We elevatored down to a wide hall, a sign above the first door saying MISSING PERSONS. Opening the door revealed a thirtyish guy with his feet propped on the desk and reading a *Hustler* magazine. He stood, six feet plus, heavy in the shoulders, with hair so blond it had to be dyed. He wore it long over his ears and down his neck. His face was oddly lopsided, and his nose slanted off to one side. He slipped the mag into a folder as if filing official business.

"Where's Lieutenant Beltrane?" Vince asked.

"Getting her ass fixed," the big guy said.

"What's wrong with her ass?" Vince said. "I always liked it."

"Beltrane busted her hip falling off a ladder. She's got physical therapy for six weeks."

The guy glanced at the clipped-on temp IDs Gershwin

24

and I had received at the desk. He made no effort to extend a hand, so neither did I.

"I need to speak to whoever's running the department," Vince said.

Big boy crossed his arms and leaned the wall. Even with full sleeves I could see the guy had guns. "So start talking."

"*You're* heading the unit?"

The guy looked irritated at Vince's emphasis. "I came here two months before the loot took the big dive. Smith retired two weeks later, Jalesco transferred to Bunco. I outranked the others, so when Beltrane hit the floor, I was in charge."

Vince simply stared like the guy was a scotch-generated mirage, the first time I'd seen Vince at a loss for words. I stepped in, glancing at the nameplate: Det. Figueroa.

"Look, Detective Figueroa, given certain insights into the case by the pathologist, the FCLE has decided to put Dale Kemp's case under our jurisdiction."

The guy scowled. Delmara's phone buzzed in his pocket. He pulled it, muttered "Got to take this. A snitch who usually pays off." Vince hustled to the bathroom across the hall, an appropriate venue for talking to a snitch.

I turned back to Figueroa, who was squinting in thought. "*Your* jurisdiction?" he said.

I tried upbeat. "Look on the bright side, bud: one less hassle to deal with."

"Fuck your bright side, mister. This is Miami-Dade,

not a bunch of county clowns with cowshit on their boots. We can handle it."

Upbeat wasn't his preferred métier, so I tried making nice. "I mean no disrespect to your abilities, amigo, but our interest in the case stems from—"

"I read the report," Figueroa interrupted. "It smells bogus. I'm not even sure it should be here."

"The victim was drugged, abducted and raped," I said, puzzled. "How's that not a crime?"

Figueroa shook his head like I was a moron. "A couple hot boys meet up at a bar, go somewhere to hook up and do drugs. They get all sexed up and time don't mean jackshit. Then one guy decides he's tired of it. The other has a hissy fit, gets his butt-buddy all dopey and drops him in the Glades to teach him a lesson. Don't say you haven't seen it."

I had encountered variations of Figueroa's scenario, and had considered it in this case, but the drug combo wasn't anything near recreational.

"You didn't see the tox reports, Detective Figueroa. He'd had some nasty stuff."

Rod Figueroa smirked, probably his default expression. "I've seen these dudes on Ecstasy, heroin, crank, ice, PCP, mushrooms, glue, cough syrup, paint thinner, and mixes of them all . . . what you got to beat that?"

I thought about explaining the calculated potency and effects of the mixture given Kemp, but it would have been like trying to open a twelve-foot stepladder in a room with an eight-foot ceiling. And anyway, I was tiring of Rod Figueroa.

"If it's your opinion that this wasn't a crime, Detective," I said, ju-jitsuing him with his own words, "then we've taken nothing from you. If you could be so kind as to send us any files you have, I'll be appreciative. Have a nice day."

I set my card on his desk and backed away. I nodded at Gershwin and we spun and left the office. I heard the sound of tearing paper, but didn't turn. We retreated down the hall and waited until Delmara appeared.

"How'd it go?" he asked.

"Figueroa doesn't seem cut out for the job, Vince, an obvious bias against gays. Most Missings cops I know are past that."

"Figueroa's an asshole. He comes by it naturally – his daddy's an asshole, too. But a high-ranking asshole in MDPD, which is why junior's got way too much pull for a guy barely thirty. Little Roddy was in Theft last I saw, but I guess Daddy wanted junior to get some Sex-Crimes cred on his way up."

"Daddy is?"

"Captain Alphonse Figueroa. A guy who started on a beat in Little Havana and made all the right moves. Knew he was making 'em, too."

"Political type?" I asked.

"Understudied with the old school macho types who ran the place a couple decades back. They pushed Figueroa upstairs, gave him a cushy desk in Community

Relations. Daddy Figueroa's a piece of work . . . I think he's on his fifth wife. Unfortunately, he's high-profile in the older Cuban community, one of the department's PR assets. So junior gets a lot of sway."

"What's wrong with Figueroa's face?" Gershwin asked. "Looks like someone scrunched it in a vise."

Delmara shrugged. "Some kind of accident when he was a kid, running a jet ski while drunk, plowed into a boat. No one's ever really said."

"Figueroa's moving up in the department?" I asked.

"Daddy says, 'Maybe my sonny boy should get experience in the Missing Persons unit' and you can hear the *yessirs* and pens filling out transfer forms."

"The asshole'll probably be Chief some day," Gershwin muttered.

Delmara slapped a hand on my partner's shoulder.

"You are indeed old beyond your years, Detective."

Gershwin and I crossed Biscayne to Miami Beach, heading to the Stallion Lounge, the last place Dale Kemp had been seen. I figured it had to open early to air out from previous evenings, the smell of beer and bodies and a gazillion drenchings of cologne thick as fog in the semi-darkness. It was booths and a few tables, half of the floor set aside for dancing. The walls were dark wood with sconces for light. A mirrored ball hung from the ceiling.

I saw four guys in a back booth. Two were in full black leather regalia, like they were rehearsing for the Village

People, the others resembled prep-school wannabes, clean-cut, white tees tucked into dark jeans. Loafers at the end of long and crossed legs. Except when they turned our way, their eyes looked a thousand years old.

A guy stood behind the long bar rinsing glasses, and I knew he'd made us from the moment our heels slapped the floor. He was inches over six feet and looked carved from a block of chocolate, pneumatic biceps rippling as he toweled the glassware, his chest broad and ripped under a blue denim vest that glittered with studwork.

We walked his way, but his eyes stayed on his drying. "You're wasting your time," he said in a sing-song voice that didn't fit the physique. "We card everyone."

He meant they asked for proof of age, though I figured a faux driver's license printed on construction paper would pass muster.

"Good for you," I said, pulling Kemp's photo from my jacket. "But that's not why we're here. Know this guy?"

The bartender flipped the towel over a cannonball shoulder, took the shot and held it closer to the light. "Dale. He's in here pretty regular, though I haven't seen him in a few days." The eyes got serious. "He all right?"

"We think he may have had his drink spiked. It would have been about ten days ago."

"That's just fucking *nasty*."

"Dale have any enemies you know about?"

He blew out a breath. "Dale could be cruel sometimes. Especially to ugmos who hit on him."

29

"Ugly people?"

"Dale never dispensed charity."

I took it that meant deigning to frolic with less attractive beings. "Anyone seem particularly interested in Dale that night?" I asked. "Hit on him?"

"Are there bees around honey? People are always scoping Dale out."

"Anyone buzzing around that particular evening?"

"I can't recall anyone who . . ." he stopped and frowned.

"What?" I asked.

"Dale got a call on the house phone. That doesn't happen much, everyone having cells. He was at a table and I yelled over that someone wanted to talk. Dale took the phone and handed it back, said there was no one there."

"Male voice?"

"Deep and kind of raspy." He lowered his voice an octave. "'Hello, is Dale Kemp a-boot?' Those were his words."

"You're using a Canadian pronunciation," Gershwin said. "Kind of."

The barkeep nodded. "Or maybe it was kind of British."

I leaned close. "Tell me this, if you remember. When Dale came to the phone, was he holding his drink?"

He closed his eyes. "He held the phone in one hand and put the other over the receiver, asked who it was. He must have left his drink behind."

"That's the picture in your head?" Gershwin asked. "For sure?"

"I always like looking at Dale."

We returned to the Rover where I tapped my fingers on the wheel. "The perp sits in the corner, watches. When Kemp's friends aren't near, he calls the landline, asks for him. The barkeep calls, Kemp gets up . . ."

Gershwin finished the scenario. "The perp hangs up and walks by Kemp's booth, pausing to spike his drink with homemade witches' brew."

I put the safari wagon in gear and we pulled into a balmy afternoon, the street a festival of brightly plum-aged youth bustling from bar to bar, called by music or hormones, the world an endless caravan of vibrant moments. They were young and beautiful and invulnerable.

Or so they supposed.

Debro left his downstairs apartment and walked upstairs with his feet crunching on the wood-plank steps. The ancient building had been a small auto-parts warehouse and the red-brick walls were crumbling on to the steps. The door at the top was metal. He unlocked it and stepped into a spacious antechamber furnished with a table beneath a wall-mounted cabinet. The far end of the chamber held a door with a small wire-reinforced window at eye level.

Debro went to the window and flipped a switch on the wall. The room beyond the chamber lit up, the light from

31

track-mounted spots screwed into the ceiling joists. After purchasing the building last year, he'd machine-sanded the floor to be an inch higher in the center, sloping down to small gutters, the gutters feeding into the drainage system from the roof. He'd then covered the floor in linoleum, caulking the seams.

All he had to do to clean up after his penitents was hook the hose into the wall faucet and rinse the floor. Debro allowed his boys twenty ounces of water a day, which was easily mopped up, food a few nutritional gel packs squirted past their lips daily, nothing solid.

It took time to do things right . . . to make things right.

Debro put his eyes to the window. Two lovely sluts were in attendance, Brianna in the corner, and his latest penitent, Harold, propped against a wall and dodging invisible birds or missiles or whatever. He tried to scream but only wet croaks emerged. Every couple of minutes he'd try to stand but even his glorious, dancing legs crumpled under the weight of the black locust.

Brianna was a different case, curled in the fetal position, pissing and emitting watery gruel from her sphincter. Brianna and her sphincter had ceased to be fun. Beside, she'd been here for over a week now, and had learned her lesson.

Debro nodded: the choice was made. He stared at Brianna for several long seconds. "Brianna's leaving us, Brother," he said. "It's time to get another."

Debro returned to his apartment to consult a map of

South Florida. Part of his extensive planning had involved sites where the punished could be sent, and over a dozen locations had been ringed in red. He closed his eyes, circled a digit over the map, let it drop. He had a place to drop a used one. Now all he had to do was get a fresh one.

No problem. It would soon be night.

6

We headed to Kemp's apartment, a furnished house Kemp rented with two male roommates, flight attendants. Both had been away during the time Kemp had been abducted. One roomie, Lawrence Kaskil, arrived as we did, pulling up on a sleek racing bicycle in a white T-shirt over black Lycra biking shorts.

"I called the police on the second day I was back," Kaskil told us, tossing his blue helmet into a closet and exchanging his biking shoes for neon green flip-flops. "It wasn't unusual for Dale to be gone overnight, but after two days I got worried."

"You got back from where?"

"Mexico City."

"Your other roommate, Tad Bertram, was where during this time?"

Kaskil flapped to the small kitchenette and studied a

calendar stuck to the fridge with a magnetic Scotty dog. "Tad overnighted in London, then to Cairo. He dead-headed to Rome for two days and is now back in London. He'll be in tonight. I dread telling him about Dale."

"Dead-headed?" Gershwin said.

"Taking a flight, but not working it. He took a couple days off to see the sights."

I took a look at the calendar, new to us, the Missing Persons unit having neglected to do any follow-up. But Rod Figueroa had it all figured out: just a case of sexed-up boys. And why work when you can gawk at nekkid wimmen in your *Hustler*?

"These notes on the calendar," I said, checking the previous month. "*Dale – Tampa, Dale – SA, Dale – ORL* . . . What's that about?"

"Overnight sales trips. Tampa, St Augustine, Orlando. Dale put out-of-town days on the calendar." Kaskil paused. "But sometimes he was gone overnight and it wasn't indicated."

"When he'd meet someone?" I said. "Like on a date?"

Kaskil nodded. "Those could be, uh, impromptu."

"You and your other roomie, Tad Bertram . . . you're gone a lot?"

"We're here maybe eight or ten days out of the month. We joke that we each pay a third of the rent, but Dale gets the place to himself seventy per cent of the time."

"When you arrived home from Mexico City, did anything seem amiss?"

Kaskil's features tightened in thought. "It was like Dale

had played with rearranging the furniture, then put it back almost in place, but not quite."

"Let's talk enemies – did Dale have any?"

"A lot of times Dale gets cruised, and if he's not in the mood he can be fast with put-downs. But no, there's, like, no one who has it in for him. Not enough to do such an ugly thing."

We asked everything we could think of, then walked to the door. Kaskil asked if he and Bertram could visit Kemp and I discouraged it, telling them to wait until he regained consciousness.

I didn't mention it was a crapshoot as to that ever happening.

We interviewed neighbors and friends of Kemp, getting nothing. When the day dwindled to dusk, Gershwin headed home and I decided to crib at the Palace, saving the hour-long drive. The Palace was a recent addition to the FCLE's ongoing accumulation of confiscations. Gershwin and I had nailed a piece of garbage who'd made big money trafficking in human beings, hiding his gains in real estate. One property was the Palace Apartments, a small building on the west side of down-town, near the Tamiami Trail.

Roy McDermott was a director of the FCLE not for deductive abilities, but his artful wrangling of funds and favors from the lawmakers in Tallahassee, a group the masterful McDermott milked like plump cows. Roy had convinced legislators to sell off all Kazankis's properties except the Palace, to be used as quarters for visiting FCLE staffers and an occasional safe house for witness-protection efforts.

I arrived and grabbed my overnight valise from the rear of the car. My ID card buzzed me through two bulletproof doors – an addition for the witness-protection aspect – and into a small lobby with framed seascapes on the walls. A clipboard on an elegant mahogany table indicated three rooms were occupied: two agents from Jacksonville and a departmental attorney from Tallahassee. They were on floors one and two, leaving the top floor, the fourth, fully mine.

My suite resembled an upscale extended-stay facility: twin couches and chairs in the main room, plus a large TV screen and modest sound system, a desk, a wardrobe, chest of drawers. The galley-style kitchen held cooking necessaries and a half-size fridge. The bathroom had both shower and Jacuzzi. The bedroom had a queen-size bed, another desk and chair in the corner.

Though a part of the FCLE's inventory for three months, the Palace had already developed a fine tradition: if a visitor brought potables to the room and had something left when departing, the beverages stayed. I held my breath and opened the refrigerator . . .

Three cans of Bud, two of Heineken, two Cokes, and seven airline-sized bottles of liquor, including two Bacardi golden rums. *Bless you,* I thought, mixing a rum and Coke – no lime, but I could rough it – then tucking the file beneath my arm, and heading out. The fourth-floor suite had one aspect I prized above all others: a stairway to the roof.

I climbed and opened the door to the night skyline of Miami. Buildings towered like glass and metal hives with a skeleton staff of bees still buzzing within, whole floors dark, others alight for the cleaning staff and workers pulling all-nighters. A helicopter rumbled in the distance as traffic sounds drifted up from the street.

On my last stay I'd purchased a sturdy folding chair, and bungeed it to a vent. I set it up, put the drink beside me and my feet on the two-foot ledge. Below my soles was sixty feet of open air and three a.m. traffic, half taxicabs. I sipped rum and Coke, pulled my phone, and took another stab at my errant brother.

Per Clair's instructions I thought so hard that my mouth formed the words *Answer the phone, Jeremy*. I visualized my brother cocking his head to the phone ringing in his office and lifting it to his ear . . . visualization another of Clair's suggestions.

Answer . . .

The phone again directed me to his voicemail. Two dozen of my calls already lay in the electronic wasteland of my brother's VM box . . . so much for synchronicity. Anger boiling in my gut, I held the phone to the night sky, growling, "God-dammit, Jeremy. Call me *now* and let me get on with my life."

Five seconds later my phone riffed an incoming call. I checked the screen and saw the name AUGUSTE and stared in disbelief: Jeremy's alter ego, Auguste

Charpentier. I wondered if I'd already gone to bed and was dreaming.

Elmore replayed the riff, too strident for a dream, and a triumph for either Clair or coincidence. My finger hesitated over the connect button, wondering whether to voice relief or ire. Given the number of messages in Jeremy's voicemail, I figured irritation was my due.

"Where the hell are you?" I snapped. "Why haven't you been answering?"

"Goodness, so testy," Jeremy said, his voice melodically Southern, not the Frenchified accent he affected with others. "I've been busy, Carson. No time for your idle chit-chat."

"Idle chit-chat? I had no idea whether you were in Kentucky or Florida or . . . worse."

"You mean back home in dear ol' Alabammy?"

"Jail," I said. "Prison. You might have been caught and I'd never know."

"Don't I get one call? I'd probably call you, Carson. Unless I used it to order a pizza."

"You're fine, then?" I sighed. "You're still in Kentucky?"

"I'll look for clues. I see endless trees outside my window, Carson. And the goddamn whip-poor-wills are screeching like banshees. Yes, I'm in Kentucky. Why do you ask?"

"Last year you implied you were moving to Key West. It never happened. The whole Key West thing . . . it's just to unsettle me, right?"

My brother was a world-class manipulator and since

39

he lived in isolation with no one to jerk around, I got to be the puppet.

"Why would I wish to unsettle you, dear brother?" he said, his voice a study in innocence.

"You enjoy keeping me off balance," I said. "It's your hobby."

"Such drama," Jeremy yawned. "I've simply been traveling, Carson. Too busy to return your calls."

"Travel is dangerous for you. Traveling where?"

My brother's face was on every Wanted list in the country. The photo was from his last year at the Institute, when he'd done a Brando before sitting for the photographer, filling his cheeks with tissue, propping his ears forward, flaring his nostrils. Though never expecting – at that time – to escape, he had planned for the occasion, the *just-in-case* kind of thinking that exemplified my brother's mind. As a result of his planning, Jeremy resembled his photo only slightly, but a seasoned eye might see through the façade, and it would be over.

"Traveling hither and yon," he said. "Seeing old friends."

"You have no friends."

"Don't be a Negative Nelly. Of course I have friends."

"Who?"

He changed course, affecting the high and tremulous voice of an elderly woman. "I'm . . . muh-muh-moldering here in the w-woods, Carson. Now th-that I'm . . . nearing my duh-dotage . . . I need h-human cuh-cuh-contact."

"Spare me the routine. You're not even forty-five yet. And human contact means danger."

"I disagree, Brother," Jeremy said, back to normal voice. "In populations where the locals are known for a live-and-let-live attitude and a *soupçon* of eccentricity, I can hide in plain sight if I've planned well."

My irritation was turning to uneasiness. When my brother grew restive, bad things occurred. He was being cryptic as well, another dark sign.

"Planned how?"

"I'm building my final chapter, dear brother. I'm coming back to the world."

He chuckled and hung up.

Coming back to the world? Heeding a shiver at the base of my spine, I folded my chair and retreated from the roof, suddenly feeling small and vulnerable under the vast dark plain of sky.

7

The megaphone on the wall of the south Miami bar is a two-foot tin cone that legend has stolen from ancient crooner Rudy Vallee while on a swing through Florida in the 1930s. If true, it's safe to say that while in Vallee's possession the cone was not embellished on both sides with a twenty-inch-long penis rendered in pink glitter, the penis aiming toward the conic apex, making the user appear to be, well . . . the point is obvious.

The bartender pulls the megaphone from its pegs and climbs atop the bar. He's wearing skin-tight black jeans and an orange bowling shirt. Those who notice begin yelling *No!* into an atmosphere of beer, sweat and a hundred lotions, potions, and colognes.

The disco music dies in mid-air. Sweat-dripping dancers flail for a few seconds as more yells of *No!* echo from the walls. The barkeep raises the megaphone to his lips to catcalls. "Last call," he says, the peniphone giving his words stentorian depth. "We close in twenty minutes. ONE drink a person . . . None of this ordering five, you ladies hear me?"

The barkeep takes a showy bow. Good-natured hoots follow him to the floor. The music returns. A dozen young men rush to the bar as a pair of waiters race from table to booth to take orders. "A last drink, hon?" the waiter passing Debro yells atop the shuddering bass line.

Debro shakes his head and averts his face to tap out a fake message on his phone. The waiter sprints away as Debro pats his knit cap and turns his gaze to a young man beside a table. The man is wearing a safari-style shirt atop coral shorts and for most of the evening kept his tanned legs crossed as he entertained a succession of friends and friend wannabees.

But now the feet are on the floor and legs spread wide as the man clutches his belly. For the second time in five minutes he rushes to the bathroom. Debro presses the illumination on his watch: forty-seven minutes since slipping across the shadowy bar and – pretending to stop and read one of the racy cocktail napkins – squirting five drops of the mixture into the young man's drink. Debro has also been watching the bathroom, empty until the man entered, everyone frantic for a final drink.

He pulls his knit cap tight and walks quickly to the restroom, hearing vomiting from the far stall. He checks the other stalls to assure no one's hooking up, arriving at the final stall as the man exits, wiping his lips with toilet paper.

"You all right, brother?" DB's eyes frown with concern.

The man leans against the stall divider for support. "I think I just puked up my liver. Jesus, all I had was three daiquiris. Ooops . . ." The man spins back for another round of vomiting.

"It's probably *Fraturna Mortuis*," Debro says, knowing Jacob Eisen has no connection to Latin or medicine. Eisen turns and blinks in confusion.

"What?"

"The virus causing it. Gut started aching ten–fifteen minutes ago? Dizziness? You feel weak, right?"

The man nods. "You a doctor or something?"

"An intern," Debro lies. "You got a ride home, right?"

"Walking. I live eight blocks away." Eisen turns green and grabs his belly.

"How about I give you a lift, bro?" Debro says. "This will pass fast, but you're gonna be too sick to walk."

"I . . . I already am. Damn . . . can barely stand." Eisen's head spins to the left as his eye widen to their limits. "Holy shit."

"What?" Debro asks.

"I just saw a fucking parrot. How'd a parrot get in here?"

Time to move fast, Debro thinks. Eisen's knees buckle and Debro keeps him from dropping. The attack passes and Eisen wipes cold sweat from his forehead and studies Debro through pain-tightened eyes. "You look fum-uliar," Eisen says, his words garbled. He touches his throat with fear. "Wha- t' fu? My froat . . . I -an't – alk."

"Laryngitis from the virus," Debro says, pulling Eisen close. "Here, lean on me. We can go out the back."

"Fanks, bruver," Eisen chokes, grateful arms encircling DB's neck like a sick child clinging to a parent. "Yura . . . life . . . saver." He starts to stumble and knocks Debro's hat to the floor. Debro grabs the hat, stuffs it in a pocket, then enters the alley. He has researched every footstep. They reach the street as a quartet of men pass by.

"Is your friend OK?" one asks.

"A little touch of the bug," Debro says. He winks.

"I know *that* bug," one says. "For me it's wine mixed with margaritas." The others titter like birds and continue. Inebriation is as common here as the cabs on the streets.

"Shhhh, Jacob," Debro says as Eisen struggles to speak. "We're almost there."

Eisen turns to Debro and swallows hard to dampen his constricting vocal cords. "I din tloo- muh nm."

I didn't tell you my name.

"You just forgot, Jacob. You're sick."

"Nuh," Eisen chokes. He tried to push Debro away. "Ehm-ee-co."

Let me go.

Debro sees only the receding backs of the quartet. He opens his vehicle's rear door and grabs Eisen by his hair. Eisen screams. Though veins stand out on his throat and forehead with the effort, all that flows from Eisen's mouth

45

is a stream of warm air. Debro pushes Eisen into the back seat and puts a knee into Eisen's spine, easily pulling his struggling arms back for the handcuffs, the man's muscles like boiled rubber bands.

"Do you see us, Brother?" Debro grins as he takes his position behind the steering wheel. "Are you with me tonight?"

8

My inability to contact my brother – combined with his odd behavior – sparked strangely concocted dreams rooted in childhood, and this night was no exception. I dreamed of my father tied to a kayak I was paddling across my cove, screaming as sharks ripped away his flesh. I turned to my deck to see a two-headed man there, one face Jeremy's, the other mine. The three of us exchanged looks of approval as my mother sat knitting silently in a chair on the strand, never acknowledging the blood-stained water moving her way.

I was enjoying the show when my phone turned the dreamscape into a shadowed pillow. I blinked my eyes, realizing I'd overnighted at the Palace, my empty glass on the bedside table with my phone. The clock said 5.48 a.m. and the phone's screen was showing MORNINGSTAR.

"Why did I buy an alarm clock when I have you?" I mumbled.

"I stopped in to see Dale Kemp," she said. "He's regaining consciousness."

I snapped upright. "What's he saying?"

"Where? What? Water."

"I'm on my way, Doc. Gracias."

Wondering about Morningstar's sudden fixation with the hospital, I found her sitting beside Kemp like a mother, her eyes scanning the chart on her lap. The heart monitor played a soft tone into the room.

beep . . . beep . . .

"He was just here," Morningstar said, patting the hand and setting it on the sheets. "A minute ago he drifted off."

"I've got to talk to him," I said, fearful Kemp might again tumble into the cavern of his mind.

"He needs to stabilize. I'll leave word with Dr Costa. Then when Kemp is—"

"I hear people talking about me." Dale Kemp's eyes fluttered open.

"Hi, Dale," I said. "I'm Carson Ryder. I'm with the police."

"I'm sorry. I didn't mean to—"

"You didn't do anything, Dale. You were drugged and abducted. But you're safe now."

Morningstar frowned and put her lips to my ear. "I'm not sure this is the best time for—"

"What do you remember, Dale?" I said, pressing ahead.

48

He tightened his eyes. "I was . . . getting ready to go out to a bar, uh, the Scarlet Fox. I'm trying to decide what shoes to wear. And then . . ."

"What?"

"Jesus," he whispered. "They're coming."

"What?"

. . . beep . . . beep beep . . .

I heard the heart rate monitor blip more rapidly.

"Dale? Memories?"

beep, beep, beep . . .

"They've got wings." He eyes were getting wider and he tried to push to sitting. "They're . . . insects. Ahhhh SHIT!"

beep beep beep beep

"Easy, Dale," I said. "It's over. You're safe."

He looked down at his arms. "They're eating me! Oh, Jesus . . . HELP ME!"

beepbeepbeepbeepbeepbeepbeep . . .

"What the hell's happening here?" We turned to see Costa, the attending physician, fortyish, dark and slender with angry eyes. "What are you doing to my patient?"

"I just asked a couple questions," I said.

"SAVE ME," Kemp howled, tubes pulling from his arms as he raised them to fend off invisible creatures. "THEY'RE EATING ME!"

Costa scrabbled in the bedside cart and came up with a syringe, deftly plunging it into Kemp's arm. Kemp's eyes rolled back and he sank to his pillow. Costa checked his vitals and looked between Morningstar and me, his eyes holding on her.

"Who's idea was this?"

"It was my fault," I said. "Dr Morningstar was against my questioning the victim. I pushed ahead anyway."

He aimed the eyes at Morningstar. "I'm not sure you should be spending so much time here, Dr Morningstar. What can a pathologist add to my patient's care, if I may ask?"

I objected to his conveniently impaired recollection. "She's the one you called in to identify the toxins," I reminded him. "When you and your people came up short."

"My patient needs to sleep," Costa snapped. "I want no one here but hospital personnel. You can question him when I say, but only when I say. Got it?"

We glared at one another for the required time, then Morningstar and I retreated to the lobby. "Sorry," I said, leaning the wall by the exit. "I should have listened. I'll come back tomorrow."

"I should have protested harder. And I was afraid it might be your lone chance to get some information." She sighed and turned her eyes skyward. "I guess I just burned Costa as a reference."

I was about to ask what she meant by "reference" when my phone rang, Roy.

"Another victim with symptoms similar to Kemp entered MD-General a half-hour back. A young male found in the Glades west of Miramar. Whoops . . . here comes the vic now."

I paid closer attention to background sounds and heard voices and clattering wheels, a gurney, probably. "You're at the hospital, Roy?"

"You got me interested in this thing."

"Roy . . . can you stop things long enough to look at the vic's back? It's important."

"Hey, Doc . . ." I heard a hand cover the phone, voices. Twenty seconds later Roy was back. "The victim's in front of me, Carson. He's as limp as a wet rag. What am I looking for?"

"Check carefully between the shoulder blades."

"They're lifting him. Uh . . . it looks like a figure eight with some scratching under it."

I blew out a long breath. "It's the same perp. I'm gonna head to the scene and see what the techs found."

I called Gershwin and gave him directions to the scene. It took me fifteen minutes to arrive beside a lock separating a pair of drainage canals a few miles west of Miramar, the landscape flat and thick with swamp grass and mangrove, the sound of birds and insects as thick in the air as the scent of water.

I saw a taped-off section along a rise between the road and the canal. The crew supervisor was Deb Clayton, a pixyish woman in her mid thirties whose button nose, large bright eyes and close-cropped sandy hair would make her a perfect Peter Pan on Broadway. But instead of Pan's tight green uniform Clayton wore a white tropical shirt, baggy brown cargo pants and red sneakers. She flanked a forensics unit step van, labeling evidence bags.

One held a fishing bobber. Gershwin pulled up in a motor-pool cruiser.

"Who found him?" I asked Deb.

She walked us to the edge of the canal, green and still. "Two guys in a boat. The victim was only visible from the water."

"Any eyes nearby?"

She nodded to the east. "The nearest house is back on Highway 27. All the perp had to do was pull off the road and drag the victim over the rise."

I checked the sightline from the road. All you saw was wild grass. I turned to Gershwin. "The guy was probably supposed to die from exposure."

Gershwin shook his head. "Not if the perp knows the area. This lock is where the Big Miami Canal intersects the South New River Canal. Heavily fished, more traffic on the canals than on the road. He was on display."

"You're sure?"

"At daybreak this becomes a parade of fishing boats."

I crouched beside the shallow water, seeing a dark garfish hunting the shoreline for minnows. It seemed we'd just gotten a glimpse into our quarry's mind.

"He incapacitates his victims and assaults them, Zigs. But maybe our boy doesn't need to kill."

"Didn't you tell me these freaks never ramp down," Gershwin said, looking into the flat expanse of sawgrass. "Only up?"

* * *

52

Debro was lazily reconnoitering bars and bistros in the near-Miami area, gauging escape routes. He'd visited most of the places, studying the seating, the lighting. The crowd. It used to anger him, the skinny little twinks finger-flicking hair from their glistening eyes as they minced from one clique to another. They'd look at him once and ignore him.

He was invisible then, too. This way was better.

Debro turned toward downtown. He'd finished his morning's work – up before dawn, take the package to the Glades, dump it.

Buh-byee, Brianna. Did the boats dock enough for you, bitch?

He drove carefully, signaling turns, stopping fully at signs, avoiding speeding through yellow lights. If he drove poorly, his invisibility would falter. But with proper care, he could remain invisible for ever.

He saw a street sign. The comic-book shop was five blocks away, too close to let the opportunity pass. He tossed his knit cap to the seat beside him and turned the corner, pulling to the curb a dozen feet from the window glowing with neon signs. He reached for the outsize sunglasses in the glove box, but paused. He had his own mask, he realized. Right here in his hands.

Even better, he could flash the sign.

Debro pulled the cap low and strode to the store. He paused beside the building, pinched his thumbs and forefingers together before lifting his elbows skyward. The mask in place, he stepped to the window and leered inside, seeing a shape behind the counter. He pushed his groin against the window, his belt buckle clicking against the glass. If the clerk wasn't looking before, he was now.

He turned and walked calmly back to his vehicle and climbed inside, pulling to the curb three blocks away. He pulled off his cap, set it on the dashboard, and once again made the mask with his hands.

Do you see us now?

9

The new victim's room flanked Dale Kemp's room and we peeked in on Kemp. He had fallen back into himself after the delirium, his face seeming a somber mask waiting only the closing of the casket lid.

We stepped to the next room and found Morningstar and, to my surprise, Roy McDermott, who offered a sheepish grin. "I couldn't help myself, Carson. After your tutorial in the case, I got interested. I've got some free time, since it ain't like I'm J. Edgar, right?"

Roy was referring to J. Edgar Hoover's involvement in every aspect of the FBI, micro-managing, they call it now. Roy was hands-off, hiring the best people and trusting them to get the goods on the bad guys. "*I don't really care what y'all do,*" Roy had once told me. "*I just want to see files stamped* Case Closed."

My eyes moved to the patient on the bed, victim two.

Light brown hair with a buzz cut. Closed eyes. Had I not known the vic was male, I would have thought him female, the features small and delicate. His hands lay outside the sheet and I saw digits smudged with fingerprint ink. The fingernails showed traces of red polish. I lifted the edge of the sheet, again the fading abrasions of ligatures on wrists and ankles.

"Got a hit on prints from a bust last year, Carson," Roy said. "No biggie, caught at a traffic stop with a half-doob in the ashtray. Name's Brian Caswell, works under the name Brianna Cass. He was reported missing eleven days ago."

"Works as what?"

"Female impersonator, drag queen. Day job is at a nail salon."

"How'd you find this out?"

"Checked with Missings at MDPD. I also called to see if anything new had come up, but nothing."

"You talked to Rod Figueroa?"

Roy nodded. "Nice guy, eager to please. He asked if we could handle it as a joint case with the FCLE in full lead. Basically it means we copy him on reports."

I shook my head in disbelief. If Figueroa had any more faces to spin he'd need gimbals in his neck. But at least it was cooperation. I studied Caswell's motionless face. He would have been good at the cross-dressing thing, I figured, given the bone structure and lips so full I suspected collagen enhancement.

"Age?"

"Twenty-seven."

"Injuries the same as Kemp?"

Roy's eyes went to Morningstar, so mine followed.

"Semen found orally and anally. Lots of tearing, like the attacks were violent and repeated."

Eleven days allowed a lot of time for attacks. "Under the influence of the datura, you think?"

"It makes sense, Carson. After feeling ill, the victim starts hallucinating violently, then crashes into semi-consciousness, unable to fend off attacks or even comprehend them. If the toxins are administered on a regular basis . . ."

"The mind could be permanently wounded."

"So even when a vic recovers," Gershwin said, "we're screwed?"

Morningstar nodded. "Ask who he saw raping him and the answer might be a purple dragon." She looked at me. "You saw the effect on Dale Kemp."

"It's insane," I said. "And yet totally rational and brilliant. After the initial capture and restraint, the perp has no need to keep victims bound. He drugs them so heavily that they're trapped inside themselves. When he tires of them, he simply trades them for fresh meat. Even if they recover, they'll never ID him."

I paused as a nurse entered the room, a guy in his mid twenties, intelligent green eyes, chestnut hair just long enough to cover his ears. He had a runner's carriage, slender and with a bounce in his steps, as if about to break into a sprint. A stethoscope hung around his neck.

"Uh, excuse me, Nurse . . ." Roy said.

"It's OK, sir," the guy said. "I'm cleared."

The exact facts of the case were being tightly managed, the suggestion being druggings with rohypnol – more common, unfortunately. We were keeping the ingredients of this particular cocktail under wraps for three reasons: keeping secret a fact only the perp knew, legal reasons there; avoiding panic when the press dubbed the altered drinks *Devil's Cocktails* or *Loco-tinis* or whatever; and avoiding nutbags wandering the woods with bad intentions and a botanical field guide.

Roy had outlined the situation with the hospital administration and the nurses were chosen for competence and ability to keep a secret. Plus MD-Gen was where ill or injured criminals were sent, so the staff were used to cops taking over rooms. It was, after all, Miami.

The nurse did nurse things, writing numbers from the monitors on the chart, checking the fluid drips and wires, listening through the steth. He popped the protective tip from one of the syringes loaded with the anti-robinia preparation and injected the victim. Roy stood and approached the nurse.

"You look familiar. Your name is . . .?"

"Patrick White. We met once before, Mr McDermott. Last fall when, uh, Mister Green was here. I was one of his nurses."

Mister Green was Sergio Talarico, a narcotics smuggler

who'd suffered a heart attack while in solitary confinement. He'd been rushed to MD-Gen where he'd had a triple bypass and seven weeks of convalescence, all without attracting the notice of his enemies, who wanted him dead so they could usurp his territories.

Roy grinned and pumped the guy's hand. "I remember now. Past midnight and the floor's goddamn security cameras blew a fuse or whatever, went black. Everyone freaked, thinking Talarico's enemies were coming down the halls with AKs. All the other staffers disappeared out the exits." Roy turned to me. "It was just this guy and two cops hunkered in Talarico's room, not knowing what was going on."

"Why'd you stay?" I asked White.

He winked and made a syringe-plunging motion with his fingers. "No one messes with a Patrick White patient, sir. I am one bad-ass dude with a hypodermic needle."

I chuckled despite the grim surroundings. The guy not only had cojones, he had a sense of humor. "You been here long, Mr White?" I asked as he turned to drop the used syringe into a receptacle on the wall.

"Trained here, work here. Now I'm going for my Nurse Practitioner license here."

The three of us wished White well as he blew out the door to his next patient, our eyes returning to the man on the bed, Brian Caswell, AKA Brianna Cass. No one spoke a word as I approached, put my hands on the bed rails, and leaned low.

59

"Where have you been, Brian? What did you see?"
All I heard back was the hiss of oxygen into nostrils.

10

Checking Caswell's digs took us to the cheap side of Lauderdale, the upstairs of a two-story on a dead-end street. The lower apartment was unoccupied and the landlord's name was Tom Elmont, a solid guy in his forties with an outdoorsman's tan and a Marlins cap over a balding head.

"He's a good kid, Brian is," Elmont allowed as he led us up the steps. "People judge them too hard. Think they're sick."

"Judge who too hard, Mr Elmont?" I asked.

"Kids that dress up in ladies' clothes. Brian explained how it's like a talent show."

He stopped outside Caswell's door. "I used to be a hardcore metalhead back in the day," Elmont continued. "Metallica, Def Lep, Sabbath, Kiss. One day I thought about all that stuff they were wearing . . . net hose, high-heel boots past their knees, ratted-out hair, black leather *corsets* for cryin' out loud . . . and started laughing. I was a tough, super-ass-masculine young buck and here I was listening to music by guys that dressed like hookers."

I couldn't stop the chuckle. I turned. "Thanks, Mr Elmont. We'll take it from here."

"Sure. I just wanted you to know Brian is a good tenant, the best. He's a gentle kid, maybe a little mixed up. But everything's been mixed up since Alice Cooper."

Gershwin pushed the door open without using the key. "Check this, Big Ryde."

The lockset was broken, the splinters facing inward, like when you slam a door with your shoulder to get past. It was a cheap lock and wouldn't have taken much. And with no downstairs tenant, noise wasn't a factor.

"Forced entry," I said, following Gershwin into the apartment. The air was suffused with the scent of sandalwood.

It was like walking into a vintage clothing store: racks of wigs, glitzy sequined gowns, feather boas, black leather undergarments, mostly *faux*. But it was a messy store, two racks on their sides, garments strewn across a battered sofa and the floor. A wooden chair was tipped over in a corner. The sandalwood came from the incense burner on the floor, spent sticks and sand spilling out and whisked with scuff marks.

While Gershwin scoped out the living room, I checked the kitchen, small and orderly, foodstuffs and spices stacked neatly in the cabinets. The provisions in the fridge were minimal, luncheon meat and veggies, a couple TV dinners in the freezer beside a bottle of Stoli. I checked the bedroom, a double bed beneath framed photos of Caswell in various stages of fancy dress or undress, vamping for the camera. A bedside table held a few gay porn mags, nothing freaky, at least compared to some stuff I'd seen.

The bedroom echoed the kitchen in its order. Books in a neat row on a shelf, his daily clothing arranged by color in the closet. Socks, underwear, tees, sweats . . . all tucked precisely in their drawers. I returned to the living room.

"Everything else this messed up?" Gershwin asked, twirling a blonde wig on his finger.

I shook my head. "Probably happened when the hallucinations started. Or Brian put up a fight. I'll tell Elmont to hang around until scene techs can get here."

We crossed town to see the person who'd called in the missing report on Caswell, Mitchell Peyton, a friend who had gotten worried when Caswell didn't meet him for lunch the following day. He'd called Caswell two dozen times – Caswell a phone junkie who always answered – then notified police that something was awry.

Peyton lived in a forties-vintage apartment complex in North Miami, seedy in a gentle way, peeling paint, a palm tumbled over in the courtyard. But the architecture was classic and bright flowers bloomed along the walkways, recalling a Hollywood idol on a downhill track, but still able to put on airs.

Peyton was in his late thirties, pudgy and losing hair and

affecting a maroon beret when he opened the door in floppy jeans and a wrinkled Aloha shirt. When we ID'd ourselves he shot a look toward an ashtray in the living room. I saw an unlit joint waiting the match, and he saw me see it.

"It's OK," I said. "Lots of people roll their own, Mr Peyton. Cigarette tobacco, right?"

"Uh, sure. Exactly. Let me just clean things up and you can come in."

Gershwin and I diplomatically turned away and when Peyton said, "Come on in," saw that the doob had disappeared. We entered, but declined sitting, instead leaning against the wall in a neat living room decorated with vintage movie posters: *Lost Horizon*, *The Wizard of Oz*, *Gone with the Wind*.

"You called in a missing report on Brian Caswell?"

"He's been found? He's all right?"

I laid out enough to paint an impressionistic picture, the scene without a lot of detail, leaving the door open for a hopeful recovery.

"When did you last see Brian?" I asked.

Peyton needed a glass of white wine to smooth out the news. "After his show at the Metro, a place on Mountrain Street. He was like, sitting at a table and receiving people, getting props for his show. Brianna burns up the stage."

"People ever buy Brian drinks?"

"Always," the beret bobbed. "It's a way to show appreciation."

"What's Brianna's act like?" I asked.

64

"He does Garland to Gaga, but his comic persona is Ivana Tramp, y'know, like from Trump. He's triple bitchy, put-downs part of the act. If someone hoots at him while he's performing, he might say, 'Girl, why are you here buying *drinks*? Save that money for *dermabrasion*.' It's all in fun. I've got a few videos of his act if you want to see."

My heart quickened. "From that night?"

"A couple years ago, back when Brian was developing the act."

No help and there wasn't much to go on in Peyton's account of the night. Caswell had been surrounded by well-wishers and drink-buyers and he'd tottered home around one a.m.

"Brian was feeling crappy and went home. He was afraid he was getting a cold and he had a show to do the next night. He's a trouper."

Morningstar said symptoms could appear within fifteen minutes following a dosing, including dizziness, dry mouth, increased heart rate, flushing and a sense of general weakness . . . similar to the onset of a cold or flu. The effects ramped up until the victim was incapacitated.

We left Peyton to his buzz and were wondering where to go next when my phone went off: Roy. The excitement was back in his voice.

"I'm back at HQ," he trumpeted. 'We just got a hit on the DNA. A name. It's over!"

* * *

65

We were three steps out of the elevator when Roy was in front of us, waving a report in our faces, his grin stretching from earlobe to earlobe.

"He's nailed to the wall," he said, snicking the page with a fingernail. "The positive on the DNA."

"Did it just arrive?" I asked. With no former hits, the only possible way to get a match was for the perp's chromo-map to have just entered the system, meaning he'd been arrested somewhere.

"Nope. It's been around for twenty-six months."

I stared. "What? How?"

Roy put a cautionary finger to his lips and motioned us to follow him to his office. We entered and he closed his door, not a typical move for Roy.

"I had a meeting with Homeland Security yesterday, the usual trading of notes. I was telling Major Rayles about the case, that we'd had no hits from the national d-base. He said he'd have our results run through Home-Sec's database which, it seems, is more extensive than ours."

"More extensive how?"

"We'll get there. The main thing is, we got a solid positive on one Gary Ocampo. Right here in Miami."

"Particulars?"

"This Ocampo is thirty. No record. I had a couple pool dicks do some fast digging. Seems Ocampo owns a small shop, Gary's Fantasy World, selling comic books and video games. He's the owner of the building and resides upstairs."

I considered the information. "No priors, Roy? A bit odd."

"Every rapist starts somewhere, right?"

I pulled my jacket from the hanger and headed toward the door. "I'll take a team and go fetch Mr Ocampo. Can't argue with the genetics."

"Hold on, Carson," Roy said. "It's not quite that easy. Ocampo was part of a health study at the University of Florida about three years back. The DNA was taken then, consensual, part of the study."

I gave him a *so-what?* look.

He said, "Those folks at HS toss a wide net, chromosomally speaking. Sometimes the net lands in a gray area."

"You're saying a smart lawyer might argue though the DNA sampling was consensual, its introduction into a nationwide database wasn't?"

Roy nodded. "I just got off the phone with the state Attorney General, wanted to know if we could bust this SOB. They promised an answer within a couple hours."

I checked my watch. We could afford to wait if it meant the difference between a clean bust and giving some shyster ammunition to muddy a case.

"I think Gershwin and I will do some shopping until the decision comes down," I said.

"Lemme guess," Roy grinned. "Comic books?"

67

11

The locale was strip malls and free-standing shops, a laundromat on the corner, a pizzeria across the street. A light breeze coaxed tree-line palms into a green hula against a cerulean sky. Down the block was a fortune teller, a second-hand clothier, a storefront taquería, a muffler shop and a uniform store. The little shops were there because the transitional nature of the street – straddling between slums and gentrification – meant low rents, but the street was a four-lane thoroughfare in and out of downtown, with ample traffic to attract customers.

Centering the block was Gary's Fantasy World, the brightest structure on the street, freshly painted and as white as snow. A broad front window beamed with neon signage pulsing *New and Vintage Comics* and *Video*

Games and *Collectors Welcome*. There were two upstairs windows, both with closed curtains.

Lonnie Canseco, a senior colleague, was a block behind. He'd assembled a unit of two more FCLE dicks and alerted Miami-Dade, who'd provided four patrol cars with two-man teams. Also, as a precaution, a SWAT unit was a block away. We could have gone with a major-league assault, but it was my call, and I preferred surgical strikes to carpet bombing. If that failed, I was fine with Bombs Away.

I radioed Canseco to pull down the alley behind Ocampo's shop in case the guy bolted out the back. My phone rang, Roy. "You're clear, bud," he said. "The AG says it's fine. Nail the fucker, but be careful, right?"

Gary's Fantasy World reminded me of an old-school record store, except the wooden bins held glassine-sleeved comic books instead of vinyl albums. Hand-lettered signs hung above bins, denoting *Superman, Batman, Fantastic Four* and so forth. A far wall held video games. Two glass counters in the rear held more comics. I took it they were the crème de la crème, priced from two hundred and fifty to over two thousand dollars.

"Two grand for a freakin' comic?" Gershwin whispered.

I heard a rustle and spun to see a young male enter from a door behind the counter, early twenties, skinny as a rail, with the bleached pallor that comes from junk food and avoidance of sunlight. There was a single tattoo inside his right arm: Spider-Man in lavish color. Per current trend he affected a knit woolen hat of thick yarn, black, pulled almost to his eyebrows. Unwashed brown hair poured several inches from the hat, ending in jagged spikes.

The kid's brown eyes stared at us without saying a word. I doubt we resembled the typical comic-book purchaser, though what did I know?

"We need to see Mr Ocampo," Gershwin said.

"He's not in."

I pulled the badge, evoking puzzlement from the kid. "Where is he?" I asked. "Mr Ocampo."

The kid looked toward the ceiling. Or maybe heaven. "Upstairs."

"Can you call him down here?"

"Gary don't come down here a whole lot."

A voice appeared in the air, wheezy and almost breathless. "*This is Gary Ocampo. What do you want?*"

My eyes went to the corners, the front door, back. No one.

"Where are you?" I said.

"*Jonathan just told you: I'm upstairs.*"

He was talking through speakers. I looked around but couldn't see the camera. "We need to talk to you, now, Mr Ocampo," I said. "We need you downstairs."

"*I can't,*" the disembodied voice said. "*Have Jonathan take you to the elevator.*"

I pulled the clerk close, figuring the store was thick

70

with microphones. "Ocampo," I whispered. "Is he armed, Jonathan?"

"Hunh?"

"Don't lie to me, kid. Is Ocampo sitting on a stack of guns up there?"

The clerk looked at me like I'd started making chicken sounds. "Fuck no. Gary usually ain't even sitting."

"What's *that* mean?" Gershwin said.

The clerk rolled his eyes and waved us through the door behind the counter and into a room of inventory, boxes of magazines and games in various stages of sorting and packaging. The kid pointed to a grated opening in the corner. "The elevator. Push 'up' and guess what . . . it takes you up."

The scene was less threatening than odd. I keyed my mic and told Canseco and the unit we were heading upstairs, then stepped into the elevator. It wasn't a freight elevator, but not one of those house-sized lifts either; a meter and a half square or so, big enough to carry a large fridge with a couple guys beside it. It groaned between floors and stopped behind a gray panel. Gershwin and I were pressed to the sides and had our weapons at our sides, just in case.

I slid the gray panel aside, finding a room so dark we were momentarily blinded. All I could see, backlit against the vertical bands of light between the blinds, was a pale hill constructed on a low table and for a split-second my mind showed me Richard Dreyfuss creating the mud tower in *Close Encounters*. At the base of the hill, against

71

the wall, was a pair of flat-screen televisions, the screens dead.

Was the rapist hiding behind the mound . . . aiming a weapon at our heads?

Someone sneezed. "Ocampo?" I said, crouching in the elevator. "Where are you?"

"Oh, for crying out loud," sighed a whining voice. "Stop your dawdling and come in."

Stepping into the room was like entering a fog made from body stink, stale air and, for some reason, a background smell of onions. Drawing closer, the mound resolved into a rounded blue sheet atop not a low table, but a large bed. The apex of the sheet fell like a ski slope to a pudgy roll of chin. The chin rounded up into a head atop fluffy pillows.

I stepped closer and heard a whirring sound as the head began to ascend, the bed mechanically inclining. Curious blue beads of iris watched me as Ocampo rose to sitting position.

"What do you think I've done that you enter my home with drawn weapons?" His voice was angry.

"May I see your hands please, Mr Ocampo?" I instructed.

"You think I have a gun? Is that it?"

"Hands in sight, dammit."

He sighed and produced two fat hands, the fingers like pink overstuffed sausages. He wiggled them. "See a gun anywhere? What on earth do you want?"

"We're interested in where you were this morning," Gershwin said.

Ocampo's eyes squinted tight in what I took as anger but instead exploded in a huge sneeze. He scrabbled for a tissue from a box beside his pillow. He blew his nose, rolled the tissue in a ball and dropped it in a basket beside the bed frame, almost full of used tissue. I was getting a bad feeling about this bust.

"What did you say?" Ocampo demanded, his eyes red and wet.

"This morning," Gershwin repeated. "About daybreak. Can you tell me where you were?"

Ocampo stared in what seemed disbelief. He snapped the plump fingers, making a *thub* sound. "Oh, now I remember. I was running a marathon."

"Be serious, Mr Ocampo."

"Then I seriously assure you I was right here. Why?"

"We'll ask the questions, Mr Ocampo," I said, studying the mass beneath the sheet. His body *couldn't* be that large. It had to be a ruse.

"What is your mobility, sir?" I asked as my hand crept toward the edge of the sheet.

Again the stare of disbelief. "My *mobility*?"

"It's important."

"I walk around the block when weather permits. Sometimes two or three times a week." He sneezed again, repeated the motion with the tissue.

I reached out and snapped away Ocampo's sheet, expecting to find the body of a football linesman padded out with pillows. Instead I saw a vast landscape of naked flesh, folded and dimpled and lolling, the man's

73

breasts drowsing down his sides like deflated porpoise heads, his genitals hidden under rumpled pouches of pimpled overhang. Several wadded tissues tumbled to the floor.

"YOU SWINE!" Ocampo screeched, scrabbling to cover himself as his face reddened. "You filthy PERVERT! You SCUM!"

I shot Gershwin a glance. Something was hideously awry. I returned the edge of the sheet to Ocampo's hand and he yanked it back in place.

"You NAZI FILTH!" he railed. "My lawyers will destroy you!"

Gershwin nodded me to the corner of the room. "This guy couldn't assault a box turtle, Big Ryde," he whispered. "He'd never catch it."

"*What are you talking about over there?*" Ocampo railed. "*What are you plotting?*"

I nodded. No matter how dangerous or desperate Ocampo's inclinations, he would be too slowed by his volume to abduct anyone. As for slyly doping someone's drink, the floor would shake with his approach, as surreptitious as a tractor.

"Somewhere along the way the DNA got messed up, Zigs."

"What do we do?"

"*Do you hear me you, you . . . fascists?*"

I shot a glance at Ocampo, his face equal measures of anger and humiliation. "First, we try to mollify him. If this hits the headlines, Roy'll tear his hair out."

"*It's harassment, pure and simple! Storm troopers!*"

We both shot glances at the huge man, scrabbling through a tabletop of crumpled tissues and allergy meds and finding an iPhone. He brandished it like a scimitar. "*I'm phoning my lawyers. Then I'm calling every news station in town.*"

My mind raced. Ocampo was taking photos of us, grist for his lawyer, no doubt. "I'm gonna call the lab and give them hell," I whispered. "Get ready."

"What lab? Who?" Gershwin said. Then, "Oh."

I retreated to the elevator and fake-dialed my cell. "Give me fucking Pedersen," I growled, tapping my toe impatiently. When I saw Ocampo's eyes move to me, the act began.

"YOU ABSOLUTE IDIOT," I howled. "We're at Ocampo's house now. GARY-FUCKING-OCAMPO. IT'S NOT HIM! Never mind why, you asshole . . . It was your goddamn lab that ID'd this poor man as the perp. NO FUCKING EXCUSES. We embarrassed an innocent man and MADE OURSELVES LOOK LIKE A PAIR OF HORSES' ASSES IN THE BARGAIN."

"What's he doing?" Ocampo demanded of Gershwin. "Who's he talking to?"

"Some lab moron whose ass he's personally gonna kick when we leave here, sir," Gershwin said.

"I should drag you over here to apologize to Mr Ocampo in person," I snarled. "You will?" I held my hand over the cell and turned to Ocampo. "Excuse me, sir, would it help if we had the guy responsible for this—"

I pulled the phone to my mouth "AMAZING FUCK-UP", then re-aimed it at Ocampo – "come over here and apologize to you in person?"

Ocampo looked confused. The invaders had become the protectors. "I'd prefer if you let me in on what was going on."

"We'll talk later, Pedersen," I hissed into the empty phone and went to Ocampo, my face set on full contrite. The phone call had been an act, the contrition wasn't. I saw a heavy wooden chair beneath a table in a dining alcove between the main room and kitchen.

"May I sit, Mr Ocampo?"

He nodded and I pulled the chair to the bedside. Gershwin leaned against the wall.

"There have been two recent sexual assaults, sir. The assailant left his DNA, which, it seems, was mistakenly identified as yours."

Puzzlement on the round face. "How do you have my DNA?"

"It seems you consented to have it tested two years back, sir. You were part of a university medical study, correct?"

"I remember signing several consent forms, one having to do with DNA."

"All DNA samples can be evaluated as part of a national database, sir. Somehow yours was obviously screwed up somewhere along the line."

He sneezed again and grabbed a wad of tissue, blowing his nose and hawking mucus into the cloth. He wadded

76

the tissue in a fat palm, put his left hand over the right like a foul shot and tossed the wad toward a can beside his bed, a meter to my right. The shot went wide and the ball of tissue rolled to the floor. I shot a downward glance at the tissue thinking a fresh DNA reading might not be a bad thing.

"Are you all right, Mr Ocampo?" I asked.

"Allergies. It's hay fever season." I looked to the window, closed tight against pollen, I assumed. Ocampo's frown morphed into a face fighting a sneeze and losing. He grabbed another wad of tissues from the box and wiped the fleshy plains of his face and cheeks. I reached out a toe and nudged the tissue closer.

"Look, Mr Ocampo, can you accept our apology? Given the DNA indication, well, we had to check you out. We had no idea you were, uh . . ."

"Too fat to move much farther than the toilet? It's OK, Detective. I'm quite aware of my body mass. I'm also aware that it makes me a poor criminal."

Ocampo's anger was draining away as, hopefully, were headlines saying, *FCLE Arrests Bedridden Man for Violent Assaults*.

When Ocampo turned away to catch another wet sneeze, I reached to the floor and snapped up the wadded tissue with my fingertips, slipping it into my pocket.

"Then I think we're set to go," I said. "We're truly sorry, Mr Ocampo."

Ocampo nodded quietly. It seemed a good exit note, hoping my ass-reaming of an unconnected phone and our gestures of kinship might keep Ocampo from contacting his lawyer.

12

We exited the store and cut between the buildings to the alley, finding Canseco in the cruiser. "Where's Ocampo?" Canseco said as we walked up. "He wasn't there?"

"Yep," Gershwin said. "He was there."

"He's not going to the lockup?"

"Not unless you've got a flatbed truck, amigo," Gershwin said.

I put the soaked tissue in an evidence bag, then called Roy and told him we were coming in empty-handed and we'd explain when we arrived. We entered his office and I gave a thirty-second rundown.

"You're certain it's impossible?" Roy asked. "Absolutely?"

"I pulled away the covers to make sure it wasn't some kind of trick."

Roy shot a look at Gershwin for his take.

"I doubt Ocampo's dick pokes out of his fat far enough to, uh, make the journey," Gershwin said. "And even if he tried to sneak up on someone, they'd smell him coming."

"Bad BO?"

"Like he was sweating onions. I figure the only way Ocampo gets a full bath is if he goes through a truck wash."

Roy turned to me. "He sells stuff right? How's he run the shop?"

"A clerk. Ocampo seems tied in via cameras and microphones."

Roy paced for a few seconds, pausing to stare out his window at the glittering skyline of Miami. The sparkling Biscayne Bay was visible between buildings, bright pleasure boats cutting white swaths through the blue water. Roy clapped his hands, turned to us. "Still, lab fuck-up or not, we need a DNA rule-out sample from Ocampo. Think he'll consent?"

"Not necessary," I said, pulling the bag from my pocket. "The guy has allergies and was pouring from his nose and eyes. This tissue went straight from his face to my pocket."

"You're beautiful," Roy said.

We headed to the lab, cursorily flashing ID at the security check-in. I'd been working with the FCLE for nine months and was known by everyone. Gershwin was known as well, especially by the young woman at the front desk, pretty and Gershwin's age, twenty-six.

"I'll run the sample back," I said. "You go fill in your dance card."

He trotted to the desk, me to the lab, a maze of offices opening to a wide expanse of tables topped with microscopes, centrifuges, computer monitors and the like. A large overhead door opened to the lot, useful when entire vehicles had to be inspected. I stopped at the day-officer's cubbyhole and was pleased to see Deb Clayton. I tossed the bagged tissue on the desk.

"Part of the rapist case, right?" she said. "You want results in a couple hours?"

"Take your time, Deb. It's gonna be exculpatory." I explained the circumstances.

"This happen much?" Gershwin asked, stepping into the room. "A mix-up?"

Deb leaned her small frame against a table. "Big testing labs handle thousands of samples daily. Sometime whole batches get screwed up."

"What if it got mixed up at the test site?" Gershwin asked. "At the university."

"Happens less often, since protocols tend to be tighter. But it's a possibility."

I saw where Gershwin was going: instead of thousands of candidates for the mix-up, it might be dozens.

"Let's head to the U," I said.

Medically oriented studies were handled, naturally, by the medical department, a complex of buildings with related disciplines. We were directed to the Office of

Experimental Research and entered a room looking more business than academe: russet carpet, peach walls hung with color-coordinated abstracts, a half-dozen chairs along the wall.

We announced ourselves to a receptionist and wandered the office, footsteps suctioned into the soft cushion of carpet. Dr Marla Roth appeared seconds later, a slim woman in her late fifties with short and graying hair and intelligent brown eyes that stared over the tops of half-circle reading glasses. When we produced badges she hid the surprise and led us down a short hall to her office, more cluttered than the entrance, three walls holding bookshelves arrayed with binders. Her voice was warm, but precise, like a friendly accountant. She directed us to sit, and I outlined the reason for our visit.

"Yes," she said. "I was in charge of that survey. May I ask what you're looking for?"

I gave her the Reader's Digest version and she frowned, probably at the implication of a mistake. She went to a shelf, fingers flicking over files until pulling one and bringing it to her desk.

"Since you're alluding to a potential mix-up in our process, I want to be exact." She read for a minute, looked up over the glasses. "The study involved two phases. The first was purely observational, accruing data from participants ranging from moderately to morbidly obese. Eligibility criteria included repeated attempts to lose twenty per cent or more of body mass, but failing. A major percentage of those who lose that much weight regain it within two years."

"Were you looking at factors other than obesity?"

"Psychological factors were a second eligibility requirement. Participants depressed by the inability to shed weight, with resultant problems. Insecurity, self-directed anger, that sort of thing. If you'd attempted suicide because of weight-related issues, you were automatically chosen. Group therapy was part of the study, both moderated and off-site, much like AA meetings."

"What was phase two?"

"That was more quantitative and involved study of caloric intake and so forth. That's when the DNA sampling was done, the intent being to determine whether obesity has genetic markers."

"Who sponsored the testing?"

"The National Institutes of Health. Total enrollment was one hundred fifty-seven, males and female, about equally split."

I looked at Gershwin. We could eliminate the females from the study, obviously. But investigating seventy-five potential suspects was a huge task.

"May I ask the name of the person you're talking about?" Roth asked.

"Gary Ocampo," I said. One name in seventy-five. "Do you recall him?"

A brisk nod. "Gary was as troubled as he was intelligent – and he's very smart. He used self-deprecating humor to mask very deep insecurities, the result of a rather nasty childhood as well as a lifetime of being mocked about his weight. As with most of our larger participants, we did the tests and interviews at his home. For the support-group work he had to come to our facility. He was hesitant at first, but something changed and he really got into it."

My breath stopped. Had we caught a break?

"How is sampling accomplished?" I asked.

"A nurse hands the patients a swab and explains how to gather material from between gum and inner cheek. The swab is immediately put into a vial and labeled with name and patient code. One swab, one pre-labeled vial. Swab to volunteer, to mouth, to nurse, to vial. No way to make a mistake."

I sighed, the precise chain-of-custody not what I'd wanted, hoping the nurse tossed Ocampo's spitty swab into a purse with a half-dozen others and didn't think to label them until getting back to the U. I thanked Roth and stood to leave.

"Happy to help," she said. "By the way, how much does Gary weigh these days?"

"About five hundred pounds."

She looked down at her records and brightened. "Five hundred? Wonderful."

"Why wonderful?"

"He must have gotten motivated. He's lost over a hundred fifty pounds."

13

Patrick White sat at the desk in his apartment, its surface covered with books: *Gray's Anatomy, Human Musculature, Medical-Surgical Nursing.* An ironing board was opened at his back, three fresh-pressed nursing uniforms hanging from the board. Music played at low volume, études by Debussy. Outside his window the setting sun had turned the sky into layers of purple and orange.

Patrick's cell shivered an incoming call. He studied the caller's name and rolled his eyes.

"Hi, Billy," he said. "What's happening?"

"You going to Kevin's birthday party on Saturday, Nurse Goodbody?"

"Hunh-uh. Gotta study."

"Bitch. All you do is work anymore."

Patrick leaned back and tossed his pencil on a book. He spun his head in a circle to loosen his neck. "I have

85

to hit the books, Billy. Got a major anatomy final next week."

"If Kevin's party is like last year's, you'll see lots of anatomy." A wicked chuckle. "Take notes."

"If Kevin's party is like last year's, I'll have a two-day hangover. Can't do it."

"Gawd . . . when did you get so *serious*? Listen, a few of us are going to the Grotto tonight, just a few drinkies. Here's an idea: close the fucking book and grab your pretty ass."

Pictures of the Grotto flashed through Patrick's head: dark corners, flashing lights, splashing drinks and sweaty dancing bodies, eyes scoping from every direction. It was a pick-up bar, raw sex seeping from the dingy, paint-peeling walls, the bathroom air bitter with the scent of amyl nitrite, any conversation quashed under waves of bass-heavy dance tunes.

The Grotto was Billy's kind of place, but not Patrick's. Not any more.

"I'm not doing the Grotto, Billy. No way."

"You want a study break, Nurse White, have a real one."

"How about D'Artagnan's instead?" Patrick said.

"Oh, puh-lease," Prestwick pouted. "Darts is so *lame*. All people do there is talk."

"I'll go to Darts, Billy. Not the Grotto."

"Oh, all right, little Miss Picky. if you're not there, I'm gonna strangle you with your own stethoscope."

Patrick flipped the textbook closed. "I'll see you around nine, Billy. But when the clock strikes ten-thirty . . ."

"You'll become a pumpkin and mice will pull you home. Buh-byeee."

Gershwin and I were grabbing a fast taco from a downtown street vendor when word arrived that Gary Ocampo's DNA sample was running through the new machine and the results were nearly analyzed. We used the siren to move traffic aside and I think there were a couple times I cornered on two wheels.

At the lab we found Roy frowning at the ceiling, arms crossed as his fingers twitched the need for a cigar. Deb Clayton had turned away to take a phone call.

"Who is it?" Gershwin asked Roy.

Roy shook his head. "You ain't gonna believe it."

"Out with it," I said. "Who's the perp?"

"The DNA says it's Gary Ocampo," Roy said, passing me the printout of test results. "Still."

"No way," I said, staring at the report. "No way in hell."

"The perp's DNA matches Ocampo's DNA," Roy said. "Somehow your quarter-ton comic-book salesman has abducted and assaulted at least two healthy men."

Gershwin thought a moment, snapped his fingers. "Maybe Ocampo's got some crazy accomplice who's . . . it's too weird."

"What?"

"Squirting Ocampo's juice into the victims. Ocampo jacks off and puts it in a turkey baster. The rapist . . ."

Roy held up a hand. "Let's wait for Deb to get off the

87

phone before we spin off the planet. She's checking with a DNA expert."

She hung up and turned to us. "It can't be Ocampo, Deb," I said, feeling like the world was upside-down. "There is no way the guy could assault anyone."

"Yet it's his DNA, Carson," she said, a twinkle in her eyes. "And at the same time, it isn't. Ever study biology?"

A long-ago memory interceded. I slapped my forehead.

"*What?*" Roy said, cigar-denied fingers twitching like he was typing.

"He's a twin," I said. "Ocampo's got an identical twin."

We were back at Gary's Fantasy World in twenty minutes, the time almost nine o'clock, the shop window bright against the dark. Ocampo was sitting and tapping at a laptop, setting it aside as we entered. The room had recently been dosed with a pine-scented air freshener, but nothing removes the undertone of too much body in too little space.

I pulled a chair to his bedside. "You have a brother, right, Mr Ocampo? An identical twin."

Ocampo's mouth dropped open. "How on earth can you know that?"

"I, uh . . . took another sample of your DNA yesterday – a tissue. Legal, but perhaps a bit, uh, covert."

He frowned and I feared another verbal assault. Instead, he crossed his arms in justification and arced an eyebrow. "What does that have to do with my brother?"

"Your DNA still matches the samples taken from the victims."

"*What?*"

"There's only one answer: the DNA came from your brother. Do you have any idea where he is?"

Ocampo looked like I was speaking backwards and he had to translate my words into forward. "Wait . . . what you mean is . . . you're saying my brother, Donnie Ocampo, is the one doing these terrible things? Is *that* what you're telling me?"

"Beyond a doubt. Your brother's name is Donnie?"

Ocampo nodded. "It was. I guess it still is."

"He changed his name?" I asked, puzzled.

"Donnie died a week after he was born, Detective," he said quietly. "He's been dead for over three decades."

14

Gershwin and I extracted as much information as possible from a confused and distracted Ocampo. He was born in a Texas border town, his father dead by the time Ocampo hit the world. He hadn't known about the brother for years, until one day a drunken and teary-eyed mother spoke of a dead twin. At first he'd disbelieved the story as an alcoholic's mutterings, but his mother had produced photos of two babies on a bed – home birth by a midwife – and the two children as exactly alike as, well, identical twins.

There was only one thing to do: go to the town of the Ocampo's birth and check the records. Though Ocampo had lived the first ten years of his childhood in Laredo, Texas, he had been born across the border in Mexico, Nuevo Laredo. I took it that his father was a Filipino who'd been working a construction project in the town when Ms Ocampo went into labor. I also took it that Ocampo's father only worked sporadically owing to a problem with alcohol.

Two alcoholic parents, I thought. No wonder the guy's got problems.

"So there are these four boys in a gay bar and they're arguing about who has the longest dick . . ."

Gerry Holcomb moaned. "Gawd, not again."

Billy Prestwick reached across the table and slapped at Holcomb. "*Don't* stop me if you've heard it. Just shut *uuuup.*"

Patrick leaned back in the upholstered booth. The place was half full, the crowd older and more professional, more paired. Several men wore suits or sport jackets from a day at a bank or ad agency. A couple of dykosauruses sat at the bar, rugged-looking women in their fifties, drinking shots and beers and grumbling about jai-alai teams. The bartender, a tall and balding man with a beret and a John Waters mustache, cradled a phone to his neck as he polished his nails with an emery board.

"The boys have been arguing about their dicks for like ten minutes," Prestwick continued, pushing silver-blond hair from his eyes, his long arms pale and slender and in constant flittering motion. "They're getting louder and more obstreperous and—"

"Ob-*what*?" Ben Timmons said.

"Ob-*strep*-er-ous, you illiterate slut. Buy a dictionary.

91

So finally the bartender gets fed up and says he'll settle the argument once and for all and to drop their pants and slap their dicks on the bar . . ."

Bobby Fenton grinned and fanned at his crotch. "You mean put them on the bar and really slap them?"

"Shut up, bitch, I'm telling the joke. The bartender tells the boys to drop trou and *set* their penises on the bar. So one by one the boys slide their jeans to their knees, scrunch up to the bar, and lay their doodles across it, pulling them out as far as they can. Just then, a guy walks in the door, glances down the bar, and yells, 'I'll have the buffet!'"

Moans and groans. Fenton said, "I'm gone. Some of us have to work in the morning." Timmons said the same and he and Holcomb filed from the booth to back pats and air kisses until it was just Billy and Patrick standing outside the booth. Billy put his arm around Patrick's shoulder and pulled him close. His breath was dense with tequila from a half-dozen margaritas.

"So there's this guy comes out of a bar after drinking beer for three hours . . ."

"I heard it, Billy."

"Shush! Not tonight you haven't. The drunk staggers to an intersection, unzips his fly and yanks out his wand. Just then a cop runs up and says, 'Hold on, mister, you can't piss here.'"

Patrick crossed his arms and waited. Billy affected a drunken voice and pretended to aim a penis at the far horizon. "'I ain't gonna pissh here, occifer,' the drunk says. 'I'm gonna pissh way . . . over . . . there.'"

"It was funny the first three times," Patrick yawned. "Four, maybe."

"Gawd, Patrick," Prestwick moaned. "Lighten up while I go way . . . over . . . there and take a piss."

Prestwick started toward the bathroom, stopped when Patrick grabbed his arm and pointed at Prestwick's half-filled glass, sitting on the edge of the table.

"You left your drink, Billy. What have I been telling everyone?"

Prestwick affected ignorance. "Don't lay your doodle on bars?"

"I'm not laughing."

"Uh, lemme see . . . Don't leave drinkies unattended?"

"I mean it, Billy. Never let your glass out of your sight."

Prestwick picked up the remainder of his drink, drained it away in a single chug, set it back on the table upside-down. He shot Patrick a wink, mouthed, "Thanks, mummy," and ambled toward the bathroom tapping at his phone to check the barrage of tweets and Instagrams and Facebook updates. He walked into a barstool, corrected, re-aimed for the dark hall holding the bathrooms.

Patrick sighed, used to Billy's hip-swinging sashays down a sidewalk, the vocal trills for emphasis, the bottomless supply of jokes. Patrick knew that some-where in the twelve years since they'd met in high school, he had become an adult. He wondered if Billy ever would.

At times Billy showed flashes of adulthood, of introspection, moments in which he realized that his youth and looks were a finite commodity, and though they carried him now, the passage was growing briefer. But such moments were always transient, the span of a meteor across the night sky, as minutes later Billy was ordering another round, or leaving to "comfort" an older man who would repay Billy with one or another generosity, or sometimes just a fistful of cash.

"Come on, buddy," Patrick whispered to Billy's retreating back. "Grow up."

Prestwick entered the bathroom and relieved himself from two feet away, allowing him to splash his initials on the rear of the urinal. He zipped up and turned to the mirror to check the magic.

A face appeared over his shoulder.

"Hello, Billy," the face said.

Billy spun. "Uh, do I know you, dear?"

"It's been a long time. You are Billy Prestwick, right?"

"Now you don't know?" Billy said.

The face didn't reply. It just stared, as if amused.

"Yes," Billy said. What did this thing *want*? "I'm me."

"And the man you're sitting across from . . ." the face continued, like filling in a space on a crossword. "The fellow with the brown hair. That's uh . . . lemme see if I can remember . . ."

Billy hated memory games. "Patrick, Patrick White. You know him, too?"

"Just briefly."

Billy frowned. "When did we meet?"

"You really don't remember me?"

"Of course I do, dear, I'm just so poor at names." Billy also hated *guess-where-we-met* games. He reached out to touch the man's shoulder but something made him stop short of contact. "Listen, dearie, great to see you again and all, but I've got a par-tay I've got to get to."

The man nodded and smiled like he knew something Billy didn't.

"Yes . . . there's a party waiting for you, Billy."

The man turned toward a urinal, unzipped as he walked. Billy started to wash his hands but suddenly realized he didn't want to be in the bathroom any longer and stepped toward the door.

Patrick watched Billy exit the restroom and walk quickly to the table, his pale face frowning he glanced backward toward the dark hall that led to the bathroom.

"You look strange," Patrick said. "You OK, Billy?"

"It's nothing. I just saw a guy who knew me. He kinda looked familiar, but . . ."

Patrick looked toward the bathroom. The guy was either burrowing in for the long haul or had booked out the back door. "Probably someone you met at a party when you were drunk. How often does that happen, Billy?"

Prestwick grabbed at his bag, missed the strap, got it on the second try and slid it over a boney shoulder poking from a purple tank-top with a sequined target centering the chest. "Don't be a nag, Nurse White."

"Where you going?" Patrick asked.

Rolled eyes. "My gawd, Patrick . . . between you and the thing in the pisser I'm playing Twenty Questions tonight."

"Someone's gotta worry about you, Billy. Tell me where you're headed."

A flash of guilt was quickly replaced by a lopsided grin.

"I gotta date, sweetums. Kind of."

Patrick frowned. "Someone you know, right? Someone safe?"

Billy shuffled through his bag, arranging phone and iPad, make-up and spare underwear. Patrick knew it as Billy's avoidance move, and pressed forward.

"Come on, Billy. It's someone you know, right? Not a stranger?"

"Oh, almost. He's like a friend of a friend, just some old bear who likes to sit on his Miami Beach veranda and tell tales about the old days, Stonewall and the Castro and whatever. I've heard that he's sweet and harmless and . . ."

"And might give you a loan you don't have to repay?"

"I make sweet old men feel young for a few hours. I think of it as charity work. You flying back to Kansas?"

Patrick nodded to the half-mug of ale. "Two sips and I'm outta here."

Prestwick affected a thousand-watt grin, teetering

96

slightly in his burgundy loafers. "You'll be running that place, one day. Head Nurse Patrick White, Queen of All the Bedpans."

Patrick sighed. "You're taking a cab, right, Billy?"

"My white knight." Prestwick kissed Patrick's temple. "Yes, girlfriend. I'm cabbing. Buh-byee!" He started for the door, but was stopped by an invisible force. Turning back to Patrick, without a word he wrapped him in a hug so tight Patrick imagined he felt the beating of Billy's heart.

"Thank you, dear," Billy whispered. "Thank you for caring."

"Some of us do, Billy. We get worried about . . . about where you're going. Where you'll be five years from now."

Billy stood back with a quiet smile verging on sadness. He flicked a comma of hair from Patrick's forehead.

"Goodness, Patrick, so *existential* all of a sudden."

"You're smart and talented, Billy. Stop wasting it and use it to do something, go somewhere."

Billy blew out a breath. His eyes went to the floor and when they rose to meet Patrick's eyes, were clouded with guilt. But then, like a bright mask clasped to a penitent visage, Billy Prestwick's face lit in mischief. He winked.

"I am going somewhere, dear Patrick. I'm going to Miami Beach."

And like smoke in the wind, Billy Prestwick was gone. Patrick righted Prestwick's glass, wiping spilled margarita with a napkin, putting the napkin in the glass and putting it aside. He walked to the window to see Billy gathered into a swooping flash of yellow taxi, heading to his next destination, never quite knowing whether it would hold danger or sanctuary.

Patrick shook his head. Had he ever been so self-consumed and moment-driven?

Once upon a time. And not all that long ago.

15

Debro sat in his car across the street from D'Artagnan's and watched Patrick White through the window. He'd slipped out the back after his conversation with Billy Prestwick. An eight-year-old movie began playing in Debro's head. The pictures still hurt. Sometimes they stung like hornets.

The movie montage comes from a trendy gay hangout long closed by the cops for underage drinking. The bar, owned by two old queens nicknamed Harold and Maudlin, kitsch collectors, was *the* place to be that spring, festooned with comic excess on the walls and ceiling: a moose head wearing sunglasses, a bent trombone, a blow-up doll dressed in a tie-dye miniskirt, posters from fifties sci-fi movies, funky birdhouses, a sagging accordion, a stuffed raccoon wearing Mardi Gras beads. The setting evoked fun and laughter.

Having spent days steeling his courage to step inside the bar, a younger Debro orders a gin-gin at the bar. The skinny, arrogant barkeep gives him a sneering once-over and brings the drink five minutes later, retreating to the far end of the bar to talk with a handsome boy in a Panama hat.

Debro is about to retreat to the safety of the street when he notices four young men clustered in a corner, one holding court as the others listen.

"... *so I said, bitch, you are not coming with me dressed like that. It's too trashy and I will not be seen in trashy company. If you're coming with me, you have to be elegant, it's like, my gawwwwd, who wears suede any more?*"

The storyteller has silver hair à la Andy Warhol and black jeans and long-sleeve black T-shirt so tight that he resembles a cartoon spider, happy and sweet, his web spun from cotton candy. The others are tittering like magpies.

"*So the slut puts on a pout like I've just strangled his goddamn canary or whatever and he goes, 'But I spent eight hundred dollars on my clothes, Billy, the shirt alone was almost three hundred dollars.'*"

Debro inches closer to the edge of the semicircle, pushing a frozen smile to his terrified face as the storyteller continues:

"*So I said, girl, if that's a three-hundred-dollar shirt, I'll trade you for two pairs of my hundred-fifty-dollar BVD's.*"

100

The tale-teller stops in mid sentence and looks at Debro, who suddenly feels naked, the other heads turning his way.

"*Well, hello there,*" the silver-haired boy chirps, "*Can I help you?*"

"*I . . . was just listening to your story. You're funny.*"

The silver-haired boy's eyes light up. "*I'm funny? Me?*"

"*Y-yes. You know how to tell a story.*"

The storyteller puts his arm around Debro, moving him into the circle and introducing him around – "*Pedro Cardinale, Randy Wilks, Patrick White*" – before leaning close in the confidence of old friends. "*Have you ever been in here before?*"

"*No. I'd just heard about it.*"

"*It's so wonderfully tacky. You like it?*"

Debro's head is bobbing, needing to please. "*I love the weird stuff everywhere. It's a hoot.*"

The silver-haired boy nods approvingly. He turns to Debro with a conspiratorial grin and leans close, his fingers falling over Debro's forearm. "*Want to want to see something funny?*" the boy says into Debro's ear. It tickles.

Debro nodded toward the goofy moose head in dark aviators. "*Funnier than that?*"

"*It's the funniest thing in this place. I'm talking fall down laughing.*"

"*Cool. Sure.*"

The silver-haired boy pivots smoothly on his heels and points toward a back room, another section of the bar.

"Go down that hall and turn left. It's on the wall, the funniest thing I've ever seen. You'll howl, I promise."

Debro makes the trip, turns and looks at the wall. It's a full-length mirror. He's staring back at himself. He tries to find a back door but can't, so he slinks past the group and rushes for the front door, his face hot and red as he tries to make his bulk invisible in the tight confines of the cluttered bar.

"What did I tell you, hon?" the silver-haired boy calls to Debro's back. *"A scream, right?"*

Debro can't keep his head from turning to them: the faces alight with humor, the storyteller with his hands on the shoulders of a handsome green-eyed boy who's smirking into Debro's eyes.

Until five minutes ago he'd had just the unpleasant, stinging pictures. But now he had names: Billy Prestwick and Patrick White. He looked up and saw White heading for the door of the bar and turned the ignition key. As he pulled away he looked in his rear-view, seeing White appear on the street.

Two in one night. He wished they could all be so easy.

16

The next day we flew to Houston and caught a twin-prop to Rio Grande City, Texas. I was met by the County Sheriff, Martin Dooley, a large and mustachioed man who topped his uniform with a brown Stetson.

"I checked with the hospital across the border in Cuidad Camargo," Dooley told us in his office, knotty-pine with a set of longhorns on the wall and a rattling window air conditioner. "They didn't record a birth, bolstering the story of a home delivery. There is a death certificate for a boy, Donald Ocampo. It's signed by a Dr Raoul Pariella. I barely recall old Pariella, musta been eighty when the birth occurred. Then there's some paperwork indicating the body was delivered to the US."

"Would it have been seen?" I asked. "The child's body?"

"You got a box going by with papers saying there's a

dead baby inside. Someone would prob'ly open it today, the drugs and all. Back then I expect they just waved it past."

"What do you remember of Pariella?" Gershwin asked.

Dooley frowned. "Mostly Mexicans in his practice and he was as likely to try and cure you with herbs as with medicine. An' he had a sideline in chiropractic. But then, it wouldn't been like he come outta UT with his medical degree. I doubt any American woulda gone to Pariella unless it was a pure emergency."

"Can we see the child's gravesite?" I said.

He stood and pulled his hat from the rack. "It's a bit of a drive because it's in a town that ain't there no more."

The drive was twenty-five minutes in the hot Texas sun, the land baked dry by drought, more brown than green, the highway an asphalt strip linking clusters of homes and strip centers broken by wire-fenced pastures of dark and heavy-shouldered cattle.

In the precise center of nothing, we skidded on to a road crumbling at the edges, winding toward a copse of trees. A cemetery lay in the distance, a hillside studded with markers, a couple hundred of them, most small and unassuming. Dooley looked at marking numbers at the edge of the lane.

"Eighty-five, eighty-six, eighty . . . Here we go."

We exited and looked down on a marker of cheap stone, the incised letters saying *Donald Ocampo*. Below that the dates framed a life spanning less than two hundred hours. Below that read, *Rest in Peace Tiny Angel*.

"How hard will it be to get an exhumation release?" I asked the Sheriff.

"Easy, since no one's gonna challenge it."

We were back by mid-afternoon as a small backhoe dug away a few feet of the cover. The operator finished the exhumation with the shovel. "Easier digging than I figured. Probably spring flooding from the creek kept it softer."

We looked down to see a small coffin. The worker cleared enough dirt to free the box and lifted it high. Gershwin and I set it on the ground, then gave the guy a hand up. He bent over the simple casket with a foot-long pry-bar.

"Hold your noses," the Sheriff advised.

"Ain't gonna be a stink, Sheriff," the worker said, slipping the bar under the lid. "Just a little mummy in baby clothes."

He pushed the bar under the lid and popped it open. The sunlight shone down as we all leaned close to peer inside.

No little mummy. No clothes.

The casket was empty.

17

"You're thinking this Ocampo woman . . .' Dooley glanced at the sheet on his desk, "Myrtle. You're thinking she kept one kid an' sold the other?"

"Maybe she doesn't even want a kid and suddenly she'd got two. Maybe the doctor's got his eyes out for such things."

I made the money-whisk, knowing how easy it could be to game the system if you either had insider knowledge, like a doctor, or wanted it bad enough. Like Jeremy, my original surname was Ridgecliff. When he'd been accused of the murders, shame made me run from my past and I disappeared from college. Over a period of months and with advice from a canny old sailor who'd escaped two previous lifetimes (and wives), I continued at another university as Carson Ryder, a test of my false structure. Six years later, although my lies were legion, the Police Academy background check found nothing amiss.

Dooley nodded. "Got reports on the Ocampo woman from those days. Four DUIs, three drunk and disorderlies. On the DUIs she was drivin' a twenny-year-old Bonneville, worth about a hunnert bucks. So she was fer-sure poor. Plus she lived out on Rock Springs Road, a poor-folks neighborhood."

"Anyone still out there?" I asked. "From back in the day?"

Dooley fixed a cigarette in his lips. "What's left is just a couple shacks, but there's a house that someone's been in for years, name's Wilkens. Woman in her late seventies, mebbe."

Miz Wilkens' house smelled of lilacs and liniment. I could see into two rooms, crucifixes on two walls. Above the couch was a rendition of the Last Supper, garish, like the replicator had added neon to the ink. Across the room a large Jesus looked heavenward, a ghastly crown of thorns dripping blood down his forehead. I took it that Miz Wilkens was devout.

"Yeah, I knew the Ocampos a bit," she said, nodding to the west. "They lived up the street from me for years."

"What do you recall of Myrtle?" I asked.

"Big girl, heavy. Homely as a mud hut. Myrtie got pregnant by a little Fil'peen guy when she was a senior. I dunno, maybe she looked sexy to them folks. He got

107

drunk one night over the border and started a fight with some Mes'cans and one of them gutted him."

"What do you recall about Mrs Ocampo?"

"One a her teachers, Miz Bellman, was a friend a mine. She was almost scared at how bright Myrtie was. Said that girl mighta gone on to college, made a big deal of herself."

"What happened?"

"To me she looked like Fatty Arbuckle in a wig, but she thought she was better'n ever'body else, always telling folks how stupid they was. Plus it was just as easy for her to tell you a lie as it was the truth, like if she could make the perfect lie, the world would come around to fit it. I think ever'one got disgusted with her uppitiness and lies and left her be."

"You knew she was pregnant. Did you hear anything about the birth?"

"She had twins, exact ones, couldn't tell them babies apart. But one of them passed away. Barely made it a week, a terrible thing. She and the living kid moved away a while later." She paused. "You know anything about the other boy? The one that lived?"

I nodded. "Yes. His name is Gary. He's doing fine, owns his own business in Miami."

Miz Wilkens thought for a moment and offered a beatific smile. "They own a business."

"*They*, ma'am? What do you mean?"

"When you're a twin like that, and one of you dies,

God puts the dead twin inside the live one. It's his way of keeping them together."

We were back in Miami by nightfall, heading to HQ. "There's no way to trace this guy?" Roy said after we provided the results of our rush trip to Texas. "None?"

"Sheriff Dooley's gonna keep digging," I sighed. "Trouble is, there aren't many places to plant a shovel."

The three of us sat in silence, thinking of how to proceed. We stared out Roy's window as if the glittering skyscape of Miami held the answer. Gershwin was first to break the silence.

"You said these guys are identical? Everything?"

"Physically, at least," I said.

"Then we know exactly what the perp looks like, right? His face, for sure."

18

I awakened Ocampo at eight the next morning. He told me he'd be "ready to receive visitors" at nine; the shop would be closed, but he'd unlock the door from upstairs, and to ring the bell.

Gershwin had to give a deposition in a previous case, so I went alone, stopping at a panadería for breakfast. I grabbed coffee and a pastry for Ocampo and was at the shop on time, in his room a minute later, staring out the open window at the streetscape below. Ocampo appeared from the bathroom, a red water glass in hand. It was a big glass and I expected a body the size of Ocampo's demanded a lot of *agua*.

He was wearing voluminous denim shorts and a bright Aloha shirt printed with palms and pelicans. His sockless feet were tucked into outsize suede slippers; I figured he could tie shoes easily enough, just not while he was wearing them.

"I thank you for the thought," he said when I offered the pastry and coffee. "But I'm on a regimen: breakfast is a half-cup of Greek yogurt and a protein bar, lunch the same."

"Supper?"

"Four ounces of lean protein and steamed vegetables."

"You like veggies?"

A sigh. "I'm getting used to them."

"According to Dr Roth you've lost over a hundred-fifty pounds, Gary. She says congratulations, by the way."

"I told her I was going to get down to normal weight. But she hears that a lot, I expect."

"Few can pull it off."

"It comes down to incentive. Picking the one thing you want more than anything in life and focusing on it. Making it the first thing you think about in the morning, last at night." He pointed to his temple. "It's something that you do in here, Detective Ryder. You need to find a need that's stronger than food."

"May I ask your incentive?"

He paused. "Travel."

"Travel in general?"

"I want to . . . I *am* going to Rio for Carnevale."

"Carnevale? What? Why?"

His voice grew soft and his eyes were seeing something far beyond the confines of the room. "Because it looks so, so free. And the people are good looking, and they seem so perfectly alive and unashamed of who they are. There's music everywhere and people dance on the beach and in the streets. Everyone is laughing. You don't see unhappy faces at Carnevale, Detective Ryder. I don't think it's allowed."

His version of Carnevale seemed as much fiction as reality, but I sensed how the myth might attract the product of a desperate childhood and lonely adulthood, a man who spent the bulk of his time confined not only within the small apartment, but within the ponderous constraints of his body.

"I like it, Gary," I said, meaning it.

When his pale blue eyes turned to mine I was surprised to see hard resolve and to hear strength in the soft voice. "It may take a couple years of work, Detective Ryder. But I'm going to Carnevale. I'm going to pull off my shirt and dance and not be the subject of jokes. I'll have nothing to be ashamed of and no one will ever know what I looked like in my days before Carnevale. I'll be new."

I realized I'd thought of Gary Ocampo as a will-deficient eating machine, doing little more than stuffing his mouth with fast food and pizza while playing video games on the screens at the foot of his bed. But it seemed there was more to Ocampo than gluttony.

"You're dieting, obviously," I said with new respect for the man. "What about the exercise?"

He nodded to the small room beside the bedroom, one

leading from the kitchen alcove. "I have weights in there. Free weights and resistance bands. I keep them there to make me walk to them. He bent his arm in the classic body-builder pose. "Don't laugh, but I'm putting muscle beneath the fat. When the fat disappears I'll be ready for Rio."

"I'm not laughing, Gary. I'm impressed."

"I ordered a treadmill yesterday," he added.

"A treadmill?"

"It's the best. A capacity of . . ." He paused and seemed embarrassed by letting me into his dreams. "I'm sorry, I don't like talking about me. What brings you here, Detective?"

I cleared my throat. "I wanted to give you a report on our trip yesterday. To your hometown."

He listened quietly as I told him about the empty grave. And, given the clouded circumstances, what Dooley and I thought it meant. All of Ocampo's former resolve seemed to vaporize and he stared at his thick hands for a long time.

"You OK, Gary?" I asked.

"My mother seems to have sold my brother. How would you feel?"

"Your mother was a troubled woman living a hard life. She had no husband, no permanent job, and two mouths to feed. She made a poor decision, but poor decisions are part of the human condition. She also seemed to have a problem with alcohol."

He swallowed hard. "Did you ever read *A Long Day's*

Journey into Night? We were living in Gainesville and Mama would go into her room several times a day and close the door. The first few times she'd come out, her eyes would seem brighter, happier. As the day wore on, the room visits became more frequent and her smiles turned to snarls and self-pity. By nightfall she would be sprawled on the couch and raging at everything she saw."

His voice had fallen to a soft rasp. "Later on, in my teens, she'd get the DTs and ramble about roaches on her robe and flying saucers and whatnot. I shut most of it out. I didn't focus on what she was saying, only hoping that it would end soon. That she'd pass out."

"When was the first mention of a brother?"

"One day I told her to stop drinking and act like other mothers. She called me a miserable little fat boy and said she wished she had the other one. I said, 'What other one?' She said the one that slid out of her b-before I d-did."

A tear trickled down a pudgy cheek and he wiped it with the back of his hand. "I said, 'What are you raving about, Mama?' She said, 'Your twin. The one that died.' I said, 'You're lying, Mama. I don't have a twin. Stop l-lying.'"

"Calm down, Gary. Relax. It's just a memory."

He took a deep breath. "Mama ran to her room and I heard her rooting through all the bottles and shit in her closet. She returned with a beat-up shoebox full of photographs and letters. She pulled out a faded photograph of two babies on a bed beside her. One was me, the other

114

was too. Identical. What she'd told me was she wished I was the one that died."

I blew out a breath, a terrible thing to hear from your mother, impaired or not.

"You still have the shoebox?"

"All I kept was the photo of Mama with Donnie and me."

"May I see it?"

He padded to his closet, scrabbled through some boxes, and returned with a yellowed envelope. When he opened it a small faded photo fell into his palm and he handed it to me. I stared at the picture: a chubby and homely woman. In each arm was a baby, each an exact copy of the other. I flipped the pic over. The blue-ballpoint script said *Myrtie, Donnie and Gary*. The date put the photo at three days after birth.

"Is there a chance it's not Donnie doing these things?" he asked.

"None. I'm sorry. He's obviously having mental problems."

"But it's not all that terrible, is it?" he said, a note of hope in his voice. "He's not really *hurting* them. Not for life."

"He's making them sick, Gary. Terrifying them with hallucinations. Raping them."

Ocampo turned away for a long moment. The face that returned was dark and troubled. "We're twins, right? Exact copies? If Donnie's a bad person and he's identical . . ."

I waved it away. "Doesn't work that way, Gary. If Donnie's bad it's because of his choices. Or how he grew up. Don't worry, Gary. You're normal – one of us."

I wanted to cheer him up. He'd been turning his life around, keeping to a tough diet, working out, planning for the future. Given the revelations of the past two days I hoped he could keep it together and not seek solace in food; to keep Carnevale foremost in mind.

19

I had just thanked Ocampo when a thought crossed my mind. We'd known about the brother connection less than forty hours and assumed his presence in the area owed to his adopter – or purchaser – being from the region. Gary had known of a brother, but we'd not considered whether the same was true of Donnie Ocampo, or whatever he'd been named. There'd barely been time to think.

"You've not had anyone trying to contact you, Gary?" I asked. "No unusual phone calls . . . or strangers loitering near the store?"

He frowned. "Last month the shop got a call from someone wanting to sell comics – at least, that's what he said. But when I picked up the phone, the caller got all weird."

"Weird how?"

"I said, 'Hello, I understand you have some issues for sale.' The guy says, 'I don't have issues. You're the one that has issues. Did you ever wonder where your issues come from?' It was odd, but he seemed to have a bit of an accent and I wondered if English was his first language, maybe that was the problem. I said, 'I buy my inventory from sources around the world. What are you offering or what do you need?'"

"And the answer was?"

"The caller said . . ." Ocampo turned white as the sheet on his bed. "My God," he whispered.

"What, Gary?"

"He laughed. And he said, 'Peace, Brother.'"

"Peace, *Brother*?"

"Then he hung up. I thought he was just some smart-ass. Then there was the incident outside. This was the day before yesterday. Some guy was being weird. That's about all I know. Jonathan was the one who told me. It kinda freaked him out."

I went downstairs. Jonathan pulled his knit cap tighter to his scraggly hair and pointed to the wide front window. "The guy was looking inside. It was fuckin' weird. He was pushing himself against the window. Like humping it. He had this big-ass grin on his face."

"His face? What did he look like?"

"I couldn't see his face because he was doing that mask thing."

"Mask?"

Jonathan pinched his thumbs and forefingers into O's,

118

pressed the tips together, then turned his hands around as he brought his hands to his face, the palms pressing his temples as elbows pointed skyward. "All the while he's pushing his crotch against the glass and flicking his tongue in and out like he's fuckin' Gene Simmons."

"What'd you do?"

"I ran over and locked the door. I was thinking about calling the cops, but what am I gonna say: 'There's some dude making circles around his eyes and humpin' a window'?"

"Then what happened?"

"I went behind the counter to grab my phone, at least get a shot of the creep. But when I turned back around he was gone."

I got Jonathan's sparse description: dark hair, maybe, blue jeans, dark T-shirt. I went to the rear and elevatored back up to Ocampo's apartment.

"I'm putting a guard on this place," I told him. "Night and day."

It took an hour to get surveillance outside the shop. I booked to HQ and found Gershwin back from his deposition.

"You think Donnie knows Gary is his brother?" he asked.

"He's in Miami, and something's pressed his button. I think Donnie's got an agenda that somehow involves Gary."

"So why'd Donnie wait until now to make contact?"

119

"Maybe he just found out an adoptive parent died and he discovered evidence while going through the estate. Maybe someone left the truth in a posthumous letter. Or maybe Donnie's known, but only recently started obsessing. A big possible is that Donnie's been in prison. You're checking that angle?"

"Three pool investigators are on it: Tyler, Ruiz and Bell. They're checking everyone fresh from prison in the past six months who has a sexual history."

"We don't have a name," I muttered. "Or a past. Not a freakin' atom's worth of info about the guy."

"We know his DNA. We know he's got some kind of accent. And we know he's six-two with blue eyes and dark hair. Not to say he looks like that now, but on that note, did you . . .?"

I pulled a sheet of paper from my pocket. I'd had the art types manipulate a facial photo of Gary, taking off weight, adding various hair styles and colors, beards and mustaches. I handed the sheet of photos to Gershwin, who smiled and nodded.

"Cool, Big Ryde: Fifty shades of Donnie."

20

Debro was pumping iron on a foam mat in his living room, the barbells rising and falling in time with his unlabored breath, the fifty-pound load for building strength, not bulk. He was naked save for a red thong and the knit cap. One windowless wall of the room was mostly mirror, so he could watch himself.

The television screen that dominated one end of the room was turned to the gay channel, LOGO, an endless procession of delicious-looking men and some lesbians. Debro liked lesbians because they had often been the target of hatred, and it had made them tough and resilient. He particularly enjoyed the young diesel dykes in their camo pants and clodhoppers, a pack of Marlboros rolled into a short-sleeved tee. It was a cool look.

Debro wasn't interested in the television, however. He was planning an event that would allow him to continue his work. It would be challenging, but reap huge rewards.

He heard a muffled thump and held the barbell at its apex and listened. Another thump, this one loud. He cursed, set aside the weights, and headed upstairs and into the room.

Jacob Eisen sprawled on the floor in a puddle of piss. Harold Brighton was at the far side of the room, lying on the floor. He was raising his leg, then slamming it down on the floor. Wham. Raise. Wham.

You never knew the reactions, different with each one. The slut on the floor, Jacob, had settled down after a day, content to be a placid fuck. But Harold had been the hardest to subdue at the capture, and since then had spent all of his time fighting to get to his feet. Even when his mind seemed shut down he rolled and moaned.

Harold had to be replaced.

Debro opened a door at the far end of the room, revealing a small utility bathroom and the bucket and mop he used for maintenance. He pulled a reinforced plastic tarp from a cabinet and returned to the large room, flinging the tarp over Harold as if covering a mattress. He gathered the ends of the tarp and yanked Harold to the floor. Harold's hands pressed against the plastic like flowers trying to break from the soil.

Debro returned to the bathroom for his supplies, filling a syringe from a small brown bottle. He preferred oral dosing while they slept, but Harold needed faster calming, his fingernails scratching at the tarp as his cries grew more frantic.

When Debro was within a step, Harold kicked, catching Debro's ankle and sending him flailing to the floor. Debro hobbled back to the bathroom, searching the cabinet until he found the steel pry-bar used to open the painted-over windows when he'd bought the place. He twirled it like a baton and went back to Harold, his harsh croaks agitating Jacob, whose head was craning from the floor.

Debro felt his anger rising as he crossed to Harold, a memory regressing thirteen years, to high school, Harold Brighton practicing for a production of *Grease*, his lithe body vaulting across the stage, his shirt off in the dank heat of the auditorium, shorts rolled up his sinewy dancer's thighs. It's after-hours and Brighton is rehearsing alone. Debro has crept . . .

into the wings and crouches in the dark behind an old piano, watching Harold Brighton cross the floor repeatedly, working to get the moves correct. Debro's hand drifts to his crotch as Brighton counts off one-two-three and again launches into his routine. Except this time Brighton doesn't stop downstage: He runs straight to the piano and stares down at the crouching Debro.

"I knew I saw someone. What are you doing?"

"I-I-I . . ." is all Debro can muster. He's wobbling, trying to keep from fainting in terror.

Brighton leans closer. "You're that pimply fat thing in Mr Kremer's homeroom, aren't you?"

Debro can only nod. He feels tears welling in his eyes.

"Why are you spying on me, you gross turd?" Brighton demands, arms crossed.

"I-I-I wuh-wasn't ssss-pying," Debro says, wiping spittle from his chin. "I wuhwuh-was . . ."

Brighton's eyes fall to Debro's khakis. Just below the belt buckle is a dark and spreading dampness. Brighton's face wrinkles in disgust.

"Oh, God . . . sick. You, you monster."

The next day all of Brighton's friends have heard the tale. They snicker in the hall.

Debro whips the tarp from Harold and swings the pry-bar at his head. *Thud.* Harold slumps to the floor. Debro crouches and sinks the needle into Harold's hip, pausing to note what a lovely, muscular, dancing hip it is. He looks down at the man's legs, strident with muscle. They're *beautiful.* But then, the man is a dancer, a special person. He'd received gifts most people could only dream of having.

But he was mean and nasty, too.

Debro's hand lingered on the powerful leg before he stood, staring down at Brighton. The man clearly didn't deserve his ability to dance. When he returned to the world he'd be as he always was – special – just as he'd return to being spiteful and nasty and causing pain.

I've been wrong, Debro thought, nudging Brighton's leg with his foot. Taking them, using them, throwing them back into their lives to pick up exactly where they'd left off: nasty little boys so smug and sure and perfect . . .

124

never knowing the insults, the put-downs, the laughter that people like Debro had to endure. People like Harold Brighton had never known pain, only adoration.

What they really needed to know was Justice.

Debro thought a long moment, then pulled off his knit hat, set it back in the anteroom, and rolled up his sleeves. The heavy pry-bar in his hand, he stepped back into the main room and closed the door.

When he emerged five minutes later, he paused in the anteroom to strip off his clothes and shoes, red with blood spatter and pieces of pink flesh. He returned to his apartment feeling like each breath was filled with sunlight. He paused and looked down at himself. A spreading wetness across his shorts. Somehow his release had gotten lost in his time with Brighton, all part of a continuous, explosive joy.

Feeling intoxicated, Debro showered, dressed in chinos and a blue T-shirt, crossing the room to pick up his knit hat, snugging it to his head. He paused, thought for a moment, then pulled off the hat and threw it to the floor.

"Debro calling," he said as he stomped up and down on the hat. He smiled. Debro wasn't his real name, but it was a name he loved, a kind of joke he played on the world.

It stood for Dead Brother.

Debro kicked the hat into a corner, pivoted on his feet like a dancer, and skipped back up the stairs to return a corrected Harold Brighton to the world.

* * *

125

We stayed in the office. I'd put an investigative crew into checking out local herbalists, asking whether anyone had expressed an interest in toxic plants, but so far the results were a big fat zero.

"There are herbalists across the area," Detective Ruiz had told us. "Datura's not something they carry. When I ask, they wonder if I've been reading Castaneda."

I recalled Carlos Castaneda from college, writing about supposed meetings between an anthropologist and a Mexican *brujo* or sorcerer. The brujo gives the anthropologist datura, which sends him to a dark land filled with terrifying creatures. But the brujo didn't keep black locust and dumb cane in his medicine bag.

At two in the afternoon my phone rang, the screen showing GARY.

"Donnie sent me a letter," Ocampo said, his voice trembling. "It's horrible."

"Put the letter down, don't touch it. I'm on my way."

Gershwin and I split up, him heading off to interview the potentials from the Missings file, me racing to Ocampo's shop. Jonathan was there, looking less reserved and cool than previous visits. Maybe the guy humping the window had broken the effect.

"Something's happening," the clerk said, rolling his eyeballs to the ceiling. "Gary's up and pacing."

I heard labored creaking of the floorboards and eleva-tored upstairs to find Ocampo in the center of the room, his legs like pink, rash-stricken phone poles. He wore a blue velvet robe that could have covered an antelope and

126

was sipping nervously from his big red bathroom cup. For some reason I detected a slight background odor of vomit.

Ocampo pointed to his bedside table. "It's there. I don't want to go near it. It stinks."

"Stinks? Why?"

"Read it."

The letter was face up, freckled with wiped-away drips like coffee. A torn-open envelope lay beside it, one of those with the bubble lining. I leaned and read the precisely inked block lettering.

I wrote this on paper I PUKED ON after seeing you. You are a FAT SLOB and make me ASHAMED. You are WEAK. You make me SICK! Things like YOU shouldn't be allowed to LIVE!!!

There was no signature, but I figured it was Donnie.

"Not allowed to live," Ocampo sniffled. "He wants to kill me."

I picked the note up in my fingernails, held my breath, and walked it to the kitchen. I returned to the living room and cranked half-open windows wide to air warm and smelling of a nearby taquería.

"You're safe," I said. "There's a surveillance team watching around the clock."

"*He's* watching, too. How else would he know I'm a fat slob?"

"He can't get close. He wants to scare you."

"Why?" Ocampo was almost in tears. "Why is he doing this?"

"He's disturbed, Gary. Listen, I've got to get this to forensics as soon as possi—"

"DON'T LEAVE!" he shrieked. He sat in the huge chair and hung his head. "At least not yet. Please . . . my heart's pounding. I feel sick."

"Do you want me to call a doctor?"

"No, just hang out a bit, OK?"

I took a photo of the letter with my phone, made a call, then pulled the wooden chair from the wall and sat, figuring I might be able to get his mind off events, at least temporarily, so I initiated idle chatter to get him talking.

"How long you owned the store, Gary? Long?"

He shrugged. "For almost a decade."

"How'd you get started? I mean, this isn't a standard business."

He looked to see if I was joking, saw I wasn't, cleared his throat. "I-I collected comics when I was a kid, buying over the Internet, selling. I was . . . am, actually pretty good at it."

"You must be, to have made enough to buy a store."

"I study things, subscribe to Hollywood news sheets. I listen for whispers of superhero scripts being optioned, movies based on comics. I buy heavily in that series. If the movie hits, the prices go way up. Especially rare issues. Then I buy all the promo items associated with the movie, because they'll become collector's items."

I smiled. "Buy low, sell high."

He nodded. "I've bought issues for forty bucks, sold them for two thousand. I got a Japanese customer spent over twelve grand last year. My biggest customer is a member of the Saudi royal family. The dude's sitting on, like, a billion barrels of oil but when I call and say I've got an early mint Marvel, he freaking flies over to get it in person."

"How about the video games?"

"Jonathan's better with the games. I do the comics and the magic stuff."

"Why magic? Is it profitable?"

He reddened. "Maybe six hundred bucks in sales last year. I like magic. It's . . . probably kind of ridiculous, but I was a prestidigitator of some note. A hit at children's birthday parties. I was called the Great Campini."

A *prestidigitator*, I thought, hearing a note of pride in his voice. *The Great Campini.*

"This was when, Gary?"

"When I was a teenager, junior high and high school."

I had a mental picture of a chubby, fifteen-year-old Ocampo standing before a half-circle of eight-year-olds in party hats, the center of attention as he pulled a stream of pennants from his mouth or produced quarters from behind ears to squeals of delight and applause, probably the only applause he ever received.

My brother had gone through a magician phase, mail-ordering a miniature guillotine that appeared to slice through his finger, a box that seemed empty one moment, dispensing a nickel after my brother tapped it with his wand, a pencil wrapped in electrician's tape. He learned to make a quarter seem to jump from one hand to another. Jeremy's magic phase had lasted about two months, which I expected was typical. That Ocampo kept the trappings of his sole youthful success seemed telling, and rather sad.

"You still do any, uh, prestidigitation?" I asked.

A sigh. "I showed Jonathan a few tricks. He yawned."

"Whaddaya got, Campini?" I chided. "Show me something."

"I couldn't. I'm rusty . . . It's been a while. I'll screw up." Though his mouth was saying no, his eyes were hopeful.

Ocampo moved faster than I thought possible, scrabbling through the closet until finding a red turban fronted with feathery eyes from a peacock's tail.

"The Great Campini is in the house. Take a seat, Detective."

I sat in the wooden chair, Ocampo the cushioned one. "Pull it closer," he said, suddenly the man in charge. "Right up to me. There . . . perfect."

I sat. He patted at his robe as if looking for something, his eyebrows theatrically raised. "Hmmm. Might you have a coin I could use, Detective? A quarter?"

"Uh, let me see if . . ." I started to stand and check my pockets.

He waved me back down. "Wait, I know where one is." He held up an empty hand, the index and forefinger

130

pinching together like tweezers. "Open your mouth, Detective."

I complied. The tweezing fingers flicked toward my lips and came away with a bright quarter between his fingertips. "You should get a coin purse, Detective," he said, dropping the quarter in my palm. "And not keep your money in your mouth."

I laughed and he took my wrist in hand and pressed the quarter deep into my palm and rolled my fingers around it as he intoned, "Now you see it, now you don't. Is it there or . . ." he tapped my hand with his, then opened it finger by finger. No coin. ". . . turned to air?"

I hadn't felt the grab and smiled. "Nice."

He bowed and circled his hand, hiding the grin but loving the moment. "The Great Campini never disappoints."

I heard a small buzzer sound from somewhere near the bed. Ocampo padded to the corner of the room and switched on one of the monitors. Its screen showed the front door downstairs, motion as someone entered.

He gave me worried look. "Are you expecting someone?"

I nodded. "Forensics is picking up the letter."

He glanced at the stained page and his face fell as he pulled off the turban. He tossed it atop the bureau and fell heavily into bed, the vomit-reeking letter again forefront in his mind.

The Great Campini had left the building.

*   *   *

131

I was back in the office in minutes. Gershwin studied my photo of the note.

"He's obviously not happy with big brother."

"The anger is so visceral – puking? – that the note seems written soon after Donnie got his first look at Gary."

Gershwin pulled a chair before my desk and sat, legs crossed, hands behind his neck. "What's your take, Big Ryde? You spent like what, two thousand hours interviewing crazies in prison?"

"My hunch is that in Donnie's megalomaniacal delusions he feels Gary thinks exactly as he does, and he wants to share his conquests, to revel in triumph. Maybe he wants them to physically share what he perceives as the spoils, like a prehistoric hunter bringing meat to a kinsman."

"Meat in the form of pretty young gay boys."

I nodded. "Somehow he discovered Gary and expected they'd become a team, the invincible twinship. He expected to find a copy of himself. Instead he found, well . . . Gary."

21

All the talk about brothers reminded me mine was doing things that were probably bizarre or dangerous and maybe both, so I distracted myself by heading to the hospital to check on our two victims. I was surprised to see Morningstar at the nurses' station, and veered her way.

"Things slow at the morgue, Doc? You must be here two hours a day."

"I make it up at night. At least until I—"

We heard a crash from Brian Caswell's room and ran the hall. I entered with drawn weapon, finding Caswell up and shuffling through the bedclothes, the IV rack tipped over on the floor. He looked at us with wild eyes. "I can't find my clothes. I've got a show to do and I *can't find my clothes*!"

He was having some form of episode. He eyes fell to

my Glock and he shrieked. I'm surprised the window didn't shatter.

"Easy, Brian," I said, holstering my weapon. "I'm a cop, she's a doc. We're here to help you."

"Then you can start by finding my fucking clothes," he demanded, lifting a pillow and looking beneath. "Someone stole them."

"Look around, bud. You're in a hospital room."

He didn't seem to hear, bending to check beneath the bed. "I've got a fucking performance. I'm doing Ivana Tramp tonight."

"It got cancelled," I said, going with the flow. "You're on next week."

He peered at me over the bed. "Really?"

"Cross my heart." Which I did.

He looked around and seemed suddenly perplexed. His knees began to buckle and I vaulted the bed to catch Caswell before he fell, laying him back on the mattress. Two nurses hovered outside the door and I waved them away, *under control.*

"Shitarooni," Caswell said, like seeing the surroundings for the first time. "It *is* a freaking hospital. I, uh, why?"

Morningstar uprighted the IV rack, the tubes still running to Caswell's thin arm. "Thanks, hon," Caswell said to Morningstar "God, you're cute. Great eyes."

"You woke up earlier, Brian," I said. Talked to a nurse, remember?"

"Uh . . . kind of. Big freckly girlie with—" he bounced invisible breasts. "bodacious breastage?"

134

I'd seen the woman a time or two in the hall, hard to miss, easy to remember. "That would be her," I acknowledged.

"What happened to me?"

I looked out the door. No sign of Costa. "You were drugged after a performance, bud."

"I did a show? How were the reviews?"

I did a thumbs-up. I didn't mention the show was over a week ago. He rolled his head, arched his back, frowned. "I ache. And unless I'm wrong, someone's been knocking on my back door."

"Uh, yes. You were assaulted."

He shifted on the bed, winced. "Gawd, tell me about it. I hope the bastard practiced safe sex."

"We know he's not positive," Morningstar said. HIV status had been checked along with the DNA.

Caswell sighed. "At least there's that, fair lady. You . . . the pensive fellow with the sexy frown. Did you catch the monster?"

I realized he was addressing me. "We're trying, Brian. It'd help if you could tell us what you remember."

He closed his eyes and searched for memories. "I'm sorry, your detectiveness, all I see is me at home getting ready for a performance, packing my dresses, accessories . . . after that it's like a switch goes off. Click."

"No weird pictures, stuff like that?"

"I see pieces of things, shapes. But mainly, it's like I fell asleep and woke up here. Listen, I gotta get home,

135

get a couple vodka tonics in my tummy and some ice on my chundini. Can you make that happen?"

"You gotta stay here, Brian. The toxins may take a while to clear. I'll have a nurse bring some ice."

"Send the one with the big bosoms. Maybe she'll give me some seeds."

"Seeds?"

He winked. "So I can grow a pair like that. Woo-woo."

"He's a piece of work," I smiled as Morningstar and I retreated to the elevator, buoyed by Caswell's recuperation.

"I think he's the type who has to keep talking," she said as the door rang open and we stepped inside. "If he stops, he'll think about what happened. It's a protective mechanism."

I smiled as the door shut. "Protective mechanism, Doc? Maybe you should add psychoanalysis to your pathology duties."

"It would be easy to make my folks lay on the couch. But this would be a good time to tell you: I won't have path duties much longer. I'm leaving the department."

I turned, trying to keep my jaw from dropping. "You're going to another city?"

We stopped and the doors whisked open. Morningstar stepped into the lobby. "I'm going into taxidermy and specializing in mice," she smiled over her shoulder. "You spend less money on filling."

"Mice? I called after her, caught flat-footed and running to catch up.

She stopped in the center of the lobby and laughed. I'm not sure I'd ever heard her laugh before.

"Actually, I want to work with living bodies for the rest of my career. In a hospital instead of a morgue."

"This idea just hit you?"

"Last year a friend was in a car accident, hospitalized for a month. I spent a lot of time in the hospital during her recovery. I started talking with the hospital staff, getting interested in cases. I saw the body's incredible ability to sustain injury and yet, with care and the latest in medical science, regain health and wholeness. It was inspiring and I wanted to be a part of it."

"You'd not seen such things during your training?"

"My late father was a pathologist. My aunt still is, up in Atlanta. When I went into medicine, my world seemed preordained."

"But that's changed."

A nod. "The people in the morgue come to me in past tense. I can usually determine why they died, but that's all I can offer. I want to work in present tense."

An orderly rolled an exiting patient between us and Morningstar disappeared behind a bobbing wall of helium balloons. On a job she could be near tyrannical. But temperament aside, Morningstar was one of the best I'd worked with, a consummate pro. I expected she'd be the same among the living.

The balloons floated past and we stepped together. "When'd you give your notice, Doc?" I said.

"Almost two months back."

It took me aback. "That long?"

"Everyone in the department knows, almost no one outside of it. I've already started some of the re-training." She grinned. "And doing observations at hospitals."

Suddenly things made sense. "You haven't been shirking your morgue duties. You're already entering the new world."

A nod. "A couple of retired paths came back to fill in my schedule. I'm doing my observations, studying, and basically considering what specialty I'll ultimately go for."

"You don't have to train a successor?"

"Roland Espy is stepping in as acting director. He's from Tallahassee, an interim administrator. We just hired a forensic pathologist from Chicago. She's worked in Indiana and then, for the past seven years, put in her time in Cook County as an assistant director."

"Chicago? She'll know gunshot wounds."

"She wants a position a little closer to the sun."

"A seamless transition. Espy takes over, you stuff mice."

Morningstar made a scissor motion with her fingers. "You use tweezers and pack batting in their tiny bung-holes. I'll mount them holding cocktail umbrellas and make a killing selling Geisha mice."

I laughed. She had a weird sense of humor, a hidden side. I decided to try something considered but never explored during our working tenure.

"It's Friday. Can I take you to a celebratory dinner tonight, Doctor? To celebrate your big jump?"

It was a long shot into total darkness. I held my breath until she responded with light.

"What a lovely thought. Of course."

I stared. "Uh, really?" was all I could say.

"I'm thinking supper club, Detective Ryder. Drinks, dining, and dancing." She turned and started for the door, her smile a thousand watts of sunshine. "Sounds like fun, no?"

22

My elation returned to tension by the time I got back to the department. Gershwin's office was a former storage room for my office, which he had to traverse to get to his space. I'd been at my desk for several minutes when he entered with a stack of files in his hand.

"I'm gonna shuffle through reports from Ruiz just to see if there's anything there."

Ruiz, Tyler and Bell were the investigative-pool dicks assigned to follow up on sightings based on the retouched photos of Gary Ocampo, potential ways Donnie might look. The photos had been sent to all law-enforcement entities in the region.

"They're overwhelmed, right?"

"Swamped. Were you the one authorized the general release of Gary's retouched photos to gay bars and organizations?"

"What? No."

"If not you, Big Ryde, who?"

"No idea."

"The hits are coming in, but the guys are barely able to check a dozen a day."

I sighed. The FCLE had dozens of active cases – murders, drug dealers, counterfeiters, bank robbers – all handled from two floors in Miami's Clark Center building. I'd been lucky Roy'd allowed me three pool investigators.

"It's a pure crapshoot," I said. "But it's gotta be done."

"Ruiz says next time you want them to check a suspect make sure he's ten feet tall with purple hair and one eye in the center of his forehead. I told Ruiz that wouldn't solve anything . . . it's Miami."

He continued for his office. I cleared my throat. "Uh, hang on a sec, Zigs. Morningstar wants me to take her to a supper club. Any recommendations?"

He jumped into his office, threw the files on his desk and was sitting across from me in a flash, leaning forward. "*Oy caramba*, Big Ryde. Give me the juicy details."

"There are no juicy details. She's resigning to re-train for standard physician-type work and I offered to take her to dinner to celebrate. The supper club was her addition."

"Does la señorita want *Latin* dancing?" I saw his grin widening. "That's pretty sensuous stuff, sahib."

"Don't start," I said. "Just give me some suggestions."

141

He snapped his fingers. "The Calypso Club, an institution. Full Latin orchestra. Low lighting, too, jefé. Candles on every table."

"What's that got to do with it?"

He put a hand above his head, one below, snapping his fingers like a flamenco dancer. "Es muy r-r-r-r-r-ro*man*tico."

I muttered and waved for him to beat it, but as soon as the Cheshire-grinning Gershwin trotted to his office I made reservations at the Calypso.

Auguste Charpentier, né Jeremy Ridgecliff, leaned back in his Herman Miller Aeron chair and looked between the computer monitors and Bloomberg terminal on his desk. The US trading day had just ended and he approximated his winnings: over eleven thousand bucks, on the low side of average.

"Eleven thousand bucks and change, Brother," Ridgecliff chuckled. He often included his brother in his talks with himself, as if the brother were there in person. "How'd you do today, Carson?"

He rolled back from the desk and took a final look at the equipment. He shut the computers down, and began removing the connecting cables, reflecting on his life since beating it from Manhattan with the police on his heels.

After moving to the backwoods of Kentucky, he'd been so fiercely bored he cataloged all flora on his ten-acre property, simultaneously teaching himself French to fit with his new guise (and to read Rimbaud, Baudelaire and Valéry without a translator's intervention). He'd also taken to watching business news in the afternoon while preparing dinner. He'd had no prior knowledge of business, a quotidian endeavor practiced by a financio-merchant class that seemed devoid of scruples, though tended to dress rather well.

While he watched the pot simmer with a rabbit ragout or whisked his *sauce hollandaise*, he flicked between Bloomberg and CNBC. At first it was gibberish, numbers and symbols and icons and a never-ending procession of men and women with second-tier minds (though conducting themselves as though they were first-tier) spouting conclusions about the markets that were immediately contravened by the next series of talking heads. Bond merchants said one thing, stockbrokers another, sellers of precious metals had their own spin.

But as he watched and whisked, listened and ladled, Ridgecliff discerned one vital trait: though comprised of thousands of interwoven parts too complex and ever-shifting to create an over-arching analysis, the market – as a whole; as an *entity* – had a personality. And because it was comprised of humans, it was a human personality, subject not to logic, but trends and phobias and false confidence and insecurities and idiot worship and self-aggrandizement and the need to see itself as the exact center of the universe.

Ridgecliff had arrived at his moment of enlightenment just as the roux in a chicken-okra gumbo had come to

143

the boil, meaning absolutely nothing, but something many people would take as a sign that gumbo was his lucky food. Which was the whole point: the market did not make mathematical sense, but humanized sense.

The market had a personality and it was neurotic.

Even better, this neurotic personality was moronically simple, with only two true states: blustering drunkard and scared child. Anything else was just transition. When the drunkard was ramping into a screaming, self-centered bender, Jeremy Ridgecliff played the bull. When conditions changed and the scared child began mewling and simpering, he played the bear. When the market was in transition, he put his winnings elsewhere, like real estate, hedges, or venture-capital funds.

It was so simple he wondered why no one had figured it out before. But then realized that a decade in an institution for the criminally insane was excellent backgrounding in analyzing the patterns of greed, dysfunction and insecurity.

Ridgecliff was setting a small monitor into a packing crate when his desk phone rang. He leaned over the screen on the console, saw CARSON listed as the caller. He sighed and shook his head as the words spread from the speaker into the room.

"JEREMY! CALL ME, GODDAMMIT! I'M WORRIED ABOUT YOU!"

The caller paused as if to add more, but clicked off. Ridgecliff rolled the chair to the phone's connection to the wall and pulled it out. "If you're worried now,

Brother," he chuckled, "I'm afraid things are going to get even tougher."

He padded the phone with bubble wrap and set it in one of the large boxes provided by the moving company, then went to the door and turned to see the entirety of his office in three packing crates sitting beside his chair, desk, and lamp. The moving company had taken the rest of the contents of his home, his office all that was left.

He started to turn off the light, but paused to take a final look at the room where his fortunes had begun and were daily changing for the better. He felt an odd quiver somewhere near his heart: a sense without analog or precedent.

My God, he thought. Is that *wistfulness*? He flicked off the light.

She was right. It could happen.

23

When it came time to take Morningstar to dinner, I first wondered if I'd made a mistake – a night of escape in the midst of a horrendous case seemed irresponsible – but I justified it with the realization that I'd been averaging fourteen-hours days for over a week. I headed home early, changed into fancier threads, made one angry and point-less call to my idiot brother, then headed back to Miami to take the simple-black-dressed Madame Morningstar to dinner. My blackened grouper, fried platanas and hearts-of-palm salad were superb. Morningstar opted for shrimp marinated in lime, peppers, and garlic over arroz con frijoles negros, and a mango-coconut salad. Being more a beer and bourbon fancier, I let her pick the dinner wine, a California Riesling she pronounced to be "bodaciously good".

When the plates were cleared we declined dessert in

favor of rum drinks, daiquiri for her, collins for me. The orchestra, which had been playing a kind of Latin swing for the first set, ratcheted up several notches, like the musicians were waking up from naps. Chairs crunched back as diners took to the dance floor. Act two had begun, heralded by flourishes of conga.

We watched for several numbers. Actually, I was watching Morningstar watching the dancers, her shoulders bobbing and toes tapping. Our dining conversation had been relaxed and delightful and without a single reference to workaday hassles. We'd spoken at length about her decision to leave pathology, and she seemed buoyed by the prospect of the intensive study and work required to enter a different field of medicine. But that had been blown away by the new volume of the band, the music now trembling with energy and intensity.

The music continued. Morningstar tapped my hand and leaned across the table. "Do you samba?" she asked, speaking loudly over the music.

"I'm a dance illiterate. I Dougie'd once." I illustrated the point by gyrating my legs and waving my hands across my hair.

She laughed. "The Dougie's not a dance, it's a series of spasms."

"Then perhaps samba is beyond my ability."

She stood and offered her hand. "The samba is about passion and fluidity. Let's see how you score in those areas."

147

Morningstar stripped the motions to a minimum and within minutes I had traded self-conscious caution for an immersion in blaring trumpets and frenetic congas. The moves arrived as if borne by music and for the first time in my life I knew what dancing was all about. We kept it up song after song, returning to our table only to finish old drinks and call for new ones.

"Are your legs tiring?" she asked as the musicians started the third set.

"I think they're finally waking up," I said.

Somehow, the hours passed in minutes and the orchestra was packing away their instruments. "Could I get you to do this again?" Morningstar said.

"I'm ready for Carnevale," I said, stealing from Gary Ocampo.

When I pulled in front of her home, the moon was rising through the palms like a beacon. The Rover's windows were open and the breeze was sweetened by dream scents rising from sleeping flowers. Her hand touched mine.

"Would you like to come in and have a nightcap?"

I opted for brandy, she for Chardonnay. Her home was light and open, the cream walls hung with bright-hued paintings by local artists. We retreated to a screened-in veranda to stand side by side and study a wild garden strung with vines and bleached by moonglow. Backyard palms swayed against an indigo sky.

"It's beautiful," I said.

"My own little paradise in the heart of the city."

She turned to me and we kissed, tentative at first, then deep and searching, our hands sliding along one another's contours. When we parted her eyes were low-lidded and her voice husky. "What do you think about making love?" she said, her hands gliding to my hips and pulling them close.

"It's like a samba, right?" I suggested. "Passion and fluidity?"

"Exactly," she smiled. "But a bit like the Dougie, too."

"How's that?"

She put her lips beside my head. Her whisper was a warm breeze in my ear.

"Correctly done, it ends in a series of spasms."

I was awakened with a hand on my shoulder and a voice at my ear. I blinked my eyes open and saw the luscious Vivian Morningstar looming above me with her cell phone in hand.

"It's your understudy," she said, holding out the phone. "Why did Gershwin call me?"

"My phone is turned off."

A raised eyebrow. "I mean, how did he know you'd be here?"

"I swear I only told him we were going to dinner."

A sly smile. "He has a lot of faith in you."

I took the phone. "What is it, Zigs?"

"Donnie's claimed another victim, sahib. Maybe."

"Why maybe?"

"There's something different. I'm at the hospital and you better come and look."

I arrived a half-hour later. Gershwin was in the lobby and had just received the latest news from Dr Costa. Ziggy had had assembled the information, scant as it was, one page in his notepad.

"Where was he found?" I asked as we rode up in the elevator.

"On a road beside the Wildlife Management Area just across the Palm Beach County line. He was lying in the center of the lane."

We went to the room to find the victim's eyes blackened and a gauze compress on the crown of his head. I knew he was Harold Brighton, having gone through the Missing-Person files so often the young male faces were imprinted in my mind. Brighton was the radiant, clean-cut visage with close-cropped blond hair and teeth no orthodontist would make a nickel from. He was smiling as if his life knew no bounds.

Dr Costa was writing on a clipboard; he turned and saw me looking at the head compress. "He was hit with something," Costa said. "Blunt object. Two stitches required. No major trauma indicated, although the blow probably induced unconsciousness."

"Is his back scratched with—"

"The infinity sign? Yes."

I turned to Gershwin. "So what's different?"

"Can I see the victim's leg again, Doc?" Gershwin asked.

When Costa lifted the sheet covering Brighton's legs, I sucked in a breath. The legs were swathed in thick wrapping discolored by seeping blood and body fluids. A tube emerged from the wrapping, dripping pink juice into a plastic bag under the bed. Two purple-black toes peeked out from the dressings on the near leg.

"It seems Donnie-boy went ballistic on the knees and ankles with something hard and heavy," Gershwin said. "Ball bat, truncheon, pipe. The soft tissue and bone were basically pulped."

Costa stepped close. "The left leg will have to be amputated," he said. "The specialist doesn't think there's much left to save."

"Brighton's the dancer," I said, staring at the ruination until Costa lowered the cover.

"Was the dancer, Big Ryde," Gershwin corrected. "He's had his last waltz."

Gershwin and I went to Brighton's street-level apartment, one of a dozen in a stucco building just north of the U of M. The landlord supplied a key and I pushed open the wooden door, stepping in with Gershwin on my heels.

"Uh-oh," he said. "I think Donnie's been by."

The walls had been covered with posters from the Dance Theater of Harlem, Joffrey Ballet and the like. They were now in tatters on the floor, taped corners still sticking to the wall in places. The same had happened in the kitchen and the bedroom, anything representative of dance stripped from the wall to the floor.

"Disarray," Gershwin said. "Like in Caswell's place."

"The disarray at Caswell's seemed from a struggle," I corrected, "things unintentionally knocked over. This is intentional, and probably very angry."

"Like, I'm taking dancing out of your life?" Gershwin mused, staring at a floor filled with torn images of flying legs, whirling arms, and faces alight with joy.

I nodded. "Though Donnie might not even have known it yet himself."

I called for an evidence unit to swing by, though I suspected the apartment would yield nothing usable. We knew the perpetrator's name, height, eye color, skin tone . . . everything. Sheets with his photo were at every regional law enforcement entity. Our secondary team along with the police auxiliary had recently dropped off sheets at every gay bar between Orlando and Homestead. We had everything covered.

We just couldn't find him.

Back at HQ we met up with Roy in his office, frowning into a newly purchased box of cigars as if wondering should he take the elevator down twenty-three floors to go outside and grab a few succulent puffs. When we entered he sighed and slipped them back into a drawer as we filled him in on the latest.

"Why the change in attack?" he asked. "The added physicality?"

"Two thoughts, Roy: this was more personal because maybe Donnie knew Brighton, had a history with him. Or . . ."

Roy lowered his head into his hands and massaged his temples. "Let me guess. You're about to tell me the perp's no longer happy just to shut off their voices and fill their heads with ugly visions, he now needs broken bones?"

"He may have intended to break a knee and just kept beating, Roy."

"You're saying . . ."

I thought back to the thick dressings covering what had once been a man's legs. In the span of three victims Donnie had moved from sexual torment to explosive physical destruction. I recalled my brother's words from a long-ago case, describing a perp as being on a reverse diet: "*The more you eat, Carson, the hungrier you get.*"

"I think he liked it, Roy," I said. "I think he liked it a lot."

"Can you stop him fast, Carson? Can you get this invisible SOB?"

I went to the window and looked out for a full minute. It was not a decision to be taken lightly.

"I want to talk to a specialist," I finally said, turning. "A guy I know who's the best at this kind of thing."

Roy showed puzzlement. "Better than you?"

"I learned the Masters-degree material on my own, Roy. But this guy gave me my PhD in Freakology."

* * *

153

I jogged back to my office and closed the door. The case was going nowhere. Even though we knew what the perp looked like and every cop in Miami-Dade and surrounding jurisdictions had a copy of his facial composite image, not to mention private security firms, university security, shopping-mall security and even – Gershwin handing out flyers at intersections – school crossing guards, we'd not had a single solid lead, and about seven hundred mushy ones.

It truly was like Roy had said: the guy was invisible.

I had no answers. But Jeremy might. I used his advice only sparingly – and when he was in the madness of his incarceration he'd made me pay with pain – but the few times he'd offered an opinion, it had helped solve the case.

Acting against my better instincts, I pulled my cell from my jacket and dialed his mobile number.

"I know you'll hear this at some point," I said, keeping my voice low against passers-by in the hall. "I need you to call because it concerns a case. I need your input. I won't ask where you are or what you are doing, who your friends are . . . I don't care at the moment, all I care about is nailing a real bad guy. Call me, Brother."

I figured I'd send another to his home landline, just to surround him with my need for his expertise. I dialed the number and heard an unfamiliar ringing followed by the connection.

"*The number you dialed is no longer in service*," a recording said.

I blew out a long breath, stood, and walked to the window to let blue sky temper the darkness gathering in my mind. Were my worst nightmares finally coming true?

When in the institute, a sort of maximum-security college dorm, Jeremy had prospered in a way, eliciting friendships with hulking, insane murderers and drooling serial rapists, making it his hobby to understand their delusions and motivations, and thereby control them, at least within certain bounds. But it was a two-way street and the madnesses of others began to infect my brother, creating a howling paranoiac who viewed my every contact as a way to control him. He was dangerous to himself and to others.

It was my greatest fear that the last few years – his calm years, relatively speaking – were only a remission, that the darkness would again rise and pull him into insanity for ever. I also knew that if he was caught and interrogated while beset with demons, he might confess my role in his escape from New York. I would be driven from law enforcement and turned into a pariah among my colleagues.

If I remained out of prison.

Nothing of late reassured me about Jeremy's condition: his joy in cryptic statements, use of other voices, avoidance of my contacts . . . all signaled a return to past ways. The only thing I hadn't caught him in was a direct lie, and in the past, almost nothing my brother said had been true. It had all been to further his control.

I thought for several long moments until recalling that I had eyes in Kentucky, if I wanted to use them to peek in on my brother.

Did I?

I checked my phone contact list, mentally crossed my fingers, and made a long-distance call.

24

After the call – which might not produce an answer for several days – I had one difficult chore remaining: informing Gary that his brother was growing more violent, and from my experience would only get worse. I suspected Gary harbored hopes of his brother being caught in a soft net and put in some therapeutic environment until gentle mental massage dissuaded him of his rougher instincts.

Gary was laying in his bed and watching one of the monitors, mouthing something to himself as a warm breeze filtered through the window. A sheet was pulled to his waist, but above it I saw the robe had been replaced with a voluminous coral sweatshirt. On the bedside table sat a plate holding the cores of two apples, a pear, and his water cup.

"Hello, Detective Ryder."

"I hope I'm not disturbing lunch."

"Just finished. Can you believe lunch used to be a bucket of chicken and a . . ." He looked down at himself and grinned. "Yep, bet you can."

"You look happy."

He pointed to the side room. "Look in there."

I saw what appeared to be six feet of rail-sided rubber track melded to the transplanted cockpit of a small jet. "Your treadmill arrived," I said.

He smiled proudly. "The first time I did four hundred feet, the second I did eight. It was tough, but I made it. Look –" He flipped off the sheet, displaying sweat pants the same color as the top, on his feet a huge pair of shoes, neon yellow with green pinstriping.

"Orthopedic running shoes," he said. "Custom made."

"I expect I'll see you in a marathon one of these days."

"Ha! Half, maybe."

I pulled the chair to his bedside. One of the monitors was dark, the other paused on something called Yabla.

"Yabla?" I said.

"It's a language program. I'm learning Portuguese."

"For Rio, or course."

He grinned. "*Sim senhor, eu sou.*"

"Nice."

"Here's another I'll be using: '*Qual o caminho para a praia?*'"

"Got me, amigo."

"Which way to the beach?"

I sighed, hating to be the bearer of bad tidings. "Listen,

158

Gary, another victim showed up. It's not good. Donnie hurt him pretty bad."

He frowned. "What do you mean, 'hurt him bad'?"

"He smashed the victim's legs. One has to be amputated. The guy was a dancer, emphasis on *was*."

Gary stared. It was like my words had to take shape in his head. "He . . . injured him. Physically? But wasn't Donnie just sort of messing with their minds, not really *hurting* them?"

It took a second to realize Gary didn't fully conceive of being raped while hallucinating as an injury. It made me wonder what he'd seen as a child if he could think that way.

"If by messing with their minds you mean several days of hallucinations and sexual violence, yes. Something's happening in your brother's head, Gary. I think *he*'s coming out."

"*He*? What do you mean?"

"Whatever Donnie's urges, he's been controlling them. But the wrappings are coming off, Gary. Donnie's probably decompensating, to use the jargon."

"What does *that* mean?"

I crossed to the window and saw the unmarked cruiser a half-block distant. "Right now it means I'm adding extra security here. I think you're in more danger than even I figured."

He swung his legs from the bed and began walking and muttering to himself. "It's not supposed to . . . this is . . ."

"What?"

He wheeled to me, his face a mix of anger and confusion. "It's not supposed to be like this."

"What's not supposed to be like this?"

He balled his hands into fists and stomped the floor like an angry child.

"I just want to go to Carnevale!" He was near weeping.

"You can't let this knock you down, Gary," I said. "You've got to stay strong. Keep to the regimen."

"He's *hurting* people. Donnie's actually hurting them!"

"He's been hurting people."

"Not like this. He took away a boy's *dancing*!"

It seemed odd that Gary Ocampo was making such a differentiation between Donnie's abductions and druggings and the physical violence, as if the former was but a pale shade of the latter, but it was a compensation mechanism: If the victims could walk away from their encounters with only a head full of horrific memories, how bad could Donnie really be? Not like a murderer, certainly . . . miles from that. He was only a misguided child, sadly wayward.

But now the twin had wreaked permanent physical damage to a victim. Gary Ocampo, his face pale and confused, padded to the window and looked out on a world that had just turned darker.

25

I went from Ocampo's to the office to do paperwork with Gershwin. It was late Saturday when we broke up after a six-hour day, making a pact to use Sunday for sleep. I fetched Mix-up from my neighbor, Dubois Burnside (who loved dog-sitting my huge pooch when I was out of town), and ended up wandering my yard with a machete, chopping brush as Mix-up splashed in the cove. I needed honest sweat, the kind from physical labor and not from the gut-wrenching suspicion that Donnie Ocampo might strike at any moment or that my brother was again surrendering to his base impulses.

I made over two dozen calls to my brother's cell, nothing acknowledged or returned, like he'd decided to live in another dimension and communicate when it suited him. I expended the anger through my machete.

When Monday came, I slept in until eight and was almost to the department when my car started talking. Gershwin had Bluetoothed my phone to the speakers and a voice in the dash said, "Call from Vince Delmara."

"Yes . . . what? Hello?" I yelled, having never dealt with a talking car before.

"Got something might fall into what you're looking for, Carson," Vince said, sounding like he was behind my dashboard. "That's *might*, like I don't know."

"I'll take anything, Vince."

"About midnight last night some uniforms were called to a disturbance off Biscayne Boulevard, white male, twenty-eight, was staggering in circles, pausing every few feet to puke. He had some fight in him and it took a Taser to knock him down. When he tried to talk he just kind of barked."

"Sounds like a typical night in Miami, Vince. How's it looking like my thing?"

"His head is clearer this morning and he's talking about things that might interest you. Says somebody spiked his drink and tried to kidnap him."

Within an eyeblink I felt my heart begin racing with the adrenalin rush and I think I raced to MPD just a little under the speed of sound.

The guy was named Derek Scott and it looked like all five-nine or so of him had been run through a wringer. Two wringers, maybe: a big knot on his forehead and torn shirt. His short blond hair was matted and his jeans were dirty from crawling on his knees. He sat in the interrogation room with his head in his hands. He was pale-skinned to begin with, and looked perilously close to gray.

"I'm Detective Carson Ryder, Mr Scott," I said, pulling out a chair across the table from Scott. "With the FCLE."

"I didn't d-do anything wrong, I swear. I had a couple beers, that's all."

"A couple beers usually make you wander the streets screaming at people?"

He looked up, his eyes red. "It wasn't the b-beer. Somebody put suh-something in it."

He had a slight stammer and I wondered if it was normal or an effect of the drugs.

"You're sure?"

"It had to be. I'm not a d-drinker, not much anyway."

"How about you tell me what happened. Everything. The truth, please, because it could be very important."

"I went out for a couple drinks. I went to Twilight Time, a bar off Biscayne . . ."

"Excuse me, but is it a gay bar? It's also important."

He looked at me evenly and nodded. "I d-drank one beer over maybe a half-hour, ordered another. I started fuh-feeling sick, like the flu or something. When I got up to leave, my legs didn't work right. I went outside to catch a breath of air and . . . cuh-couldn't find my car."

"You forgot where you put it?"

163

"I knew exactly where I put it, the lot on the corner. But – and this I s-s-swear – the lot wasn't there any more."

"Wasn't there?"

"It . . . it had turned into a suh-swimming pool."

I looked at Vince, standing against the wall with his arms crossed. He raised an eyebrow.

"Go on," I said.

"I think . . . I remember a car pulling up next to me. It made a sound like a jet landing . . . rrrrrooooosh! Like that. A man's head leaned out the w-window and asked if I needed help. It sounded like he was talking from the bottom of a well. I said that my car was in a swimming pool. He knew where it was and told me to get in. The next thing I know is we're fighting and then I'm in the s-street."

"You jumped from the car? Fell?"

"I don't know. The street just appeared. And . . . I think that's all I remember until I wuh-woke up this morning."

"You don't remember screaming? The confrontation with the cops?"

"Nothing. I know you must hear this a lot, but I'm sure I only had t-t-two beers."

Vince had checked deeper and found the guy was a veterinarian's assistant, no criminal record.

"The man whose car you entered, do you think you'd recognize him?"

"I-I honestly don't know. Everything in here—" he pointed to his temple "—is all jumbled up."

164

I retrieved a sheet of Donnie's retouched photos from my briefcase. Scott leaned forward and turned grayer.

"It was that one, the one in the corner."

Not noting the faces were variations on a theme, Scott had picked the photo retouched to show Gary Ocampo's face adjusted to normal size, given neatly parted brown hair, and outfitted with glasses, pencil mustache and pointed goatee. He looked politely evil, like one of Hell's sales staff.

"You're sure, Mr Scott? As sure as you can be, given the circumstances?"

"Uh . . . it's hard to explain, but yes."

"Why hard?"

"It's like . . . like my eyes aren't sure it's him, but suh-something inside my body is screaming, *That's the guy.*"

I liked the answer, figuring Scott's subconscious held the truest picture of Ocampo. I nodded to Vince, meaning, *the guy is the real deal.* I turned off my interrogator voice and went to empathy, what I felt now that Scott's story jived with everything we knew thus far.

"We're going to transport you to the hospital, Mr Scott. There's no reason for alarm, but I you've probably been dosed with a powerful hallucinogen."

"Hallucin . . . you mean like LSD?"

"Kind of. Plus other things to make you easier to abduct. Anything else you remember?"

"It's an exploded jigsaw puzzle in my head," he said plaintively. "Pieces of pictures."

I told him I'd be in touch, but to call if any of the puzzle pieces started to fit together. It was a major break in the case and I waited until an ambulance came to take him to the hospital, then called Morningstar.

"I have a forensic tech heading to the hospital," I said. "Scott recalled having a fight with his would-be abductor."

"I'll make sure the tech gets under-nail samples. And I'll bag his clothes for analysis."

Scratching at an assailant's flesh could pick up DNA, even if the skin wasn't broken. And a single blood smear from a scratch could make a case stick. When it came to forensic evidence against Ocampo, we needed all we could get.

I was returning to the department when I remembered my cell phone was switched off for the hospital. I pulled into a small city park, passing a couple kids on skateboards and one big guy lazily pedaling a plump-tire bicycle. I stopped beside a picnic bench, enticed by the sun on my windshield and thinking a few minutes of fresh breeze might clear the antiseptic air of the hospital from my lungs.

I sat on the bench and activated my phone. It buzzed and I squinted to see the messages displayed on the screen: *Missed Call. Voicemail.* It was from Jeremy.

Heart rate rising, I pressed my VM button. "*One new voicemail,*" the nice lady's voice said. My brother's message had arrived a half-hour ago.

"*Stop filling my voicemail box*," Jeremy intoned. "*I need the space for important messages.*"

His message repeated. And then again. And again.

I listened to the same eleven words for three minutes until I got the point.

26

The rest of the day passed with no contact from my brother, and I added nothing to his voicemail. Not only did I lack inclination, I had zero time: the day contained two meetings with Roy, two with the pool investigators, one with the day-watch commander at Miami-Dade PD, one with Vince Delmara. Snitches were contacted. Bartenders re-interviewed. Recent parolees with a sexual history were reexamined for a third time. An updated sheet of Donnie-reconstructions was created and released.

On the positive side, Brian was released (although the recommendation was for another day's stay). Announcing that "The show must go on", he was wheeled across the hospital lobby surrounded by cheering friends, one of whom had brought Brianna a screamingly red wig ratted so high the attendant had to lean sideways to guide the chair.

It was one of the rare moments of levity in the case.

Despite the investigative frenzy on a dozen fronts, the case produced no new leads, nothing from the pool, nothing from MDPD, and I had found my way to the Palace near midnight, just enough strength left to press the "up" button on the elevator, and I swear I sleep-walked the final feet of hall.

The night seemed to blow by in seconds, and dawn was breaking through purpled cirrus when I returned to the hospital to check on Derek Scott, alone, Gershwin attending the funeral of a third cousin on his half-uncle's side. Between his Cuban mother and Jewish father, the kid seemed related to half of Miami. I was hoping Scott's memory was improving. Both Morningstar and Costa had said pieces might return as the botanical deliriants metabolized and left his system.

I jumped into the elevator. As the door closed I heard, "Hold, please!" I jabbed the button as Patrick White bolted into the lift, breathing like he'd been sprinting for blocks. He leaned the wall and caught his breath.

"You ever try walking, Patrick? Some people actually like it."

He grinned. "I could say the same thing to you, Detective Ryder. I think I saw you sit once. The rest of the time you either pace the floor or you're running in or out like Usain Bolt."

Busted. "Some cases I get to sit and think, Patrick. For this one I need track shoes."

He watched the floor lights blink and cleared his throat.

"I, uh . . . can I ask how the investigation's going? Is that allowed?"

I turned to him. "It affects your world, Patrick?"

He nodded. "I'm not big on the bar scene myself – I have too much going on right now – but I have friends who spend too much time in party mode. I'm concerned for their safety."

"Tell your friends to keep their drinks in hand at all times. And be wary of everyone."

"I have been."

The door slid open, and we entered the long hall smelling of antiseptic. White flicked a wave and resumed his sprint, dashing to the nurses' station to check in. I continued past the station, checking my watch as I picked up speed. It had been two hours since Scott's admission. Morningstar was in an alcove talking to Brianna's favorite nurse and I figured the lovely pathologist wanted to check Scott's condition before heading to the morgue.

She saw me and hustled over, looking stunning in a blue summer dress that showcased the long legs. Her dark hair was unbound and flowing to her bare shoulders. At the morgue or in the field it was always pulled back and held by a scrunchie or, in a pinch, a rubber band.

"I got the lab report," I said, trying to keep my eyes off the gorgeous pins, "with Scott's tox screens."

She nodded. "Datura and robinia, but at lower levels than Kemp and Caswell, especially the robinia, which supports the idea of daily dosings in captivity. Scott was weakened but not incapacitated, and the hallucinations

170

seem gone, though I wouldn't want him driving for several days."

Others were nearby and, except for a wink, I maintained the businesslike demeanor, nodding and progressing to Scott's room, peeking inside and watching unobserved from the hall. I was pleased to see Scott sitting up in a chair with a copy of the *Herald* at his side. His color had gone from gray to pink. Patrick White had come on duty, the two chatting merrily away as White held Scott's wrist and checked his watch. "Your heart rate is down fifteen from yesterday," White said. "To sixty. Is that close to normal?"

"Maybe a bit higher than usual."

White studied Scott's chart. I'd noted the nurse seemed totally absorbed in every case, trying to add something rather than just going through motions. It was good to see.

"So your rate's in mid-fifties, generally?" White said, eyeballing the pages. "That's good. Are you athletic?"

"I b-belong to a gym. I try to go at least three times a week. And call me Derek."

"Make it four gym trips, Derek, and I'll give you the Patrick White gold star for achievement." He hung the chart back on the bed and smiled. "Outside of that, you're much improved. But I expect Dr Costa already told you that."

"I much prefer hearing it from you, Nurse White. You're s-so much nicer."

Was that a shadow of flirtatiousness in Scott's voice?

171

White was turning to tap a shunt on Scott's IV drip and Scott seemed to be evaluating the attractive nurse. It lasted but a split second. When White turned to his patient Scott's eyes broke for the wall. It was the same veiled flirtation I'd given attractive nurses when I was the one in the bed, and White did what all those female nurses had done, that is, ignored it, resetting the water pitcher and glass on the bedside table.

I shot an appraising look at Scott. One of our theories was that Donnie had an anger toward attractive males who were most likely to have more sexual activity – sex figures into a lot of things, overt or sublimated – than less gorgeous specimens. Scott blew that one out the door, unfortunately. Unlike the two other victims, attractive to the point of pretty, Scott was average shaded toward plain: widely spaced blue eyes, thick nose, flat cheekbones. Where the others were slender, he was husky and thick shouldered, and it may have been strength that helped him elude his potential captor, even as his mind raged with distortions.

"Howdy, Derek," I said, finally entering the room. "You're looking good."

"He's doing good," White said, greeting me with a nod. "I think the toxins have about cleared Derek's system."

I nodded at a used syringe on the bedside table. "So the antitoxin's working?"

"Less an antitoxin than a boost for protein synthesis," White corrected. "But it seems to blunt the effect."

"Now that your head's clear, Derek . . ." I pulled a chair to bedside. Patrick White nodded and raced off to his other charges. "Anything you can add to your recollections? Like your assailant's vehicle make and model?"

He closed his eyes and thought. "I don't really know cars. It seemed silver . . . uh . . ." His voice sounded like he was trying to bring something into focus.

"What, Derek?"

"I think . . . I think I see a-a metal thing on back, like a b-bike rack."

"Bike rack." I jotted it into my notes. It jived with a work-out type and I'd have the pool guys take Donnie's pics to bike shops. Anything.

"I'm not sure. It could have been on a car nearby, or a luggage rack or—"

"It's all right, Derek. You were messed up."

"I want to stop this bastard." There was sudden anger in his voice. "I hated being taken so . . . so easily."

"We'll nail him, Derek, with your help. Do you recall the vehicle's interior color?"

"Buh-black or at least dark. But it was night."

"And the parking lot had turned into a swimming pool," I grinned, trying to move him past anger, which muddied recollections.

"Yeah," Scott nodded, a small smile returning. "Th-that too."

I pulled out the photo sheet. "This still seems the face?"

He winced. "He seemed big, too. Tall. Strong."

"Any idea about weight or build?" I needed as much

173

confirmation of Donnie's size as possible, concerned about a future trial using witnesses with hallucinogen-influenced minds.

"It's still fuzzy and—" He paused, pointed out the door. "There. The guy who just went past. He s-seems about the size."

I saw a blue-garbed orderly pushing an empty gurney down the hall. "Hey, partner," I called, jogging after him. "Do me a favor and step back here a sec, would you?"

He shrugged and followed me to Scott's room.

"This?" I said to Scott, nodding at the perplexed orderly.

Scott walked to the guy, looked up. "He reminds me of the guy somehow. He was taller, I'm sure." Scott held his hands three feet apart. "And his chest seemed huge."

The orderly carried a chest more barrel than flat, and wide shoulders. It was how I expected Gary Ocampo would look if he lost a couple hundred pounds. Was Scott's subconscious speaking again?

"How tall are you?" I asked the orderly. "Weight?"

"Six three. Two forty, give or take. What do I win?"

"My eternal gratitude," I said, sending him back to his labors. "A confirmation of our suspicions," I told Scott. "Anything else coming through?"

He stared at his hands a long time, thinking. Then turned up his arms and studied his forearms. "I saw . . . drawings. One on each arm. Maybe it was when we were . . ." He squeezed his eyes tight. "I think he tried to choke me, then hit me with s-something. I saw the inside of his arms."

"Tattoos?"

"Inside . . . the elbow. The same thing, but one was ruh-red, the other blue. I'm trying to get them in focus."

I reached to my briefcase for another sheet of paper, the one where I had taken a black Sharpie and replicated the scratchings found on the victims' backs. "Like this?" I said.

"That's it!" He stared wide-eyed like I'd performed magic. "Gemini. The Twins."

"Gemini?"

"Except for the circles or whatever on top, they were like Gemini symbols. One was red, the other, uh, blue." He adjusted his thumb and forefinger to the size of a quarter. "Abuh-bout this size, I guess."

"How do you know that? The symbols?"

Scott did sheepish. "I used to be into astrology, getting my birth chart made, ch-checking forecasts before I did anything major. Cost a fortune. These day I think it's pretty much b-bunk, though I uh, check the paper for the daily forecast." He took another look at the symbol and raised an eyebrow. "You know what the top part reminds me of, Detective?"

"An infinity symbol?"

"Looked at one way, sure. But if you look at it another way, it's like two p-people kissing."

I looked. It was like one of those optical illusions where you don't see a shape until someone suggests it, then it's

175

all you see. I thanked Scott for his time and went to disseminate the information to Ruiz and beyond.

Morningstar was still at the station and I wondered if she was getting psyched for the big jump. She waved me over, like the big eyes didn't have a gravity of their own. The intern waved and hustled away.

"He give you anything useful?" she asked.

"We've now got an identifying feature: tattoos. And an idea how Ocampo looks, at least for now. It also appears one methodology is to dose the vics in a bar – like we thought – and follow them until they start to become disoriented, when he lures them into his vehicle."

"Bold, but appearing benign? Doesn't that also say something about his personality?"

I nodded at her insight. "It says that when he feels in control, he's fearless. Also that he can portray himself as harmless, perhaps even charming. Both are hallmark traits of an intelligent sociopath, by the way."

Her cell rang and she pulled it from her pocket, answered, listened, said, "Thanks, I'll tell him."

"That was the lab, Carson. The scrapings from beneath Scott's nails? The DNA came from Donnie Ocampo. But you knew that, didn't you?"

We had another piece of evidence. Now all we needed was Ocampo.

After giving the pool detectives the heads-up on bike possibilities, I headed to Roy's office to give him an update. He was tucking a shiny black fishing reel into a box on his desk, the Miami skyline shadowed and dramatic in the window at his back.

"A new Hatch Finatic 7," he said, lofting the box. "Maybe one of these days we can get out and test it."

I sat in the chair before his wide, clean desk. "We caught a break on the abductions."

He tossed the box aside. "Gimme, gimme."

I laid out the latest: Donnie's stealth and aggressiveness, the dark vehicle, maybe a bike rack, and especially the tats.

"The twins?" Roy said. "That for real?"

"Scott saw the sign for Gemini before he saw an infinity sign."

"And kissing, too. You believe his memory about the ink?"

"He saw one sign as blue, the other as red. That may be the drug. But I'm convinced Donnie's twin-tatted himself. It fits."

"Why does Scott remember and the others don't?" he said.

"Scott had a single dose, the knock-down dose. The others were pumped with the stuff on a daily basis. Plus Morningstar says the toxins affect people differently. Body chemistry, weight, age, all can make a difference. Scott weighs twenty pounds more than any of the other victims. Scott got lucky."

"Otherwise Scott might now be somewhere getting his head pumped full of nasty visions?"

"The victims are subjected to days of induced delirium.

Lingering hallucinations could destroy a trial. Even if a victim points to Ocampo in a courtroom, a smart lawyer will prove the witness remains prone to mental instability, an open door to reasonable doubt."

"How about Scott?"

"Right after Scott testified that his abductor resembled Donnie Ocampo, cross-examination would reveal that seconds before seeing Donnie, Scott saw a swimming pool where there was a parking lot."

"Think Ocampo figured this all out beforehand? Tell me it was accidental."

"Donnie is Gary's exact replica, and Gary Ocampo's made a good living by selling comic books. He knows the market and plays it like a first-rate stock-picker. He's shrewd and canny, and leverages it to his advantage. I figure Donnie is just as smart."

Roy sighed. "Scott's memories are messed up, right? Even though he got away?"

I nodded. "Scott got lucky. We didn't."

I started to the door but Roy called to my back. I turned. "Correct me if I'm wrong, bud. But doesn't Scott's escape mean Donnie's now got an empty space on his dance card?"

27

I was heading to my office when my phone went off. When I saw the name DONNA. I cut into the restroom, ducked into a stall and hit the *Talk* button, hoping she'd been able to come through.

"You answer your own phone down there at the FCLE, Carson?" the amused voice said. "I figured you'd have a secretary for that. Or a valet."

"Funny, Donna."

Three days back I'd called Donna Cherry of the Kentucky State Police, a special investigator now based in Jackson, Kentucky, about thirty-five miles from Jeremy's mountain hideaway. When Jeremy had lured me to Kentucky several years ago, I'd found myself involved in a local case. Cherry and I had started out as adversaries and evolved into something altogether different. I had called to ask a favor: that she personally contact Dr

Auguste Charpentier and request he call me. She knew Jeremy only as a retired professor of psychology who had provided a bit of assistance on the case, and assumed I wanted to re-establish contact with a question about a new case. Of course, what I wanted was for Jeremy to open his door to a cop asking that he call me.

It would make my point: I'm serious.

"Like I said," Cherry continued, "I've seen Doc Charpentier a time or two, once at the Campton library, once at the grocery in Stanton. He was his usual reserved, polite self. Plus he looked super great, like he'd been working out. But then, he was always a kind of sexy dude . . ." She paused. "For a middle-aged guy, of course."

As Charpentier, Jeremy used simple tricks to age himself. Though almost forty-five, my brother's clear blue eyes and flawless skin made him appear closer to my age of thirty-nine. Charpentier looked in his mid-fifties.

"You finally got a chance to personally pass on my message?"

"I needed to run down the Mountain Parkway into Slade, so I dropped by his place. You've got bad luck, my friend. That big ol' cabin was as empty as a ghost town. I peeked in every downstairs window. The only thing inside were echoes."

"Damn," I whispered, feeling my heart sink.

"I stopped by the local post office. He cancelled his box last week and left no forwarding address. You missed him by days, hours maybe."

"Nothing to say where he's headed, Donna?"

"Zippo. I figure he got tired of retirement and took another university position, Crown Prince of Oxford University, maybe. Charpentier had way too much candle-power to wither away in the woods, Carson. That guy could be anything he wanted."

Debro flicked on the lights and peered through the window in the metal door. Jacob Eisen was naked on the floor and seemed to be trying to swim. But instead of a foamy path in his wake, he was leaving blood. It looked like someone had followed him with a paint-smeared mop, spreading red in a foot-wide swash.

Eisen stopped paddling and tried to push up on his arms, his mouth, chin and chest glistening red. His hands slipped in the scarlet viscosity and his face banged to the linoleum. One of Eisen's trembling fingers slid into the red hole of his mouth, digging deep until stopped by his thumb.

His eyes grew as wide as if seeing a demon and he tried to crawl from the hideous vision, slipping and sliding in his own fluid, blood spattering from his mouth as screams came out in a red and silent spray.

Debro stood at the window, but his mind was far away, tumbling back in time and as it tumbled, his body grew round and clumsy and his knees quivered with its weight. His hands swelled until his fingers were as plump as sausages, his knuckles like dimples in the fat . . .

the hands atop a barroom table with a half-consumed daiquiri beside them.

181

"Hey, you," *calls a voice from a dozen feet away.* "Yeah, you – Chubby. Does your ass beep when you back up?"

He's in a bar trying to make friends. It's late and the boys at a table across the way have noticed him. They're tough boys in paint-tight jeans and leather jackets, hard little monsters who make themselves big by making others small. Debro had seen them noticing him and laughing among themselves, but it's the wiry boy with hard dark eyes under kinked red hair who's been laughing the hardest. He's the leader. The others are as meaningless as dust.

"You're in the wrong bar, tubs," *he smirks.* "The chairs are only rated for four hundred pounds."

Debro smiles and waves, like he's enjoying the sport. But inside, fear and shame.

"You know there's a superchub bar in east Lauderdale, fat boy. Shouldn't you be up there mixin' with the Michelin Men?"

Superchubs were enormously obese gay men with a fetishistical following in some circles. Debro went to the bar once and it sickened him. Their look, their smell, their hairy grossness. Their joy at being fat. He wasn't one of them.

"My crew and I have a bet, beefy. They think you need to put a bookmark in the flab rolls to find your dick. I think you wrap a string around it and let the string hang out. Which is it?"

Debro forces a grin to his face and mimes pulling a

182

cord in front of his ponderous belly. "You win. It's the string."

Laughter, but not with him, at him. At his simpering, broken smile, at his self-loathing weakness. He should get up and punch the leader, beat his smirky face into a slimy puddle. He looks at his hands, but instead of balling into fists, they retreat beneath the table.

The red-haired guy spins to his companions and smirks, then turns to Debro. "We got another bet, doughboy. When you come, do you shoot lard?"

Over the years, Debro had been on the savage end of many nasty tongues, but Jacob Eisen had the nastiest of all, an acid-edged tongue that reveled in spewing insults and meanness . . .

Which was why Eisen no longer had the tongue. Twenty minutes ago Debro had reached into Eisen's gaping mouth, snatched the tongue with pliers, pulled it as far out as possible. The tongue had offered less resistance than gelding a hog.

Eisen had started choking and Debro had rolled him to his belly where he moaned and gurgled and dug at his face as blood spilled across the floor. But now he seemed to have mostly forgotten the tongue, swimming around the room like a fucking mermaid. Justice had been done, and Eisen could go back to his filthy world. There were others awaiting punishment.

Debro returned to his apartment below, turning the TV to the LOGO channel and stripping off his shirt, preparing to pump iron, get the guns warmed up for the next challenge. He started to reset the weight on his 'bells, but stopped . . . hadn't he just had a major triumph? It had been glorious, removing the little bastard's instrument of hate, and as he had sawed at the slimy tongue, Debro had struggled to stay on task through a monumental orgasm.

A celebratory drink was called for.

Debro rolled the barbell back to the corner and went to the kitchen, catching his reflection in the glass of his cabinet doors. He was smiling. Debro studied himself as if seeing a well-done portrait, then stopped and admonished himself. Best not get too pleased. After all, hadn't he fucked up his latest attempt by letting the pathetic, stuttering troll named Derek Scott escape into the street? Allowing him to run to the police?

It had been a major mistake on Donnie's part.

Debro started laughing. He reached into the fridge and plucked out a beer. He was more invisible than ever.

28

Another fifteen-hour day became another fifteen hours lost in the crime-solving department, and the brother side of things was no better. It appeared Jeremy had decamped from Eastern Kentucky on a permanent basis.

After he'd escaped from everything the NYPD could throw at him (including, at times, me), his year-long disappearance had been one of the most difficult times in my life, with every phone call ringing the potential for life-changing horror: *Hello, Detective Ryder? Captain Ralph Stewart here in Pittsburgh. We've caught a killer named Jeremy Ridgecliff. You ain't gonna believe this, but the freak's telling us you're his brother and the reason he's out on the streets. I know he's bug-eye crazy, but you can appreciate we've got to rule out all the manure this loonie is spreading . . .*

The thought of living that way again felt like a punch

in the gut. But I concentrated on the single pleasant thought in my life, tonight's dinner with Vivian Morningstar. I felt like a kid watching his Christmas tree burn from the bottom up: At least I could focus on the lovely angel up top until the flames arrived.

The restaurant was an intimate family place with six tables and a single waiter. I ordered a brew to sit across from her vino and we both ordered *ropa vieja*, that hearty Cuban dish of shredded beef cooked with tomatoes, onions and peppers and often served, as this was, with *platanas maduros*, black-ripe plantains sautéed in butter and demerara sugar.

We ate slowly to savor, speaking as we dined.

"How are things coming with the department?" I asked. "Prepping for the exit scene?"

She buttered a piece of steamy, fresh-baked bread. "The incoming path will share duties with Fontova and Nelson until getting a handle on things, then hopefully move into an upper-level position." Pop . . . between her wide and lovely lips went the bread.

"Clean and efficient. How's your staff taking it?"

"They'll be happy to see the gorgon go."

"Horsecrap. They revere you, Vivian."

Rolled eyes to hide the embarrassment. "Misplaced, but yeah, some do. It'll be hard, Carson. I've been there for a decade, and we hit some home runs."

"You'll hit more. Any thoughts on specialty?"

"I've not even started my courses. I can't think about what I'll—"

"You already have, Viv."

Her fork paused mid-lift and the hazel eyes – shaded brown today – regarded me curiously. "Am I that transparent? Or are you that good at reading people?"

I smiled. "Some people."

"Trauma appeals to me, working in an emergency room and making decisions, weighing alternatives, fast-running a list of potential solutions through my mind . . ." she paused and her eyes darkened. "The only thing that worries me is, what happens the first time I make a wrong decision and someone dies?"

"You answered yourself by saying 'the first time'. You've acknowledged that death will happen – in that milieu it can't *not* happen – and it's a part of the job. All you can do is work the stats in your favor, which you'll do by becoming one of the best there is."

Another pause. "Have you ever made a mistake that cost someone's life?"

"Yes. Usually by not getting to a solution quick enough. But when I mull over my mistakes, which I do in darker moments, I leaven them with counts of lives saved. There are more names in that column, Viv. A lot more."

She thought for a moment and nodded. Then, as if feeling the conversation had gone far enough down that road, her face brightened and she reached for my hand. "I was thinking this afternoon . . . I basically only know about you from your college days onward. Aimless for a couple years, the odd jobs. Until your friend Harry

Nautilus convinced you to become a cop. But what about family? Do you have siblings?"

I took a sip of beer to dampen my upcoming lies and revisited the "only-child" scenario I'd glibly espoused dozens of times before. Only three living people knew of my brother: Harry Nautilus, Clair Peltier, and a troubled and alcoholic Mobile pathologist named Ava Davanelle, fired long ago.

Jeremy had injured me during a trip to the institute for advice on a case – he exacted a horrific price back then – and when Ava nursed my wounds I had confessed my secret. Ava had seemed fascinated by the depressing horror of my childhood and the claws by which it still clutched my daily life, and she demanded to accompany me on my follow-up trip to the Institute, where more information from Jeremy would require another payment of pain.

The confrontation between Jeremy and Ava had been searing. Made a hater of women by our mother's retreats from responsibility, Jeremy had circled Ava like a hawk, belittling her with every swooping pass: "*A tender li'l thing like you wading through DEAD BODIES, Miz Davanelle? Ha! Do you pick at them . . . a pinch of tissue here, a strand of sinew there? Or do you just watch as a LOWLY MAN DOES THE WORK? What DO YOU do with bodies, sweet thang?*"

Ava had refused to be cowed by his taunts, and actually seemed to enjoy the dangerous confrontation with my erratic, angry brother. "*I do a lot of things with dead bodies, Mr Ridgecliff,*" she'd calmly replied. "*But most of all I like to slice open their bellies, climb inside and paddle them around like canoes.*"

I had been amazed by the power with which the formerly shy and meek woman had constrained and confounded my brother. Every lie he threw she turned into wounding truths and threw back harder, and I had watched breathlessly, afraid Ava would finally push Jeremy into violence. But somehow – through instinct or luck – she sensed where Jeremy's boundaries lay, and we all survived that dark evening. In the end, Ava had won: Jeremy was confounded and silenced by her courage, which kept him from injuring me further.

In retrospect, I think Ava forced Jeremy to look within himself during the following days, and in that time he began to change. And though he would never be normal, he ceased to be the lit stick of dynamite that had darkened our relationship since his incarceration. I received no more shrieking midnight calls. No more babbling, incoherent threats. And he never again needed to cause me physical pain.

I looked up from my memories into Vivian's expectant eyes. The old lie was on my tongue: *A happy childhood*, I'd say, ending with the unfortunate revelation that my father had been lost in a plane crash when I was ten and my mother perished quietly from cancer.

But the old lies got stuck in my throat. "I, uh . . . that is—"

Morningstar giggled, thinking I was playing a game. "What? You've forgotten if you have brothers and sisters?"

189

I set aside my glass and measured out my words. "I have a brother, Vivian. He's six years older than me and we've had some difficult times. I'm a little worried about him right now, but I'm hopeful things will work out."

"What's his name?"

Thomas . . . Eliot . . . Blake . . . William . . .

"Jeremy."

Everything I'd said was factual, though ninety-nine per cent was missing. Still, it was the first time – outside of the aforementioned trio – that I'd admitted to a brother, much less spoken his name.

Morningstar held her wineglass in toast position. "To you and your brother, Carson. May everything work out between you two."

I tapped her glass with mine.

"To us, then. Brothers."

29

Morningstar and I spent the night at the Palace and rose as dawn painted the sky with pastel shades Degas would have envied. The day might have been perfect had not Donnie Ocampo been eluding capture at every turn. Morningstar had early meetings at the morgue, and I wanted to find something, anything, that would put me in Donnie Ocampo's path. I dropped her at her office before nine and was racing to the Clark Center when my phone rang: Roy.

"I just got word, Carson," he said. "Donnie's left another one."

I pulled into a parking spot, heart racing.

"Is it bad, Roy?"

"He's, uh . . . Christ Jesus, Carson. The vic was being rushed to Baptist North, but MDPD intervened and the bus went to MD-Gen. I'll meet you there."

I was at the hospital in twenty minutes, my time from car to hospital wing about one minute, running the stairs and arriving at the room with tongue and shirt tail hanging. Roy was leaning the door frame and simply looked at me and blew out a breath. I went inside and saw the patient in the bed had the lower half of his face under thick gauze, tubes running into the padding. Costa was at the man's side, pumping medicine into a shunt. He looked at me with sad eyes.

"He can't talk to you, Detective Ryder. I mean that literally."

"What happened, Doc?"

Costa swallowed hard. "He's had his tongue cut out."

I felt my breath leave my lungs. "How is he?"

"There was major loss of blood, but not life-threatening. The amputation was recent – in the last twelve hours – so infection hasn't had time to set in. Other injuries included contusions on the knees and elbows. A large swelling on his forehead."

"How about the drawing on his back?"

Costa shook his head. "It's not there."

"*What*?"

"His posterior is perfectly clear, unmarked."

I blinked, unbelieving. Everything I had theorized about Donnie Ocampo told me he had to scrawl the figure. It was part of his inner mythology.

Did we have a copycat?

"You've run the rape kit?" I said. "Started the tox screens?"

"Rush on everything. Results within two hours."

I pulled my sheet of missing men from my briefcase, though I was familiar with every missing man between the ages of sixteen and forty. Given the hair and eye color – and a floral tattoo on his right forearm – our victim was Jacob Eisen, twenty-eight, a worker at a local Amazon shipping center. He'd been reported missing by a roommate and was last seen at a bar just south of downtown. That much jived with Donnie's previous captures.

I turned to Roy. "Where was he found?"

"Tossed out behind a strip mall in Lauderdale, exact time unknown."

"In the city? Not out by the Glades?"

"In the concrete heart of Lauderdale."

Another anomaly. The possibility of a copycat marauder grew larger. The media had carried stories about the abductions, but thanks to intentionally vague police reports and close-mouthed hospital employees, we'd managed to keep starker details from the newsies, knowing the perp would be dubbed Loco-Man or whatever and turned into a media sideshow. Idiot kids would go into fields looking for jimson weed, thinking they'd get a nice high. Dieffenbachia sales would spike city-wide. I'd once made a press-conference mistake of mentioning the brand of wood chipper used to shred a body, and the manufacturer called a month later to thank me, saying regional sales had risen thirty-seven per cent.

But the full truth would come from the rape kit. Only

193

two people had Donnie's DNA, and one of them was incapable of the crimes.

"How'd the victim get found?" I asked Roy.

"A delivery guy was pulling behind the buildings to drop off chemicals for a laundromat and nearly creams a naked guy walking in circles with dried blood running from his mouth to his toes."

"How'd you find out so soon . . . Vince Delmara call?"

"No. It was Rod Figueroa."

"Figueroa? What?"

"Eisen would still be on the Missings list, right?"

"Yep. But with the urgency I don't see the street cops saying, 'Hey, why don't we call ol' Rod in Missings and tell him he can pull one off the list?'"

"He must be keeping an eye out for similar crimes. Is it important?"

I waved it off. "What's important is getting into Donnie's head, Roy. Before even he doesn't know what his next move is."

Roy hustled outside, needing a cigar to calm his restless fingers. I called Gershwin and told him I'd handle the scene and to start scoping out Eisen's digs and canvassing neighbors.

I flipped on the screamer and burned up I-95 to Lauderhill, cut east to Sunrise Boulevard, passing blocks of newer development to an older section of strip centers, car dealers, fast-food emporia. The strip mall was called Sunrise Commons and in the process of renovation, most stores empty with signs promising something new within weeks. There were several active businesses including a dry cleaners and a little pizza joint. As directed, I pulled around back where I saw a forensics unit mobile lab.

I saw Deb Clayton beside huge trash bins, directing techs taking scrapings from the pavement. I pulled to the scene tape and hustled to Deb, currently wiping her shades on the tails of a blouse the same pink as her crime-scene booties.

"Find anything?" I asked.

"Lots of spatter and footprints where he stepped in the blood. We can trace his path, which was basically a ten-foot circle. We'll go through the damn trash," she added, pointing at a big container marked GMSC. "But your boy hasn't left anything at previous scenes, so I expect all we'll get is stinky." She nodded at the surrounding buildings. "Not quite rural here, Carson. From the backcountry to the back of a strip center . . . It's like he did a one-eighty."

"I'm afraid we might be seeing a copycat, Deb."

"Because of the change in dumping venue?"

"And a couple other aspects that don't jive with the previous attacks."

I jogged to the front of the long building, passing a defunct bowling alley and two empty shops, ending at a strangely wide door with the letters GMSC painted on it in ornate letters. I stepped inside to the sound of Lady Gaga on a jukebox beside the door.

The outside sun was bright and my eyes had to adjust to diminished lighting. As objects resolved I saw less a tavern than a fraternal organization, like an Elks club. A small bar in a corner fronted a rack of liquor bottles and three beer taps. I turned to a wall of booths, but mostly it was tables and chairs. The chairs were big and wooden and sturdy and a few overstuffed lounge chairs were scattered about. A television above the bar was playing a silent Food Channel, a handsome and heavyset woman layering cheese and prosciutto and olives on to a slab of bread.

"Go, Contessa!" someone yelled. "Pile it on, baby."

I turned to a man of four hundred or so pounds sitting in a lounge chair in a corner and thumping its arm with the butt of a bottle of beer. His remark generated applause and laughter from four other similarly large men playing cards at a nearby table. In all, I counted eleven men in attendance, nine of them morbidly obese, and two of normal size. Most were in their thirties, a couple guys nearing forty. Three were so large I wondered if they'd had to butter themselves to slip in the door, wide as it was.

Puzzled, I walked toward the bar where an obese, thirtyish man was stacking washed glasses in a rack, enough material in his Hawaiian shirt to cut placemats for a luau. Behind him were several framed eleven-by-seventeen photos of huge men holding loving cups or award ribbons. A banner behind a man so obese his features seemed to have sunken into his cheeks proclaimed *Chubby Champion, 2012 Southeastern Convergence*.

"Excuse me," I said to the guy racking glasses. "Is this like a Weight Watchers meeting or something?"

He seemed to think my remark appropriate for the house. "Hey, everyone . . . the gentleman here wants to know if this is a Weight Watchers meeting."

Laughter. Hoots and howls and slapped knees. One normal-sized guy pointed to a huge man and trilled, "Yes it is, hon. I'm watching *his* weight." He blew the mammoth a kiss.

I sighed, pulled my badge and handed it to the barkeep. He stared between me and the badge, puzzled. "I just made you a detective for ten seconds," I told him. "What do you detect in my expression?"

He looked into my face and frowned. "Uh, confusion?"

I plucked the badge from his fingers. "Very good, Sherlock. How about you help me out here?"

30

I left GMSC after discovering the place had only been open a half-hour, no one there when Eisen was dropped. The lab was my next destination, and I found Morningstar in the room holding the new DNA-analysis machine. It was a major advance in crime diagnostics, and I expected more.

"That's it?" I said, looking at a stand-in for an office copier, just a big box with a read-out panel.

"What did you expect?" Vivian asked. "More chrome?"

"Here comes the report," Gerri Haskins said. She was the tech trained on the device, sitting at a desk beside the machine, her hand on a sheet of paper as it rolled from a printer.

"And . . .?" I said, leaning behind Gerri like I was cribbing on a test.

"I don't know if it's what you want to hear, Carson,"

she said. "But the match is loud and clear. It's Ocampo DNA."

I whispered some expletives to myself.

"What?" Viv asked.

"Patterns," I said. "Patterns lead me inside minds. Donnie's veered from two established patterns."

"The new violence?"

"Violence was always inherent, just ramped up. But he's stopped making the sign on the victim's back, and he's no longer dumping them in out-of-the-way locales."

"Getting bolder . . . at least with the latter?"

"I have no idea. It's all screwed up."

I hightailed back to the hospital and found Eisen on a ventilator, Costa saying he was having difficulty breathing. Patrick White was there and Costa gave him instructions and went off to handle another case.

"I know you can't tell me anything confidential, Detective," White said when he'd finished checking tubes and wires, "but are you getting any closer to this crazy?"

"It's a tough one, Patrick," I admitted. "The guy seems invisible. We know what he looks like, we just can't find him. You're telling all your friends to watch out, right?"

"It's my new mantra. Plus the pictures of the suspect are in most bars."

"You never heard anything about how they got there, did you? The photos?"

We'd recently sent out the photos to the bars, but someone had gotten there before us in many cases, the photos already posted.

Patrick hung the stethoscope around his neck and shook his head. "They just appeared. The guy looks . . ."

"Yep. Like half of Miami. Plus it's about a hundred per cent chance he saw the photos and gave himself a makeover."

White finished his ministrations and left at a run. I took a final look at Jacob Eisen, wondering what his connection was to Donnie Ocampo. Or was it just a wrong place–wrong time scenario?

I heard racing footsteps and turned to see Lonnie Canseco run into the room. It surprised me, since he'd not had anything to do with the case.

"Tell me it's not true," Canseco said, staring in dismay at Eisen.

"He got his tongue removed, Lon."

I saw Canseco's hand ball into fists, his teeth clench in anger. "*Fuck!*" Canseco said through gritted teeth, his fist pounding the wall.

A nurse passing by stepped inside. "Is everything all right here?"

I assured her it was and nodded for Canseco to follow me out into the hall. He did, shooting backward glances at the victim.

"Why you here, Lonnie?"

Like Jeremy, Canseco liked looking sharp. He wore a

summer-weight suit the color of ash, a shirt the blue of a Denver sky, a scarlet tie with a knot so perfectly triangular it could calibrate electron microscopes. With handsome, angular features and Latin coloration, he resembled the actor Jimmy Smits at age thirty-five.

"I know the kid," Canseco said. "I do some counseling, a volunteer. I met Jake at a session."

"Counseling?"

He looked down the hall and winced. "I hate hospitals, Carson. I know a laid-back bar a couple blocks away. I could use a drink."

The bar was three blocks distant, the Brass Key, a quiet tavern with soft light and dark wood, a place where the barkeep wears a black vest over a starched white shirt and keeps his distance until you need something. We ordered, double Scotch neat backed with soda on ice for Canseco, a shot of bourbon with a beer back for me, then stood at the railed bar, the sole customers save for a quartet of suited sales-types at a back table. I waited until Canseco had a blast of the Scotch, then got into it.

"You said you met the vic at some counseling thing?"

"Young gay men, guys who've had a hard road, gotten in trouble. I try to divert them to a more productive lifestyle, like furthering their education and getting jobs or better jobs. It's a big-brother kind of thing, and I do it a couple hours a week." He gave me a look. "And yes . . . I'm gay."

I wasn't taken aback by Canseco's sexual identity, only by my ignorance. He put his hand on my shoulder, gave it a shake. "You are slow on the uptake, amigo."

"You know him well, then? Eisen?"

"I started with the program six years back. Jake was one of my first charges. We've kept in touch . . . I guess I see Jake every couple months. We'll grab lunch or a beer, shoot the shit."

"OK to talk . . . or is it confidential? The program?"

"Nothing secret. Oh, Jake used to hook some, shoplift, peddle smoke; the usual petty crap. All in the past."

I lowered my voice. "The tongue cut out . . . that could mean he's spoken when he shouldn't have or, in some circles, told a lie. Jacob a big liar?"

"Like pathological? No. I mean, he'll fib or tell white lies if a situation calls for it. Like if I said, 'Jake, do these slacks make my ass look fat?' He'd say something like 'No, Lonnie, not at all.' And yet I'm sure they do."

I leaned back and checked. "I don't think so."

"Cool. Thanks."

I downed beer and thought about the other victims, about Brian–Brianna in the Ivana Tramp persona, with supposedly acidic comedy. And Harold Brighton was reportedly caustic as well.

"Could Eisen be sharp with the tongue, Lon?"

"He was a pissed-off kid, Carson, trying to lessen his pain by belittling others. He came up in an Orthodox Jewish family, got tossed out of the house by Daddy when he was eighteen. He dropped out of school with three months to go, worked the streets, got beat up a few times. I think Jake sometimes insulted people just so they'd belt him in the chops."

"What he thought he deserved?"

"Self-loathing. A lot of that going around."

"What'd you do?"

"Convinced him he had value. He did the rest."

Harry Nautilus used to counsel poor and angry urban youths riding a one-way flume to a life of drugs and incarceration. Convincing such kids they had merit took courage and insight, and though I already respected Lonnie Canseco's skills as a detective, I was gaining new appreciation for his humanity.

"How'd you meet Eisen, Lon?"

"He got busted for slapping around some poor old queen. The judge gave him six months for A & B. I told the judge if he suspended sentence in favor of anger management and Jacob finishing high school, I'd make sure the kid followed up."

"Eisen must have done pretty well."

"It was rocky until he realized I'd been through many of the hassles he had, substitute Catholic for Jewish. Jacob's a smart guy, and he started to let himself learn things about himself. He got his GED and went to a community college and earned a degree in business. Now he's got a decent job and a future."

"No more Mister Nasty?"

"The new Jake is secure in his skin. He likes himself, so there's no need to piss on others."

We finished our drinks and put money on the bar. A question occurred, now that I knew Canseco was gay.

"Hey, Lon . . . just by chance. Did you distribute any Ocampo pics to gay bars?"

He turned, a puzzled look on his face.

"No. I figured that was you."

Roy would be anxious to get the latest so I ran back to HQ. He had an upcoming meeting in Tallahassee and was memorizing background information on a group of legislators added in the wake of a scandal that saw several others go to jail. Venal lawmakers are in every state, but Florida seemed a particularly fecund hothouse for their incubation.

When I entered, Roy pushed aside his "cheat sheets", information compiled on legislators that allowed him to feign interest in their interests. His study paid off: We were one of the best-funded agencies in the state.

"Jesus, Carson," Roy said, taking a final glance at one of his sheets. "This new assemblyman, Coronado . . . his hobby is collecting yo-yos. What do you say to a guy like that?"

"How they hanging?"

He closed his eyes – probably counting to ten – then got down to business.

"You looked weirded out when Doc Costa said Eisen didn't have that goofy mark on his back. Reason?"

"Making the mark filled a need Donnie doesn't seem to have any more. The same with his dumping methodology.

204

He went from the Glades to dropping Eisen behind a superchubs hangout. Couldn't be a coincidence."

"I'll bite. Superchubs?"

"The place is called GMSC, for Girth and Mirth Social Club, a hangout for obese gay men. It's a kind of subculture, like men who have a thing for really big women."

"How you know all this stuff?"

"A chatty bartender."

"What's it mean . . . Eisen dumped behind this place?"

"Maybe some message to Gary Ocampo. Or a slap in the face. Only Donnie knows."

"No mark, different dumping ground. You're sure it's Donnie at work?"

"DNA is a match. Plus I heard from the lab on the way over. Same nasty brew: datura, robinia, dieffenbachia. No way a copycat would know that."

"Why's he changed MO?"

"He's seeing things in a different way, Roy. He's changing."

Roy thought a moment. "You were going to talk to an expert, your super specialist. How'd that go?"

"I can't seem to reach him. He, uh, travels quite a bit."

"Hell, Carson, this is the FCLE. Grab a couple guys from the pool and have them track him down." He pulled a pad close and picked up a pen. "You're busy, I'll handle it. What's the guy's name?"

My alarms went off. I'd made a mistake mentioning the possibility to Roy. Normally he was hands-off in a case, but the oddities here had piqued his interest. "I've, uh, got him covered from every angle, Roy. He'll turn up soon. But thanks."

He tossed the pen back on the desk. "You got it, bud. But if you can't get him, I will."

I shot a thumbs-up. "Cool. I'll let you know."

I headed back to my office, closed the door, and pulled my phone. "Call me, you stupid, self-aggrandizing son of a bitch," I hissed into my brother's voicemail. "Or else you're gonna have a head honcho of the FCLE trying to track you down. How's that sound, Brother?"

31

Gershwin arrived in late afternoon. I was at my desk when he tossed his briefcase on my sofa, yanked off his tie and collapsed in the chair across from my desk. The AC had died in his beatermobile, a third-hand F-150 pickup that kept running despite shedding another part every two or three miles. He hadn't had time this morning to get to HQ and grab a cruiser from the motor pool.

"I checked Eisen's place," he said, unbuttoning the top three buttons of his shirt and flapping air across his sweating chest. "It's an apartment near Hollywood. Lock intact, no signs of a struggle. Looks like Eisen's picky about his fashion, had two pairs of pants and three shirts laid out on the bed like doing mix-and-match."

"What's the location like?"

"He lives in a complex at the end of a long hall, not a good place to deal with a hallucinating person, even if he can't talk. The parking-squad zealots found Eisen's 2009 Rav just two blocks from the club where he was last seen, so I figure Donnie plucked Eisen from the street."

"OK, Zigs. Nice work."

Gershwin ran down to the promenade outside to get an iced papaya juice from a cart vendor and I heard the intercom crackle on my desk phone.

"Carson, you there?"

Bobby Erickson, a retired Florida State Police Sergeant who worked the internal desk.

"Sure enough, Bobby. Whatcha need?"

"You got call on line three, a Dr Touring. Says you been looking for him?"

It was Jeremy using another of his identities. But why hadn't he called my cell? What could he gain by . . . It hit me: he would know calls to the FCLE, as to most law-enforcement agencies, were recorded. I couldn't rant at him for his antics, or ask questions that might sound suspicious. It was brilliant, irritating, and totally Jeremy.

I'm not sure why, but I went to the window and drew the blinds, plunging my bright office into soft shadow. I picked up the phone. We'd both be playing a word game.

"Hello, Doctor," I said, keeping my voice even. "Good that you could find the time to call me."

"Ryder! My good man! What do you need?"

"I, uh, was talking to my boss about a case of mine. A difficult case. I mentioned you might consult and when

208

I couldn't track you down, he thought he might put some of our people on it."

A pause. "You're renting me out now? Do you get a commission?"

"It was an off-the-cuff remark. My boss became interested enough to ask more about you. Before that happens, we should meet. Where are you at present, Doctor?"

"I didn't mention that I'm now in Key West? I thought I told you last year."

Serving up the same old slop. "Key West? I thought you were in Kentucky."

"I'm afraid my old Kentucky home is in the past, Detective Ryder. It is still detective . . . you've not advanced in your career?"

Bastard. "Still detective, Doctor. I need to see you soon. Like tomorrow."

"I'm extremely busy with my foundation. I might work you in late next week."

I couldn't understand why he wasn't jumping at the chance to see my files. Nothing intrigued my brother more than a case that gave me difficulty.

"Listen, Doctor, I really need to—"

"Plus I have work pending on my new abode. We're deciding on color schemes."

"Oh? Who is we?"

"My girlfriend is visiting for a few days."

"Girlfriend?" I said, trying to keep disbelief from my voice. My brother detested women and, as far as I knew, had never had sexual relations. The only females that interested him were those I dated, Jeremy clamoring for intimate details – "*Do you put your tongue in them, Brother? Does it taste like bile?*" – and pouting when I refused to answer.

"Yes, Detective. My girlfriend and I are decorating my new abode. Peaches."

"Your girlfriend's name is Peaches?"

"That's the hue she's selected for the kitchen: Peaches. Oh, wait . . . she's telling me it's actually Sunrise Peach. I don't know how that differs from Twilight Peach, but I'm new to this. Give me a call midweek or so, Detective, perhaps we can work something out."

"I . . . don't think that will work. My boss will continue to press."

A sigh. "Let me check my calendar. Hmm. Here's what we can do, Detective Ryder: hang tight for a day or so. Tell your grand imperial whatever I'll soon be consulting and to muzzle the bloodhounds."

"Here's another idea, Doctor. I'll be in Key West soon. How about I drop by your place and you can show me—"

He hung up. I stared at the phone. I'd worked with the Key West police last year and called a contact. If my brother had bought property, it would be in the residential database. I'd drive the ninety minutes to Key West and show up on his doorstep, files in hand. Maybe a ball bat in the other.

"Sorry, Detective," Lieutenant King Barlow said after checking my request. "No Charpentier listed."

"Auguste Charpentier?" I spelled it again.

"Not even listed on the sales-pending reports."

Jeremy had left Kentucky. The Key West home was a lie. Where the hell was my brother? What was this "foundation" he was supposedly building? Plus my brother never did or said anything without a reason.

What was the purpose of a fictional girlfriend and a peach color scheme?

32

"Pretty is as pretty does," Billy Prestwick sighed as he set aside the facial moisturizer. "And right now pretty tweezes."

It was eight in the evening. Billy Prestwick leaned closer to a mirror bordered with light bulbs and plucked hairs above the bridge of his nose. If he didn't tweeze, he'd grow a grotesque *unibrow*, gawd, the indignity.

He finished his follicular ministrations and studied his image, pursing his lips and winking to himself. "Showtime," he trilled, a lift from Roy Scheider in *All That Jazz*. He fluffed his trademark silver hair – the idea stolen from Andy, but *très chic* in a retro way. And no one else was doing it.

His phone pounded out the drum riff from "Let's Have a Kiki". He checked the caller and grinned.

"Why, Nurse Patrick, are we coming out to play?"

He listened. "No, I'm not letting you drag me to a yawn bar. I spent my entire weekend with a lovely gentleman, but he was sixty-four and gawwwwd . . . I need to par-*tay*. We'll start at the Stallion and, if we play our cards *purr*-fectly, get invited to some simply stunning soirée in Miami Beach. Pack your swimsuit," he giggled. "Or better, still, don't."

He listened again, sighed. "If you must study, I can't stop you. So I'll at least see you at Stallion for a drinkie or two. We'll buzz around for a bit and I'll leave you to your books while I swim off to the action. Gawd, Patrick, one day you'll be finished with all this *future* nonsense and return to the living, right? Yes, you will, yes, you will. Kiss kiss, bye bye, girl, see you at nine."

Prestwick went to his bedroom to craft his look, opting for cranberry jeans that molded to his ass, a burgundy suede belt with the word *Diva* repeated in silver studs around its length, and a skin-tight purple T-shirt with a silver-sequined star in the center. The shoes were gray loafers, Italian, the expensive leather like warm butter – a gift from an admirer.

For visual depth he added a black silk vest. Oriental in style, with frogs instead of buttons and dragons embroidered in an iridescent black thread down the front panels. Subtle, lovely, and inscrutably expensive, the product of a renowned Taiwanese designer and another gift from another admirer.

He did have the perfect life, did he not? He could be himself, mostly, which he knew was a wonderful thing.

Another wonderful thing was his visage, once described as, "Brad Pitt, the early years".

Billy checked the mirror again. *Brad never looked so good*. He pirouetted like a ballerina, chuckled to himself, and trotted to the living room to finish the joint he'd started prior to tweezing. Outside his front window the sky was moving from orange to cobalt, the air holding that particular magic of late twilight that grants all color five minutes of a soft and surreal incandescence, a gift before the dark. He toked at the weed until it was a smudge in his fingers, tapped it out. When he turned for the door he heard a voice in his head, small, yet clear as bell.

"*Where are you going, Billy?*"

Patrick's voice, asking one of the questions he'd been asking more and more of late. "*Where are you going, Billy?*" "*What will you do in ten years?*" "*Who will pay your bills?*"

Patrick telling Billy he wouldn't stay Billy forever. For a moment Prestwick felt like something heavy had bumped the far side of the planet, and he fought to keep his balance as his vision blurred. He sat on the couch and waited it out. *Fucking Patrick,* he thought, wiping his eyes on his sleeve. *What a downer.* What Billy needed was some good drinks and some good laughs and gazes following him in disbelief. Patrick, too.

Billy dried his eyes again, whispered "*party time*" and started for the kitchen door that led to the garage, where his Corolla sat, a 2004 model. He simply had to get someone to gift him with a new ride, something precious, like a Miata convertible.

When he opened the side door to the garage, the doorway framed in trellised vines, he saw not the garage, but a chest, above it a face covered in a black ski mask.

"You're looking stunning, Billy," a voice said.

Something struck him in the face. The incandescence flew from the night, leaving only a suctioning dark, the sensation of being carried, and the prick of a needle in his thigh.

33

Traveling home and back was not normally difficult, two hours I could use to mull over cases. Often I worked from home, advising smaller departments about what to look for in cases where mental aberrations played a role. I became almost adept at teleconferencing, and had even taped a large map of Florida behind my desk at home – a few random pins affixed – giving my televised image a gravitas beyond my initial efforts, backgrounded by a large portrait of Miles Davis holding a trumpet and looking mildly stoned.

But to put the hours to better usage, I had spent last night at the Palace, taking Miz Morningstar to the roof, she to sip wine as I had read reports by flashlight and tried to find method in Donnie Ocampo's madness.

We were up early in the morning and Vivian went to work and I to the hospital to check on our victims. Dale

Kemp had pulled from his stupor, his mind dark save for recollections of alien insects with giraffe legs and being trapped somewhere under a pyramid. When shown the altered photos representing Donnie Ocampo he had stared blankly and shaken his head.

Harold Brighton was being kept sedated as he underwent various operations on his remaining leg, basically a tube of mangled meat filled with bone meal. If all went well he was to be awakened tomorrow.

Jacob Eisen was still deep within himself, Lonnie Canseco at bedside whenever time permitted. I had twice called Brian Caswell, Brianna, who reported he was trying to get back into performing, but found difficulty recalling lines. He had no further recollections to report.

I was walking from Eisen's room when I saw Patrick White waiting in the hall, anxiety written in the green eyes. He cleared his throat. "Can I talk to you for a moment, Detective?"

"Take all the time you need."

He spoke low, his voice touched with fear. "I'm worried about my best friend, Billy Prestwick. He was supposed to meet me last night at a bar, but he never showed up."

I nodded to a vacant waiting area, a couch, two chairs and a table scattered with *National Geographic* and *People* magazines. I sat in the chair, him the couch.

"He's gay?" I asked. "Your friend?"

"I guess you'd say very."

"You've tried to reach him everywhere he might be?"

"His home, friends. I've sent him text messages,

Facebook messages, tweeted for his whereabouts. No one's seen him."

"First off, has this happened before?" I said. "Not showing up for a get-together?"

"Yes, but not for months. He's become more reliable, or maybe less erratic."

"Has he been under any stress . . . financial, personal? Anything that might make him want to get away for a while?"

"Billy doesn't do stress. He's so carefree he cures stress in others."

"This bar you were supposed to meet at . . . was he there before you, maybe went off with someone?"

"He wasn't there. People know him, plus he's hard to forget."

I was about to give him my mollification speech, but the fear on his face was past that. "Being a best friend sometimes implies a key," I suggested.

"You mean to his place? Sure. I use it to get him inside when he's had too much to drink."

"How about we go check out his digs."

Maybe giving White a task would help allay his fear. And from my experience, we just might find the errant Prestwick in his home, too drunk or drugged to answer the phone, or with a lover. Or perhaps Patrick was being less than candid and got into a tiff with his friend, who was now engaging in the no-speak offense. Or maybe the guy had something he wanted to hide and didn't feel like talking.

I knew that one from my brother.

Prestwick lived near Highway 953 in a small house with a garage a few trellis-lined paces from the dwelling. I heard the house's air conditioner wheezing as we exited the Rover. Palmettos flanked the rickety front porch and White opened the door. I checked the lockset: intact.

I followed White into a living room furnished with a leather couch, overstuffed chair, table, a bookcase in the corner. The walls were a pale green, an old but decent Persian carpet on the floor. The table held an empty wine bottle, a couple spent beer cans, a full ashtray, a nail file and one rolled-up white sock.

"Check it out, Patrick," I said. "Anything look out of place?"

He disappeared down a short hall to the bedroom, bath, returned a minute later. "As messy as usual."

"No sign of a fight, struggle? Furniture out of place? Things fallen off shelves?"

"It's like he was here a minute ago."

"Any messages on the phone?"

"Billy doesn't have a landline, just the cell and tablet."

I drove Patrick back to the hospital. The temperature was in the mid-nineties, and we spoke with the windows closed and our conversation backgrounded by muted traffic sounds as I wove through downtown Miami. "The perpetrator has been snatching folks from bars after spiking their drinks, Patrick," I said. "That's been his MO. If Billy wasn't seen at any bars last night, it's a good sign."

"That's what I keep telling myself. But Billy's a social-media junkie. Not responding means he's been away from his phone and tablet. It's not normal – they're his lifeline to, well, life."

"I gotta ask . . ." I said, cutting the wheel to pass a city bus. "You're sure you guys didn't have a lover's quarrel, Patrick? That Billy's avoiding you? It usually blows over."

"We're not involved sexually, never have been. Maybe it's one of the reasons we're so close. And whenever Billy has a, uh, problem like that, I'm the one he comes crying to."

I looked at the clock in the dash. "Your buddy's been gone since nine last night?"

"That's when I was supposed to meet him."

"How about I take you to the station and you can file a Missing Persons report. Technically, it won't take effect for several hours, but I can schmooze it past. It means local cops will be on the lookout for Billy. Be great if you could come up with a photo, head shot is best."

He pulled his phone as I turned to MDPD headquarters. "Gimme a minute, Detective. Billy's filled every social medium out there with selfies."

"Selfies?"

"Shots of himself. In every possible outfit and expression." White flipped through files and angled the phone my way. "How's this?"

I stopped at a red light and leaned to look at the

220

phone. Except for the unruly mop of tinsel slightly less strident than a fresh dime, the guy looked like a young Brad Pitt. His head was cocked and the wide mouth held a know-it-all grin.

"Perfect," I said.

I'd had no contact with Rodrigo Figueroa since our initial dust-up, but Roy had found the guy easy to deal with. I saw Figueroa standing by the coffee urn in the center of the room and wandered that way, wondering which version I'd get. He was on the phone smiling until he seemed to glance our way. He glared at the phone and booked for the door, pulling his jacket off as he went.

"Detective Figueroa!" I called. But he was moving fast and disappeared through the door, the jacket seemingly stuck between his head and arm, Styrofoam coffee cup clenched in his lips. Must have been some phone call.

"Who's that?" White asked as the door swung shut.

"Speedy Gonzales, by the look of things."

We went to the Missings desk where a young officer named Juanita Rosell appeared. I explained the situation, embellishing only slightly, and she took the report and Patrick's downloaded photo, promising to get the info processed and out as fast as possible.

"My good buddy, Rod," I said, again embellishing. "He was here one minute, gone the next. You know where he went?"

Rosell shrugged. "Got me. Rod doesn't usually move that fast unless it's quitting time."

Billy Prestwick now an official Missing Person, White and I continued to the hospital. "Have faith, bud," I called to his back when I dropped him off and he slumped away.

Truth be told, my mollifications had worked on me about as much as they had on White. He knew his friend well, and was worried sick. So was I, but there was little to be done but hope William T. Prestwick showed up soon, guilt in his eyes and an apology on his lips.

34

My next stop was at the comic-book shop to see how Gary was faring. The ubiquitous clerk, Jonathan, was meeting with a gaggle of young customers holding skateboards. Like Jonathan, two of the boarders were wearing heavy knit hats. Ninety-four degrees out and they've upholstered their skulls; fashion is a cruel mistress.

When the boarders trouped from the store with comics under their arms, I went to Jonathan. "Gary's upstairs, I take it?"

"He hasn't been down in days."

"He taking his walks around the block? Using the treadmill?" I figured Gary Ocampo on the rolling track would make a sound like a cement mixer filled with marbles.

"I hear the bed creaking. The TV. And then there's these guys."

223

I followed his eyes to the front door and saw a delivery truck pull up outside, magnetic roof sign saying Angelo's Pizza Express. A wizened old guy pushed through the door with a huge pizza carton in hand.

"Got a super-large pep-saus-mush, ex chee and anchovies," he said. "Be twenty seventy-five."

Jonathan paid the guy. I could hear a muffled television from upstairs and figured Gary was too busy watching to turn on his downstairs monitor.

The delivery guy left the shop and Jonathan sighed and started toward the elevator with the box.

"I'll deliver it," I told Jonathan, taking the pizza from his hands.

I exited the lift to see Gary propped up in bed staring at a blaring television, a hodge-podge of newspapers at his side. "Run to the fridge and grab me a mango cola, will you, Jon?" Gary commanded, eyes not leaving the screen. "Put it in my big red cup."

I stepped forward, lifting the box like a prize. "Howdy, Gary. I brought lunch."

He saw me, registered surprise and hid it quickly. He flicked off the television as I shot a glance at the trash can: fast-food bags, two crumpled pizza cartons, Chinese takeout cartons.

"Uh . . . thanks," he said, a child caught with a hand in the cookie jar, grunting from his bed in voluminous denim jeans and a gray sweatshirt Morningstar and I could have used as a hammock. His feet were in dirty-soled white socks.

I shot another glance at the trash bucket. He'd slickly covered it with a newspaper in the split second when I'd glanced away, sneaky-fast when he needed to be. Not being his aunt or his counselor or his conscience, I didn't mention the ele-pizza in the room.

"I was reading the paper," he frowned as he lowered to the chair. "A missing man showed up injured. It doesn't quite say how, just 'serious'."

"It was Donnie, Gary."

"I fucking *knew* it," he moaned. "What really happened?"

"The victim had his, uh, tongue removed."

His eyes closed and he was seeing terrible things. "Why?" was all he could whisper.

I went to the window, needing to see beyond this cloistered room smelling of fish and meat and garlic. "The victim used to be a kind of a wise-ass, big on insulting people," I said. "Maybe he ragged on Donnie in the past. Or called your brother names when he was abducted."

"HE'S NOT MY BROTHER!" Gary screamed.

I spun, surprised by his outburst. "What?"

He stared at me, huge fists balling and releasing. "Whatever he is, he's a nasty fucking *monster*. My brother wouldn't be a monster. He'd be A FRIEND!"

"We've discussed this, Gary," I said. "Whatever Donnie is, it's no reflection on you."

He started to say something, paused, slumped to the bathroom and slammed the door. I continued to stare out the window, spotting the unmarked surveillance unit a few parking slots down the block. MDPD didn't have the manpower, so I used FCLE newbies undergoing the FCLE version of Police Academy. The majority were already cops, hired away from other departments. But they were learning the FCLE way of doing things, strict and stringent and by-the-book professional, at least until you made it to my level, where you could do about anything you wanted, as long as it seemed to fit legal boundaries and worked. It was like writing or painting or architecture: you had to learn the rules before you could break them.

I heard the toilet flush and a minute later Gary reappeared, sucking water from his red cup, his burst of anger drained into sorrow. He re-sat the chair. "I was thinking, Detective Ryder . . . uh, do you think the victims would meet with me when they recover?"

I frowned. "There a reason?"

"I'm responsible for their pain and troubles."

"That doesn't make sense, Gary."

The massive shoulders shrugged. "Not like I tried to kidnap them. But it was . . . my twin, Detective, my flesh and blood that did the terrible things." He thought a moment and gave me a hopeful look. "Maybe . . . could you ask if they'd see me, just for a few minutes. It would make me feel better."

"They've been wounded, Gary. Physically and mentally. It's not time for meetings."

I felt sorry for Gary Ocampo. He was trying to do

something decent, and I was shutting him down. He canted his head as if taken by a sudden thought.

"What about the fellow that got away? He wasn't injured, right?"

"Derek Scott? I'm not sure he'd understand why you—"

"Please ask him. *Please*? All he can do is say no, right?"

"You should expect it."

He frowned, as if figuring a way to sweeten the deal. "DVDs – tell him I've got some of the coolest movies around. He can have his choice if he comes to see me for just a couple minutes. I'll fill a box for him. Or if he wants comics he can have all the new releases he wants. But mention the DVDs. Tell him I have videos."

DVDs. Comic books. Gary using a currency he knew. All I could do was ask. Maybe it would help keep Gary from a fast-food self-blitzkrieg.

I pulled my phone in the Rover. When on a case I create phone directories of all pertinent parties, so Derek Scott was listed. He answered on the fifth ring.

"Hello, Detective. I've been trying but so far nothing new."

"Keep trying, but don't worry if the memories don't come. How you feeling?"

"Almost normal. Sometimes I'll h-hear a voice and turn to see no one there, b-but Dr Costa thinks that'll eventually go away."

"Doc Costa knows his stuff. I think you received excellent care."

227

"A-around the clock . . . from all the doctors and nurses. I s-sent everyone thank-you notes."

I smiled, figuring Derek was referring to one nurse in particular, the good-looking Patrick White. "It's not memories I'm calling about, Derek. The man who tried to abduct you is named Donnie Ocampo. He has a twin brother in Miami named Gary. Gary's been completely distraught through the whole affair. It's way off base, but Gary feels a responsibility for his brother's actions. He'd like to meet you for a few minutes."

Silence. Was it shock, or did he need time to process the information? Seconds ticked by. "Gary never knew he had a living brother until recently," I added, hoping to enlist Scott's aid. "By the way, he says he'll give you some videos."

A pause. "Excuse me?"

"He says you can have a choice of videos. Or comic books. You can take your pick."

I held my breath as Scott mulled the offer.

"How can I p-pass that up, Detective?" he said after several seconds ticked by. "Tell Mr Campos I'll stop by this afternoon. No, let me call him."

"Sure," I said, relieved. "And it's Ocampo."

"Oh-camp-oh. Let me write that down. And the address t-too."

I called Gary with the news that Scott would set up a meeting. Gershwin was continuing to check Eisen's background and comparing it to the other victims' histories, hoping for points of convergence. It was needle-in-a-haystack work, but had to be done.

It was mid afternoon and I was about to call Vivian. Desperate for a break from the case, I could free maybe forty-five minutes for dinner and needed to see a friendly face across the table. I was pulling my phone when it rang.

"I've freed a slot in my schedule, little brother," Jeremy announced. "Come out tomorrow and we'll talk. Say eleven a.m."

"Out where?"

"Key-freaking-West, Carson. I need an abacus to keep track of the times I've told you that."

"I checked. You don't—"

"You're getting tiresome. While you're on your way, I'll message you the address. It's in a ritzy part of town, so if anyone stops you, tell them you're auditioning to be my valet."

"*What*?"

But again, I was speaking to an empty phone.

35

I took Vivian to Tiki Tiki, a restaurant owned by Connie Amardara, one of Gershwin's many aunts; *the* aunt, she'd told me the first time we'd met, *tia numero uno*. She had raised the kid for much of his young life and I had never asked the circumstances.

We exited the Rover beside a sprawling single-story brick building painted pink and expressing its Polynesianality via an ersatz thatched-straw bouffant shaded by tall palms. We entered though a foliage-filled courtyard, a fountain spraying water over stones. A sound system played "Over the Rainbow" by the late Israel Kamakawiwo'ole.

Flaming torches flanked a gangplank to a front door more Camelot than South Pacific. Inside were weathered wood walls, ropes and hawsers strung from the ceiling, with false windows fashioned like giant portholes overlooking Gauginesque women carrying coconuts to the ocean.

"I love it," Viv said, echoing my words when first entering a year ago.

We saw a roped-off booth in a far corner, the table set, a fresh candle burning brightly beside a vase holding a huge spray of tropical flora, the only table so embellished. Though the place was only two-thirds full, a squat and muscular waiter of Hispanic extraction stood before the rope line with arms crossed as if daring anyone to look that way, much less sit there. Viv studied the scene. "Looks like the place is expecting VIPs, Carson. The Queen of England, maybe."

I sighed. "It's our table, Viv. Get ready."

"For what?"

"Carson!" a voice trumpeted and I braced myself as a short woman nearly as round as tall rushed up and wrapped my middle in a hug that would have embarrassed an auto-crusher. Per usual, she was dressed in a floral muumuu, her wrists and ears clattering with bangles, jangles, and various thangles.

"My amigo, mi mensch, mi Sherlock Holmes de azúcar," she crooned to my chest.

"Sherlock Holmes of sugar?" Viv said.

I unwrapped the woman from my midsection, and presented Connie Amardara to Vivian Morningstar.

"Oy caramba, such pretty eyes, this one." Connie took Vivian's hands. "But then, I had heard already in advance that Carson's lady doctor could shame the stars with her beauty."

231

"Ziggy," I said.

She crossed her heart. "Ignacio told me almost nada, I swear. Just that you spent a whole year sneaking looks at her backside until she stole your heart while dancing."

Morningstar giggled. I whispered, "*I'll kill him.*"

"Such a spread I've prepared for you two lovebirds . . . puerco browned in schmaltz then roasted in rum and lime, arroz con chopped liver . . ."

"Liver?"

"I add just a smidgen of chopped liver while sautéing the rice." Connie kissed her fingertips. "Magnifico! Plus your favorite platanas in mantequilla con azúcar y crèma."

"It sounds incredible, Ms Amardara," Vivian said.

She canted her head as if hearing an unknown sound. "Ms Amardara? Who is Ms Amardara? To you, Señorita Morningstar, I am Connie, always Connie."

"And I am always Vivian. Or Viv."

"The name means life, no? Vivian?"

"Si."

Connie turned to me and waggled a no-nonsense finger. "The name is a sign to you, Carson. And not to be taken lightly." Connie bustled away to the kitchen and the waiter, transformed into a smiling man named Oracio, took our drink orders and zipped away as we wriggled into the booth.

"Sneaking looks for a year?" Morningstar said as she unrolled her silverware from a linen napkin. "My backside?"

232

"Connie exaggerates. It was more like ten months."

"The woman obviously thinks the sun rises and sets with you, Carson."

Oracio returned with Consuelo's Delights, rum drinks that were Connie's secret specialty. I pushed my lips through froth and sipped the blend of three rums, fruit juices, and a touch of cloves, magnifico.

"I think Connie believes me responsible for Ziggy's good fortunes at the FCLE. Like everyone else, she probably expected him to last about a month."

Morningstar sipped her drink and looked ceilingward in ecstasy. We'd have one, then switch to lighter fare. Two Delights would loosen your knees and unhinge your eye-strings.

"Is Connie right, Carson? Are you responsible for Ziggy's success?"

"I put his feet on the ladder. He's done all the climbing."

The food arrived and we lost ourselves in gastronomic delights. But even the incredible meal and company of Vivian Morningstar lacked the force to push tomorrow's supposed rendezvous with Jeremy from my mind. Somewhere nearing dessert it hit me why he would text his address when I was well on the road: to keep me from calling the local constabulary and asking who'd bought a house at that address.

His manipulation was irritating, but upped the odds that he might actually be in Key West. Of course, he might know I'd think that, thereby lulling me into thinking he was there when he wasn't . . .

Circles containing circles set spinning within a Mobius: my brother at work.

I felt Morningstar's hand touch mine. "You suddenly seem distracted, Carson. Are you all right?"

"It's my brother. He's cluttering my thoughts. I'm sorry."

"Don't be, you're concerned about family. Is Jeremy all right?"

It was a jolt hearing his true name from another's lips. I nodded. "He's just being his usual cryptic self. And elusive. He enjoys playing games."

"But you're still hopeful of a reconciliation?"

"I don't know what I'm hoping. Or expecting."

The dinner got back on track. I pushed aside my bleaker thoughts and concentrated on the moment: I was in a restaurant owned by a woman who thought I pulled the sun into the sky in the morning while sitting across from a woman who actually did, at least by my lights. *Your life is assembled from pieces of magic*, I thought as we walked to my car and I tossed Viv the keys, two drinks past driving, *If it ends tomorrow, you're still one of the luckiest humans to ever walk this beleaguered planet.*

36

I rose in the morning with the first roseate hues of the sun across the cove behind my home. Morningstar and I didn't spend the night together, she having a meeting with her staff and several new personnel members to prepare for her fast-approaching departure. I had headed back to my home with my own agenda to consider: I was destined to travel to Key West, starting the trip at eight a.m.

If my brother's vanity showed anywhere, it was in his dress, always fashionable, and after twenty minutes of study I selected a cranberry-hued seersucker suit purchased years ago from Lansky's in Memphis, a crisp-collared white shirt, no tie. At the bottom I tied tan bucks, at the top I set a straw Panama embellished with a blue bandana knotted in back. I stood, knees-bent, before my mirror and experimented with the hat until finding the perfect, rakish angle.

Valet this, Brother . . .

Driving from Upper Matecumbe Key to Key West became a trip back in time, starting at the present and regressing. When I turned west on to Highway 1, I was thinking about Jeremy's current games and obfuscations somehow involving "foundations", "girlfriends", and a presumably fictional existence in Key West. I figured he would either not be there, or have a temporary residence at a rental cottage or hotel. My money was on the former.

When I passed through Long Key, I'd moved into the near past, to Kentucky, my brother living in backwoods isolation and working the stock market.

By the time I crossed Marathon Key my recollections had moved two years earlier, Dr Evangeline Prowse mysteriously helping Jeremy escape from the Institute to New York, sparking a fierce manhunt for my brother, who wreaked havoc before vanishing.

By the time I passed through Big Pine Key, I had just started college and learned my older brother had been arrested for the savage killing of five women and would be incarcerated for life. I quit school, invented a new life and name, and returned to college to gain a Masters in psychology. Only now do I understand that I undertook the study to make sense of my family.

Touching Big Coppitt Key, I recalled the day the police found our father's disemboweled corpse in a nearby woods. I was ten, my brother sixteen.

When my tires crossed the bridge to Key West it was but one week earlier and my wild-eyed father was holding me to a wall by my neck, telling me, "*I made you, I can kill you*."

I don't often drink to calm down, a dangerous path. But my first stop in Key West was at a tavern where I chased a double shot of bourbon with a beer. Though it was not yet ten in the morning, I was far from alone, but it was Key West, a locale the writer John Dos Passos once described as "agreeable, calm, and gently colored with Bacardi".

I had left earlier than needed and while rising from the bar stool heard my phone signal a message. Expecting the worst, I was surprised to see an address. I shifted to my map function and was further surprised to see the address was real, on a side street on the southwest side of the island, near the ocean.

My heart generating a mix of dread and anticipation, I crossed the island. Nearing the site, I moved from an avenue of bungalows tucked within greenery to a street bearing stately, capacious homes I judged to be worth at least two million dollars if on the smaller side.

I stopped before a tall and imposing home of pastel yellow, its vertical orientation enhanced by a wide cupola topped with a conical spire and rising above the roofline. The structure was half concealed behind sixty feet of landscaping, azalea and bougainvillea spanning the bases of regal palms. A white picket fence ran the front of the property and turned, but midway to the back of the lot it stopped at high white walls which I figured surrounded a rear courtyard.

I exited my vehicle to the buzz of the gate lock disengaging, my brother wanting me to hop to his whim. I ignored the gate and jumped the fence. Instead of walking to the door I meandered the front yard, sniffing flowers and finally leaning against a towering Royal palm and studying the street. After a minute I heard the front door open.

"You've made your point, Carson, whatever it is."

I climbed several steps to a full porch furnished with rattan chairs and a swing. The door swung fully open and I saw my brother. Per sartorial expectations, he was resplendent in an ice-cream suit, blue shirt, a red tie patterned with tiny parrots, his loafers the hue of café au lait. Gone was the whitened mustache and goatee and hair, gone were the facial wrinkles deepened by a light daily rubbing of mascara. His hair was now its natural sandy blond, neatly cropped, and his dancing blue eyes outshone the Key West sky. His new infatuation with exercise was obvious in his thickened arms, neck and chest. All in all, Jeremy could have passed for forty, and given the stress of the recent case, I probably looked like the older brother.

Because few things pleased my brother more than startling me, I hid my surprise behind a false yawn. "Hello, Dr Charpentier," I said, patting my mouth, stepping inside the entryway, and handing him my hat. "I take it your name's not on the deed."

Without looking, he neatly Frisbee'd the Panama atop a rack a dozen feet distant. I yawned again.

"You really thought I was lying about moving here?" he said.

I jammed my hands in my pockets and glanced at the surroundings. "Seeing it, I still have doubts. Auguste Charpentier owns no land in Key West."

Jeremy walked into a high-ceilinged and mostly bare living room: a long blue sofa of creamy leather, matching chair, a low teak table. A stack of unopened packing boxes ruled one corner. "Charpentier has dissolved into the wind, Carson. Those few who believe they knew him think he has moved to France. He never allowed them close enough to care to check."

"You've changed your name, then?"

"*Oui, mon frère.*"

"To what?"

An enigmatic smile. "How about I give you the nickel tour, starting upstairs? You'll have to pardon the disarray."

We climbed stairs and he displayed several unfurnished rooms, bright and high-ceilinged. The polished wood floors shone under light streaming from the tall windows. "How long have you been here?" I asked.

"I purchased it three months ago but had to handle tasks elsewhere. I've lived mostly here the past month."

He took me to a gorgeous oak staircase spiraling to the top room of the cupola, his office, a round space with a half-circle desk before a view of the ocean framed by palms, two computer monitors on the desk, two more on a flanking table. Additional boxes sat to the side.

"You're still operating on the assumption that the

market has just two states, scared child and boastful drunkard?" I said.

"It continues to make money. I've also reached the point where just money makes money."

He showed me the main bathroom, containing a shower in which I might have parked half of the Rover, a dozen heads angling in from every direction but below. There was a Jacuzzi sized for two, a standard toilet and a bidet. The floor was white marble flecked with green, the walls gently olivine. A white silk bathrobe hung on a brass hook inside the door.

We returned to the first floor and he took me to the spacious kitchen – where he expected me to comment on the pleasant peach color of the walls, but I did not – then led me through a dining room to a two-story solarium overlooking a walled-in courtyard bright with flowers and shaded by palms.

"Here's an interesting item," Jeremy said, a strange note of pride in his voice as he pointed above my back. High on the room's sole non-glass wall hung a painting at least six feet tall, five wide, a semi-abstract rendering of strident, multihued flowers against a jungle-ripe background of flowing greens. Color gave it presence, composition gave it force, and the piece seemed perfect for the venues, both Key West and the room.

I thought I figured out the pride in his voice. "A designer didn't select that painting," I said, impressed. "You picked it out on your own."

"Actually, I painted it last week."

240

"No way."

He smiled. "My artistic side seems to be opening up, Carson, though it did take two tries to get right. Would you care for a drink? Or did the ones you've had suffice?"

I had chewed a pack of gum on my trip from the tavern to cover the scent of alcohol. My brother had entered the Institution with normal senses, but something inside had honed them to a preternatural state. I figured it was a self-preservation mechanism. He had once told me he could detect psychosis by its smell, and I'd never argued.

"An ice water for now."

He strode away and I ambled through the downstairs to the front window, seeing a herd of camera-laden tourists walking the avenue. In one day in Key West my brother would encounter more humans than in a year in Kentucky. I wondered how he would deal with it.

He found me and handed me a tumbler of water. It hit me that he'd not made a single allusion to his vaporous lady companion.

"So where's your girlfriend today?" I said. "Peaches?"

"Don't be so dismally cute, Carson. I told you Peaches was paint. My friend has various chores in Miami, including shopping for furniture. She'll return early next week. You probably passed her on the way, though she would have been several thousand feet above you."

"Does not-Peaches have a real name?"

He walked to a mirror and straightened his tie. "I'm beginning to think you don't believe in her existence."

241

"Photos then, a shot of you and your paramour lazing on the beach and making dreamy eyes at one another."

He turned from his image. "Our relationship doesn't resemble your body-centric succession of temp workers, Carson. It's more . . ." he frowned in search of a word.

"Fictional?" I supplied.

"Cerebral."

I smiled and made the motion of advancing a pawn. "No sex then, just endless games of chess?"

He started to speak, stopped, changed course. "There was a reason for your visit, correct? Have you brought me something to consider?"

I pulled the materials from my briefcase and handed them over. When I started to add my comments he asked me if I'd been to Key West recently.

"Two weeks ago I drove out to kill a Saturday."

"Go see if anything's changed," he said, nodding toward the door.

37

I stood in the diamond-bright sun and pondered my choices. I might tour the Hemingway house, but I'd done so twice before and exited discouraged. Though the home had been the residence of one of the most influential writers in American history, it seemed the bulk of the visitors were mostly interested in the six-toed cats.

The raucous Duval Street was a few blocks distant and I might grab a beer in one of the bars, but this time of day Duval would be dense with milling clots of tourists released from the cruise ships like camera-strung cattle. I turned to study the imposing home, noting its address on the brass mailbox: three numbers and a street name.

They were all I needed to discover what name Jeremy was using.

I drove to the police station, hoping Lieutenant King

Barlow was working. It turned out that King was not only on duty, he was in the station house, all six-nine, one-hundred-eighty pounds of him.

He brought me to his office, a small room beside the squad room, and I stood while he sat and towered over his desk. After a couple minutes of small talk, I got to the point.

"Are the recent real-estate transactions easily accessible, King?"

He held his index finger above his keyboard. "Tap tap. You want me to check something for you?"

I made a deal of looking outside the door, then closing it. "It's, uh, one of these things that's still in the early phases, King, if you get my drift. Hush-hush."

He raised an eyebrow. "Drugs? Or more human trafficking?"

"Can't say yet. If anything comes of it, you guys will get a piece."

He grinned. "Hey . . . we're still wearing laurels from last year."

Ten months back I'd handled a human-trafficking case that ended up in Key West. Though King and his people had a small walk-on near the finale, at press conferences Roy McDermott insinuated a supporting role. Many law enforcement entities seized any opportunity to grab headlines, often at the expense of other agencies, but Roy spread the accolades around, thinking it bread on the waters, returned multifold.

Like right now. King pecked at the keys, stood, offered

me his chair. "I'll grab a coffee. Take it away, my man, and happy hunting."

I entered the address of Jeremy's home. It would provide the name my brother had used to purchase the property, assuming it wasn't one of his corporations, dummy and otherwise, like C&A Associates, the one holding the mortgage on my home.

A screen came up with the addresses in sequence. I ran my finger down the list until coming to Jeremy's house number. He hadn't used a corporation to buy the house; it was a private transaction.

He had used his new name.

I stared in disbelief. My mouth was probably drooping open.

This was the way it was meant to be . . .

Debro withdrew from the body beneath him, his breath ragged with exertion and climax, sweat dripping from his brow on to the suck bruises on Billy Prestwick's neck.

Just me and him. One of them at a time . . . It was the way.

This way was more intimate. More care could be given to their punishment. He still held their words, looks, dirty smiles in his memory – in his very heart – after all these years. But here he'd been putting them back into their lives unscathed. He'd allowed the kindness of his nature to deprive himself of his true due. This, finally, was the real deal: Justice. It was a pity he'd not realized it when he had the simpering, nasty Brianna or pretty-boy Kemp. Brianna liked to banter with the audience, then turn it into mean barbs. He should have driven sharpened pencils into her ears.

Try to hear what we're saying now, bitch.

And Kemp? The blond slut sold something to doctors. After finding him – not hard, he remembered his name and it was in the directory – he'd followed Kemp locally for several days, watching him park his shiny silver Camry outside physicians' offices and medical clinics, pull a big rolling bag from the trunk, and scamper inside for an average of fifty-three minutes. What was a salesman but a talking machine?

It should have meant another tongue gone . . . just like that.

Debro toweled sweat from his face and chest and went into the anteroom. Locking the door, he studied Billy Prestwick through the window: naked, his small hard buttocks gleaming with lubricant and semen. His eyes were wide open and his mouth opened and closed slowly, a line of spittle running from his chin to the floor. Even in his sloppiness, he was beautiful.

Prestwick's skin was like fine china, Debro thought, almost glowing. His silver hair was a glorious mop. His slender back was red and chafed from Debro's half-hour ride, but otherwise unmarked. It would remain so . . . the Gemini Project officially abandoned. Gary was no longer allowed to share. But Donnie had done his part.

246

Which meant Debro was alone. Or soon to be.

The way it was meant to happen.

I walked the area around the cop house for twenty minutes, trying to make sense of my finding. To purchase the house, Jeremy would have had to create the kind of identity echoed in a multitude of government offices, meaning that cross-checking would create confirmation and not questions.

It was a monumental undertaking, much riskier now than two decades back, when I'd crossed from one life into another, though Jeremy's money might make it less reliant on paperwork trickery and more on well-placed bribes.

Still . . . why *that* name?

When ninety minutes had elapsed I returned to Jeremy's house, surprised to find a large orange van out front, the lettering saying *Island Electronics*. In front of the van were two green pickup trucks with covered beds, the logo stating *Fioptics Ltd*. Across the street was a panel van from Harrow & Son, General Contractors. A short man in a blue uniform closed the back door of the orange van and strode toward the house with a coil of wire over his shoulder and a toolbox in his hand.

I heard hammering from inside, took the front steps three at a time and entered without knocking. The sound of sawing was added to the hammering and I saw two men cutting a section of wall from Jeremy's kitchen. He was standing behind them, talking to a third man.

I pointed upstairs. "Can we go up to your office and talk?"

"We can go to my office."

Climbing the steps I saw a woman in the rear room assembling an electronic console. The home held the sudden industry of a beehive. We entered my brother's office and I saw the man who had carried the wire from the van. He was drilling a hole in the floor near the wall as a young woman wearing protective glasses looked on. Both wore *Island Electronics* uniforms.

"We need to talk," I whispered to my brother.

"By all means, Carson, talk."

"Not here, dammit. The bedroom."

He shrugged and we backed into the hall and stepped into the empty bedroom. Or almost empty, another of the electronics crew pulling away floorboard with a pry-bar.

"I'm updating the security system," Jeremy said. "And adding high-speed fiber optics. Putting new arteries in an old body, so to speak. Plus upgrading the smoke and carbon monoxide alarms. I want it all completed soon . . . my girlfriend has furniture deliveries scheduled."

"Where can we go to speak?" I said, feeling my jaw clenching.

"About the cases?" He sighed. "With all this clamor I haven't been able to get to it today, Carson. I'll call in a day or two."

I willed my hands from his neck. All of this work had been scheduled and from the git-go my brother had no intention of reviewing the cases today. I could have e-mailed the materials. But that wouldn't have let him jerk me around in person.

"Screw the cases, Jeremy," I hissed. "I need to talk about something else."

"I've really got to stay here, Carson. I want to make sure everything's done to a T."

The bathroom was across the hall and when the workers looked away I yanked him across the hall and into the bathroom, closing the door behind us.

"You can't use the facilities on your own, Carson?" he grinned. "Is it ageing? Your prostate?"

"I know you know I know your name," I said. "You know I know that, right?"

My brother held the grin, not needing to unravel all the knows. "You're so predictable, Carson. How are things at police headquart—"

"Tell me your name," I interrupted. "I want to hear you say it aloud. Just so I know I'm not dreaming."

He paused, eyes sparkling, savoring the moment.

"Jeremy Ryder."

"Why *that* name?" I said. "WHY?"

"Shhhh," he said, lowering the lid on the toilet. "Have a seat, Carson."

My legs were wobbly with everything that had unfolded in the past two hours: his magnificent house, his artwork, his original given name combined with my concocted surname. I sat. Jeremy leaned against the wall beside the long vanity and crossed his arms, a picture of elegance.

"Your brother is returning to you, Carson. You can call me by my given name in public. I, in turn, intend to start calling you Alphonse, just to see how it feels to always have to think before addressing one's beloved brother."

"The idea is crazy. You've truly created the identity?"

"Day by day I add to Jerome Alan Ryder . . . a peripatetic financier type who moved from Alabama as a teenager and has since resided in various cities abroad. Have you checked your invented past lately?"

"Why?"

"Jerome A. Ryder's past seems intertwined with yours, as if our fictional selves went separate ways years ago and recently reunited."

I stared. My brother was beyond belief. "You mean . . .?"

"A few places in your invented background mentioned *only child*. You'll now see a brother is casually noted."

"You've combined our false backgrounds?"

"Our real ones are inexorably linked, Brother. It seems so right."

I shook my head. There were no words for what he was attempting. Chutzpah, balls, brass . . . all woefully insufficient.

There was but one fatal flaw.

"You're still a wanted man, Jeremy," I pointed out. "Every law-enforcement agency in the country has you in their database. Thousands of cops go to work daily with your photo on their bulletin boards and computer screens. There's nothing you can do to live a normal life.

You think you can alter the past? What's your alteration for that?"

"You're a man of moving water, Carson," he said. "You need it nearby to make you flourish, right?"

I had been surrounded by water in Mobile, surrounded by water on Matecumbe Key. Flowing water seemed to soothe my soul and I could no more live in a desert region than on the moon. I stared as my brother opened the huge shower stall and turned a handle. Torrents of water poured from every direction, splashing, mingling, the floor speckling with overspray.

"Yes, I like moving water," I said, perplexed. "So what?"

He turned off the water, put his hand on my shoulder and guided me toward the door.

"Then always trust a river, Carson."

38

Debro was in his apartment considering the proper punishment for Billy Prestwick. He sat in a chair with a laptop on his thighs, studying Prestwick's Facebook page. The posts were little more than drivel, self-absorbed twinks jabbering to other self-absorbed twinks.

So gud 2CU last nite at Stallion, Billy. Where did U get cool shades? I NEED a pair like. Kisses.

Why is Life so HURTFULL? Cant Peeple be NICE? Someone send me FLOWERS.

Heading 2 Bink's Lounge 10 minutes . . . any U sluts want 2 par-tay?

He opened Prestwick's photos: Twenty-one separate albums holding a total of 312 photos. They were all basically the same: Billy Prestwick grinning in a bar, smiling on the beach, making gangster fingers on a street corner, sticking his pink tongue out at the camera, standing shirtless beside a mirror. His pretty face smiling beside a dozen different drinks.

Selfies, mostly . . . pictures of Prestwick that Prestwick had put on Facebook.

Look at me, they said. *See how pretty I am.*

On my ride eastward I was in a fog of Jeremy's making. Any trip to see my brother ended up giving me a few answers, while generating even more questions. He was actually living in Key West. He had changed his name to reflect mine, and intertwined our fictional histories. For better or worse – as far as anyone caring to dig deep into my history was concerned – I now had a brother.

I doubted Jeremy had come to Key West to hunker down within his house, thus becoming subject to tens of thousands of eyes. All it took was one sensitive pair to see him, log into one of several law-enforcement sites, and call the local cops.

"Yeah, this is Johnny Baker . . . a county cop in Spitwhistle, Oklahoma. Me and the missus are here on a vacation and – you're gonna shit – but I think I just spotted Jeremy Ridgecliff from the FBI listings. I followed him to this big-ass house. Hang on, lemme give you the address . . ."

And after Jeremy was hauled away, curious detectives would dig into his fictional past to see how he had pulled it off, finding his lies looped around mine.

If he went down, I followed.

I had spent almost a year with the FCLE, a dream job I hoped would carry me to the end of my career. But into the bright Florida sun had a come a shadow: my brother, using fractured logic to bind his dangerous past to mine. I had thought I was safe. In fact, I was supremely vulnerable.

I was crossing Duck Key when my phone gave the ringtone for case contacts, a four-note theme from an ancient television series called *The Twilight Zone*, which, given my cases, seemed appropriate.

My smartphone let me speak while driving. As could my vehicle, which said, "*Call from Derek Scott*" in the voice of a friendly lady.

"Answer call," I said, then heard the connection establish.

"Detective Carson Ryder here, Mr Scott. What can I do for you?"

"*Hello, D-Detective. You wuh-wanted to know how things w-went with m-my meeting with Muh-Mr Ocampo?*"

I hadn't specifically asked that Scott call me with the results of his meeting, but I figured he'd picked up on my concern for Gary when setting up the meeting and was doing me a good turn by reporting back.

"No big deal, Derek, but sure . . . I'd be interested in how he is. I'm concerned about what the stress might be doing to his health. How'd things go?"

"*I, uh . . . fine. We t-talked. Sure, he's got his troubles and all, but, uh, it was n-n-nice of him to want to see me and . . .*"

His mild stammer verged on full-blown stuttering, which often happened with stress. I cleared my throat. "I'm getting the feeling there's something you're not telling me, Mr Scott."

A sigh. "*The meeting with M-Mr Ocampo w-was, um, unsettling. Maybe embarrassing.*"

"Can you talk about it?"

"*Uh . . . it's sorta, uh . . .*"

He was obviously uncomfortable. I checked my watch. I hadn't planned on going into Miami, but there was time.

I said, "Sometimes these things are best discussed face to face instead of on cold little plastic devices."

"*I hate them,*" he said, "*phones. Always have. That doesn't mean I don't use them all the tuh-t-time, we have to, right? Otherwise we'd be living in 1910 and never talk to anyone who w-wasn't in front of us.*"

Even though I could talk at my steering wheel and have my voice heard in a phone a thousand miles distant, I felt the same way.

"You want me to come see you?"

"*I live in B-Belle Glade, over an hour away. I'm not*

there, anyway. I'm in a b-bar, the Cool Melon, just a bit north of downtown, you could come here a lot faster. It's a regular bar, buh-by the way."

"Doesn't make a difference, Derek. Save me a stool."

I was there in fifteen minutes, a neighborhood pub near Miramar. Scott was at the end of the bar with a beer mug at his elbow.

"What went on with Gary?" I said as I pulled up a stool. "You said something about embarrassing?"

"Everything w-went like I expected at first. Mr Ocampo apologized several times, telling me he wasn't like his brother, that he was s-sickened by what was happening. I told him it was fine, there was no way he could be responsible, even if the guy was a twin, Gary was a d-different person."

"What I pretty much expected."

"I was there maybe ten minutes, hoping maybe tuh-talking to me made him feel better. But when I got up to leave he still seemed so sad. I felt terrible for him, for all that s-seemed wrong in his life. I leaned over to g-give him a hug, kinda wondering how to do it . . . all that buh-bigness. And he – he . . ."

"What happened, Derek?"

"The p-poor man t-tried to kiss me. I wasn't expecting it and when I p-pulled away he started crying, apologizing for how disgusting he was. I tuh-tried to tell him it was all right, p-p-perfectly natural. But it was a very emotional scene, d-difficult for both of us. I h-hope he's all right."

I thanked Scott and started to depart when he called my name. I turned.

"You should know . . ." he said, "the fuf-first moment I saw Mr Ocampo?"

"Yes?"

"I f-felt a strange shock, like recognition. I know, I've seen all the different pictures of the man who tried to abduct me, and I know he's Mr Ocampo's brother . . . but I felt something deeper."

"Like a visceral resemblance between the two?"

He tapped his chest. "Something in here got scared for a split second."

Another confirmation that Donnie couldn't eradicate his resemblance to his brother, and maybe wasn't even trying. I retreated to the Palace to try and puzzle it out, but fell asleep in the chair.

39

"*Muchos gracias, amigo*," Sergeant Leo Bander said, taking the bag of Cuban pastries from baker José Murano. Bander flicked open the tab atop the Styrofoam cup of coffee with his thumb and took a sip. Morning needed strong coffee and baked goods.

"*Jugo?*" Murano asked. *Juice?*

"A man can only take so much health, José," Bander said, eyeing the fresh pastries cooling on a rack behind Murano. "I'll have an orange juice mañana."

A grin from Murano. "*Pero tu esposa . . .*"

"My old lady's got me eating salads five times a week, José. Or fucking stir-fries." Bander patted the two inches of belly leaning over his belt buckle. "She's got the idea that when I retire next month, we're gonna go hiking in the fucking Alps or something. Never marry a woman ten years younger, José. They'll wear you out."

"Sometimes that can be a good thing, Leo," Murano winked.

"Sometimes, amigo," Bander sighed, handing over his money. "And sometimes it's just tofu and goddamn carrots."

Bander left the small panadería reluctantly, its atmosphere thick with the smell of fresh bread and iced cakes and dense black coffee. Though dawn was an hour past, its echo tinged the sky with pink. Gulls flicked between palms on the avenue and squabbled over crumbs on the sidewalk.

Good morning, Miami, Bander thought, fresh caffeine and the promise of pastry kicking his brain into a higher gear. *You're looking beautiful today, babe.*

A dozen pounds of gear squeaking on his utility belt – pistol, pepper spray, folding baton, radio, cuffs, ammunition – Bander climbed into his cruiser and pulled into the parking lot of one of the ubiquitous shopping centers a block down the street. He rolled into the shade beside a furniture store, put the cruiser in park, and buzzed the seat back to give him more room. He downed one of the sweet pastries in two bites and chased it with a swallow of coffee.

One month, he thought as he removed another pastry from the bag and took a bite. *One freaking month more.* He figured he'd die in the saddle, but his wife of five years now, Marilita, had other ideas, like hiking the fucking Alps.

And maybe she was right. He'd have done his full

259

thirty when he pulled the plug, every day of it on the streets of Miami. "Fuck a desk job," he'd once told a partner. "The street is where the action is, the glorious fucking weirdness, the insane sideshow."

Leo Bander thought he'd seen all the sideshow had to offer in his thirty years. He had once stopped a guy doing a hundred-twenty on Interstate 95, the guy saying he'd just washed his car and was drying it off. He'd busted a whorehouse to find a famous television preacher drunk, stoned, and buried under a naked and writhing clot of male and female bodies, the righteous reverend later explaining it was simply research, that he had to know sin in order to preach against it.

Bender had arrested a seventy-year-old woman for shotgunning a rooster in the middle of Flagler Street in Little Havana, the woman explaining that the rooster held the spirit of her late husband, and had recently had amorous relations with a neighbor's hen.

He'd once watched a guy in a silver lamé bodystocking – and wearing a beach blanket as a cape – take a nine-story dive from the balcony of a Miami Beach hotel on to the hood of a stretch limo, the limo filled with a half-dozen Atlantic City gamblers. He'd walked up to the pale and shaking group and nodded at the broken body cradled in the vehicle's roof, cape dangling over a smoked rear window.

"So what're the odds on that one, boys?" he'd said, as seriously as he could muster.

He'd seen bodies mangled in car crashes, people

jumping from buildings to escape fire, babies roasted in hot cars while parents sat in a cool bar two dozen feet away. A man killed with a roofer's nail gun . . .

Thirty fucking years, Leo Bander thought, staring at the sky through the windshield. *I've seen it all. There's nothing left.*

He checked his watch: time to get back on patrol. He radioed his return to service and pulled to the rear of the buildings, no attempts at forced entry, just the usual gang signs on the brick.

Bander passed a stand of trash receptacles, a corpulent rat darting from one bin to another. Motion ahead caught Bander's eye and he blinked to see the pale back of a naked man with exceptionally bright hair. The man was staggering from a loading bay at the rear of a store. He looked wasted, stoned or drunk or both.

Bander sighed and rolled the cruiser a half-dozen feet behind the guy's skinny white ass, the guy oblivious to the sound of approaching tires. Bander gave the siren a hit: *Whoooooop.* He leaned out the window. "OK, buddy, let's put a stop on it right there."

The man twitched. Moaned. Turned around.

Leo Bander's heart stopped in his chest. He was wrong. He had seen everything in thirty years . . .

Except that.

40

I awoke in the chair at two a.m. and moved to bed, too tired to remove my clothes. I arose at seven, showered and performed three days' worth of shaving, then dined alfresco on sausage, eggs and grits as workers filed into the surrounding buildings and buses whined from stop to stop. Rain had passed through before dawn and the air felt renewed, at least until a bus sizzled past.

I was finishing my coffee and wondering if Morningstar had gone in early this morning – the new pathologist was in town, ready to be filled with knowledge – or if she was still abed. I pictured her tan body across snow-white sheets (I'd never known anyone who could sprawl so picturesquely) and felt the need to hear her voice, thinking it a good way to start a day likely destined to fall downhill from here.

My phone riffed and I hoped she'd been on the same thought track, just a faster dialer, but it was Vince Delmara.

"Howdy, Vince. You're out and about early, and on a Saturday."

"Like days have any meaning any more. Listen, Carson . . . you filed a Missings report day before yesterday, right?"

"It was filed by Patrick White. I was just making sure it moved quicker and—"

"Thirty minutes back a male of Prestwick's approximate age and size was found southwest of Florida City. Hair's silvery?"

"The photo should have ID'd him, Vince. They check it?"

A pause. "Um, unknown."

"How's his condition?"

"Vitals are stable, I hear. Uh, listen, Carson. You know this guy, Patrick White very well?"

"He's a nurse at MD-Gen. He's a good guy, solid. Why?"

"You may want to be there when he visits his buddy. Gotta go, Carson. I'm on a fast track today. Stay sane, OK?"

Something in Vince's call – *stay sane?* – ramped my heart up and I turned on the screamer and flashers, pulling into the Emergency intake. An ambulance was in the bay with rear doors open and I wondered if it had delivered Prestwick. I entered to see four medical types studying a chart, their faces tight and tentative. I shoved the badge and ID in the air.

"I'm here about a recent intake, young male, silverish hair. Can anyone help me?"

It was like everything stopped. All faces craned to me. A fortyish man I assumed to be a doc – green scrubs, stethoscope around his neck, intense expression – ran my way.

"Prestwick's down the hall. Name's Doc Brown, yeah, like the soft drink."

I followed Brown to the first room. Stepping in I saw the lower half of Prestwick first, legs sticking out, fine there. My gaze continued upwards to a head completely wrapped in gauze and stained with seepage. A breathing tube was inserted into the mask of gauze. A pale arm was strung with tubes and wires and a nurse was changing out an IV bag. Two other doctors were conferring in a corner. One was shaking his head in what seemed disbelief.

"What happened to his head?" I asked Brown.

"Not his head. It's . . . his face."

"Injured?" I asked.

"Removed."

The words didn't fit in my head and I stared at the gauze orb, a slit over the mouth emitting low moans.

"Explain that to me, Doctor."

Brown blew out a breath. "Think of the face as a mask of flesh over the skull. Someone incised a line under the jaw line, ran it front of the ears to the top of the forehead, grabbed the mask and pulled it off."

My stomach upended itself and I only barely got it righted.

"My God," I whispered. "What's left?"

"Underlying tissue. Muscles. Have you ever seen the Chinese exhibit, *Bodies*?"

I had and closed my eyes. Prestwick was moaning louder. Brown looked at the nurse. "Fentanyl, quick."

"*Dr Brown*," said the paging system. "*Dr Brown to Emergency.*"

"Shit. Gotta go." Brown shot a look at Prestwick as the nurse pushed a plunger on the syringe. He shook his head.

"Someone must really hate him."

Feeling poleaxed, I drifted into the hall and realized it was up to me to call Patrick White. He answered halfway through the first ring, like the phone had been in his hand, waiting.

"Patrick? This is Detective Ryder."

"I can tell by your voice . . . it's bad. Is he, is Billy . . ."

"Billy Prestwick is alive, Patrick. He's in no danger of dying."

A released breath. "Thank God. Oh, thank God."

"Can you come to the hospital, Patrick? I think it'd be a good thing."

White arrived twenty minutes later. I had been by the elevators hoping to catch him and break the news, but he used the back stairway and I only knew he'd been in Prestwick's intensive-care room when I saw him exit it.

He looked drunk, his legs loose and his head drowsing and he leaned the wall for support. I got to him just as his legs looked ready to buckle.

"Come on, bud," I said, steering him to a visitor alcove and easing him into a chair. His mouth was open and his eyes closed, and I knew they were seeing horrors. I booked to the nurses' station and got a cup and ice water.

"Drink this, Patrick."

He drank clumsily, water dribbling to his shirt. He set aside the cup and shook his head. "Who could do that to another human?"

I pulled a chair across from Patrick and sat. "The man who did it is sick, Patrick. His mind has cancer."

He turned to me. "You've got pictures. Why can't you find him?"

"All we really know is his basic size and his underlying facial structure. He's likely changed everything else."

"But it's your job, right? This is what you do?"

"We're trying, Patrick. It's just that this guy—"

His fists pounded the couch, his face reddened. 'NO! I don't want to hear what you can't do! You want to see what you did do? Go look down the hall!"

"Patrick . . ."

"MY BEST FRIEND IS DOWN THE HALL AND HE HAS NO FACE! YOU DID THAT! YOU KEEP SAYING YOU'RE TRYING . . . SCREW TRYING. HOW ABOUT ACTUALLY GETTING SOMETHING DONE!"

White's anger echoed down the hall. Nurses' eyes looked our way, two physicians leaned from Prestwick's room. I wanted to disappear, to be anywhere but in this hospital hall filled with pain and despair and the results of my failure. When Patrick White sunk deeper into the chair and began sobbing, I started to walk toward the station, but realized it was the coward's instinct and it was my penance to keep within the umbra of White's grief, to feel the negative power of my ineptitude.

So I sat on a couch beneath the alcove's window. My head fell into my hands and I tried to find a place of quiet for just a few seconds, a place where all my chaotic thoughts might resolve into an insight, a possible solution. And there I sat until I felt a hand tremble on my shoulder and the weight of another presence on the couch. I turned to Patrick White, his eyes red and cheeks wet.

"I'm sorry," he said, swallowing hard. "It was cruel and terrible and I didn't mean it. I'm so sorry."

"It's all right, Patrick. It's been a terrible last few hours."

He pulled a handkerchief and wiped his eyes. "I know you're doing everything. I've never seen anyone more determined."

I put my hand on his shoulder. "He's your best amigo, Patrick. You have every right to your anger."

"Not when it's misguided. I can't imagine how it must be to deal with the kind of creatures who can do something like, like . . ." He could only nod toward Prestwick's room.

"Creature is the right word, Patrick. But this one's uncannily smart. We can't find him by his looks, so we have to find him by how he thinks. Like why did he select Billy as a target? That's where you can help, Patrick. You told me a bit about Billy the other day. Tell me more."

White moved from the couch to the chair, pulling it close as he measured out his words. "It's . . . it's difficult because there are two Billys. One's outrageous, over the top, vain as a peacock . . . almost a cartoon character. That's the Billy most people see."

"The other?"

"Caring, intelligent. He's good at hiding that one, because he's insecure. Billy thinks if he's not the center of attention, he's failed. Not so much failed himself, but failed everyone. If there's not a crowd surrounding him and laughing, he's doing something wrong."

"Can he be hurtful with his words? Insulting?"

A long pause.

"Patrick?" I prodded.

"Years ago, when we were in our late teens, early twenties, Billy could say hurtful things. So did the crowd he hung with . . . like they had to be mean to be cool. They were a bunch of nasty little bitches." He paused. "I was one of them, Detective Ryder. I can't believe I could have been so terrible."

"You grew up. How about Billy?"

"Growing up? He equates it with being serious, and being serious with being a drag. But he's turned being mean into being funny, always clowning."

"What's he do for a living?"

"He dresses windows for a few small shops, really creative set-ups. He's got flair. He also relies a lot on the kindness of strangers, to lift a line from Tennessee Williams."

"He hooks?"

"He accompanies. Some men hate getting older, losing their youth and virility. They enjoy walking around in public with someone young and attractive. Others like to talk, to bask in his, his . . . Billyness. He makes them feel a part of things again, and in exchange, they give him clothes, liquor, money. And yes, sometimes there's sex involved."

"He uses his looks."

A nod. "He once told me he couldn't imagine looking regular, that it would be such a drag to have an ordinary face." White paused, and tears began rolling down his cheeks.

"Cosmetic surgery can do a lot these days," I said, trying to be comforting. "The pros will fix his face."

He looked at me and swallowed hard.

"But to fix a face, Detective Ryder, you first need to have one."

The scene investigators were still on site when I arrived. Prestwick had again been dumped in an urban area, again behind a strip of shops. It was as private a drop zone as a city offered and I found Deb Clayton studying a standpipe, as if wondering whether she should finger-print it.

She pointed to a loading dock holding broken pallets. "We found a blood trail starting below the dock. An MDPD cruiser was patrolling, saw the victim, called for a bus."

"What was the vic's condition?"

"Stunned, staggering. Naked. According to the patrol officer, Leo Bander, it was the freakiest thing he's ever seen. And Leo's about to finish thirty."

I climbed the steps to the rear door and banged. When nothing happened I picked up a chunk of broken pallet and did a timpani solo. Seconds later the door opened and a balding fortyish guy in a brown suit stuck an angry head out.

"What the fuck is going . . ." He saw the copmobile and forensics unit. The anger dissolved. "Oh shit, another fucking body?"

I shouldered past him. It was cool inside and I saw a lot of wooden crates and boxes. "That a frequent occurrence?" I said. "Dead bodies in the backyard?"

The guy shook his head. "Just once, a homeless guy. It was last year and the paper said his heart gave out. Poor fuck was forty-two. I found him, and I coulda swore he was eighty."

"It's a hard life," I agreed. I looked at the rows of wooden and cardboard cartons, sized like they could

270

hold all sizes of picture frames. "What do you sell here, by the way?"

He walked toward the front, waving for me to follow. I caught up with him as we passed through a door to the retail area. It was bright and cheery and filled with dozens of Carson Ryders.

When my mouth dropped open, so did theirs.

41

I went to the office. Roy was in Tallahassee, probably schmoozing the yo-yo legislator. Gershwin had been out with the second team, taking Donnie's picture to the chemistry and botany departments of local colleges and universities.

"Please tell us you know this guy . . ."

Gershwin returned and reclined on my sofa with hands behind his head, staring at the ceiling as we discussed recent events, Jeremy not included.

"Donnie left Prestwick behind a mirror store?" Gershwin said.

"A discount mirror outlet, every size and shape of mirror you could ever want."

"Meaning?"

I pushed aside the mess on my desk to give me a place to rest my heels. "Donnie knows. I don't. Appearance, mirror to the soul, a reflection of whatever. It may make no sense to us even if we knew what it meant to him."

"You said he's changing shape?"

"His madness is changing shape. Something spurred him into extreme violence, and he liked it."

"Enough that his next move is cutting out a man's tongue?"

"Violence is replacing sex, or they're now the same. He's probably getting more release from suffering than sex."

"Donnie took Prestwick, tore off his face, and dumped him. He kept him what, sahib . . . thirty-something hours?"

I blew out a breath. "The more violence, the less time he needs to keep them."

"Concentrated thrills. You have my next question figured out, right, Big Ryde?"

I pulled my feet from the desk and leaned forward, nodding at Gershwin.

"Donnie's next step, Zigs? It's when he discovers that murder is the ultimate thrill."

Debro was in the second bedroom of his apartment, the room he'd filled with flasks, bottles, a water-cooled condenser and a compact centrifuge, all ordered from Edmund Scientific three years ago, before he moved closer to Miami. The few chemicals he needed were simple, set off no alarms, and were easy to acquire.

He pulled the propane burner from the base of the flask

and checked the output from the condenser: fourteen cc's of yellowish fluid, the product of ten pounds of the seeds and inner bark of black locust trees, extracted via centrifuge, unnecessary adjuncts precipitated out, the remainder distilled to a concentration containing the glycoside robitin, and the alkaloid robinine, both toxic, the solution ready for final filtration.

Debro wore a respirator over his mouth, nose and eyes. Connections could not be perfect in his makeshift lab, and a sniff of vapor would turn his muscles to rubber and he'd puke the floor, shit his pants and pass out. When he awakened hours later he'd be nearly unable to stand, and for days would feel like he'd been hit by a train.

That was the black locust. A single drop of his jimson weed extract – seven hours of work to turn a bushel of leaves and stems into a half-ounce of extract – and a brain would generate pictures that made nightmares look like Disney cartoons.

The dieffenbachia? Chew it like gum and pretty soon all you could do was make a croaking sound. Getting to its essence was an old-school process: run the leaves through a food processor, put the mush into alcohol until the active chemical leached into the C_2H_{60}, then process it to a kind of syrup with just enough viscosity to flow, a single drop turning your voice into a cold croak in minutes.

Debro knew this all from experience: he'd been his own lab rat.

He only tried the smallest doses for himself . . . he

wasn't crazy. And he hadn't had anything else to do back then but gain knowledge. But his pursuit had needed a larger sampling of effects, allowing him to gauge results from flu-like illness to incapacitation all the way to . . . well, the ultimate overload.

Luckily, Florida was chock-full of lab rats available for experimentation. He'd known many of them by name and exactly where they lived or hid. They were called illegal immigrants. The *indocumentados*.

Debro had conducted his special experiments many months ago, his sombrero-topped lab rats supplying the major input in dosages of his magic potion. It took under a week to discover the outside parameters . . . from mild sickness up to death. You basically just averaged the two extremes.

Olé! he thought with a smile. A very instructive week. *Gracias amigos!*

Debro decanted the black locust extract into a small bottle, ready to mix with the other compounds. If he knew his quarry – weight, age and fitness level – he could pre-fill the dropper with his mixture and not have to go to a bar's bathroom and make adjustments on the fly.

Or, like Prestwick, Debro could knock him unconscious outside his home, jam a needle in a thigh, hold him down when he came to, sick and terrified. You put more in a syringe because you wanted them to drop fast. A bar you wanted sick first, frozen throat, then the visions. You watched them clutch their bellies and run to the bathroom. If circumstance allowed, you could control from there. Or wait until they went home and simply climb in a window or break down the door. By then they were usually sprawled on the floor in their own puke and swatting the air or picking invisible things from their skin.

And when they regained consciousness, days later, their memories were empty. It was a triumph. And the triumphs would soon continue.

Debro set a syringe and a dropper on a white mouse pad on his table, his staging area. He closed his eyes and ran a picture of his quarry through his head, a recent photo: 155–165 pounds. He'd average the weight and load his equipment for 160 pounds.

Debro picked up the syringe and felt a tingle of delight. He would soon have another.

All that remained was gauging the punishment.

Patrick White stared at the mask of bandages covering the former face of Billy Prestwick. Throughout the morning various specialists had been in, cosmetological surgeons, mainly, carefully peeling back the dressings to study the area. Several of the seasoned physicians had winced when beholding the damage. They retreated to the hall where Patrick heard them talking in low tones, comparing the relative merits of several procedures.

Billy was starting to have moments of consciousness, though he was heavily sedated. When Patrick asked Dr Costa why Billy was coming around while the others had taken much longer, he'd speculated since Billy had only been kept for three days, his abductor hadn't pumped so much of the incapacitating mix into him. The others had been dosed for days longer, the toxins accumulating over time.

"Ohhh fuuu-ck," Billy moaned, a tube-laden arm reaching toward his face. Patrick stopped the hand, set it back on the sheet, patted it.

"It's me, Patrick. You're in the hospital and you're safe."

"Ha' happ'n?" Prestwick said, recognizable words: *What happened?* Patrick breathed out in relief, only then realizing he'd been holding his breath. It was the first indication Billy was returning to Billy. That was both good and bad.

"You were, uh, kidnapped, Billy. Like the others. But you're alive and back safe and sound."

"K'nap?"

"The others were gone for a week or more. You came back after three. Guess he got tired of you."

The hand started to rise again, Patrick holding it tighter.

"Hap'n face?" Prestwick asked. "Cn't see."

"Your eyes are fine, Billy. The monster beat you up a bit. Just rest, right? Get better and we'll get you back to barhopping in no time, right?"

"uh, uh . . . y cn't I tlk?" *Why can't I talk?*

Patrick closed his eyes and shook his head, feeling his eyes well with tears. Now was not the time to tell Billy he had no lips.

"It's the bandages, buddy. Don't talk. Just relax. Sleep and get better."

Prestwick's head rolled to the side, worn out by the effort of communicating. His breath settled into the rhythm of sleep and a slight snore rattled from the dark mouth-hole of the dressings. Patrick set Billy's hand on the bed, choked back his emotions, wiped his eyes on his shoulders, and stopped in the bathroom to rinse his face with cold water. He looked at himself in the mirror and made a bright smile rise to his face. He slapped his cheeks to make them remember the smile's shape.

Time to go to work. It would be a long day.

42

Prestwick's story was too grisly to cover up. Though the depth of the horror was not conveyed – "extensive facial wounds" was the phrase repeated by radio and television newscasters – the story was widely disseminated. I knew that a man with three TV monitors in his room couldn't miss seeing the story.

Rather than call, I went to the shop. Jonathan sat behind the counter, staring disconsolately at a stack of video games as he stuck price tags on the cases. It was the first time I'd seen him without the knit cap, his dark hair highlighted with green.

"I'll be damned," I said, trying to lighten the kid's long face. "I thought you were born in that hat, never took it off."

"Gary wants to be alone," he said. "He shut me off this morning, first time ever."

It was an odd remark, but I chalked it up to the kid's eccentricities. "You look down, Jonathan," I said as I walked to the counter. Save for me and Jonathan, the store was empty.

"Gary's acting like he used to. He makes me run to fast-food joints. He had three bags of McNuggets for breakfast. Not that I'll be doing it much longer."

It sounded like the long-time clerk was thinking of quitting. "C'mon, bud," I said, "don't give up on him. He needs friends more than anything."

"It ain't that. Look."

Jonathan tapped the keyboard on the checkout counter, then turned the monitor my way. It's an industry e-newsletter. This is in the advertising section."

I leaned close to the page and read a block of text highlighted in a red box.

RENOWNED COMIC-BOOK SHOP FOR IMMEDIATE SALE

An established South Florida comic-book store with an international reputation and sideline in games is immediately available as a turnkey operation. Over $385,000 in current inventory (prices conservatively estimated), 1900-sq-ft store has same-sized full living quarters above and is for sale or lease, with excellent terms. Superbly maintained building is priced 20% below market value for quick sale.

This is a once-in-a-lifetime offer for the serious
collector who has always dreamed of owning a busi-
ness. Owner must leave business for health reasons.
No reasonable offer refused.

The reply address was a Gmail account. "That's Gary's addy?" I asked.

"He's got fourteen of them, last count. He never uses this one, but I knew about it. The description can only be this place."

"I want to talk to him, Jonathan," I said, looking for the hidden cameras. I'd caught glimpses of the video feed on Gary's upstairs monitors and saw the camera swing to catch the forensics techs when they'd entered.

"He don't wanna talk to anyone, not you, not customers. Like I said, he even shut me off."

"Tell him I'm down here."

He shrugged. "Whatever."

I walked to the front window. The surveillance had changed position to the far side of the street. When I turned back, Jonathan had slipped the hat back on and was staring at me. I jumped as speakers in the walls bloomed with Gary Ocampo's voice.

"I don't want to talk today, Detective Ryder." He sounded defeated.

"Gary . . ."

"Go away. Please just . . . go away. I'm sorry. I fucked up."

"If it's about Scott . . . that's just life, Gary. If I had

to count the times I've hit on women who shut me down, I'd need an accountant."

"What are you talking about? I didn't do ANYTHING! What I TRIED TO DO WAS . . ." he stopped.

"Was what?"

"I DON'T WANT TO TALK TO THE POLICE. I CAN'T."

"I'm not here as a cop, Gary. I'm here as a friend."

"YEAH? HOW LONG IS THAT GONNA LAST, YOU THINK?"

"We have to talk, Gary. It's about Donnie."

I heard his voice break down. "I'm . . . shutting you off, Detective. Turning my monitor off. For the last time, go away and leave me alone."

I looked at Jonathan, cocking his head like listening for the buzz of the mics. "Gary's gone. He shut it all down."

"Can I elevator up to see him?"

"Not unless he wants. He turns the downstairs off when he wants to be alone."

"He get depressed like this often? This kind of mood?"

"I been working for Gary for six years, since I was seventeen. He used to get sad or crabby a lot. Some days he'd just lay up there and watch TV and eat. Then he hooked up with that weight thing at the university."

"A change?"

"He started to lighten up. Both ways. No more bags of White Castles and football-sized burritos. People visited at night, y'know . . . heavy people working on their shit together. I was sometimes still here and heard

282

people laughing. It was cool. Not only did Gary go out for group meetings, he even wanted to . . . he got all excited the last few months."

I rapped the counter with my knuckles and flicked a wave. I was halfway out the door when Jonathan called, "Detective?" I turned.

"He likes you," the kid said. "You think maybe you could talk him outta selling the place? I mean, like when he gets outta this pissy mood?"

"He'd know you found out he was selling the biz, maybe get pissed off."

"If he stays in business he needs me to run the place. I know everything that goes on, stuff even Gary don't know I know. It's like it's my place, too."

"Gary ever talk to you about his dreams, Jonathan? About going to Rio?"

"He never told me. But it comes in the mail, the travel brochures and cruise stuff. All that Brazil and Rio stuff. It started back when he was doing that group thing with the weight. I think he sends for the same stuff over and over just because he likes getting it."

I retreated from the shop more worried about Gary Ocampo than when I'd entered. Behind the anger was a deep sense of depression, like his world was falling down a rat hole and there was no way to save it. It seemed his fingersnap decision to sell the shop was, like the broken diet, a form of running away.

I turned down the block and walked past the FCLE surveillance team, saw Michael Rasmussen and Terry

Longo hunkered down in a gray van with AAA Appliance Repair on the side, every day a new vehicle. I paused a half-dozen feet from the cruiser and put my foot on a hydrant, pretending to tie my shoe.

"How's it going, boys?" I said, barely moving my lips.

"Like watching paint dry," Rasmussen said from behind a newspaper. "How about you bag this fucker so we can live somewhere besides a tin can?"

"You're getting paid to sit on your ass and watch pretty girls walk by," I said. "How bad could it be?"

"I'll let you know when we see our first pretty girl."

I spun back toward the Rover and climbed inside. I was figuring out my next move when my phone rang. It was Jeremy. I pulled into the corner of a seedy car-wash lot, not wanting to yell at my dashboard, and took out my cell. "I'm in my car," I said. "How about I get somewhere quiet and you can fill me in."

"I like to look at those with whom I consult. It's a professional courtesy."

"No time, Jeremy, I'm—"

"I can work you in tomorrow. Same time as last time, and no stopping in bars."

He hung up. I called Gershwin and said I had private business to deal with and it would take all of tomorrow. Then I drove to Matecumbe and sat on my deck and watched Mr Mix-up romp and roll in the yard, deciding there were worse things to be than a dog.

43

The next morning I hit Key West at ten a.m., stopping for a cup of coffee at a diner by the docks. My brother had actively returned to my life days ago and was already dancing me around like his private puppet.

I forswore jumping the gate for a more formal entrance. He opened the door in a white linen shirt, sky-blue slacks and tan bucks and I stepped inside. "When do the plumbers arrive?" I asked.

"Plumbers?"

"Or the roofers. Or the crew that's gonna rewire every lamp in the joint."

He pulled an iPhone from his pocket, tapped the calendar and studied for moment. "No one's working on the house today, Carson. Some furniture is being delivered this afternoon, that's all."

"Will your girlfriend be here to supervise?"

A pause. "Is she supposed to?"

"It's what women do, Jeremy. Point and say, 'I want the couch here.' When the couch is there, they study it for a few seconds and say, 'No, I think it's better over here.' This goes on for an hour or so, then it's time to position a table. If you're going to invent a girlfriend, Jeremy, you need to know how they act."

He thought a moment. "Do they really do that?"

I nodded. "It's genetic, something to do with nesting."

His lips pursed and his brow furrowed; my brother was truly intrigued. "Fascinating, Carson. I'll watch for signs."

I checked my watch to emphasize my hurry for the information. "You asked me here for a reason, right? Your take on Donnie Ocampo?"

He put his hand on my shoulder and turned me toward the rear of the house. "Let's repair to the backyard, Carson. Care for a libation?"

A minute later we were in the large courtyard, lemonade for my brother, sweet tea for me. We sat at a thick glass-topped table beneath drifting palms, a wall of vines and orchids at our backs. Jeremy had the file on the table, waiting. He folded his hands under his chin.

"The whole affair is a discord, Carson. It's out of tune."

"I need more than that."

"You've concluded Donnie's angry at El Blimpo. So why doesn't he show it?"

"Didn't you read the reports? The phone call about

286

Gary's issues, the threatening letter." I did the hands-as-mask thing. "The mask at the window?"

My brother rolled his eyes. "Goofy faces at the window? An angry man would toss a brick through the glass. Or fire a shotgun through it. And only one call from Donnie to his hated brother? Why not buy a burner phone, make a vehement call, toss it out and buy another? Why not a call a day? An hour? Where's Donnie's hate, Carson? His need to punish Gravy Ocampo for being a disgusting bag of lard?"

"It was in a threatening letter, Jeremy. Donnie *puked* on it."

My brother waved an invisible fan at his face, Scarlett O'Hara preparing to faint, right down to the voice. "Voh-mit on a let-tuh? Oh, mah goodness, Mistah Cahson, how very thee-atrical." He switched to his regular voice. "I'm becoming diabetic from the sweetness of it all. The cuteness. Making sport of Captain Chubbywumper's *issues*? That's a pun. How many hate-addled poisoners have you heard pun, Carson?" He did the hands-mask thing. "And did you happen to notice what this is besides a goofy gesture? It's the goddamn twin sign, Gemini. Just upside-down."

"You're reaching, Jeremy."

"I never reach. Answers drop into my hands. Donnie's not sane, Carson, not even close. He is, however, fiercely unhappy. Just not with El Gordo, at least not in the beginning. Donnie's punishing those he feels have wronged him – likely a big list, at least in his mind – and his revenge is becoming deeply personal. I expect he's

287

approaching the point where he won't need to drag victims off one at a time. He'll set fire to a gay nightclub on Tank-top Tuesday, hide nearby and masturbate to the screaming." He paused. "Do you think when gay men burn they give off rainbow smoke?"

"You said Donnie wasn't angry with Gary, not at the beginning. What did you mean?"

Jeremy folded his hands behind his head and stared at the palm fronds above. "The two started as one, Carson, bruvers in armsies. But Donnie got tired of sharing. Or the boys had a falling out. So Donnie stopped making the sign. It was how he told Gravy they were no longer a team."

"Sign? Team? What are you talking about?"

Jeremy leaned forward, riffled though the case materials, and held up the Gemini symbol. "This goofy, childish sign was *for* Little Lard Fauntleroy, not *at* him. Did you happen to notice the twinnies were kissing?" He performed the vapors thing again, waving at himself. "Oh, Mistah Cahson, if this whole af-*fair* got any moah sugary, I do b'lieve I would fay-ant dead away from the sweetness."

I shook my head in disbelief. "You can't be saying Gary and Donnie were in contact the whole time?"

"Not the whole time. Only until . . ." He shuffled through the photos, coming up with the shot of Harold Brighton. "Dancing boy. Here's where Donnie stopped making the sign. They had a falling out and Donnie dissolved the marriage."

"Donnie made the sign. Brighton was marked."

"Because that was the first thing Donnie-boy did – mark them. I'll bet he did it within five minutes of pulling them into his lair, even before he grabbed his first backdoor bonanza. It made the victims *theirs:* property of the twins. But some time during Brighton's captivity, Donnie took another road."

"Why?"

"He reached his bottom floor and found out what he truly needed. Fat twin became extraneous, an impediment."

I stared at my brother. His theory was too wild, too improbable. I knew Gary Ocampo, Jeremy didn't, thus he was postulating events that could never have happened. I wondered if he was just trying to humor me.

"Maybe you should take another look," I said. "Fresh and in the morn—"

But he was up and heading for the door, looking at his watch. "I have to visit the docks for a few minutes, Carson. I'm auditioning various sea captains and inspecting their vessels. I won't be gone long, so wipe that pissy look off your face."

"Interviewing local skippers? Why? For what?"

"Speed. Seaworthiness of craft. Range. Amenities."

I stared at him. "Don't forget discretion."

"Whatever for?"

"You're planning for what happens if you get spotted, right? I imagine a fast and long-range craft might be nice. With a discreet and highly paid skipper taking you to . . . where? Mexico? Honduras?"

289

"Get spotted? You mean like a leopard?"

"I keep trying to tell you . . . your face is on the wall in cop houses across the country. If you insist on going outside, it's not *if* you get seen, but when."

My brother buttoned his jacket, flicking something unseen from a lapel. "You have such a creative imagination, Carson. Perhaps you should take up painting as well." He tucked a knuckle under his chin and regarded me. "You'd be a Pointillist, I expect, using tiny dots to build your pictures."

"You didn't answer the question. What do you want from a boat?"

"To go fishing, of course."

I waved him away. Hopeless.

44

Just like a coin once did in Gary Ocampo's palm, Jeremy disappeared. I twirled my drink in circles, positive Gary knew nothing about his brother's crimes. Jeremy was distracted, off his game. My trip was a waste of time, but at least I could honorably tell Roy I'd consulted with my expert and that he'd unfortunately been stymied.

Needing more than lemonade, I went inside and mixed a modest Scotch and soda and returned to the floral pyrotechnics of the courtyard, the noon sun dancing through the palm fronds. Gulls swooped and keened in air so blue the color alone could have kept them aloft. The tall vine-covered walls absorbed sounds of the street. I thought I heard a sound like a door closing, but when I listened toward the house all I heard was the whisper of fronds in the breeze.

A few seconds later I heard the rear door unlatch,

followed by gentle footfalls. I didn't turn, but waved my hand over my shoulder. "That was speedy, Brother," I said. "Did you find a boat that can carry you to Ecuador?"

"Hello, Carson," said a voice to my back.

It was a feminine voice, low and husky, and I turned to see a woman stepping my way with a glass of minted lemonade in hand, her hair as white as snow, though her motions were lithe and youthful. She wore a bright sundress and her skin was cream, seen in long arms, supple legs and a gentle face with eyes behind large sunglasses.

Something in the motion halted my breath. She removed the sunglasses.

"Ava," I whispered.

It was Ava Davanelle, the alcoholic pathologist I'd worked with – and made love to – a decade ago. Lovely, brilliant Ava. Troubled, dark Ava. The woman who'd faced off in battle with my brother when his demons were their strongest, and who had sent them scurrying back beneath their rocks.

"It's been a long time, hasn't it, Carson?"

She continued my way, framed in sunlight, orchids at her back. Except for the hair, white where once lay waves of auburn, little had changed. Her eyes were the green of a placid sea, her mouth wide and built to surprise when it smiled, her neck long and graceful.

"I . . . what are you . . ." The reality hit as I stood, the ground unsteady below my feet, trembling. Or maybe it was me. "You're Jeremy's . . . girlfriend?" I said, my voice barely a whisper.

"Girlfriend? That's the term he's been using?"

"It's wrong?"

The surprise of a smile. "It's limited."

I needed motion and arranged chairs around the table, pulling out a chair for Ava. She nodded and sat, the legs crossing as she relaxed.

"You realize I'm a bit taken aback," I said, sitting. "And more than a little curious."

She plucked a spring of mint from her lemonade and twirled it. "I'll start at the beginning, when you took me to the Institute to meet Jeremy." The smile again. "You recall that day, I expect."

"I'll never forget it. Jeremy lashed at you with every mind game he had, and you whipped him back with his own words. You were fearless."

"Not fearless, Carson. As terrified as I'd ever been. I'd never seen anyone like Jeremy, felt an energy like that. The all-consuming emotion, the raw and blazing anger."

"He might have killed you that day, Ava. I might not have been able to stop him."

"I felt that threat, Carson. Could you understand that beneath my terror I also felt an exhilaration. That I felt joy?"

I wasn't sure I heard her correctly. "Joy, Ava? That doesn't make—"

She stopped me with a raised hand. "Maybe it's because I had nothing to lose that day, Carson. Or just didn't care . . . busily drinking away my career. But the day became branded inside me, the most interesting of my life. The most interesting to Jeremy, as he later told me. Confusing to him, but . . ."

"Yes," I nodded, a long-ago puzzle finally solved. "Jeremy would be fascinated by something that confused him. It explains why he always begged me to bring you back to the Institute, Ava. I told him you had moved away. When I lied and said I didn't know where you were, he was distraught, but hid it under anger."

"Then you know I went to Fort Wayne, Indiana. I'd found a job as a path assistant. I had a new life to build and I wanted to make sure I didn't screw this one up. I worked in Fort Wayne for a couple years, then found a position in Illinois."

She took a sip of the lemonade and continued. "Four years ago, Jeremy phoned in the middle of the night, finding me through a professional organization. He said you'd just helped him escape from the police in New York. He said he had used all of you he dared use."

I stared, nonplussed. "He told you the full story? Everything?"

"I hung up. Then was sorry I did. A few days later Jeremy called and asked if he could see me. I asked where he was, and he said on my front porch. I pushed aside the curtain to see him sitting in the porch swing and smiling at the window. He was holding a bouquet and a box of candy."

"He's one of the most wanted men in the country. Why didn't you call the cops?"

She studied the sprig of mint. "Could I not ask the same question of you, Carson?"

"I didn't think him guilty of the crimes, Ava. Not to an extent to justify life-long incarceration."

"He told me that was your judgement. I thought if that's what you believed, it must be true. And if you could no longer keep Jeremy safe, perhaps I could."

"You believed my brother? Trusted him?"

"Jeremy showed up on my porch knowing a single phone call could end his freedom. He trusted that I'd listen to his story before making that call. We spoke through the door for an hour before I opened it. By then, yes, I believed his every word."

"You kept him safe him for me?"

"In the beginning. I owe you everything, Carson. You saved me from myself."

"You saved you from yourself, Ava. I simply helped you find AA."

A puzzled lift of eyebrow. "How is that not saving me?"

I had no answer and Ava continued. "Jeremy stayed with me for three months building the Charpentier persona. Chicago was unsafe and he never went out. We decided a rural setting was his best bet for safety."

"Thus Kentucky."

I heard the door slam at my back and turned to see my brother stepping outside with a lemonade in hand. "Which worked for years, Brother. But the times they are a-changing."

He sat beside Ava and slung one long leg over the other, grinning, knowing seeing Ava had fried my circuits, at least for the first couple minutes.

"Find the right boat?" I asked my brother. He wanted rattled, I gave him nonchalance.

He lifted his glass in assent. I looked between my brother and my former girlfriend, stopping on Ava. "You're going to live here, I take it, Ava? Key West?"

"I'm moving to Miami."

Jeremy sipped and winked at me. "It's not our nature to rub against one another on a daily basis, Carson. We've been meeting twice a year on average. It will now be several days a month."

Ava had said she'd worked in Illinois, and was now moving to Miami. I hadn't made the connection when she'd said *Chicago*, Illinois.

"You're the new pathologist," I said.

A beatific smile. "I start next week. Can't wait."

We talked for another half-hour, lighter conversation. Ava was staying in an apartment in Coral Gables until finding a home. She detailed several strange cases from Chicago and I felt at home discussing a world which intersected mine. Jeremy was, of course, equally fascinated, since the crimes Ava described involved mental aberrations.

After an hour I looked at my watch and stood, uncertain whether I was entering the real world or leaving it. Ava and Jeremy walked me back through the house, Jeremy stopping at the staircase. "See our esteemed visitor to the door, please, Ava." He grinned at me. "I'm creating a painting for the living room and must get into zee arteestic mood. Do you think I should wear a beret?"

He laughed and headed upstairs, Ava walking me to the door. I opened it, turning to her. "It's gonna take some getting used to, Ava. I still can't quite understand you and my broth—"

She stilled my lips with her fingers. "What I learned in AA, Carson, is that I'm a hopeless drunk and will always be a hopeless drunk, rabid for the alcohol swoon, craving to fall into the delicious swirling well of booze. Alcohol made me feel loose and warm and free. But each time I took a drink, I also entered a world of dark shapes inside myself, fears and revelations and pieces of the past that crawled behind the shadows."

"You stopped drinking because of the fear, Ava?"

She gave me a sad smile. "I loved alcohol's comfort, Carson, but even more, I loved its danger."

I absorbed her words, and had my own revelation. "Jeremy is your alcohol, Ava. Your drug."

She closed her eyes and nodded her head.

"He keeps me ceaselessly drunk, Carson. And I love it."

45

I started my drive back with the intention of going into Miami to salvage the remaining day, but a growling stomach pulled me into a seaside bar-restaurant on Marathon Key, ordering a beer, a flounder sandwich overhanging the platter, and a side of fries. I ate on a deck, dining to ship's horns and gulls as I arranged my experience at Jeremy's house into three distinct stacks of thoughts.

The first concerned Jeremy's relationship with Ava. The surprise would take time to assimilate. Given Jeremy's strange attraction to Ava so many years ago, it should not have been a total surprise that he had needed to see her again. And given Ava's dysfunctional, addicted history, that she had needed to see him.

The second pile of thoughts related to Jeremy's move and reshaping of his identity and history, especially his tying it to mine. I was deeply troubled by his attraction to a community of prominence, with thousands of eyes wandering the streets on a daily basis. I would not have been so worried if I knew my brother planned to live a hermit's life, locked within his walls, but he seemed to be planning to venture into crowds, to live a normal life.

It could never happen. I had to convince him of that – for his sake and now Ava's – but that lay in the future.

The final pile was his analysis of Donnie Ocampo, the stack of most pressing concern, and where my thoughts focused. That Donnie was not sane – my brother and I were in harmony there – but Jeremy's conclusion that the Brothers Ocampo shared communication made no sense to me.

But as I ordered a second beer, I considered the times I'd gone to Jeremy for advice. They were few in number, and his analysis often made little sense at the moment offered, but in the end had been preternaturally accurate. So I sat and focused on feelings sparked by Gary, replaying the time I'd spent with him in my head, recalling moments when something had seemed a shade askew.

I had been surprised at Gary's initial position that Donnie wasn't really harming the victims, as if abduction and rape were lightweight crimes, and it wasn't until Harold Brighton's legs had been demolished that the horror of Donnie's actions seemed to register in Gary's mind.

"*It's not supposed to be like this*," Gary had wailed after I told him about Brighton. "*He's hurting people. Donnie's actually* hurting *them!*"

What wasn't supposed to be like *this*? What was *It*?

Then there was Gary's request for a meeting with the victims, the one I'd quashed, Gary then asking if he could meet with Derek Scott, since he had eluded Donnie and been only lightly wounded. What had Gary put as his reason to meet the victims?

"I'm responsible for their pain and troubles."

He wasn't, Donnie was, and it seemed strange to put first-person-singular before the victims' pain. I'd felt some of his words and perceptions were discordant myself, but the world itself veers from pitch, and I'd allowed latitude, perhaps because I felt sorry for Gary Ocampo.

I checked my watch: two hours had passed. I'd head home tonight and confront Gary Ocampo first thing in the morning. It was time to throw hardball questions and see how he responded.

46

It was almost three in the morning. The Miami moon soared high above Gary's Fantasy World, FCLE investigators-in-training Mike Rasmussen and Terrence Longo back in surveillance position. They'd been spelled for six hours by a second unit, returning for a midnight-to-dawn stint, this time in a fifteen-year-old beater Caddy with smoked windows.

Rasmussen zipped up his fly – made difficult by the steering wheel between his thighs – and snapped the lid on a twenty-ounce Styrofoam coffee cup, now filled with urine. He set it carefully in a bag, turned in his seat and wedged it in a box with five other cups. Two held coffee.

"Don't get 'em mixed up, partner," Terrence Longo said. Both were in their late twenties and had been pulled from the investigative-trainee reserves on the twenty-second floor of Miami's Clark Center, which they shared with the full-time investigators, whose ranks they craved to join. The twenty-third floor was reserved for the Big Dogs – like Roy McDermott – and the senior investigators like Lonnie Canseco, Celia Valdez, and the hulking, grunting Charlie Degan.

A couple of the major specialists also had offices there, like Carson Ryder who, it was rumored, could detect psychosis by the scent of one's breath. The twenty-second-floor dicks laughed at that one, but several held their breath when passing Ryder in the hall. It was Ryder who had requested the surveillance, and both had been impressed that the guy had spoken to them that afternoon, cool trick, tying the shoe and talking perfectly clear without moving his lips.

"We buy coffee in the cups, drink it," Rasmussen mused, "piss it back into the same cups. Then we go buy more coffee and it starts all over. You think coffee ever laughs at us?"

Longo started to respond, froze, his eyes staring down the street. "Motion," he said, lifting the night-vision binoculars to his eyes.

"What?"

Longo lowered the lenses. "Nothing. Just Dirty Hairy out for a moonlight stroll."

Dirty Hairy was a nighttime regular on the street outside Gary's Fantasy World, an alcoholic vagrant who drifted between trash cans looking for things to eat, drink or turn into cash. He wasn't big on bathing or shaving, a pair of bloodshot eyes peering from above a piratical beard littered with remnants of previous meals. Like many street denizens, his age was indeterminate; he looked Paleozoic, but could have been thirty. Hairy trash-picked his way toward the cops, pausing to open crumpled fast-food bags in the gutter, hoping for errant fries.

Headlamps appeared on the deserted avenue as a vehicle pulled from a side street and turned toward the shop. Dirty Hairy hobbled to a brick building and flattened himself against it. The vehicle slowed as it closed in and an MDPD cruiser pulled beside the pair, its window rolling down.

"Moonlight becomes you," MDPD officer Jason Bogard said to Rasmussen. The cop at the helm of the cruiser, Silvio Balbón, chuckled. "Still watching for the same guy, right?" Bogard said.

"Donnie Ocampo," Rasmussen said. "You've got the photo?"

"Yep. Problem is your boy ain't real distinctive: six-foot or so, kinda around two hundred pounds, blue eyes if he ain't wearing color contacts, and a couple tats hidden with a long-sleeve shirt."

"That's why we're hoping he'll show up here. To make it easy."

"Y'say he's got a grudge against the guy owns the funny-books store?"

"What I hear."

Bogard shook his head. He stared down the street, smiled. "Hairy still thinks getting flat against things makes him invisible, I see."

Longo squinted toward the vagrant frozen to the wall. "Hairy who? Hairy where?"

Bogard knocked his knuckles against the side of the cruiser. "Well, keep 'em hanging loose, boys. We're back to the mean streets."

The cruiser rolled away and ten minutes passed, with Dirty Hairy peeling from the wall and drifting away, Rasmussen kvetching about coffee's hijinks, Longo lifting the glasses to spot a mongrel dog working the same containers as Dirty Hairy.

Pops in the distance.

"The hell was that?" Rasmussen said. "Firecrackers?"

The radio crackled on an MDPD band. "*Shots fired!*" screamed the speakers. "*Officer down! Help! Officer down, 223 Garret Street.*"

"Jesus," Rasmussen said. "It's just two blocks away." He looked to Longo. "what'll we do."

"We're suppose to stay here," Longo said, jaw clenched.

"*Need help bad, here. Anyone! Officer down!*"

The sound of more shots. Longo nodded toward the comic-book shop. "This'll keep. We got a cousin on the ropes."

The engine roared and Rasmussen smoked a U-turn in the street, racing to the address.

47

The next morning I was up with the earliest gulls and herons to swim in the cove. The case had broken my rhythm and I'd missed my pre-work swim and run. I needed them today: they refreshed my head and gave me more room for thinking, and I would need all my gray matter this morning. For better or worse I was going to assume that Jeremy was right and Gary and Donnie had some form of relationship and/or communications.

Which would mean that Gary Ocampo had been playing me from the git-go.

I got to downtown Miami at nine and headed to the department. The comic shop didn't open until ten. I could have gone over early, but I wanted to waltz in like usual, laid back and buddy-buddy.

Then, when Gary was distracted by bonhomie, I'd try to tear his story apart.

Roy was back from Tallahassee and standing in front of his desk, a translucent yo-yo tied to his finger as he whipped it up and down.

"Watch this, Carson . . . I'm gonna walk the dog."

Roy flipped the yo-yo at the floor, but instead of spinning above the carpet, it zinged back up at his head, Roy ducking a split-second before getting bonked. The yo-yo wobbled disconsolately to the end of its little rope.

"Crap," Roy said, staring at the toy. "I had it last night."

"You'll get it back," I assured him. "Listen, Roy, I talked to my consultant."

He disentangled the toy from his finger and dropped it in a drawer. "Can he help us nail this mad fucker?"

"My guy thinks the Ocampo brothers have something going on together."

"Whoa . . . no shit?"

I held up my hands. "Nothing's proven. But I'm gonna go beat on Gary Ocampo and see what happens."

I was two steps down the hall when Roy yelled, "Hey, Carson! Speaking about Ocampo, you hear about the hoopla near there last night?"

I spun on my heels. "Hoopla?"

Roy gave me a twenty-second synopsis about gunshots and an unclaimed call going out over the airwaves. It didn't make a lot of sense. I stopped him in mid-sentence. "Hold up, Roy. The dispatchers get a call about gunshots and put it over the air to patrol units . . ."

He nodded. "They hear the dreaded 'officer down'. It's red-zone panic and every unit within miles races to the address. They cordon the house, figuring there's a shooter inside, maybe a hostage. Everyone's trying to figure out who's down, who called it in. MDPD's got over a dozen patrol units on scene, the tactical team, a command car, two medical squads, a fire truck, and Longo and Rasmussen."

"Wait . . . They left the shop?"

"They were two blocks away and heard *officer down*. What would you have done, watch a goddamn building or maybe save a fellow cop?"

I'd seen this before. What you wanted was a measured response, what you often got was an over-response, too many people running in circles, emotions running high, exactly when mistakes were made.

"How many MDPD cops were on scene, Roy? Probably a quarter of the street force, right? What did Longo and Rasmussen add?"

Roy sighed, seeing my point. "Yeah . . . our boys had a job and they blew it."

"Go on, Roy. So . . ."

"So everyone's stacked up waiting for someone to make sense of things. Longo and Rasmussen see they're excess baggage and book back to the store."

"How long were they gone?"

"They say forty minutes max. Meanwhile, back at the house, it's a three a.m. cluster fuck. Took two hours to get a tac team inside. They find the homeowner, Elma

Aguilla, taped tight in a back bedroom, a string of blown-up M-80s on the living-room floor."

"The gunshots."

"Someone entered the home, punched Aguilla out, taped her tight, and left a string of M-80s on a long fuse. The perp split and when the fireworks went off neighbors called them in as gunshots. Then someone comes on the police frequency and starts screaming about an officer down."

I could envision the scene in my mind. I just couldn't envision why. "What the hell was happening, Roy?"

He upended his hands. "Someone thought it might have been a diversion, but no crimes were reported in the area. Weird, huh?"

I headed to my office, running Roy's words through my head.

Someone thought it might have been a diversion, but no crimes were reported . . .

"Diversion," I whispered, grabbing my phone and calling Gary Ocampo, my heart suddenly on full adrenalin.

He answered on the second ring. "I'm sorry about yesterday, Detective. I'm just . . . trying to sort things out."

I blew out a breath. "You're fine?"

"I'm just finishing breakfast." I heard him take a sip of coffee or water. A pause. "Why?"

"There was a commotion in your neighborhood last night. You hear it?"

"I, uh, heard sirens and stuff, like a fire somewhere. I went back to sleep."

"OK, just checking, like I said."

"Detective Ryder?"

"Yes?"

"Donnie's evil. I didn't know, you've got to believe me. I'm scared."

"What do you mean, didn't know?"

Silence.

"Donnie can't get to you, Gary," I said. "I've got you under constant surveillance." I didn't mention last night's half-hour lapse and heard a long pause on his end.

He said, "There are other things to be scared about."

Gary Ocampo was being cryptic and discordant. One half-hour meeting with my brother and I heard it.

"Other things like what?"

He said, "I gotta go."

"HANG ON, Gary," I barked. "I'm coming by in fifteen minutes. There are things we need to talk about."

"No, I mean I gotta *go*. To the bathroom. NOW."

I was in front of his store in minutes, starting inside when I looked down the street and saw a bakery truck, its side painted with a loaf of bread. The more I'd thought about the pair leaving their post, the more irritated I'd become. They should have known that every MDPD officer within a three-mile radius would drag race to the address the second the call crackled off.

I saw anxious eyes watching through the tinted side window. There was no shoe-tie hydrant beside the vehicle, and anyway I wanted my wishes directly stated. I rolled back the passenger-side door and saw the pair. They gave me sheepish and Rasmussen took the lead.

"Uh, Detective Ryder, about last night . . ."

My hand chopped down: *shut up*. "I will be in the building for one hour," I said quietly. "Use it to piss, shit, get food, get coffee, get laid, whatever. Then I want you back here until the Second Coming or I have someone relieve you, whichever comes first. Do you understand?"

Averted eyes and *yessirs* in perfect harmony. I strode to the shop where Jonathan was dusting books and DVDs. He looked at me expectantly. "You gonna talk to him about not selling the shop?"

"If it comes up. He mention anything about feeling crummy?"

"Haven't heard a word. At least he's not ordering a load of pizzas."

I went to the elevator, parked upstairs, and pressed the button to bring it down. Nothing. I jabbed at it like flicking bumpers on a pinball machine.

"The elevator's not working," I called to Jonathan. "Gary turn it off?"

He walked over and looked at the panel beside the Up/Down buttons. "No. There'd be a red light on."

I mashed the key a half-dozen more times. The damn thing was dead. I needed some answers to questions

310

sparked by my brother and was going to get them this morning.

"Is there another way up?"

Jonathan nodded to the rear. "Back stairs. They're real tight. And kinda cluttered cuz we use them for storage."

He pointed to a door near the back. I walked over and yanked it open, seeing steps jammed with boxes.

"Gary!" I yelled up the dark staircase. "GARY!"

No response. I pictured him on the toilet and eating cold pizza, the door closed until I left. His return to fatty foods and huge calories had probably given him diarrhea, food exiting as fast as it entered.

I was turning for the front door when a thud shook the floor above.

"What the fuck?" Jonathan said.

I knew it was five hundred pounds going down. I ran back to the tight staircase, grabbed the handrails and jumped boxes, tripping, kicking them down the steps. Comic books spilled everywhere.

"Call 911, Jonathan," I yelled, dread clutching my heart. "Then get up here."

I kicked some boxes from my way, jumped over others. I tripped, fell back a few steps, retook them. The door at the top was locked and I stood on the shallow platform and pounded the door with my fist.

"GARY . . . TALK TO ME. GARY!"

Nada. The door was old and wood and solid. I grabbed the stair rails and catapulted my body into it, getting nowhere, the steel lock-pin deep in the casement. I considered shooting out the lock, but had no idea where Gary was in the room. I kicked the door, which only knocked me backward, falling halfway down the steps, cartons tumbling after me.

Jonathan finished his call and stared wide-mouthed. "Tools?" I said. "Hammer? Axe? I need something heavy."

He bolted to the back door, opened it and bent to pick up something in the alley. He came in holding a heavy masonry brick, the veins popping out in his skinny arms.

"We use it to prop open the door for deliveries," he panted.

I grabbed ten pounds of cast concrete and re-climbed the stairs. The knob fell away on the third blow, the lockset broke loose on the fifth. I pushed through the door. There, beside his bed, was Gary Ocampo, sprawled face-down on the carpet, wearing blue pajamas, one slipper on his foot, the other still under the bed, like he'd been trying to get dressed. The buttocks area of the fabric was stained with stool. I felt his neck and thought I detected a faint heartbeat.

"Gary!" I yelled, slapping his fat cheek. "Wake up, bud. Stay with me."

His only response was a quiver of lip and a white froth that fell from his open mouth to the floor. I turned to see Jonathan in the room, eyes wide in terror. "Help me get him turned over," I said.

It was like trying to flip a beanbag chair filled with

312

pudding. "Grab his arm," I said to Jonathan, "Let's see if we can leverage him over."

The kid slipped under Gary's arm and I wrestled beneath a huge leg, bracing my heels on the floor. "Count of three," I said. "Lift and push. One . . . two . . ."

On three we threw everything into it, Jonathan grunting with effort, veins protruding on his forehead as I stood with Gary's leg over my shoulder and simultaneously pushed forward.

Gary Ocampo rolled over, Jonathan falling across his chest as I tripped and fell across his legs. But Gary was on his back. I checked his pulse again, nothing this time.

"Come on, Gary," I said, hearing sirens in the distance. "Think of Carnevale."

I told Jonathan to bring the medic up the staircase, then started rescue breathing on Gary Ocampo.

A minute later the paramedics came through the door, man and woman, cases in hand. The guy was new to me but I knew the woman, Teresa Bardazon, as one of Ziggy's on-and-off girlfriends.

I stood and she saw me first. "What you got, Carso—" the eyes fell went to Gary. "Jeee-sus, he's huge. Heart attack?"

"No idea. Light, reedy pulse, getting lighter. No breath response."

With choreographed precision the pair put an air bag over Gary mouth and nostrils, the guy squeezing air into

313

his lungs. But that needed a pumping heart to move the oxygen to the brain. "We gotta get him to a hospital quick," Bardazon said, eyeing the elevator. "The four of us can get him in there."

"The elevator's dead," I said.

The male medic, a powerful-looking guy named Ted, ran to the elevator and pushed *Down* a dozen times before realizing I was right. Bardazon tore open Gary's pajama top and pressed a stethoscope to his pale flesh. "I'm not getting anything." She balled her fist and slammed his chest, setting the huge breasts and belly into quivering motion.

"The fat's like a shock absorber."

I knelt and pounded Ocampo's chest like John Henry throwing his sledge, except Henry's hammer didn't sink into the rail. Bardazon leaned in with the scope again. Shook her head, *nothing*.

"Last resort," she said, scrabbling though the med bag, stripping the wrapper from a wicked-looking syringe, the thick needle longer than my index finger. She looked between Gary and the needle.

"It won't sink deep enough," she said, meaning it wouldn't reach his heart with the jump-start of adrenalin. "It won't clear the adipose tissue."

Ocampo was turning blue, starving for oxygen, cells dying in his brain. I ran a fingernail over Gary's breast like the point of a knife.

"What if we . . ."

Bardazon understood, grubbing through the bag and

314

coming up with a bottle and a wrapped scalpel. "But we gotta be fast."

I poured topical antiseptic over Ocampo's chest. Bardazon leaned in with the scalpel and made a deep slice in the fat above Gary Ocampo's stilled heart.

"Pull it open, Carson," she said.

I took a deep breath and opened the wound, seeing the thick cushion of gelatinous yellow fat growing red with blood. "Farther," Bardazon whispered. "Rip it open if you have to."

I put my weight into spreading the inflicted wound, opening it down to the fascia and musculature above the cardiac cavity, giving the needle access. Bardazon lifted the syringe above her head, whispered *three-two-one* and plunged the needle into Gary Ocampo's heart.

I put my hand to his neck. "It's started!"

Bardazon leaned in with the scope. "Go baby . . . tick you MUTHAFUCKA!"

I retreated to dial the FCLE's Resources Division, semi-retired agents who could put FCLE agents in touch with any expertise needed, from snake handlers to the electronics pro who'd help me save a young girl last year. We had to get Gary Ocampo to an emergency room and it was either get the lift running or knock down a wall.

The RD folks said they had their "elevator consultant" on the way, a guy who'd retired after thirty-six years with Otis. I turned to Bardazon. The former light in her eyes was replaced with resignation as she set the scope back in the bag.

My eyes gave her a *what's up?* look.

"He's gone, Carson," she said. "The heart stopped and that was it."

"What?" You always hope you heard it wrong.

"He's dead, bud."

I felt lightheaded, outside of myself, in a dream. Bardazon rose on stress-weary knees, using Ocampo's body to push herself standing. "There might have been a chance, Carson. There's an ER five minutes away at Mercy North. But with the elevator on the fritz and the stairs so tight . . ."

"Yeah," I said, staring into space.

Bardazon and the other medic, Ted Fuselli, called for a special gurney. Ten minutes later I answered the door to a black guy about the size of Harry Nautilus. His name was Washburn Kincaid, and he was one of the FCLE's elevator pros. I sat and waited until he summoned me to an open box beside the furnace/AC unit, a grouping of thick cables running to the panel.

"You know what this is, don't you?" Kincaid said.

"Sure, a breaker box."

"Controls power to the electrical systems. A short or overload happens, the breaker shuts off the juice and that circuit goes down."

I looked at what was simply a larger box than the one in my home: a dozen or so switches all canted to the right. In the case of a short or overload, the breaker closed down the circuit and the switch flicked to the left to indicate a problem. Fix the problem, reset the switch, power continues.

"They all look fine to me," I said, seeing an opening at the bottom of the panel, a rectangle half the size of standard brick. "What goes down there?" I asked. "At the bottom?"

"That's the space for a larger breaker, two-twenty volts." Kincaid tapped a switch assembly to the right of the hole. "Like this one, which protects the furnace and AC circuit. But one breaker is missing."

"Someone pulled the entire unit?" I said.

"Not hard, Detective. They pop out for replacement or repair."

I closed my eyes. "The breaker for the elevator, right?"

He nodded. "As soon as it got pulled, the elevator went to its safest mode. In other words, it shut off. Powerless. Totally dead."

Gary Ocampo had been murdered.

Kincaid bridged the circuit and the elevator was operational. The bus arrived and the heavy-duty gurney went upstairs. Three minutes later it returned bearing a huge body under a sheet, no one having XXX-Large body bags. Jonathan followed the medics from the elevator, sniffling and wiping his eyes with his sleeve.

Bardazon stopped and turned to me. "Sorry it had to go down like this, Carson. The stairway was just too narrow."

"Yeah," I nodded, looking out the window and seeing Longo and Rasmussen pulling in. "Excuse me," I said.

317

I was in the street seconds later, the pair of surveillance cops wide-eyed at seeing me striding toward them with my fists clenched. Their eyes widened further when I kicked the mirror off their cruiser. I was trying to yank the locked door open when the two medics and Kincaid wrestled me back to the shop.

48

An hour later I entered the pathology department, knowing it was going to be an unhappy occasion. I flicked a wave at the woman behind the counter, thirtyish, attractive, and another of Gershwin's occasional companions.

"Where's Ziggy?" she said.

I patted my pockets like he was in there somewhere. She laughed, good, because I needed to hear a laugh before my next stop. I bypassed Morningstar's almost-former office, now just a desk and a chair and a single brown box, continuing to suite six, the one with the outsize autopsy table. They had another on order, corpulent bodies becoming so common.

I entered to see a gowned Vivian almost hidden behind the rise of Gary Ocampo's mountainous belly. Because of the situation, his autopsy had gone to the top of the list. He was naked, hands at his sides, eyes closed. The slice over his heart gaped like a leering mouth, yellow fat puffing out like the mouth was chewing.

I'm sorry," Vivian said, pulling a tray of instruments to her side. "I know you liked him and were trying to help him."

I shrugged, not liking to talk about failures. "Anything in the screens?"

"A huge dosage of black locust in his blood." She nodded at the body. "I just finished the visual. No needle punctures like Prestwick."

"Oral, then?"

She nodded. "The forensics team is checking every item in the living area as a possible source." She picked up a scalpel. "I'm starting now. Are you staying?"

I went to sit a chair against the wall. I'm not sure why, but I felt I owed it to Gary to be here. The task took almost three hours, slowed by the necessity of removing quivering blocks of yellow adipose tissue.

When she finished, a trio of assistants moved the remains to a cooler compartment. It hit me that next of kin was usually notified regarding disposition of the body. The only next of kin was Donnie, who was our killer, a thought that took a minute to shake from my head.

Morningstar hit the locker room and slipped from the surgical wardrobe, and I followed her down the hall toward a meeting room.

"I took the liberty of running the case by our new shining star," she said as we approached. We stepped through the door. "Dr Davanelle, I have someone you should meet . . . if you haven't already, that is."

Ava was seated with a stack of manuals and forms before her. We both performed eyes-wide amazement. "Dr Davanelle," I said, reaching to take both her hands in mine. "What a surprise!"

Morningstar smiled. "I wondered if you two had met. Dr Davanelle's resumé mentioned working in Mobile for a few months."

"It was a long time ago," Ava said. "But Detective Ryder and I were together on a couple of cases."

"Interesting ones, if I recall, Dr Davanelle," I said.

A wisp of smile, but only if you knew Ava.

"Yes, I think they were."

"Looks like the Ryder–Davanelle alliance is back at work," Vivian said, her words carrying more weight than she'd ever know. "A pity it reopens with such an ugly case."

I crossed my arms and leaned the wall. "Any thoughts, Dr Davanelle?"

"I gotta get my post-mortem recording logged in," Viv said. She gave me an unpurred purr, but only if you knew Vivian. "Nice seeing you again, Detective Ryder."

I nodded politely as she headed door-ward. "Likewise, Dr Morningstar."

Though our relationship was not strictly verboten by official rules, working the same cases was frowned on. But Vivian had almost made it to the end of her pathology career before taking up with a colleague. We figured when she was a month or so gone we'd – presto! – seem to discover one another.

A pair of young lab techs were across the hall discussing a case, in earshot and preventing Ava and I from overt appearances of familiarity. I pulled out a chair and sat. Despite our strange history we were at work, we had a case to solve, and – despite her background – Ava was an extremely bright and talented person.

"What's your take on the plant toxins, Dr Davanelle?" I asked. "Odd, right?"

"The effects on humans are roughly analogous to the effects on cattle, Detective Ryder."

"Cattle? How would you know that?"

"In Fort Wayne I worked at a municipal office complex. Northern Indiana is a big farming region and a state agriculture agent worked there as well, John Kepes. He had a degree in bovine-ology or whatever."

"Cows."

She nodded. "John sometimes ran off to inspect livestock found dead or sickened. Jimson weed was a problem. Black locust less so, but I recall him mentioning how some horses were chewers, drawn to the shoots or bark, and if the farmer didn't remove or fence off black locust trees, animals might die."

"Scary plants sound like a big deal up there."

"It's pretty much what every farmer does, since toxic botanicals are everywhere. John would issue warnings to the agriculture community to check fields for jimson weed, snakeroot, sneezeweed, larkspur and a dozen other toxic species."

"You saw no human exposure?"

She shook her head. "Most people don't graze in pastures. Which brings up what I find the most interesting aspect of the case."

"Which is?"

"How do you figure out a human dosage that incapacitates but doesn't kill?"

I shrugged. "Probably just a madman's roll of the dice."

She looked dubious. "Helluva lucky roll, balancing three different forms of toxin without a single death."

Across the hall, the pair of techs moved on, laughing about something. Ava tinkered with a button on her jacket and gave me a sly, eye-batting smile, one I remembered from when she was sober and in a puckish mood.

"What's with the Cheshire Cat face?" I asked.

She glanced to the door to make sure the techs were distant and lowered her voice to a whisper. The smile remained. "You and Viv have a thang going on, right, Carson? Isn't that the current term, *thang*?"

"Uh . . . Viv?"

"That's what you call Dr Morningstar outside of work, right? Viv or Vivian. Or do you have pet names?"

Jesus, a *thang*? I swallowed hard and tried a dodge. "I have no idea what you're talking about. What pet names do you and Jeremy have for each other?"

"I call him Lady Brunhilda and he calls me Spot."

"*What*?"

She laughed, a chime-like sound I also remembered from her better times. "Come on, 'fess up, Carson – am I right? You're seeing Dr Morningstar?"

I learned long ago never to argue with a woman who said you were seeing a woman. Their detection equipment was calibrated in the Beyond. I cleared my throat. "Uh, yes, Ava . . . Vivian and I have been keeping company."

"Ah, keeping company. For very long?"

I pretended to check my watch. "It's countable in hours. How did you know?"

"She walks differently when you're near. Her voice changes. Jeremy would wonder if Dr Morningstar needed saving."

"Saving?"

"From alcoholism, a difficult past, anger at the world. Jeremy believes you're attracted to women who need to be saved from something. He says that's the driving force in your life: saving people from their wretched pasts. It's how you deal with your own past."

I rolled my eyes. "Projection. Jeremy's the one controlled by his past."

I expected Ava to push back with the *It's-different-now-that-we're-together* argument. Instead, she calmly nodded.

"That's very true, Carson. It's also about to change."

"Oh, really? When?"

She mimicked my watch-glance.

"It's countable in hours."

* * *

I left Ava to her study and climbed into the Rover, uncertain where to go next. It had been a long day, starting at the office, moving to Gary's Fantasy World, where I had watched a man die, then to his autopsy. I felt frazzled, drained, and on the verge of passing out. I realized I hadn't eaten anything in over a dozen hours.

It seemed there was only one thing to do: go to Tiki Tiki and chow down before my head dissolved. A drink was a nice thought, too. I got to the restaurant and found Connie Amardara was at home. I'd thought she lived at the restaurant, maybe in a refrigerator, waiting to ambush Zigs and me with platters of food. I missed her exuberance, but it made my entrance quieter and easier on my ribs.

I ordered a platter of carnitas, tortillas and salsa verde, plus half a pastrami on rye, and called Gershwin.

"Where you at, Zigs?"

"The forensics department. Guess I just missed you. Hey, I hear you knew the new pathologist back in the old country. She's a cutie. Did you give her the white hair way back then?"

I winced; it was more nearly the opposite. "Negative. I'm at Tiki Tiki working on a Consuelo's Delight. Join me."

"*Muy bueno*. I just found out how the poison got into Gary Ocampo's mouth, by the way."

"I'm not hearing any more bad news until I've got several ounces of rum in my belly."

Gershwin arrived twelve minutes later, grabbed a mug

of draft from the bar and hustled to the booth. "Well?" I said.

"You ever see a big red cup in Ocampo's place? Seems it got painted with the black locust stuff. He was drinking Dr Pepper from it when the stuff hit."

"Oh Jesus, Zigs."

"You think Donnie got in while the surveil unit was gone?"

I finished the sandwich and started on the carnitas. "It was the only time he could have managed it. But there was no sign of forced entry.

"But Donnie was in there. He had to go upstairs to paint the inside of the cup with poison."

"Go with it, Ziggy," I said. I wanted to see if Gershwin gravitated toward Jeremy's conclusion.

Two minutes later he looked at me, a frown in the dark eyes. "Do you think Gary might have been hiding certain things about Donnie, Big Ryde? Like they knew each other?"

I pushed my plate away. "Try this, Zigs: Donnie created the diversion that pulled the surveillance. He knew the lock code or Gary let him in. Sometime in there he went to the bathroom and swabbed the cup with hyper-concentrated black locust. When the meeting was over, he crippled the elevator, knowing if the poison didn't kill Gary outright, his only salvation was getting to a hospital immediately."

"What did they talk about?"

I went quiet while the waiter cleared the plates. When he left I leaned forward and spoke quietly. "My guess?

Donnie had crossed a line. I think it was the escalation of violence." I was cribbing from my brother, who had read a break-up in the cessation of the Gemini symbol.

"But if the Ocampos were in this together, why did Donnie kill Gary?"

"I think they'd agreed upon certain rules," I said. "But Donnie changed the game with Harold Brighton."

"And Donnie was afraid Gary would squeal."

"I think Gary was getting close to telling me, Zigs. The guilt was too heavy."

Gershwin nodded and sipped beer. A thought hit: in all of my communications with Forensics, I'd assumed Gary was innocent. His potential involvement meant we needed a microscope on Gary Ocampo's trappings. I called Forensics.

"I'm interested in his computers and anything related," I told Deb. "Disks, memory sticks, whatever. Especially files created in the past month."

A pause. "Sounds like you don't think he's solely a victim."

"Dawn comes slowly."

"The night shift just checked in. I'll send a team there now."

As I'd spoken, Gershwin had been running his finger over the condensation on his mug. He turned it to me and I saw the sign of the twins.

"Brotherly love, Big Ryde. They were in something together until Donnie went rogue. But where the hell is Donnie?"

I couldn't answer so I ordered another Consuelo's Delight, which meant I couldn't drive. Because I wasn't going to be driving, I ordered a third. Gershwin ended up taking me to the Palace. He got me to the elevator and pressed my floor and I took it from there. As I studied the enigma of my clothes and tried to remove them – difficult while sitting on the floor – I recalled Ava's thoughts about the difficulty in figuring out dosages. I'd made a flip response, but the longer I sat on the floor, the more sense it made.

I grabbed a pen and scribbled some words on a pad, and crawled toward the bed.

49

In the morning I arose with snatches of dream floating in my head – Jeremy in one, a faceless man in another, in a third a dancer leapt into the air and when he landed his legs became red paste. I showered them away, dressed and chased a couple of power bars with coffee. I was slinging on the Glock when I recalled a dream about making a note last night.

Or was it a dream?

I jogged back to the bedroom and found nothing on the nightstand but a pen. I dropped to my knees and saw a scrap of paper that had fallen to the carpet. I picked it up and read my worst handwriting:

Ask Ava: farm guys

Farm guys? It hit me: I'd been thinking about Ava's thoughts on Donnie's need to test the toxins. And her experience with the agriculture guy in Indiana. Aspects of it made sense, but it wasn't my world. First, I had to check with the path department–morgue to see if anything had been found on Gary's computers.

I stopped by the computer-analysis section first, saw Gary's computers on a long desk, a large monitor between them, files blowing across its screen like *The Matrix*. I heard footsteps and turned to see Lee Clark, head of Computer Forensics, enter with a cup of coffee in his hand, Jerry Garcia, the slim, thirty-year-old version, in khakis and a blue dress shirt.

"Anything showing up, Lee?" I asked.

"A shitload of movies and games. We've run searches for words like 'brother' and 'donnie' and names of the toxins. Nothing yet. No file marked 'diary' either, but you know . . ."

"Yeah, never that easy. Keep on truckin', and thanks."

I moved to the pathology part of the complex, seeing Ava exiting an autopsy suite, making notes as she walked. A dark dress made her hair seem as white as snow and her face was that of a kid at Christmas. She saw me, smiled. "This place is incredible. All the latest."

"You see the new DNA box?"

She nodded. "The future has arrived."

"Chicago have one?"

"On order. I sent my last DNA sample to the national

330

lab last month, doing it old school. The results should be back any day now."

"But you're here now. In the future."

"And loving it."

I saw an empty meeting room and guided her inside, closing the door and leaning against it. "I've been thinking about the perp needing to test the toxins. Any further thoughts?"

She sat, mulling it over. "You've checked local colleges, right? Chem, ag, and botany programs?"

"Nothing came up."

"Thing is, there are all sorts of weird chemical concoctions that could be used to subdue victims. A budding chemist might even make something like 3-Quinuclidinyl Benzilate, or BZ. It's listed as a weapon of mass destruction, but it's basically a powerful deliriant. That might have the same effects."

"Your point?"

"Why did the perp use actual plants? Because he knows them. And like I said, the effect must have been tested on humans. There are two ways to go with such trials, Carson: start lethal, drop back, or go light and ramp up. The first choice is probably faster. Kill someone, halve the dose, try again."

"That's grim, Ava."

"I can check with the CDC to see if there've been any poisonings reported nationwide. That might take a few days."

"I can put the word out locally."

331

Both avenues would likely dead-end like the others, but we were running out of streets. I thanked her and started away, but paused.

"The last time we spoke, you told me Jeremy's being controlled by his past was about over. Care to elaborate?"

She held out her wristwatch like it was in countdown mode. "I said the time to that moment was countable in hours."

"You did, indeed. And?"

"I guess there are now fewer of them."

I walked out to the parking lot and called Gershwin, who was in his daily meeting with the pool investigators, checking input, trying to find new ways to get the info out on Donnie, and generally doing heavy-duty legwork.

"Anyone send out info on Donnie to county agriculture agents, people like that?" I asked.

"Uh, it's not exactly top of mind, Jefé. Why?"

"An idea sparked by Dr Davanelle. We've sought input from every urban venue from Orlando to Key West, nothing. Let's e-mail a packet to every ag agent and farmer's co-op in South Florida. The folks in Resources can get you listings."

"You think Donnie's next move is rustling cattle?"

"We've turned over every other stone, might as well blanket the countryside with Donnie's pix. Ask about any strange poisonings that might have cropped up over the past couple–three years. Plant-based toxins in

332

particular. Animal deaths, human poisonings – anything. Check with rural hospitals, clinics, anything medical."

"You got it, Kemo Sabe."

"You up for a late breakfast after you get that done?"

We met up at a Southern-style diner south of downtown, scratch biscuits, gravy to make you weep. We ate, drank coffee, and pored over our notes. I studied the jumble in my open briefcase. "What are we missing? What am I missing?"

Gershwin looked at me over a honey-dripping biscuit the size of a hockey puck. "It worries me, too, Jefé. I go over the stuff at home, a different vic every night."

"Who was last night?"

"Brian Caswell, Brianna."

"You find any new stone to turn?"

He sucked honey from a glistening thumb. "Remember the guy who reported Caswell as a missing, Mitchell Peyton? He had some old videos of Brianna starting out. I dunno, rehearsals or whatever. We never checked them out."

I nodded. "We passed because we figured we'd nail Donnie fast. And stuff that old wouldn't be relevant."

"Well?"

"It's probably still not relevant, but let's have Peyton give us the Brianna retrospective."

50

Debro sat in his vehicle on the wide avenue bordering a side of Miami-Dade General Hospital. The engine was running to keep the AC cranking and the sizzling midday sun made it necessary for Polaroid sunglasses when whipping the field glasses between his lap and his eyes, sneaking glances at the employees' entrance to the facility.

Patrick White worked twelve-hour shifts, six a.m. until six p.m. That was for three weeks, with the fourth week off. White took his lunch at 11.30 a.m., returning at 12.10. You could set a clock by the little bitch. When researching White, Debro had considered taking him during his lunchtime walk, but deemed it too dangerous. Debro had made himself impossible to see, and continued success depended on his invisibility. It was his shield, his armor.

Today, he simply wanted to see White. To refresh his

memory of the man's cruelty. And to savor what was inevitable. The employee door opened and Debro flicked his glasses to his eyes as a trio of female nurses stepped from the building. False alarm. He scanned the glasses up to the fourth floor, the wing where White worked, studying the windows one by one.

Come out, come out wherever you are . . .

The glasses paused at the fifth window from the end of the building. Where Kempie had been kept, little Jakey-boy Eisen probably still next door . . . guess they didn't have a tongue ward . . . And there, the third window? That had been the room holding the One That Got Away, the spitting, stuttering Derek Scott. "Duh-Duh-Derek," Debro chuckled, shaking his head.

He raised the glasses anew. Let's see . . . he didn't know where Dancing Boy Harold was kept, but wouldn't it be cool if he shared a room with Eisen . . . and Prestwick makes three? Debro wondered if he could visit them. It would be easy to pull off once he—

Motion! Debro pulled the glasses to the side. Patrick White was stepping from the door. He held it open for a couple of other employees, then took out his phone, checked for messages, tucked it back. White paused for a moment, looking like a lost child. He took a deep breath and leaned forward, starting to jog to the street. Patrick's butt was small and tight in the blue scrubs, and Debro made a mental note to stop at Walgreen's for more K-Y.

* * *

335

Gershwin called Peyton, who was a booking agent for a cruise line and on his day off. He professed delighted at displaying his collection of Brianna memorabilia and was all smiles when we arrived, ushering us into his home. The ashtray formerly holding the joint was now squeaky clean and the room smelled of clove incense.

I sank into Peyton's couch, Gershwin taking a lounger. Peyton checked a date on a DVD, pulled it from the case and slipped it into the player. "This is early, when Brianna was just getting started. It's from a dumpy club up by Fort Pierce."

Segments of Caswell's performance appeared on the fifty-inch screen, a younger Caswell mimicking various female celebs. It was pretty bad overall, missed lip-sync cues, clumsy moves, odd costume choices – although the Madonna bit seemed dead-on, the silver cones, maybe.

"The camera's all on Brian," I said. "We're interested in audience shots."

Peyton sighed, addressing a Philistine. "You need to get a sense of who Brianna is. Her drama, her feeling, her *heart*."

I bit my tongue and sat back, thinking if Caswell had a hundred followers as devoted as Peyton, he'd never buy a drink again. We finished the recording and Peyton slipped another disk into the player. "This is classic," he said, picking up the remote. "Some day the History Channel will be bidding on it."

"And it is . . .?" I said.

"When Brianna started developing Ivana Tramp. Prepare to be blown away."

A shaky shot of a stage, Caswell entering as Elton John's "The Bitch is Back" blasted from the sound system, hips in full-swing sashay. He wore a red sequined gown slit high up one side, silver high heels, a wig the color of polished brass, and enough jewelry, bangles, extended nails and make-up to make Dolly Parton envious.

Caswell had been working on his craft. The moves were fluid, the persona hugely outsized but controlled. It was basically off-color jokes and insults – religion, culture, sex, much of the humor gay-oriented and beyond my ken – but the crowd seemed wildly appreciative, noted by both the laughter and the faces when Peyton panned the crowd.

"You're showing more audience in this one," Gershwin said to Peyton.

"To get their reaction. This is when Brianna learned to play them. To make them howl. Isn't she the Bitch Queen deluxe?"

"Can you pause on audience scenes?"

"Sure."

"*How many fags does it take to screw in a light bulb?*" Brian or Brianna or Ivana asked.

"*How many?*" the crowd yelled.

"*Two. One to hold the bulb and the other to smear KY on the threads.*"

Caswell mimed the bulb-greasing action to roars of laughter. The camera panned to the audience and Peyton hit pause. We scanned for anyone resembling Donnie Ocampo. Most faces were in shadow or backs turned to us, the room maybe three dozen round tables glutted with beer bottles and drink glasses.

"Anything?" I asked Gershwin.

"Nada."

Peyton continued and the camera returned to Brian or Brianna or Ivana. He was striding across the stage with a hand porched over the lavishly decorated eyes, staring past the lights into the crowd. "*You, in the blue shirt, stand up so we can see you, girl.*"

The camera highlighted a rope-thin man in a blue shirt and chinos doing a *who-me?* gesture as his tablemates push him to standing. He's at least six-six in height, a beanpole.

"*Well, well, well . . . what do we have here?*" Caswell mimed putting a phone to his ear. "*Hello, Oz? Did you lose your scarecrow?*" Laughter. Peyton stopped the scene and we studied the crowd. No Ocampo look-alike. The motion re-started with Caswell studying the man. "*You know, if dicks followed body type, you'd have a two-foot soda straw.*"

"*Be nice!*" someone yelled, sounding good-natured and half-drunk. "*Don't be such a bitch!*"

"*Who yelled that?*" Brianna pouted. "*Be brave and tell Mama.*"

"*Him,*" someone yells. "*The guy in back.*"

The camera panned over the crowd and zooming in in a halting motion. I saw a guy sitting at a table alone, heads turning his way. "Freeze," I said. Gershwin and I leaned in to look at faces in the crowd. It was mostly the backs of heads.

"Nothing," I said. "Keep going, Mitch."

The camera resumed with Brianna's hand over her eyes again. "*Who said that? Oh, stand up back there, hon. Lemme look at you.*"

The camera swooped to the back table and I saw only the shadow of a figure stand slowly, exhorted by nearby patrons. It was a big person, heavy.

"*Oh, wait*," Ivana said. "*I need to see you better.*" She reached into her purse and retrieved outsized reading glasses, put them on. "*Wide-angle lenses*," she said to hoots of laughter. She turned back to her target. "*I'm not saying you're heavy, dearie . . . but do you use a cast-iron toilet?*"

Howls and heads craning to see the unfortunate subject. No one was there, the guy had moved or booked. Ivana mock-confided to the front row. "*Have any of you people heard the rumor? Fat people don't fuck . . . they dock.*"

The camera again drifted over the crowd. "Wait," Gershwin said. "Stop. Back up a few frames." Ziggy popped from his chair, walked to the monitor, tapped the screen.

"Anyone you know, Boss?"

I leaned forward to focus on a big guy in a tank top, with heavy arms and blond hair. His hand crossed the forearm of a young man beside him, both laughing like it was a shining teeth competition.

"My, my," I said. "Rodrigo Figueroa. Our big

339

gay-bashing boy from Missing Persons." I turned to Peyton. "You know that guy, Mitch?"

Peyton nodded. "That face is hard to forget. He's been at a couple shows up by West Palm. And I think in Tampa. Is it important?"

"It's certainly interesting," I said.

51

We bolted from Peyton's place with a bag of suppositions in hand, ending at a Po' boy shop run by an expatriate Louisianan named Big Ted. I ordered fried shrimp and Gershwin boiled shrimp and we drank sweet tea and huddled like gamblers figuring odds on a horse they'd never noticed until it blazed into view an hour before.

"Figueroa's about the size of Donnie Ocampo," Gershwin said. "Six three or four."

"Barrel chest, wide shoulders. It fits." I held my hands wide, like Derek Scott had done in describing his attacker. "The guy's almost the exact size of the orderly Scott thought was built like Donnie."

"Plus Figueroa tried to block us from the case."

I nodded, stacking more wood on Figueroa's fire. "When it was unsuccessful, he asked Roy to be kept copied on the files, in the loop."

"He knew where our eyes were, who we were scoping out."

"There was the way he bolted when White and I entered his department, like maybe White knew his secret life." Another log for the stack.

"But he called Roy when Eisen showed up. Why?"

"Simple, Zigs," I said, chopping more fuel for the blaze illuminating Rodrigo Figueroa. "Rowdy Roddy made himself look good, maybe even pumping Roy for any additional info. It didn't do anything to harm him."

"The face, though. It's not much like the pictures."

"Figueroa's face is distorted. Maybe the jet-ski accident, whatever, he got banged up so badly that we're seeing a reconstruction."

"Nice place for Donnie to hide. In the police force."

"*If* it's him. Big if, Zigs."

But I felt a bonfire burning in my gut and my heart. We had a convincing suspect, the first one in two weeks of slogging. Had the Invisible Man finally shown himself on a two-year-old tape?

"He's the kid of a MDPD captain."

"Someone adopted Donnie. Cops can do those things, too."

"Figueroa's working now. We take a look at where he lives, you think?"

I made the motion of separating blinds with my fingers. "Maybe take a peek in the window and see if he's got guests."

Rodrigo Figueroa lived in a trendy apartment complex

342

a little below Hollywood, landscaped grounds, big bright pool, central clubhouse. "I used to date a woman who lived here," Gershwin said. "It's singles-ville, the units off central courtyards. That's Figueroa's wing over there, all studio apartments. Tiny. No way to get a captive to the place, and nowhere to keep them."

"Then if he's our boyo, he's got a hidey-hole somewhere. Let's see where Roddy-boy heads after work. It may be time for him to water his livestock."

We found Figueroa's lime-green Dodge Charger in the MDPD garage and parked between it and the exit. He exited precisely at 5.02, one of a long line of departing employees. Gershwin had grabbed a nondescript sedan from the motor pool and hung a half-block back as Figueroa burned his tires north.

"In a hurry," Gershwin said.

Rush-hour traffic poured from every direction, but Gershwin had a New York cabbie's gift for slipping between vehicles with millimeters to spare. Rain started, the hard and straight stuff that turns the world gray, but Figueroa was as slowed by the rain-addled traffic as we were, so the tail held.

"He's not going home," I said when Figueroa passed his exit.

The Charger veered from the four lane and Gershwin slowed as Figueroa pulled to a liquor store. We entered the lot and headed to the side. A minute later Figueroa was exiting, hunched against the rain with a bagged six-pack under his arm.

"Looks like our boy's gonna relax with a few brews," Gershwin said. "And maybe some friends, you think? Unwilling friends?"

We followed our bent-faced boy to a neighborhood between Tamarac and Oakland Beach where he entered the driveway of a single-story ranch, white with yellow trim, a pretty place, with neatly sculpted bushes interspersed with palmettos. We passed the house just as Figueroa pulled into a three-sided carport beside a tan Prius.

"What'll we do, Big Ryde?"

"The house is too open to scan. Let's check his wheels for anything with DNA."

"Gotta be a comb in there, given that mop on his head."

It was almost as dark as night, purple-black thunderheads dumping at a two-inch-an-hour rate. We swung to the curb and scanned the neighboring houses. When no eyes seemed at windows, we sprinted to the carport.

"Crap," I said. "My slim-Jim's in the Rover." I was referring to the strip of notched metal used to pop locks. Gershwin grabbed the door handle and opened the door. Unlocked. We looked at one another.

"Musta been in a real hurry to get inside, Jefé."

"Let's grab and git."

Gershwin dove into the front and I took the back. Unfortunately, Figueroa seemed real prissy about his ride, the interior showroom-clean, not so much as a candy wrapper.

"Got anything?" I whispered.

"Ashtray's clean, nothing on the floor. I'm looking for blond hairs."

The carport lights came on and a voice yelled, "Get your hands in the air, you fucks!"

Busted. I wondered if the carport had a sensor. We rose to see Figueroa in the doorway, a small, cocked revolver in his hand as his eyes registered Gershwin and me.

"What the hell are you doing in my car?"

I climbed out with my hands in front at shoulder height, Gershwin doing the same. We were ten feet from his trigger finger.

"It's cool," I said.

The muzzle raised from my belly to my head. "No, it's not cool. What are you doing in my car?"

"We've got your DNA, Donnie," I told him. Better if he thought we already had him nailed. "It's over. You'll just make it worse."

The lopsided face twisted further. "Who's Donnie? What the fuck you mean, DNA?"

"Dude, we already checked it," Gershwin said, following the narrative. "Positive. We were getting a back-up sample. If you go in with us, we'll keep you safe."

I'd never seen a face appear so confused. But he was Donnie Ocampo, right? He had to be good at faking it.

"Make some fucking sense!" he yelled. The muzzle didn't waver.

345

"We saw you at a gay bar, Rodrigo," I said. "Watching Brianna Caswell perform."

He looked like I'd reached across a dozen feet and punched his gut. "Gay bar? It wasn't me . . . no, I mean, I-I was undercover."

"No . . . we're saying we know who you are. It's over. Put down the piece and we can—"

He stared, his lopsided face a mix of fear and flat-out confusion.

"Who do you think I am?"

"Donnie Ocampo."

It took a three-count to sink in. Figueroa looked about to faint.

"You think I'm the guy abducting those men? FUCK!" he screamed. "FUCK FUCK FUCK. You *bastards*. That's why you're here?"

He'd gone from anger to confusion to fear and now, resignation, shoulders slumping, head shaking. The gun lowered. I was getting the same feeling I got when entering Gary Ocampo's room to arrest him. Like something was hideously awry.

He said, "I'm putting the piece away, though I should probably shoot your goddamn kneecaps off. You've fucking ruined my life."

I looked at Gershwin. He was thinking the same as me: Rodrigo Figueroa wasn't acting like a guy who used toxic drinks to abduct and torture men. Figueroa decocked the piece – his back-up, I figured – and tucked it into an ankle rig.

"You were lying about having my DNA," Figueroa said. "You're here getting it."

I shrugged. "Best I could do."

"You thought I was Ocampo because you saw me in a . . . gay bar?"

"We had to check. You've done some odd things."

"Watching a drag show?"

"Trying to hang on to the case. Wanting access to the reports. Doing a gazelle when I brought Patrick White to Missings. Calling in a vic, which could have been a smokescreen. And you're the right size and build."

He rubbed his face in his hands, shaking his head. "Jeez . . . You might have just asked. Here—" He pulled a hank of hair. "Got an evidence bag?"

I reached to my pocket. "Uh, yes."

"Run your goddamn sample. It'll say you're a moron."

We heard slapping footsteps and turned to see a man in his mid-thirties, short brown hair, polo shirt over running shorts, blue flip-flops. He peeked tentatively around the corner of the carport, a blue umbrella over his head.

"What's going on out here, Rod? Who are these men?"

"It's fine, Anthony," Figueroa said quietly. "I work with these guys. We're talking about . . . a case. I'll be there in a minute."

"They can come inside, Rod."

"I'll just be a minute."

The guy looked between us, nodded, and flip-flopped back to the house.

"I didn't choose what I am," Figueroa said, suddenly looking defeated, though I was unsure by what. "It chose me."

"We're not looking for explanations, Rod. We're just looking for Donnie Ocampo."

"I went out with women," he continued, like he had to justify that he'd tried to not be gay. "Dozens of them. I *made* it with them. I lived with a woman for almost three months. I've been to three counselors and two shrinks. I even went to that church therapy to get straight. But it's still here. I can't escape it."

He was pleading a case and I hadn't even known we were holding court.

"Maybe it's your father you can't escape," I said.

He stared, his mouth ajar, eyes wide in the misshapen face. Then the eyes closed and Rodrigo Figueroa blew out a long and resigned breath.

"Yeah . . ." he said, almost a whisper. "Papa thinks real men are a cross between John Wayne and Johnny Wadd, women are just . . . Jesus, women are like my poor mother . . . there to spread their legs and fix supper afterward. Every time I think I can get free, I can come out, I get freaked at what's gonna happen and, and . . . ah shit," he choked, "who'm I kidding? I'm just yellow."

"No one knows you're gay?" I asked. "I mean, in the department?"

He shook the bright mop. "Hunh-unh. I never go near Miami bars, always above Lake Worth. Or go for weekends in Tampa, Saint Pete, Fort Myers. I never get drunk, out

348

of line, anything that might get me noticed. If word got to my father, I'd be . . . I don't even know. In the department I do the horny dude thing, leering at the women, keeping straight porn in my desk, centerfolds in my locker. My old man thinks I'm as masculine as a goddamn stag. I *am* masculine . . . I'm just not his kind of . . ." He looked at us with sad eyes. "You really thought I was Ocampo?"

"We're pretty desperate. This is one bad dude out there."

"I know, and I tried to do my part to get the word out."

"Word out?"

"I saw your sheet on Ocampo, the photos. I figured they should be thick in the gay community, so I got some buddies to distribute them."

Question sensibly answered. And I had two more. "So why were you so hardcore about keeping the case, Rod?"

"I figured if it was gay-oriented, I might quietly tap into it quicker. Then I did some digging and heard you knew your stuff. As far as wanting the reports, the cases affected my world."

"That time I came into Missings so Patrick White could file? You saw us, right?"

"I'd seen the guy you were with. I didn't know him, but if I recognized him . . .'

"He might recognize you. And say something."

"Most of my life is being worried I'm gonna get found out." He nodded at the bag in my hand. "Like when you run that sample . . ."

I tossed it back to him. Rod Figueroa wasn't Donnie

349

Ocampo. Gershwin and I slumped out the garage door. I paused, turned back inside, writing a number in my notepad. I tore it off and handed it to Figueroa.

"A guy named Canseco," I said. "He usually works a younger crowd, but I think you might want to sit down with him."

52

The phone rang its way into my sleeping head. My hand was bringing the bedside receiver to my lips before I realized I was at Morningstar's house.

"Hello?" I said.

A pause. "This is Robert Costa. May I speak to Dr Morningstar?"

I looked at the digital clock: 6.42 a.m.

"I, uh . . . hang on a second."

I put my hand over the receiver and shook her sleeping shoulder. Her eyes blinked open. "Costa," I said. "On the phone. For you."

She gave me a puzzled look and took the phone. I stood and wandered to the window, trying not to eavesdrop. I could hear her voice, low, a conversation. The phone hit the cradle and I turned to see Vivian looking away, her eyes on the floor.

"Viv?" I said. "What is it?"

"William Prestwick's dead, Carson. He—"

"My God. What happened?"

"Prestwick somehow stood in the bed and tied a cord to the sprinkler and . . ." She shook her head. "And I guess he just relaxed his knees."

All I could see was Prestwick in the bed, the gentle and consoling Patrick White at his side. "How did he . . . when . . .?"

"He was found an hour ago. Though heavily sedated, it appears he managed to unwrap his dressings. There's a mirror in the room."

We dressed in a quiet funk and drove to the hospital, arriving at half-past seven. I saw Patrick White sitting alone in an alcove, his face in his hands.

"Gimme a few," I said to Morningstar.

She gave my hand a squeeze, which it needed, and went off to find Costa. White was on a small sofa in an alcove and I nodded as I entered his space.

"What makes someone do these things, Detective Ryder?" he asked, his voice ragged from grief. "Hurt someone like Billy was hurt?"

I crossed the room and looked out the window, the sun too bright and the day too clear to have to deal with another human tragedy sparked by Donnie Ocampo. But here we were.

"I think it's self-loathing, Patrick. Filtered through insanity and directed outward. If I could, I'd issue every

352

gay man in town an anti-Donnie Ocampo potion, because the bastard seems to be invisible."

White nodded and retreated into himself for a long moment. "You know the saddest thing in all this, Detective Ryder?"

"What's that, Patrick?"

"It was destined to happen. No matter how Billy's face was rebuilt, he'd never have been Billy again. If he hadn't killed himself last night, it would have been next week or next month. From the moment that monster put his knife into Billy's face, Billy was dead."

I found Vivian and we left the hospital, driving in silence until I dropped her off at her office. My trip to the department brought me within a few blocks of the comic shop and my Rover veered that way, like I needed to see the place one final time. The scene crew was working, but I figured they were about to close up shop.

I noted a sad-eyed Jonathan leaning against the side of the shop with his arms crossed. I parked and crossed to him.

"I can't get in," he said, nodding toward the yellow-taped door. "They won't let me."

"It's a crime scene, Jonathan. What do you need?"

"I got some games in there. My skateboard. My iPod."

"I can get you inside for a few minutes."

A young tech unlocked the door. It was cool and quiet, except for the sounds of feet upstairs, the techs cleaning up. Jonathan leaned behind the counter and grabbed a skateboard, the surface printed with a graphic of the Hulk. He bagged a stack of video games, then reached into a cubbyhole under the counter and came up with an iPod, dropping it into his pocket. "That's it," he said, eyeballing the place and figuring he'd never be back.

His knit hat was hanging on a wall peg and I nodded to it. "You want your hat?"

"Gary's gone. I don't need it."

"You lost me, partner. Don't need it?"

He snatched the hat from the peg and turned it inside out, revealing a small black box glued to the fabric.

"A camera?" I said.

"The kind bike racers wear so people can see what they see on the bike. Tiny, huh? The lens looks out between the yarn."

I turned the hat right-side out. The lens was smaller than a pencil eraser and poked between strands of fiber, as close to invisible as it got.

"You were Gary's camera downstairs," I said, figuring it out.

"There's a camera outside the door, another by the register. But this was Gary's favorite. When someone talked to me, it was like they were talking to him. He thought it was cool, like he could see things through my eyes."

We heard a sound through the floorboards, a piece of furniture being moved.

"What are they looking for?" Jonathan asked. "Nobody ever told me shit."

I leaned the wall and explained the situation in edited detail. Jonathan was wide-eyed.

"You say you think Gary was, like, in contact with his crazy brother?"

I shrugged. "Gary never mentioned anything?"

"He just told me not to worry, it was his business."

I shouldered from the wall, time to boogie. "Anyway, that's why all the people are combing through the place, Jonathan. Plus we're looking at his computers."

"For what?"

"A diary, maybe. Notes about his brother. Things Gary wanted kept secret."

He looked toward the ceiling. "They won't find anything."

"You don't think Gary had secrets?"

"If he did they're not on the computer. Gary sent special files to his cloud account. You know, like a server somewhere. Cloud stuff doesn't live on the computer."

"You know where this, uh, cloud stuff is?"

"Like I told you, I know where everything is. But the cloud account takes a special password."

I stared at him.

"I know that, too," he said, studying his fingers.

An hour later, sitting beside one of the department's computer whizzes, a twenty-five-year-old woman named Tonya Sparrow, I watched as Gary Ocampo's cloud-shrouded files came tumbling to earth: six years of business records, a half gigabyte of porn, mostly pretty young men having rather typical sex, all things considered, and a multi-gig file named *Debro*.

"What's in Debro?" I asked Sparrow.

"Dunno yet," she said. "It's the only one that's encrypted."

"Can you break it?"

She studied a screen dense with computer language, then looked at her watch.

"Gimme twenny minutes."

Ninety minutes had passed since Patrick had spoken with Detective Ryder, unable to lift himself from the sofa, to make his legs work. His insides felt scooped out. Solicitous staffers had offered food, drink, comfort, but he'd waved them away with small murmurs of thanks and they finally stopped asking, walking on tip-toe when they passed.

Patrick gathered himself to standing, took a deep breath, and entered the room that had held Billy Prestwick. The facial wrappings had been removed from the floor, but everything else remained: the IV bottles, the monitors on their wheeled stand, the bedside table holding the medications Costa was using to counteract the robinia and lessen the effects of the datura.

After learning of the substances affecting his patients, Patrick had looked up the toxic compounds in the black locust: the protein robin, the glycoside robitin, and the alkaloid robinine. Costa had been giving Billy activated charcoal and a combination of drugs to jump-start the protein synthesis inhibited by the toxins. The

356

combination – formulated in conjunction with Dr Morningstar and a toxicological specialist at the University of Miami – seemed to have an effect. No one had died, at least. The concoction was administered via injection. Four syringes – prepared in the hospital pharmacy – waited by the bed, intended to heal a man beyond healing.

Patrick stared at the empty bed. The monster who had killed Billy was still out there. He might be out there forever. Some of the saddest but truest words he'd heard had been spoken an hour and a half ago by Detective Ryder:

I'd issue every gay man in town an anti-Donnie Ocampo potion, because every one of them is at risk.

Patrick crept to the door. The hall was quiet, the nearest staffers at the nurses' station, a hundred feet down the hall. Patrick hustled back to the table. He took a deep breath, not knowing quite what he was doing, only that it was against every hospital rule and procedure.

He removed a syringe and slipped it into his pocket.

53

Sparrow had been a bit optimistic, the cracking of the encryption taking closer to an hour. Gershwin had arrived, torn up at hearing Donnie had claimed another victim, his death toll now two in the past day. He leaned against the wall as Sparrow off-loaded the decrypted files to a DVD. They were video files.

"How much video?" I asked.

"A couple gigs, maybe an hour's worth, pretty low resolution."

"You watch any of it?"

Sparrow frowned as she slipped a disk from the computer. "I don't think it's an Adam Sandler movie."

She set Gershwin and I up in a small room with a large monitor in the corner and handed us a remote. We grabbed coffees from the machine down the hall and came back to see what Gary Ocampo had been hiding in the cloud.

"Ready?" I said, flicking the screen into life.

"As I'll ever be."

We saw stuttering, murky images: dozens of moving male bodies, some alone, others in groups, dancing or crowded around tables. The audio was low, the party-fueled voices reduced to a sonic blur. I noted a long bar running to the right.

"The Stallion Lounge," Gershwin said.

The camera tilted down and I saw a hand and a glass. "It's Donnie," I whispered. "He's wearing the camera in a hat. I'll bet it's a knit cap."

"A hat?" Gershwin said. "We'll never see his face."

The camera panned the room and stopped on jerky images of men chattering around a table filled with glassware. Two went to the dance floor, two remained. One smiled, his face angling toward the camera.

"Kemp," Gershwin said.

The camera veered wildly as Donnie looked around the room, returning to Kemp.

"*Do you see us, Brother?*" said a rasping voice. "*Are you there?*"

Donnie's voice. The first time we'd heard it . . . cold, clinical, amused. No accent.

"He's talking to Gary," Gershwin said.

The two dancers returned to pull the others toward the dance floor. One stood, everyone chiding Kemp for sitting. Seconds passed and Donnie's voice returned.

"*Could you tell me if Dale's a-boot? Dale Kemp? He is? Can I talk to him?*"

"The call," Gershwin said. "Donnie's calling the bar. He's faking an accent."

The camera panned to the barkeep, the bar's landline at his ear. He put his palm over the receiver and yelled into the crowd.

"*Dale!*" Almost lost in the rumble of voices and music.

The camera returned to Kemp, hand behind an ear as he pointed to his chest, "*Me?*" He crossed the floor. The camera elevated and Kemp's table grew closer. Then the table and solo drink, so close I could reach out and lift it.

A blur of motion over the glass. The room spun wildly and the camera reset in its original position. "Donnie spiked the drink," Gershwin said, breathless. "Then went back to his table."

I wanted to yell *No!* when Kemp returned and lifted the drink. Ten minutes passed before he patted his belly and went to the restroom. "He's getting sick," I said, needlessly.

Kemp returned for ten more minutes and downed the final ounce of beverage. He spoke to his dancing companions.

"*Damn flu,*" I imagined him saying. "*I'm heading home.*"

The last shot was his back going out the door. When the video picked up again a naked Kemp lay on the gray floor of a long room with brick walls, his eyes wide with terror as he batted at invisible demons in the air. Hands reached in and rolled the kid over and roughly etched his back with a ten-penny nail. When his mouth opened in a scream, all that exited was a spray of spittle.

"*The bitch is branded,*" Donnie said. The Gemini sign filled the screen as Donnie leaned close. I aimed a silent nod toward Key West. My brother had theorized that the victims were marked upon arrival.

Then, rape. Kemp's shoulders shook with impacts as his arms flailed against the ground and his face howled soundlessly into the floor.

"*Are you with us, Brother?*" Donnie grunted. "*Are you turned on?*"

The scene turned to black. It was cool in the room, but I was pouring sweat.

Gershwin swallowed hard. "These were sent to Gary live?"

"Think of concert-goers sending video to friends."

The next recording started: Brian Caswell after a performance and vamping at a table, a feather boa floating over a sequined purple blouse, leather miniskirt, diamelle-studded high heels. Donnie didn't even have to sneak up and spike Brian's drink: he simply handed it to him in a flute of celebratory champagne. "*Great show, you earned this.*" The video blanked out and resumed with a hallucinating Caswell being marked and assaulted.

"*Are you there, Brother?*" Donnie grunted. "*Are you enjoying the payback?*"

Next came the abduction and initial abuse session with Jacob Eisen, sickened and met in the bar's bathroom by Donnie, posing as a doctor.

"It's probably *Fraturna Mortuis*," Donnie tells the pale, red-eyed Eisen.

"Dead brother," Gershwin translated, his Catholic-school upbringing giving him knowledge of Latin. He checked the time remaining on the DVD, scant minutes. "Looks like we're nearing the end."

"It's Brighton," I said as the pictures resumed, seeing the dancer amidst a cluster of men beside a table. The camera lifted and closed in. As the point of view passed the table it paused to show a highball glass filled with a foamy drink. A hand waved across the top of a glass as if blessing it.

Minutes later, Brighton left the bar and the video resumed at Donnie's lair with the marking and initial assault. The scene faded into a second one, Brighton in distress but, perhaps because of the dancer's fitness and muscularity, more mobile than the others. One leg slammed the floor like remembering part of a dance.

"*Harold's got to go*," Donnie whispered. "*The bitch is a nuisance*."

Donnie Ocampo suddenly had a pry-bar in his hand. When Brighton kept struggling, the truncheon blurred past, deflating the tarp.

"Jesus. Is he going to . . ."

The camera scanned down Brighton's covered body. A hand slipped the tarp up the long and sinewy legs and administered an injection. The syringe was set aside and the hands returned to caress the legs. Then, as if a decision had been made, the camera went black. The end of the downloaded files.

362

The end of the Twins.

"Go back to the injection," I said.

Gershwin retracked the scene. I watched a length of arm enter the frame, broad hands guide the syringe into muscle, press the plunger. The hands caressed the legs and the screen again went black.

"What don't you see, Zigs?" I asked, pointing at arms bare to the round biceps.

"Tats. Scott saw Gemini symbols tattooed on Donnie's arms."

"Did they go somewhere?" I wondered aloud. "Or were they never there?"

54

Patrick sat in the Brass Key, angry with himself. He should have stayed with Billy's other friends gathered at D'Artagnan's, helping console them, deal with the horror, the loss, but the grief turned into too many people having too much to drink, ending in waves of tears and maudlin excesses.

He'd needed somewhere quiet, but not his home, wall to wall memories of Billy: dancing in front of the stereo, primping in one of the mirrors, pacing the floor and exhorting Patrick to *hurry up*. Billy was always in a hurry to get somewhere, and once there, in a hurry to get somewhere else.

The never-ending quest for fun.

Patrick rarely visited the Brass Key and only when seated did he realize the cool and shadowy bar was three blocks from the hospital, like he needed distance, but not that much. Patrick's phone rang. He checked the name, winced. Another of Billy's friends wanting to commiserate. He silenced the phone – he'd check in tomorrow, when people sobered up and regained composure.

He rarely drank liquor, but had ordered Amaretto and soda. He raised his hand to order a second when he heard a familiar voice at his back.

"L-let me take care of it. I owe you one, Patrick."

Patrick turned to see Derek Scott, his former patient. "What a surprise to see you, Derek. You don't need to do that."

"I owe y-you for all the care."

"What brings you here?" Patrick asked.

"It's one of my f-favorite places. Q-quiet. I l-like to sit and watch TV. How about you?"

"Same reasons. Plus it's close to the hospital."

"You looked s-sad when I came in. I almost tuh-turned around."

To tell the truth would invite compassion, perhaps sympathy. All Patrick wanted was quiet. "A, uh, patient of mine passed away. It's never easy."

"I'm s-sorry," Scott said. "I'll leave you to y-your thoughts."

"No, it's fine, Derek. I'm just having a quick one. Gotta work tomorrow." He nodded to the stool beside him. "Join me, please."

Scott was a nice guy, if a bit self-deprecating, the touch of stammer, perhaps. Maybe it would be better to have someone to talk to, give him a few minutes from his thoughts of Billy.

Scott ordered an amaretto for White, a light beer for himself. The drinks arrived and the vested barkeep moved to the end of the bar. Scott sat and they talked, jobs, mostly. Scott was a veterinarian's assistant and told amusing tales: the dyspeptic burro, the racehorse that went faster after drinking rum, the cow that grazed on chives and gave onion-flavored milk. Patrick talked of his studies and upcoming exam. Twenty minutes passed and Patrick ordered a round, then stood.

"I gotta hit the head, Derek. Watch my drink and phone, would you? Not that they're in much danger here."

Scott turned to see a table of business types huddled in conversation, the barkeep watching a muted boxing match.

"You bet I will, Patrick."

Patrick returned a minute later, the businessmen leaving in a single file. They seemed to signal his own time to leave. He downed his drink and bid Scott good night, thanking him for his company.

The good-hearted Scott flicked a wave. "Take care, Patrick. Hope to see you soon."

Patrick climbed into his Honda compact and belched, tapping his stomach with his hand, indigestion, the stress of the day. Derek Scott been a decent addition, though. Maybe Scott had been destined to be at the bar to keep Patrick from tumbling too deeply into his sorrow.

Patrick rented a bungalow west of downtown, a crummy place overall, but at least he didn't share walls

366

with others. When he made the jump to Nurse Practitioner he could look into buying his own home. He pulled into the drive and unlocked the rickety front door. The house to the left was vacant, the one to the right blared with guitars and trumpets, the renter a Mariachi who learned new tunes by cranking up the volume and sitting in front of the speakers.

Patrick passed through the living room – avoiding the book-laden desk in the small living area, guilt – and went to his bedroom. When he removed his shirt, his hands felt clumsy, inept. *Jeez, did I drink that much? Three amarettos over ninety minutes?* His guts started cramping and he headed for the bathroom, but his knees collapsed, the floor seeming to rise into his face. He pushed himself to standing and wobbled into the hall.

What the hell is happening?

A knocking at the door. Patrick stumbled into the living room and fell down again. He tried to yell *Who's there?* but his words hardened in his throat and all he could do was croak. A coal-black iguana skittered across the floor and exploded into musical notes. A second iguana followed. How did iguanas . . .

Hallucinations, Patrick realized, fighting to keep focused. *I've been poisoned.*

The knocking again. Patrick grabbed for his phone, his fingers almost useless. A third black iguana raced across the carpet and exploded.

"Cm un," he rasped, staring at the dead screen.

Thunder at the door and Derek Scott appeared in the

room. He was green and smiling and holding something bright in his fingertips. His voice wavered up and down like someone was playing with his volume.

"I REMOVED the BATTERY from YOUR phone, PATRICK. How WAS your COCKTAIL, buddy?"

Patrick tried to kick himself backward across the floor, but Scott crossed the distance in an eyeblink, a pry-bar in his hand. The bar flashed and Patrick's head exploded into stars and his back slammed the floor.

A hand grabbed his collar, trying to turn him over. Patrick pulled the hand to his mouth and bit. A scream and the hand wrenched away, Patrick tasting blood. Without knowing how, he was standing and running the short hall to his bedroom, bouncing from the walls like a drunk. He shut the door, pushing the lock with his knuckle.

Footsteps. A voice outside the door.

"COME on, BITCH," Scott said. "IT'S gonna HAPPEN."

Nothing. Then a slam from the door. The door cracked at the upper hinge. A second slam . . . the crack widened almost the length of the cheap door. A dozen glittering purple worms emerged from the split and began flying around the room.

Patrick squeezed his eyes shut. His guts screamed with pain and his heart jackhammered in his ears. Purple worms buzzed past his eyes. But there something he was supposed to know . . . something he had done.

"*WHAT IS IT?*" he screamed to himself, the words making spittle on his chin.

He heard his closet door open at his back. Patrick spun to see Detective Ryder stepping from between hanging clothes. Ryder pointed to the dresser and his voice made the sound of a siren.

Patrick yanked his bedside drawer open and saw the syringe stolen from Billy's room. Pulling the plastic cap from the needle, he looked at Detective Ryder for approval, finding only a wisp of blue smoke spiraling in the air. Patrick sunk the needle into his thigh and threw the syringe aside. The shattered door fell from its hinges and a gigantic scorpion entered the room.

The monster's immense claws lifted Patrick into the air and pinned him to the wall as black, stalk-mounted eyes inspected him from all directions. The scorpion's stinger floated above Patrick's head, a curved and dripping dagger. The creature's mouth was a wet slit beneath the swirling eyes, pursing open and shut and dripping sour fluids. When Patrick screamed, he heard nothing but the voice from the scorpion's reeking mouth.

It said, "Do you want to see something really funny?"

A thousand years passed. Patrick opened his eyes. He was naked and bobbing in a gray ocean, the looming sky made of wood, and the stars were too bright to view.

"Hey, Patty boy," a bright and familiar voice said, so loud it seemed inside his head. "How about you put on your swim suit? We're going to Miami Beach tonight."

Patrick spun his head to see Billy at the end of the room. "Billy, help me," Patrick screamed. The room

369

answered with a soft echo: *"Bu-uh h'me."* Billy smiled, pirouetted, and his face disappeared, replaced by quivering tendons.

He's not real, Patrick thought, swallowing his horror. *Don't get lost in the hallucinations. Stay calm and think. First, check your systems . . .*

Patrick looked down and saw his wrists crossing his belly and bound by handcuffs. His legs felt heavy, but mobile. He closed his eyes and scanned for his heart rate: elevated, one-fifteen, one-twenty. BP had to be high as well. Pain radiated through his abdomen and his head throbbed. Dry mouth. Occasional muscle spasms, currently minor. Probable pupillary dilation.

How much had the stolen mixture helped? A blunting effect hopefully, on both the robinia and datura. The dieffenbachia had to wear off. The other victims had reported visions so potent it was all they could remember. Patrick had hallucinations, but if he kept telling himself they weren't real, he might stay in control. There was also limited muscular function.

The floor began to ripple like a waterbed and he made himself ignore it, *not real.* He closed his eyes and focused. The madman was Derek Scott. It had to be. But all the photos, all the descriptions . . . they were someone else. Were there two madmen? The Donnie one and Derek Scott?

He heard the sound of a door opening. Derek Scott entered the room. Except for a slight glow he didn't look like a hallucination. *What am I supposed to look like to him?* Patrick asked himself. *How should I act to keep the monster from knowing I'm still in me, at least for now?*

Patrick stared into the air as if seeing a terrible vision. He choked out a scream and began knocking the back of his head on the floor . . . *easy, not too hard.* Scott looked pleased and approached, slipping from his clothes as he went. *You will be raped,* Patrick told himself, a flashing glance seeing Scott kneeling beside him, naked and aroused and twisting the cap from a tube of lubricant.

If you fight, Patrick's mind said, *he'll administer more poison. You can't fight.*

He didn't.

55

I overnighted at the Palace, which was getting tiresome. At home I looked out over water; the vista here was steel and brick and glass, nice for a couple days, but I needed deck time beside the cove, Mix-up cleaving the water like a furry, bobbing barge. But that could only happen when Donnie Ocampo was behind bars or in the ground. After yesterday's events at the shop, I would have been delighted to shovel dirt over the monster.

I slept all the way to seven a.m. before the phone rang, Vivian. "I'm sorry to wake you, Carson. I'm at the hospital. I think there may be a problem . . . I'm not sure."

My heart dropped. "Another victim?"

"No. It's, well . . . nothing, maybe."

I said I was on my way, arriving at the hospital twenty

minutes later. Morningstar was standing by Marjorie, the Rubenesque nurse.

"It's Patrick White," the nurse said, her hands twisting in one another. "He didn't come in for work this morning. I thought maybe it was the emotional toll of his friend, but he has a major exam today. It's not like Patrick."

Patrick had told me of his aspirations and I knew that even with the death of Billy Prestwick, White would follow through on the exam.

"I'm worried," Marjorie said. "This is the first time he's ever—"

"Give me his address."

I met Gershwin at White's rental house, a shabby little bungalow in a neighborhood of the same. I saw a small red Honda in the drive, his. Gershwin got to the front door first.

"Not good," was all he said.

The door had been opened inward by force, wood shards littering the carpet. A desk by the front window held open books and pads, like he'd been there minutes ago. I saw a dark stain on the rug and leaned low to realize my worst suspicions: blood. I heard Gershwin call from a hall.

"The bedroom door, Jefé. It's busted down, too."

After issuing the BOLO, we had spent two hours talking to White's friends and colleagues, but just because I knew the victim made me no less impotent in finding

Donnie Ocampo. We returned to the department where I was lying on my couch with my hands over my eyes, empty. Gershwin was on the floor, case files spread around him like fall leaves. We both had nothing left.

Gershwin's desk phone rang. He jogged to his office and I heard mumbled conversation. He was back in a minute.

I kept my hand over my eyes. "And?"

"You wanted me to query medical facilities in country locales about possible plant-related poisonings. That was Dr Clark in Hardee County. Says he saw an incident a couple years back. Robinia. Black locust."

Morningstar had said black locust poisoning in humans was rare. I sat up, feeling a tingle in my spine.

"How far is Hardee?"

"Three-hour drive. There's no direct route."

"Not by car."

One of the perks of being in the law-enforcement elite was fingersnap chopper service. Forty-five minutes later we were a half-mile above western Okeechobee and following Highway 27 until we veered to a locale just below Placid Lakes. It was farm country, dotted with cattle and horses and citrus groves.

We landed in the lot of a single-story brick clinic, TriCounty Medical Services. Dr Clark was in his late sixties, medium height and weight, his thinning gray hair counterbalanced by a bristle-brush mustache. Clark took us through a waiting room jammed with sad-looking people of all shapes, sizes, and ethnic backgrounds, leading to an office crammed with files. He sat atop the small desk, Gershwin and I in folding chairs.

"It was maybe three years ago," Clark said, gnawing the arm of his reading glasses. "A man presented at my clinic, too sick to walk. He was brought in by a friend, himself barely able to stand. They said a third man was back at their camp, unconscious."

"Camp?"

"They were migrants, cutting brush, repairing fences. We dispatched an ambulance and discovered a dead male, age forty-three. When the body was autopsied, the pathologist suspected a toxic substance, and sent tissue to the FBI lab."

"What about the others?"

"I ran activated charcoal through them and kept them hydrated and nourished until they recovered. The Sheriff found no foul play and it was assumed they'd been in contact with either a natural toxin or man-made one, like a pesticide. Six weeks later the FBI results indicated robinia. I've seen equine and bovine black locust poisoning, but I grew up on a farm. Never saw it in humans."

"The surviving workers have any idea how it got in their systems?"

"They had finished their suppers a while before and started vomiting and having trouble standing."

"Where can I get in touch with them?"

He shook his head. "They were *indocumentados*,

Detective. Illegals. They're somewhere between Chihuahua and Seattle."

Long gone. "You know most people around here, Doc?" I said.

"Been here twenty-two years. I've seen or treated about everyone in the county."

I pulled my increasingly worn sheet of photos and held it up. "How about this guy? Ever see him?"

Clark slipped on the glasses. "Looks like a lot of folks. But no, doesn't ring a bell."

Out of politeness I didn't kick anything. "Any other crimes of note around that time?" I asked.

Clark gnawed the glasses for a few seconds. "Nope . . . unless you want to include a disappearance: José Abaca, low-level thief, con artist, pimp, dope dealer, whatever made fast money. No one misses him."

A nurse opened the door and wanted Clark to take a look at something. He said he'd be right back. I turned to Gershwin. "You thinking what I'm thinking, Zigs? About the three poisonings?"

He held up three fingers. "Three doses: low, medium, high. Papa Bear's moving, Baby Bear's dead, Mama Bear's passed out on the floor. Mama Bear becomes the benchmark dosage."

It looked like Ava had called it, dead-on, so to speak. Clark returned and I asked him if there was anyone we could talk to who knew the poisoned men.

"There's a camp for the migrants. A few older guys

are always there, sort of like permanent uncles. They probably won't talk."

"Can you come and make introductions?"

"Did you see my waiting room?"

Clark directed us to the camp. We passed several miles of pasture before seeing a cluster of graying wooden houses with small porches. A fiftyish Hispanic man sat on one porch, sipping beer from a can as chickens pecked in the sparse grass. When we pulled into the dirt drive his head turned away, like if he didn't see us, we weren't there.

"Excuse me," I said. "May we speak?"

His eyes went blank. "No Ingles, señor."

"Uh, Big Ryde . . ." Gershwin said, stepping in front of me. "How about you go reorganize the glove box and I'll call you in a few."

I headed to the car as Gershwin sat on the steps. I watched him pull his badge and ID, point to the ID, likely explaining that we weren't inmagracíon. The guy finally nodded, and they started talking. After a couple minutes Gershwin waved me from the car.

I discovered that Gershwin was a miracle worker; Señor Ronaldo Vasquez had learned English in under five minutes. After the requisite pleasantries, I asked what he'd heard about the illnesses and the death.

He thought a moment, like framing his words. "There were rumors about the sickness, about a man's death. There are always rumors."

"That the men had been purposely poisoned?"

"That is a likely thing to think."

"By who? Was that speculated?"

"A greasy snake named Abaca. He had been visiting the men at their little camp. He was all smiles and brought beer and a bag of tacos for each man. Not long after, they were sickened."

Abaca was the low-life Clark said would do anything for a price, a sociopath, I figured. No conscience, no qualms. I looked at Gershwin. Was Abaca our killer? Was Abaca Donnie? Feeling a surge in my heart rate, I pressed forward. "The workers knew this for certain, Don Vasquez? That Abaca had given them something bad?"

"They were eating and bad food is a problem always. Especially in this heat."

"But weeks later, after the tests came back as poison? That's when Abaca became a suspect?"

"When your soul is black, you open yourself to such thoughts."

"What happened to Abaca? Do you know?" I mentally crossed my fingers, hoping the old man had an idea of Abaca's whereabouts. I looked at Gershwin, he was staying cool, but thinking the same.

The man paused for a long moment, as if gauging internal distances. "You are not of the police here, Señor Ryder. That is what Señor Gershwin told me. Nor do you have any interest in the inmagracíon. Or even . . . *locale* crimes?"

378

"All true, Don Vasquez." *Come on . . . please God let this man know where we can find José Abaca . . .*

But Don Vasquez went another direction.

"One of the men was the son-in-law of the dead man," he said. "The other was his good friend. Honor was involved and they went to . . . speak to Abaca."

"But Abaca was gone by then, right? Perhaps to Miami?"

"You are sure, señor, that you have no interests here?"

"All we want is the truth, Don Vasquez."

The man paused for a long moment, as if gauging internal distances. His eyes found mine. "No, Señor Ryder. Abaca had not disappeared. He was dead on his floor, his face a terrible thing to behold. He died while eating."

I started to speak, but used my head instead of my mouth. The men had probably intended to injure or kill Abaca, revenge, but found him dead. Figuring they'd be prime suspects, they'd made the body disappear. I suspected Abaca was weighted down beneath four feet of Everglades water, a fate he likely deserved.

"Why did Abaca poison the men?" I asked. "Was it known?"

The man shrugged, at a loss. "It is strange, as they were very pleasant men, not given to making enemies."

"You have lived in this area for long, Señor Vasquez?"

"For eighteen years. I know everyone here."

For what had to have been the two-hundredth time in three weeks I pulled the photos of Ocampo from my

379

jacket. Held them to a pair of eyes and held my breath. For the two-hundredth time the eyes scanned the pictures, thought carefully . . .

And a mouth said, "No."

56

Before we lifted off, Gershwin phoned the department to check our calls. "Anything?" I said, dreading that Patrick White had appeared, injured in some hideous fashion.

"You had one call, Jefé. Someone named Folger."

I frowned. *Alice Folger?* Four years passed like a blur and I was racing through Manhattan trying to get to my brother ahead of the NYPD, while simultaneously appearing to assist their manhunt. Lieutenant Alice Folger started as my adversary, ended up as what Ava might call a *brief thang.*

What could Alice Folger want?

We were edging toward Okeechobee when I put the air call through my helmet and dialed Bobby Erickson, the ex-FSP sergeant who handled 23rd-floor calls.

"Gershwin told me about a call, Bobby . . . Folger?"

"Yeah," he said, chomping something as he spoke. "Name was Alice. With the NYPD."

"She say what she wanted?"

"Only that an old friend of yours had finally surfaced." He swallowed. "She sounded real happy, Carson."

Debro stared through the window at his newest penitent, Patrick White. The man was lying on his back, his head slowly tapping the floor as his eyes rolled slowly in his head. White looked at Debro but, of course, could not see him. He was probably seeing dancing body parts. It was something he had said at the bar: "*I've got a test coming up tomorrow, anatomy. It's a toughie and I've spent two weeks cramming my head full of body parts.*" He had pointed to his head with a laugh, "*They dance in there all day, livers, spleens, colons – ascending and decsending, you know – veins, arteries, capillaries . . .*"

"*I thought we were solid straight through,*" Debro had said. "*Like potatoes.*"

White had thought that was funny.

Debro felt at his crotch. He'd had two good sessions with White, but the most recent had been two hours ago, and Debro wasn't back to full heat yet. It was best when you pictured them in your head for an hour or two – imagining it, maybe bringing yourself close with your hand – then stopping and letting it build.

At first he couldn't get enough – why he started with

three in the first week – but since Brighton, one at a time was better. You could focus on things besides sex, like the bad things they'd done and the ways they should pay.

Assuring himself that White was still deep within the triplicate prisons of hallucinations, weakness, and a dead throat, Debro headed downstairs, where the LOGO channel was beaming a trio of female impersonators yammering like lovely little magpies and for a moment Debro savored the thought of putting the whole trio on his floor and beating them with a ball bat.

Debro grabbed a beer, muted the sound, and sat on the couch, feeling relaxed, pleased and, as always, invisible. The cops would be looking for Donnie even more intently, of course. The dead-and-then-alive Donnie, the six-foot-four Donnie, the hospital-orderly-sized Donnie. They'd be looking for dark-complected Donnie. Blue-eyed Donnie. Donnie of the twin tattoos.

Debro smiled to himself. The tattoos had been a stroke of genius, not only bolstering the dead-brother deception, but throwing another wrench into the cops' machinery.

What was happening with the investigation? He wondered. The only real advantage of having Gary alive was the occasional peek inside Ryder's head. But the lump of chickenshit had turned pure yellow when Debro finally administered true justice. The fat bitch should have been cheering.

"*You took away a boy's dancing,*" Gary had whined the last night of his worthless life. "*It was never supposed to be like this.*"

"*It was your idea, Gary.*" Derek had reminded the pouting moron. "*Revenge.*"

"*Not hurting them forever. You started thinking about it that first day!*"

A group meeting had just ended at the University, Phase Two, a dozen fat turds sitting in a circle and mewling at Dr Roth. It broke up and it was just Derek and Gary hanging out and talking. Another wave of fatties started in the front door like a parade of elephants, Roth directing them into a side room holding chairs with arms, like when you gave blood. Derek had asked what was going on.

"Those are participants in phase two, the clinical phase," Roth had said. "There's more physical monitoring involved. Lipids, cholesterol, insulin levels . . . tests related to metabolism. There's a DNA test as well."

Derek had studied DNA in veterinary school. Like chemistry, it was interesting stuff. Botany, too. A lot more interesting than studying a bunch of stinking animals.

"Why DNA?" he had asked, his senses prickling like he was seeing the future.

"An investigation into genetic aspects of weight."

"I don't know much about DNA," Derek had said, doing his best *naïve*. "Do the results like, become available for cops to look at? Are they like fingerprints?"

"It's likely that law enforcement can be granted access to DNA testing, Derek. I should also mention that tens of millions of people are in DNA databanks, so unless you're planning a life of crime, it doesn't make a big difference."

Roth entered the blood-draw room as the pair watched the nurse hand corpulent participants a wood-handled swab so they could brush their teeth for a few seconds, then hand it back.

The Idea appeared in that one, beautiful moment.

What if . . . Derek had thought. It was just floating-in-his-head kind of thinking. Like when he'd see a cute boy in the street and wonder *What if I could tie him down on my kitchen floor and kick that smug look from his face?* It was like that. *What if you put someone else's spit in your sample jar. What would happen? You'd be someone else, right? Or someone else would be you.*

What if . . .

It was that very night when Gary – flirting like they were a pair of slender twinks and not a six-hundred-pound monster coming on to a then-three-hundred-pound man – said he was going to enter the Phase Two program. Then he'd put on that ridiculous fucking hat and made all sorts of shit disappear and reappear, Derek pretending it was the coolest thing he'd ever seen but all the time thinking, *What if someone else's spit was on Gary's swab? What would that mean? What could happen?*

Derek had responded to Ocampo's flirting. Within three nights of sweaty emissions into the rolling bag of

fat – Gary sometimes giddy, sometimes weeping – Scott
learned the darkest details of Ocampo's life: the whispers,
the insults, the betrayals . . .

The dead brother.

57

We arrived at the department. The elevator opened on the twenty-third floor and I was four steps into the hall when I heard Bobby Erickson's voice.

"Call on line one, Detective Ryder. Her again: Captain Alice Folger, NYPD."

"I'll get it in my office, Bobby."

Gershwin went to talk to Roy. Somehow I made it down the hall. I closed my door and picked up the phone. "Yo, Carson," Folger said. "You're a hard man to track down. I tried Mobile, they directed me here."

I forced a smile to help fake a cheery voice. I probably looked like Dr Sardonicus. "Alice, damn! Great to hear your voice. Did I hear the title 'Captain'?"

"It's your doing. After that ruckus you dragged me into I was too out of control to keep on the street, so they made me Cap."

"Come on."

"OK . . . after our dance with Crazy Jeremy I took classes in psychology. Got a Masters, actually. I'm spearheading a unit like that one you ran in Mobile. You doing the same thing in Florida . . . tracking the hardcores?"

"Sure enough. Stop sending them here."

"Ha! Why'd you book from Mobile? You piss someone off?"

"The Chief of Police."

"Glad to hear you haven't lost your touch. Why I'm calling . . . have you heard the news?"

I swallowed hard: here it came.

"Heard what?"

"Speaking of good ol' Jeremy Ridgecliff . . . guess who just showed up?"

I closed my eyes. The worst had happened: Jeremy spotted in Key West, or somehow ID'd in Kentucky, a background check for the property sale maybe. Had he been arrested? Was he again on the run? In three seconds a dozen questions zipped through my mind.

"Come on, Carson," Folger prodded. "Guess who surfaced after all these years?"

I could feel sweat dripping inside my shirt. I swallowed hard and forced nonchalance into my voice. "Jeremy Ridgecliff, I take it. What about him, Alice?"

"I figured you hadn't heard. The news came across the wire, the pull notice . . . I was always afraid he was hiding in one of the boroughs, waiting."

"What haven't I heard, Alice? What do you mean, 'pull'?"

"Ridgecliff's dead."

It made no sense and I replayed the words in my head. It was like Folger was talking from a land of crystalline focus and I was surrounded by black fog, blind and lost.

"Dead?" I rasped.

"The Feds just pulled him from the Wanted listing, Carson. He's history."

"I . . . how? What's the story?"

"I told an agent buddy to fax me the full packet to close out our file. Seems last month a body was dragged from a river during a bridge project, rotting meat in clothes, dead for months. A DNA sample went to the FBI, got backlogged, and yesterday came back as Ridgecliff."

"Dead for months?"

"I imagine they'll put the carcass in a potter's field somewhere. Or maybe toss it back into Lake Michigan as fish food."

"Lake Michigan? What?"

"I forgot to mention: the soggy remnants were in a river channel leading to the lake. Ridgecliff died in Chicago."

In the span of a city's name, the fog blew away.

"Always trust a river, Carson." My brother's cryptic words illumed.

"The packet you requested . . ." I said. "Did it include an autopsy report, Alice?"

"You wanna make sure he's officially dead? Me too, cuz I read it twice. Says right here: Deceased. It's signed by one Dr Ava Davanelle. Guess Doc Davanelle got the world's last look at crazy Jeremy."

I hung up and understood what Ava had meant by "days countable" and headed to the morgue. Ava was in a meeting room poring over a procedural manual. A tech called a greeting and I flicked a wave, then stepped inside the room and closed the door. Ava wore a dark blue dress, white hair at her shoulders, dark eyes intent on her reading. She was turning pages, her purse and note-pads on the table, a cup of coffee at her elbow.

She shot me a *What's-up?* look as I shut the door.

"Seems the countdown's over," I said.

She closed the manual and pushed it to the side. "How'd you hear?"

"A detective in Manhattan called to say the FBI had pulled Jeremy from the Wanted listings. Death does that."

"Yes, it certainly does."

One wall of the room was glass and I walked to it and let my eyes wander the clear sky, pushing the last wisps of fog from my mind. When I turned, Ava was redoing her lipstick, a light gloss.

"What was it, Ava . . . a simple substitution?"

She made a kissing shape, dropped the lipstick and mirror back into her purse. "A rotting corpse no one wanted to go near, just bones and shreds of meat. The skeleton was approximately six feet in height."

"You kept some of Jeremy's tissue on hand."

390

"In my purse for months. A shred of skin, some hair follicles."

"Jeremy didn't, uh, have a hand in . . ."

The hint of a frown. "I assure you, Carson. The deceased was a total stranger, another lost soul delivered to the morgue."

"It's why Jeremy's been noncommittal about when he'd come to Florida, talked about how laying a foundation took time. You were waiting for the perfect corpse."

She nodded. "Decomposed past visual identification and of correct height and gender."

I crossed my arms and leaned against the wall, considering the process. "And in law enforcement agencies across the land, Jeremy's pictures are traveling from wall to wastebasket, his computer records dragged to the trash. Case closed. The hunt is over."

"Jeremy Ridgecliff is dead, Carson, which means Jeremy Ryder is free."

I nodded and turned for the door with much to absorb. I paused and turned back to Ava.

"You violated your professional oath. You misrepresented the facts."

She was again studying the manual. "Which I have to live with," she said, not taking her eyes from the book. "Perhaps one day you'll tell me how it's done."

58

I left the morgue unsettled, yet feeling an odd calm. I returned to the department wondering how Ava had felt when she made the switch of Jeremy's tissue for the man found in the river. Surely she had realized she would be forever changed by the deception. She must have believed it worth the price.

I pictured her with the decayed carcass on the gleaming autopsy table, water rinsing beneath the ragged, necrotic flesh. Were other autopsy tables nearby? I wondered, pathologists speaking into recorders, assistants weighing, marking, bagging, maybe a cop nearby to observe a procedure.

I wondered if the substitution had been dangerous, Ava having to slip Jeremy's tissue from her clothes as the dead man's sample was pocketed, her face a mask of innocence as her fingers broke the law.

Was her face as calm and natural as Gary Ocampo making a quarter disappear from my closed palm? *Gary Ocampo holds my hand at the bottom, touches it on the top.* I know exactly where the quarter is, and yet I do not. All my attention is diverted, exactly how he wants things. He's pulling the old sleight-of-hand switcheroo.

Switcheroo.

Gary Ocampo sneezes into the tissue, closes his hand around it, turns to the wastebasket, opens his hand and the tissue is flung into the can at my side . . .

And then I had flashers blinking, sirens blasting, as I headed to the pathology lab at Daytona 500 speed. The on-duty pathologist was Bernard Hackett, a humorless drone who viewed every request as an imposition. Morningstar would have loved to have sacked him, but Hackett was a state employee with twenty-five years in grade, and enjoyed a sinecure shared by popes and Supreme Court justices alike.

I found Hackett hiding in an autopsy suite and reading a sailing magazine. When I told him what I wanted, he glared like I'd pissed in his grits.

"You want *what*?"

I tapped the cooler holding the Great Campini. "Gary Ocampo. I want a DNA test done, Bernie. Get some tissue from him and—"

"It's Dr Hackett. Two complete DNA screens were already performed. One at the university, one right here and less than three weeks ago. Both showed that—"

I grabbed a scalpel from a tray and opened the drawer holding Gary Ocampo, lifting a fat hand.

"Will a finger do?"

Hackett's magazine dropped to the floor. He decided to go back to work.

I had the *Invisible Wires* feeling. Harry Nautilus, my former partner in Mobile, coined the term years ago: you feel unseen wires all around you connecting pieces of a case. But you can't see them, you can only grope blindly. Then one day – by perseverance, intuition or blind luck – you trip over one. And pull yourself hand over hand to the conclusion.

I called Gershwin to the morgue, then sat in a quiet autopsy suite until the results arrived, running the water on a nearby table to give my ears something pleasant to hear. A half-hour later I heard the door and looked up to see Roy enter the room.

"Jesus, it's cold as a fucking morgue in here," he said, pulling on the seersucker jacket he'd been carrying. His white shirt was unbuttoned at the neck and his blue tie loosened. "I got a whispery call saying someone from our department was over here wasting taxpayer dollars. It sounded so amusing I figured you were involved."

I sighed. The twit Hackett at work. He obtained the tissue sample and took it to the lab, but thought he'd snipe back at me for making him perform what he judged a redundant test.

"So what's going on, bud?" Roy asked, checking the cigar count in his pocket.

"I was gonna drop a dead guy's finger in the new DNA machine, Roy. See where it pointed."

"Excuse me?"

I waved it away. "I'm re-testing Gary Ocampo's DNA."

The pumpkin face turned puzzled and I was about to explain when Gerri Haskins entered holding a read-out. "The DNA is not his," she said, perplexed. "Ocampo's. I mean, yes, it is his: Ocampo's. No, I mean . . ."

"It's Gary's DNA now," I elucidated. "But before, it was Donnie's."

"Someone care to fill me in?" Roy said, pulling a wrapped cigar to twirl.

"Gary used sleight-of-hand to force-feed us the perp's DNA," I said. "He switched it at the university, and repeated it with me."

Roy frowned. "He gave you Donnie's DNA? But I thought you already—"

"I doubt the perp's name is Donnie, Roy. He's certainly not Ocampo's brother."

"Don't perps prefer we not have their DNA? Why the switch?"

I displayed the photo sheet for the two hundred and first time. "So we'd put everything we had into chasing this guy. Except he doesn't exist."

Roy paced the floor until he got it, the cigar spinning like a tiny baton. "But aren't you back to square one, Carson? No Donnie, no suspect, no nothing?"

"Nothing can be good when the only something is false, Roy."

"I'd sure like to understand that."

"Gary gave us a misdirection designed to close our eyes to every direction but this . . ." I tapped the sheet of photos. "But now they're open in every direction."

I called Dr Roth at the University, where the first switcheroo had occurred. Our initial trip had been fishing baitless in the dark, concerned with procedures, not participants. Things had changed.

As I'd told Roy, by opening up, they closed in. Ziggy arrived and I whistled him to the Rover, filling him in as we drove, his eyes widening as I detailed the scheme.

"Gary gave the university someone else's DNA?" he said.

"The Great Campini at work. When the DNA test came back positive for Gary, we went to bust a strong, stealthy perp."

"But presto . . . it's the Goodyear Blimp."

"Gary and his partner figured the cops might want DNA confirmation, so Gary's pouring DNA, red eyes, nose dripping, sneezing into tissues and dramatically flipping them to a basket a meter from my hand. He figured I'd—"

"Onions!" Gershwin said, slapping the dash.

"What?"

"We smelled onions that day. I'll bet the moment we elevatored up he took a snootful of onion powder. Hocus-pocus and on us is the jokus: instant tears and a nose dripping like a faucet."

I shot a thumbs-up. "The perp spits on tissues and they go into the wastebasket, more tucked under the sheets. Gary sneezes into a tissue, palms it and substitutes one with the perp's DNA. It matches the U's sample, and the only answer is an identical twin that died but didn't, with an emptied grave to ice the cake. It's insane. It's brilliant."

Roth met us in the lobby and sat us in her office. She'd heard that Gary had died, but the poisoning aspect hadn't been revealed. I didn't bring it up, not yet.

"So sad," she said, shaking her head. "A heart attack?"

"They're still running tests. Did Gary have any close friends among the test participants? I'm betting yes."

"You *are* a detective. Gary was thick as thieves with an early participant. How'd you know that?"

"An inkling. What was the friend's name?"

"Derek Scott."

"Pardon me?"

"Derek Scott. Their friendship started on day one, like they had some sort of bond."

I shot a look at Gershwin. His face was cool, emotionless. But I knew his breath was like mine: locked in his throat. "Bond?" Gershwin asked Roth.

"Their histories, maybe. Derek seemed a big influence on Gary, like the friend Gary always wanted, someone to talk to, to share confidences. They became inseparable after a couple of meetings, but maybe . . . maybe Derek needed Gary as much as Gary needed him."

397

"Did I hear disapproval in your voice, Doctor?" I asked.

"Derek Scott could be negative, Detective," Roth said carefully. "There was a darker side to him. I did worry a bit about the kind of influence he might have on Gary, who seemed to see a soulmate in Scott. Sometimes I sensed a manipulative side to Derek, so I wasn't so sure."

I felt faint, breathless with the thought that we'd just stumbled over the central wire. Derek Scott was Gary Ocampo's *soulmate?*

"How much did you see of them?" I asked evenly.

"More of Gary, since Derek was only in the first phase of the program."

"The first phase was the peer groups, support groups, whatever?" I said.

Roth nodded. "Social support, shared purpose. I moderated the first two meetings. After that, participants made their own decisions about where and when to meet. How deep to go into their problems."

Down to the bottom, I thought.

"You mentioned the pair were together from day one, Dr Roth," Gershwin asked. "Any record of that day?"

"I videotaped the first meeting. But participants have an expectation of privacy, Detective Gershwin. I can't make it available."

I told her what had actually happened to Gary Ocampo.

"I'll set up a conference room for viewing," she said.

Ten minutes later we sat in a conference room and saw fifteen obese men in a circle of wooden chairs, one of several phase-one male support groups, the thought being that participants would open up more to their own gender. The camera was distant and unobtrusive.

Roth was having the participants introduce themselves, tell why they over-ate, and what they wanted weight loss to accomplish. Roth was a comfortable and concerned big sister, radiating warmth. After nine introduction-*cum*-confessions, she came to Gary. He pushed to his feet, not making it on the first try.

"I'm sorry," he mumbled, trying again.

"You can stay seated, Gary," Roth said.

"My name is Gary," he said, looking at the floor. "And I, uh, have been fat all my life and people have made fun of me all my life. I'm here because I hate me and . . ." he paused, swallowed hard, and brought his eyes up to meet the other eyes. "And because my mom hated me, too. Sometimes, at least, when she was drinking. I eat because I always feel empty."

Silence. The other introductions had been shy and halting and general. Ocampo's confession was deep and obviously painful and I wondered if it had surprised Gary as much as it surprised the others. Roth came back with a follow-up.

"Why do you want to lose weight, Gary? Your goal."

"I want to travel without people looking at me and laughing or whispering. Everyone here knows what it's like to be looked at like a freak."

Murmurs of assent. The introductions continued until the last man took his feet. He was obese, but not the size of many of the others who, like Gary, stayed in their chairs during the intros. His hair was neatly parted and his eyes looked toward Gary as he made his introduction.

"My name is Derek Scott and, like Gary, I've been big all my life . . ."

"No stammer," I said, hearing a different voice. "That was for us."

"My old man was a mean drunk," Scott continued, "and my mama was too. She left without so much as a goodbye. When she left I started to get fatter. I'm tired of carrying all this shit around and that's why I'm here."

"Thank you, Derek," Roth said. "And do you have a specific weight-loss goal?"

"Yeah. I wanna say 'Fuck you' to all the assholes who laughed at me."

A moment of surprised silence. Then chuckles and the kind of applause that comes from a shared, but generally unstated, wish.

We left the building at a run.

59

Scott's address was bogus, which pretty much nailed him as the perp, not that we had any doubts. He'd evidently dosed himself with enough toxins to show up in his system, but not so much he couldn't control actions designed to get him busted by the MDPD and – as he no doubt knew from his *my-drink-got-spiked* routine – routed to me, where he'd sent us every direction but straight.

Gershwin handled a revised *Be On the LookOut*, the new BOLO heading to every law-enforcement venue in South Florida. When that was done, he sat quiet for a moment and turned to me.

"The night the surveillance team left their watch. Nothing happened, right? At the shop?"

I thought it through. "The cup got poisoned when Derek Scott visited Gary. I figure Gary was trying to get

401

Derek to stop the ultra-violence. Derek probably listened and maybe made mollifying noises. Then went to the cupboard and did his thing. Then called me and made a big deal of Gary trying to kiss him, like Gary was an emotional wreck."

"He was."

Another brilliant move by Scott: poison Gary's cup during his visit, then create a diversion so we'd think Donnie had entered: there'd be no suspicions of Scott as Gary's sole visitor before the poisoning.

"The BOLO should be widespread in an hour," Gershwin said. "Where from here?"

I called Dr Clark at the Hardee clinic. "I just sent you an e-mail photo, Dr Clark. Could you take a look?"

I heard a chair roll, fingers tapping a keyboard. "I'm opening my mail now . . . Damn, is that Derek Scott? Jesus . . . how much weight has he lost?"

Clark knew Scott. Another wire made visible. "Over one-fifty. Tell me what you know about Derek, please. It's important."

"Derek in trouble?"

"More than I can explain right now."

A sigh. "Derek's old man was Rudy Scott, a veterinarian who had a large-animal practice here for decades. Rudy was a gentle and soft-hearted fool who was, I think, confounded by his son."

"How so?"

"Derek was bright as it gets, maybe got it from his mom. She was local, from a dirt-poor family, but had the kind of smarts a lot of folks call cunning. She targeted Rudy with bright eyes and big boobs, nailed him with a pregnancy, probably thinking marrying a guy with Doctor in front of his name meant a cushy life."

"A country vet not a high-pay position?"

"If you run it right. But Rudy was the type of guy to take payment in eggs instead of dollars and probably got paid in full about half the time, too meek to go after what he was owed. I think Rudy felt more at home with critters than people, understood them better. That woman used to give Rudy hell, call him names in public, berate him."

"Where's Mama Scott now?"

"She screwed about a quarter of the men in the county and ran off when Derek was fourteen. Not long after, I started hearing rumors about the kid. Folks tell me things they need to tell, but don't want to travel further. Nasty stuff."

"Explain, please."

"Derek was fat, but not a jolly fat boy or whatever the stereotype is. He was a bully and a heavy drinker. I'm sure a lot of his weight came from drinking, but he ate to excess, too, not big on self-control."

"That's not all that nasty of a rumor, Doc."

"I'm getting there. When Derek got to high school I started hearing that he could discern young men who were homosexual and hiding it, ashamed. The whispers were that Derek'd zero in on troubled young men and take advantage in many ways. Sexual was one of them. He knew he wouldn't get caught."

"If the victims told on Derek, they outed themselves."

"I think Rudy knew his kid was screwed up, Detective Ryder. But if you don't look directly at a problem . . ."

I nodded. "It doesn't exist."

"Rudy died three years back, drove off a pier into Okeechobee. Witnesses said he made no attempt to brake, like he saw a road that wasn't there. But he had a solid practice developed over years and it sold for over a million bucks."

"Derek would have known about toxic plants?" I asked.

"There are million-dollar thoroughbreds at some of these farms, Detective. Brahma breeding cattle. A vet around here knows every toxic plant by sight and symptom. And Derek went to vet school three years."

"How much chemistry would Derek know?" I asked.

"Chemistry classes would have been in the first couple years, so he knew plenty."

"Could Derek have known José Abaca?"

"Everyone knew the go-to man for bad things. But I doubt Derek ever had any business with Abaca."

I expect you might be wrong there, Doc, I thought, wondering how much Scott had paid Abaca to deliver tainted tacos. And did he find any money remaining when he poisoned Abaca?

I ran out of questions, thanked Clark, hung up.

"Think Daddy Scott was an experiment, Kemo Sabe? With datura?" Gershwin asked when I detailed my call.

"If it was, it made Derek a millionaire. And killing a misguided, harmless father for money is pure sociopath territory, Zigs. Maybe toxic plants gave little Derek his first real experience with power. So he made them his study."

"He may not have finished his degree," Gershwin noted. "But he sure did his fieldwork."

Debro sat naked in his living room smelling himself, nose bobbing from one armpit to the other, entranced. He loved to smell himself; it was like his whole body was breathing, every pore. He'd just put in a session with Patrick White followed by a session with the weights and he smelled like heat and energy.

At first he'd ridden his boys like carnival ponies, one after the other, riding until his thighs were chafed and his balls got so empty it hurt to squirt. Sex was good – no problem there – but it was limiting: You felt good while it was going on, then there was a big *snap* and it was over. But punishing his bitches? That was best because the glow hung on for days, even after they were gone. It was like his hand could still feel the pry-bar smashing Brighton's legs, ears hearing the beautiful wet *thup* of the metal hitting meat.

And Eisen's tongue? Debro had only to pinch his fingers together like pliers to feel the slippery resistance of the twitching organ, Eisen going "*Errr . . . arr . . . arghhh*" as the sweet pink meat was sliced from its roots.

Bliss.

405

Prestwick? Pretty, pretty Billyboy. That had been the finest event of Debro's life: a single-edge razor blade outlining the face, tiny blood pearls rising from the incision like datura pushing from the ground. Debro's hand closed into a fist as he felt the cup of flesh beneath Prestwick's chin, hot and wet as his fingers burrowed beneath and . . .

Debro owned a face.

That was it, wasn't it? You owned them. And the more you took from them, the more you owned.

It was time to understand what it was like to own one completely.

The lights had been turned off in the room and Patrick suspected he was being watched, his peripheral vision catching a shape in the small window in the door. But he couldn't be certain the head-shape wasn't a delusion. Sometimes visions rose in his head: snakes on the floor, balloons in the air, flames skittering across the linoleum.

The door opened; he'd been right: Scott entered. Patrick forced himself to stare at the ceiling, appearing drugged, dulled, sunk into delirium. A floorboard squeaked and Patrick inadvertently turned to the sound, his face rising to meet eyes looking down.

The eyes locked.

"I think it's time to hit you again, bitch," Scott said. He wore only a jock strap and crouched and waved his hand in front of Patrick's eyes. Patrick made himself stare dead ahead. *Hit*. It could only be an injection.

Scott straightened and sipped from a can of beer. Patrick tried to move his arms, felt them twitch and stutter, the control erratic; no way he could take the muscular Scott, a man in full control of his mind and his body.

And if Patrick revealed his awareness, what would happen? There was but one course of action: accept the dose and hope the countering pharmaceuticals retained some blunting power.

Scott passed his chair, smacking the back and setting it into rocking motion, then disappeared out the door. He returned within two minutes, his right hand holding a syringe and a fifty-cc vial of dark brown glass. In his left was a small leather bag. A bouquet of green balloons bobbed behind Scott as he walked, popping with every step. When they popped they left black smoke roiling in the air.

They're just hallucinations, Patrick told himself, again tapping his head against the floor and letting a strand of spittle fall from his mouth.

Scott set the syringe and vial in the lounger and approached Patrick, the leather bag bouncing from hand to hand.

"You've been a bad girl," he chided, looking at Patrick. "You were mean."

Patrick's lips bubbled at the ceiling and he slowly thudded his head against the floor. He had no recollection of ever seeing Derek Scott before he came into the hospital, a supposed victim. Never.

Scott set the leather bag next to Patrick and strode casually to the chair, beside it the sixteen-ounce Budweiser. "I've figured it out, Patty," he said, picking up the bag and tapping its contents into his hand. "I'm gonna help you prepare for your exam."

A hand appeared in front of Patrick's face. It was holding a blade as curved and as wicked as the tip of a scorpion's tail. A linoleum knife. "You're interested in anatomy, right?" Scott said. He laughed and reached for the vial, loading the syringe and setting it on the floor beside the vial.

"Just some locust for the muscles," Scott said, bending over Patrick with his finger on the plunger. "I want you nice and soft and ready to learn all about insides."

Patrick saw a luer lock IV syringe. He waited until the needle was sliding into his thigh to mime a spasm, his right arm jerking in what seemed an involuntary motion, catching the syringe and snapping off the needle in his leg.

"Fuck!" Scott screamed, jumping back from Patrick's flailing limbs. His face screwed up in rage and he threw the useless syringe at Patrick and stormed from the room.

He's getting another needle, Patrick thought. *Move!*

Patrick pushed himself up on his hands and started toward the chair. Fighting to make his flaccid limbs move in unity . . . *left*, dammit, now *right* . . . *Come on, move* . . .

He crawled to the brown vial beside Scott's can of beer and tried to pick it up, but his fingers had stopped working. Patrick put his head on the floor and used it as a backstop, wedging the vial between his index and middle fingers.

Hang on . . .

He lifted the vial and shakily poured several cc's into Scott's beer, hoping his eyes were telling him the truth and the liquid was entering the can.

"WHAT ARE YOU DOING!"

Scott's voice filled the room, bouncing between walls. Patrick's hand froze, the vial stuck between his fingers. Scott's face was golden and glowing. A broad grin came to his face. Scott strode to Patrick . . .

60

And dissolved into a pile of black cats. They howled and skittered across the floor and ran up the walls, disappearing as they reached the ceiling.

A *hallucination,* Patrick realized, his heart hammering in his ears. He looked at the can and saw dark beads of toxic liquid at the opening, a giveaway to the tampering. An army of cockroaches appeared on Patrick's arm but he ignored their clacking, metallic legs and dropped a shoulder, rolling back to his original position.

He resumed the slack-mouth staring, trying to ignore the insects crawling across his body. The door opened again and a second Scott entered, naked and aroused and bearing a new syringe and a pair of handcuffs. It took seconds to lock the cuffs in place. Patrick felt the needle sting his thigh. "Fifteen minutes," Scott whispered, setting the glowing linoleum cutter on Patrick's belly.

"Then we'll have an anatomy lesson, Patrick. Just you and me."

Scott retreated to the chair. He picked up the beer can, rolled it between his palms. Held it toward Patrick like offering a toast, tipped it back . . .

And drank.

"Think," I said to Gershwin. "Where would Scott be?"

We were on the streets, too restless to sit at the department. We had every damn invisible wire in hand except the one that led us to Scott's lair. Night was falling, and what would normally seem a pleasant orange cast to the sky seemed like a blanket of fear turning darker by the moment.

My phone was in my lap and I kept wishing it would sound, a cop saying he'd just spotted Derek Scott's 2012 maroon Explorer. We'd been looking for a silver sedan, possibly with a bike rack. Scott had moved us like chess pieces.

"How would Scott acquire property?" Gershwin asked as I turned on to I-95 and headed south. "Without using his name?"

"He might rent it," I said. "Pay enough and there's no questions asked."

"There's a risk the owner might show up to check out the property. Scott is risk-adverse, Big Ryde."

Gershwin was right. I replayed his relationship with Gary. A thought hit.

"Gary's cloud data. He kept business dealings there."

411

I saw the nearest exit and took it, pulling into a clothing-store parking lot. I dialed Sparrow at computer forensics.

"Yo," she said. "S'up?"

"The download from Ocampo's cloud account. There were some business records with the videos, right?"

I heard her scratching through files. "Usual stuff, tax records and whatnot. Inventory. Plus some property papers."

"More than the shop?"

A minute of keystrokes. She told me what she found.

I hung up and looked at Gershwin. "Eleven months back Gary Ocampo bought a building in Kendall. Two stories, almost three thousand square feet. How far is Kendall?"

"Fifteen minutes from here," Gershwin said. "But I know a shortcut."

Scott left the room and returned with another beer, sitting in his chair and playing with himself as he studied Patrick. His hand made an ugly squeaking sound as it rose and fell, an aural hallucination, Patrick knew. He also knew the anti-toxin was overcome, the floor now glowing as if lit from below. Lightning had started crackling against a far wall. Sickly purple clouds sped across the ceiling.

Derek Scott rose from his chair, fifteen feet tall. He lifted the knife.

"Time to study anatomy," he said, his voice coming from inside Patrick's head. Scott pulled the cushion from

412

the lounger and propped Patrick's head high, Patrick staring at his chest, his open and bare belly. Scott's hand closed around the linoleum cutter's wooden handle, its wicked curve echoing the curve in Scott's smile as Scott made the blade draw circles in front of Patrick's eyes. The blade left trails, like a sparkler.

"Wonder what we'll see first . . ."

Scott paused. His eyes flashed to a corner. His head cocked, like hearing a distant voice.

"Gary?" he said. "*Gary?*"

Scott stood and walked tentatively to the corner and waved his hand in the air, like trying to touch something only he could see. He turned slowly, looking between Patrick and the can of beer on the floor, the vial at its side.

"*YOU BITCH!*" Scott screamed. "I'LL *GUT* YOU!"

Lightning crackled through the room as Scott stumbled toward Patrick, the knife glowing and buzzing in the sparking air. Scott dropped to his knees at Patrick's side, his face black, his mouth dripping fire. He slipped the knife under Patrick's chin. NO Patrick croaked, trying to roll away as the room spun like a wheel and the glowing blade burrowed toward his heart. PLEEEEASE NO . . .

Lighting exploded again. Two blinding flashes, like twin suns exploding. Waves of thunder spun the room so fast it turned inside-out.

Time stopped.

Took a breath.

Re-started. Patrick blinked his eyes open to the sound of wind blowing inward from the door, turned his head into the wind. Superman stood at the door, his cape flapping in the breeze, his dark hair rippling, and smoke drifting from a hole in his palm. He lifted from the floor with a *swoosh* and flew to Patrick. But it wasn't Superman's face above the massive cartoon shoulders, it was Detective Ryder's face.

"I've got to get you to a hospital, brother," Superman Ryder said in a voice that sounded like trumpets. "Hang on."

Clouds surrounded Patrick and he could not tell if he was rising or falling.

61

Four days passed and I'd actually gotten some sleep. Derek Scott was chained to a hospital bed, recovering from datura and two gunshot wounds in his abdomen. After healing he would go to trial and thereafter to a maximum-security prison, where he would no doubt wreak sexual havoc on handsome young men gone afoul of the law.

Patrick White would be the key witness at Derek Scott's trial. We had enough to lock Scott up and White's testimony would let us throw away the key. Patrick had an inch-deep, two-inch-long slit in his upper chest, but would soon recover. He had re-scheduled his missed exam and I knew he'd be a superb nurse practitioner.

Gershwin and the lovely young woman who worked the desk at the morgue went to Memphis to soak up a few days of blues and barbecue. I ordered him to visit the National Civil Rights Museum, saying it would be one of the most profound experiences of his life. After that, I said, go to Gus's for fried chicken.

And me? I was looking toward a horizon where two blues met, the back-lit blue of the sky, the wet-jewel blue of the sea. I heard Ava and Vivian speaking behind and above me, both marveling at the odd stroke of Fate that had made my brother an acquaintance of the incoming pathologist at the morgue. According to my brother's new backstory, he had passed through Mobile on business at the time Ava was there and I had introduced them. They had reconnected when he'd recently learned – through me – that Ava was in Miami.

Jeremy Ryder's false history wove through my false history like the graveyard rose of Sweet William and the briar of Barbry Allen, however you want to translate that.

I heard a door close and Jeremy sat beside me, a fresh glass of lemonade in his hand. He wore a linen safari shirt and tan cargo shorts that looked pressed, a creamy straw Panama hat providing shade. We'd been discussing the cases, and I'd detailed the video where the pair had met.

Jeremy had been delivering his commentary, which he gleefully continued now that he'd refreshed his glass. "Scott recognized vulnerability in Gravy from the moment he gave his sad little *Mummy Hates Me* speech," my brother grinned. "Scotty probably wondered, What can I get from this whimpering doughball?"

"Everything he wanted, I think. Scott even adapted his intro speech to align with Gary's. He drew him in."

"Scott was a predator who sought out weakness, Gravy a sad widdle chubbins with mommy issues and repressed anger. Needy-boy Gravy bared his adipose heart to Scott, including little dead Donnie, his need to bare his boobies in Rio, and his magical ways."

"All of which Scott used from day one."

"Scott's an inventive sort. The only problems were building his secret lair – which he loved doing, by the way, exercise while he dieted – then going to Te-jas to empty a casket. What do you think Derek-boy did with little Donnie, Carson?"

"He was in a freezer in Scott's garage."

Even my brother looked surprised at that one.

"Stage set, the abductions begin," Jeremy continued. "Scott leaving spermy evidence everywhere. But in the data banks it's listed as Gary Ocampo's juice. And folks like you –" he winked – "are looking for the Invisible Man."

"It gets weirder," I said. "Scott moved to Miami twenty-seven months ago, where, you'd think, he crossed paths with the victims. But none recall seeing him. Only when we showed them Gary Ocampo's photo – the real version – did the memories kick in: Brian Caswell vaguely remembers picking on Gary during a performance. Dale Kemp made some cutting remarks at a theater, Harold caught Gary spying on him in high school and broadcast the incident, making Gary a butt of widespread joking.

Prestwick and White jerked Gary around in a bar years ago, an incident with a mirror. Eisen also gave him a pretty bad verbal rough-up in the same time frame."

Jeremy absorbed the information and nodded. "Little weepy Gravy tells Derek tales of humiliation. Crazy Derek absorbs every detail of Gravy's woe and adds it to his own, then puts on his magic sharing hat and goes a-hunting for the nasty trolls who poor-mouth sweet widdle fat boys. Think it's coincidence Derek tracked down the slimmest, prettiest little meanies?"

"He had money and time. And Gary's humiliations, which he no doubt shared."

"Derek Scott was an opportunistic predator who found the perfect opportunity to live the dream, Carson. If he'd kept his anger in check he'd still be out there. But of course . . ."

I heard Vivian and Ava laughing again. They were swim-suited, sunglassed, and eight feet above us on the boat's flybridge where they'd been sunning. Jeremy and I sat in the stern. The craft was seventy feet of gleaming Viking motor yacht, hired with captain and three crewmen out of a Key West marina.

Jeremy had wanted to go fishing.

I'd brought about four hundred bucks' worth of salt-water angling gear. My brother had a dime-store cane pole, the kind we'd used as kids, holding three meters of cheap monofilament with a tiny hook and a shiny red-and-white bobber, the tiny bobber floating astern like a joke.

418

"Catch us a fish," Viv called down, nodding to a gas fueled grill. "We need lunch."

"It's problematic," I called back, pointing at a pair of black triangles cleaving the water two dozen feet from the boat: sharks. They were ten-to-twelve-footers by the looks, and even if I hooked a fish, they'd tear it to shreds in an eyeblink.

"No excuses," Ava chided. "If you boys can't catch a fish, we'll have to eat burgers. We want fish, y'hear?"

I sighed – fish sounded good to me, too – and wandered to the rear where Jeremy's bobber floated forlornly in the mild chop. I was turning away when the bobber disappeared, reappeared, quivered . . .

Then zipped beneath the water like a bullet.

"A bite!" I yelled. "You've got a fish on!"

Jeremy yawned and picked up the cane pole. It bent in his hands as he pulled up. I watched six pounds of red snapper break the surface and splash to the boat. The women whistled and applauded as lunch flopped on the deck.

I stared at the snapper, a deeper-water fish rarely found near the surface. As the women dug out cameras, I heard splashing and leaned out over the gunwale to look down the hull toward the distant bow. Two of the crewmen were yanking the swim-finned and scuba-masked third crewman up a boarding ladder, the man scrambling aboard like hellhounds were snapping at his heels.

The scenario was clear. The snapper had been caught previously and kept in the yacht's live well, an aquarium, basically. When my brother had gone inside he'd signaled his need for the fish. I wondered how much Jeremy'd had to pay for someone to swim through shark-infested waters just to hook a fish on his line and give it a yank. I shot a glance at the circling sharks, then quietly studied my brother, doing a doffed-hat bow as the women giggled and cameras clicked.

Jeremy was free. He owned his life. He had scads of money and could do whatever he wished: Endow a charitable foundation, collect Pre-Columbian artifacts . . . hell, he could even buy rare comic books. Instead, he'd just put another human being at great risk for the sake of personal amusement.

How much had he really changed?